WHO HUNTS THE HUNTER?

★ ★ ★

Cap didn't sleep, simply watched and waited, though the day had been draining and disturbing. Patience was a tool of the hunter. The Enemies tossed restlessly before slipping into disturbed slumber. Cap moved without hesitation.

He leaped over a log, dropped into a slight dip, and exploded out of it.

Cap caught Jaime on the back of the neck and bit, hard. A swiping pawful of claws tore Jaime's throat out and quieted him to a wet, breathy sound, and Cap dragged the body up the slope and into the dip.

A shout, the cough of a Gun, and a Bullet cracked past his ear. He ran as fast as he could, hampered by the limp weight of his kill, and felt a sting in his tail. There were other shouts and shots, but none came close, and he ran until his legs and lungs were on fire.

Cap took a look at his tail, and found some short length had been shot away by the stray Bullet. It stung badly, and throbbed. He would accept it. He had the Comm, and had done what his friends wanted.

"Jaime has the rebel comm!" one Enemy shouted.

"You make it sound like it chose him on purpose." Sergeant replied.

"I tell you that cat thing is hunting us, and knows *exactly* what it's doing!" was the response.

"And I tell you ~~that~~ ⟨...⟩, look. Here's a blood tra⟨...⟩ ⟨...⟩w it."

"Are you insan⟨...⟩

Duty"

**Baen Books by
Michael Z. Williamson**

★★★

To purchase these and all Baen Book titles in e-book format,
please go to www.baen.com

TOUR OF DUTY:
STORIES AND PROVOCATIONS

★

MICHAEL Z. WILLIAMSON

TOUR OF DUTY

Copyright © 2013 by Michael Z. Williamson

A Baen Book

Baen Publishing Enterprises
P.O. Box 1403
Riverdale, NY 10471
www.baen.com

ISBN: 978-1-4767-3676-1

Cover art by Bob Eggleton

First Baen mass market printing, October 2014

Distributed by Simon & Schuster
1230 Avenue of the Americas
New York, NY 10020

Library of Congress Cataloging-in-Publication Data:
    2013010546

Printed in the United States of America

10 9 8 7 6 5 4 3 2 1

Contents

★★★

Acknowledgments
★★★

"Naught But Duty," © December 2005 by Michael Z. Williamson, *Crossroads and Other Tales of Valdemar*, DAW.

"The Humans Called It Duty," © March 2007 by Michael Z. Williamson, *Future Weapons of War*, Baen Books.

"The Sword Dancer," © December 2008 by Michael Z. Williamson, *Moving Targets and Other Tales of Valdemar*, DAW.

"Wounded Bird," © December 2009 by Michael Z. Williamson, *Changing the World: All New Tales of Valdemar*.

"The Price," © May 2010 by Michael Z. Williamson, *Citizens*, Baen Books.

"The Groom's Price," © December 2010 by Michael Z. Williamson, *Finding the Way and Other Tales of Valdemar*, DAW.

"Heads You Lose," © Janet Morris, August 2011, *Lawyers in Hell*, Kerlak Publishing, reprinted by permission.

"The Brute Force Approach," © August 2011 by Michael Z. Williamson, Baen.com, Baen Books.

"The Bride's Task," © 2011 December by Michael Z. Williamson, *Under the Vale and Other Tales of Valdemar*, DAW.

"A Hard Day at the Office," *Rogues in Hell*, © July 2012 Janet Morris, Perseid Publishing, reprinted with permission.

"Desert Blues," © August 2013 by Michael Z. Williamson.

"One Night in Baghdad," © 2006 by Michael Z. Williamson. Appeared in a slightly different form on michaelzwilliamson.com.

"Port Call," © January 2003 by Michael Z. Williamson, michaelzwilliamson.com.

"April Fool," © April 2006 by Michael Z. Williamson and Brad Linaweaver, *Locus Magazine Online*.

Crazy Einar's articles first appearance *The Pennsic Independent* at the Pennsic War between 1999 and 2005. All are © August 2013 by Michael Z. Williamson.

"My True Encounters With the Indianapolis Police Department," © August 2013 by Michael Z. Williamson.

"Inappropriate Cocktails," © August 2013 by Michael Z. Williamson.

"On Reparations Generally, for the Descendents of People Long Departed," © 2003 by Michael Z. Williamson, michaelzwilliamson.com.

"The Manly Way To Cook Meat," © October 2007 by Michael Z. Williamson, ManlyExcellence.com.

"The Ten Manliest Firearms ," © 2007 by Michael Z. Williamson, ManlyExcellence.com.

"Ten More Manly Firearms," © 2008 by Michael Z. Williamson, ManlyExcellence.com.

"The Mosin Nagant," © July 2009 by Michael Z. Williamson, ManlyExcellence.com.

Dedication

★★★

For my brother and sister veterans of OEF/OIF.
With respect.

TOUR OF DUTY:
STORIES AND PROVOCATIONS
★ ★ ★

How I Got This Job

★ ★ ★

AS I SIT HERE finishing this collection and sipping fine Scotch, I still wonder, "How the hell did I get here?"

I was born in the UK, to a Scottish father and English mother. They got married, so I'm Scottish. If Scotland ever does declare independence, I will gain yet another passport.

I remember growing up middle class in the UK. My father had a motorcycle, and eventually a car, while he alternated electrical work and school. My mother waited tables evenings. We had a "flat" with no heat, and a transistor radio. Lunch for me was usually a boiled egg or a slice of bread with jam. In 1969 we got a black and white TV so we could watch the moon landing. Since my father was an electrical engineer, he re-programmed the set and we got *four* channels, though BBC1 and -2 usually showed the same thing. I remember the occasional *Doctor Who*, *Tom and Jerry*, and yes, *Sesame Street*.

Eventually we moved to a real house (well, a duplex), with plumbing. We were lucky. The row houses behind us had bathrooms tacked onto the back, with pipes running up to deliver water, and I believe the sewage dumped down into a semi-open system. They were a hundred years old and predated modern plumbing.

Every day, my mother would walk me the half mile to school, and pick me up afterward. The school toilets were also outside. After three years, the school built a brand new bathroom, still outdoors. However, we no longer had to urinate in a gutter or crap in a hole. When school wasn't in session, my mother would take my hand and, with my sister in a pram, we'd walk most of a mile to the town market.

Now, in early 1970s Britain, she had to argue with the grocer, who wanted to get rid of the oldest food first for the same price as the fresh stuff. Then she'd load it in a small cart and pram in front, pulling that behind, or having me push one, we crossed a couple of four-lane roads to walk home.

We moved to Canada, because the mid-'70s economic climate in the UK didn't look promising. My parents were young, but they were correct.

My father went ahead of us, secured a job, and sent for us. As we departed England, there was a bomb scare on our aircraft. It only took a few minutes to resolve, but I'll always remember it.

Upon arriving in a hot, sunny Toronto, I was loaded into a Pontiac Parisienne, a Bonneville with a Canadian accent, where my feet didn't even reach off the seat, and there was a radio in the car. THERE WAS A RADIO IN THE CAR! I was driven to an A&P, where there was a hundred feet of fresh produce. It was really odd, because there was no glass and no grocers. You could take whatever you wanted and put it in a bag, then they'd load it all into the car for you. You could just leave what didn't look fresh, and they'd do something with it. I was sure they didn't waste it, though.

You'll see hints of this in my writing. Do not ever make the mistake of thinking that a shared language equals a shared culture. Certainly, there are likely to be more similarities than for people who don't share a language, but even common words can change. For example, the first day of work, my father asked the office's secretary for a "rubber," by which he meant "eraser." In Canada in the 1970s, this was easily understood and corrected. Use that term in America today, and there could be legal repercussions and EEO action.

I liked Canada, mostly. The bullies were worse than in the UK or the U.S. and traveled in packs. That surprises people who want to believe all Canadians are polite and kind. I have two words for you: "Ice hockey."

It was quickly determined that my British education at the hands of the Anglican Church put me far ahead of my peers. I could write in cursive, do long division, basic wood crafting and needlepoint, and had a good grasp of both grammar and science. That paid off later, of course. At the time, I was placed a grade ahead.

Most Canuckians in Mississauga, Ontario are apartment dwellers, though the apartments have a lot of nice features—pools, squash and tennis courts, underground parking. It wasn't a huge change for me in that regard— the apartment was at least as big as the house in England, and there were lots of kids to play with. TV was easy—we could reach Toronto and Buffalo, and get *Sesame Street* in English, French and Spanish, and about thirty channels.

Actually, I could have learned a lot of languages. Twenty-seven of thirty students in my fourth grade class were immigrants.

Then I found out about something called "Trick or Treat." Rather than wear sheets and papier maché masks while munching treacle around a fire on the commons, it was encouraged to visit other apartments asking for candy. When you realize these apartments were 13-25 floors of 15-40 apartments per floor, with five buildings within easy walking distance, I still don't remember how I managed to cover them in only a few hours, but I do remember entire pillowcases (plural) full of loot.

I did take up skating, and ice hockey, and street hockey, and gym hockey, having an entire bag of sticks of different types at different lengths for skates vs. shoes, and both left and right handed.

It was in Canada where I started writing my first book. I'd been studying up on rockets (that moon landing was still with me), writing text and sketching pictures of fuel systems, gantries, rocket staging, telemetry charts. I had dozens of pages finished, all done with marker and ruler.

Canada wasn't quite what we were looking for, apparently. A few years later, my father found another job, and we wound up moving to the U.S. and settling in Central Ohio, where it was explained to me that we should have two cars, since we had two adults in the house. A friend's parents were unable to properly discipline their son, because if they sent him to his room, he just watched TV there instead. Same language, different culture.

The teachers frowned at the complication I offered, and tossed me into class. That first day, I took an American history quiz and aced it. They were surprised. I was surprised to find it was specified as "American" history, and more so to find that the name was redundant, as they didn't really teach other nations' histories.

I could have skipped another grade, but I was already far ahead, skinny, and facing maturity issues. We all decided I should stay where I was.

There were bullies in Ohio, too. I was a small kid, but I always fought back, and eventually got better at it. At first I got the crap beat out of me, and I really didn't know how to fight back. By the time high school rolled around I was a pretty decent brawler, but for some reason—probably being skinny, too smart for my own good, and mouthy—kids kept trying to beat on me. A few of us came to terms. The rest seem to have wound up the way most congenital bullies do—as not much of anything.

There was another turning point about then. It seems our immigration attorney was sneaky. He never actually put in writing what he was advising us to do by phone. We'd gotten a temporary visa for a year, moved to the U.S., bought a house, settled in, and applied for a permanent visa.

The temporary visa expired. That left us in limbo. You can't leave the country and reenter without a visa, so we couldn't visit family. We had no legal status at all, though we were still paying taxes. But you know those silly things kids do, like shoplifting, breaking curfew, et cetera? If I'd been caught doing stuff like that, my entire family could have been deported, our future stricken. In theory, it takes a pattern of such behavior, and a few misdemeanors aren't an issue. It has to be a crime of "moral turpitude." But legal immigrant teens are *very* cognizant of this standard. And, once the visa expired, we had no status. Any slip could have ended the trip. I sympathize with a lot of "illegal" aliens, because it's very easy to be illegal even without intent. I know of several variations that friends have slipped into by accident.

Three years later, we finally got in to see an immigration officer. She looked at our papers, considered, looked at us, and said, "The problem is that what you did is illegal." (It is legal now. It was not then.)

Even for a teenager, that's a pretty heavy blow. By getting a temporary visa, we'd stated an intent to leave. Applying for a permanent visa contradicted that. And no, good intentions make no difference to the law in a case like this. All that matters is your papers. The easiest thing for this agent to do was to stamp a sheet and send us back to the country before the country we'd left, with a bar on reentry to the U.S. for ten years, and sucks to be you. We'd have had a few months, but would have had to sell the house, uproot, see if Canada would take us back as residents, or else relocate back to the UK again, at the height of the late 1970s troubles, and re-adapt to a culture we'd left behind.

The hardest thing for her to do was for her to write a letter to her superiors explaining that she believed we had honest intent and faulty advice, and that we should be granted the opportunity to apply for permanent visas.

She did this.

Ma'am, whoever you were, THANK YOU. I can never repay that kindness, that very nonbureaucratic thoughtfulness.

We were allowed to become American Permanent Residents, and don't ever lose that green card.

My parents divorced when I was fifteen, and my mother, sister and I were on tight rations while my mother sold real estate and tried to find something more lucrative. My paper route money often went toward food. At sixteen I started cleaning and detailing cars for a few bucks.

Adulthood is a turning point for many people, and it was for me, but with a difference: Our citizenship hearings came up. I was barely an adult, still in high school, and had to be debriefed.

As immigrant nonrefugees, the bar we had is somewhat higher than it is for native borns or those seeking asylum. For example, proof of literacy is required. One couldn't belong to any subversive or communist group, must not have a criminal background, must demonstrate "adequate knowledge" of U.S. history and government, and, yes, much of this applies to teenagers as well as adults. That last is the cutout—if they're sure you're some kind of enemy plant, they can ask who the fifteenth vice president was (Hannibal Hamlin) and when you don't know, they can boot you.

It was ironic that the kid from England was required to write on the form, "I can speak, read and write the English language."

In the meantime, I realized I didn't have the focus for college, and needed out of the house. I didn't get along well with either parent, and needed something. The Army recruiter probably could have hooked me if he'd shown more perseverance, but the Air Force recruiter won out. I took the ASVAB test—Armed Services Vocational Aptitude Battery—and demolished it, as I had the ACT and SAT. I got 99th percentile across the board. I showed up at the Columbus Military Entrance and Processing Station and was offered a huge list of jobs, including things like "computer security," which were in their infancy. I gleefully selected a dozen choices.

Then the counselor said, "Wait, your paperwork indicates" something negative. "Are you a felon?"

"Uh . . . no . . . "

It turns out there'd been some questionable security clearances that had allowed spies into various places. Immigrants were held to the same standards as felons, until naturalization was complete, and mine wasn't.

That list of a hundred jobs shrank to a dozen, including things like "Plumber." Now, plumbing is a worthy profession. But it wasn't as glamorous as what I'd been shown moments before.

I wound up in an engineering specialty that changed over time, being largely a glamorized air-conditioning and cryogenic plant mechanic on the peacetime side, though it did include some weapons and vehicle training for deployment purposes.

Sometimes, you take what you can get. It worked out in the end.

I entered the Delayed Enlistment Program, and prepared to finish school. I finished, I graduated, and it was very much anticlimactic. I wasn't any smarter, any richer, or any more employable.

Then the second immigration hearing came up, the important one. We scraped enough money to buy me a suit, and my mother and younger sister wore church-worthy dresses.

This time, the waiting room was full of dozens of people. There were Czechs, Chinese, Argentines, Rhodesians, Malians, a couple of other Brits and others we never met. I have never felt what I felt in that room. None of us had anything in common, but we all had one thing in common. We talked about our former homes, the differences, the opportunities. Everyone was dressed for the occasion.

When my name was called, the immigration official required me to confirm previous questions. He asked, "Since your last hearing, have you joined or belonged to any organizations other than the Boy Scouts and Civil Air Patrol?"

"Yes," I answered.

He looked up at me, a bit surprised, because this was supposed to be largely a formality at this point.

"Which organization?"

"The U.S. Air Force."

It took him a moment to process that, then he grinned hugely and said, "So you're definitely here for the long haul."

"Yes, sir, I am."

He had me sign the papers, then he signed.

A while later, all of us together wound up in a courtroom, in seated rows, silently and politely awaiting our Immigration Judge.

The judge came in, very cordially, noted this was the most enjoyable part of his job, and he was proud to see us. He even knew which countries some of us were from, which was both very thoughtful, and very professional.

Then we raised our hands, and he administered the Naturalization Oath. There was a quiet cheer, and we all shook hands and patted each other on the back.

Fifty people entered that courtroom. Fifty *Americans* came out. If you are an immigrant, you understand. If not, I cannot explain it to you. At that moment, after a decade, I was once again, and at last, home.

I still have that suit, by the way. There is no way my chest would fit in that skinny jacket anymore, nor my arms, and to be fair, the waist is at least three inches too small. But that suit is mine.

Three months later I left for Basic Training, and it took the USAF three years to straighten out the paperwork from Permanent Resident to Naturalized Citizen, complicated by the fact that it was illegal to make any copy of the document in those days.

If you see me at public functions, you will find a lot of immigrants, including me, congregate. No matter where we came from, we share the bond of having chosen, and worked, to be Americans. Skin color, religion, political affiliation, have far less interest or impact to me than that unique connection. I noticed this in the military, where lots of immigrants wound up in my unit, and at science fiction conventions, which I started attending.

At my first convention, I managed to break my watch. I have never replaced it. It didn't really matter what time it was, and I threw myself in headfirst. No one knew it was my first convention. I've always fit into that crowd.

I had lots of letters to editor, recipes, and such published from age eighteen, with a very high hit rate. I wrote stuff for KeepAndBearArms.com that went viral, and eventually got reprinted for money. I sold some erotica, and got requests for more.

I wrote a short story, which I submitted to several

magazines, only to have it rejected. It wasn't great. I did eventually salvage some of the characters and elements for other stories.

It's almost a stereotype that science fiction authors have an odd employment history. I got caught in the first round of military cutbacks in the late 1980s, wound up getting my reenlistment cancelled, and was out the gate on a week's notice. I had to get all the essential stuff I didn't have—an apartment, a bed, kitchen utensils, a cat—on credit. Then I had to find a job in a sucky area for jobs. Champaign-Urbana being a small town with a large college has lots of well-educated, needy, underpaid applicants for jobs. I took some hourly positions in fabrication shops, and doing machine maintenance, and even as shift manager at a pizza place, until I could get enrolled for school with the GI bill to help. I also enlisted in the Army National Guard.

During this time, I hung out a lot with the Society for Creative Anachronism, and someone with a small business asked if I'd both craft armor and weapons for them to sell, and be a sales rep for those and other products. Every weekend, I was at Drill, or a convention, or a reenactment. I stopped working day jobs and did school weekdays. The money wasn't great, but it was enough to see me through classes.

A funny thing happened on the way to my degree. I went to a convention in Minneapolis. I arrived after a day of school, a night of driving, and no sleep, so I wasn't really lucid after ten hours of setup and selling. A friend of mine introduced me to a friend of hers, wearing leather and spandex and nothing else except boots and a sword. We got to talking, and talking some more, and had a great time. She was curvy and cute, great to talk to, and almost psychic. While I was trying to come up with a clever way to say "Is there somewhere more quiet we can go?" she asked me, "So, should we find somewhere more private?"

Good idea.

I actually was dating someone at the time, though not exclusively. I made a point of saying so, that I was free for the weekend, but couldn't promise more than that. So we had the weekend.

A funny thing about one night stands. They don't always last one night. A month later, she drove all the way to Milwaukee to join me at a convention there, and a month after that, she stopped by the apartment in Illinois on her way to Florida.

She never got to Florida, and still hasn't. She managed, very politely, to divert my date for that weekend into an accomplice and roommate, move us into a rental house, find another roommate, and wind up my Significant Other.

Twenty-two years later, twenty of them married, Gail is still here. The bitch just won't leave. On the other hand, I haven't had any reason to throw her out. But it's a one night stand. Honest.

I paid my way through college several ways. I had the GI bill. I had National Guard drills and volunteered as support for whatever extra days they needed people for. I was a stripper (yes, really) for decent money, though not often enough. The small enterprise I worked for moved and folded. We started our own small business. I worked on blades—repairs, sharpening, custom crafting, and selling retail at SF conventions, SCA events and occasional other events. She helped with sales, costumes, and the tax paperwork.

Gail went back to school, too, having previously attended University of Minnesota and a local college. She managed fast food, then wound up doing office management.

Winters were the slow season, and I spent those times trying to build up inventory, scrape money from what small events there were, stringing my wife's income along into a fine thread, and writing.

I left school without a degree, though I have more than enough credit for a master's. The problem is, it's in electronic controls, history, English, physics, and none of it complete as a program. I was making enough from events, and enjoying it, that I didn't miss the official stamps (I do hold a Journeyman's certificate in HVAC, and a certificate in electrical controls).

Gail's research suggested that if we moved, we could keep the same cost of living but earn more money. I wasn't tied down to any location. The only complication was that I had transferred back to the Air National Guard at this point, and would have a four hour drive for drill. It was workable, until I could find a slot in a unit closer to home.

So we moved to the Indianapolis area, staying with friends until we got settled, and yes, managing to earn twice as much money for the same cost of living.

So I kept doing it, we managed with some great years and lean years, and in the late '90s, my firearm articles started getting published. Summers were, and still are, hectic with events. I took four years of winters to write

Freehold, which is not my best writing, of course, but was heartfelt and earnest at the time.

SF, though, especially military SF, is not a sellers' market. Several experienced authors advised me to "write short stories," build up a following with sales, then get a novel sold. It used to work that way. That was falling by the wayside at the turn of 2000, and is pretty much no longer valid advice, in my opinion.

My shorts got rejected, often because they sucked. I knew my grasp of language was sufficient. I knew I had good plots and characters, but something in the construction was missing.

By the time I wrote the short story that begins this collection, I thought I had a reasonable grasp of the art, and the friends I could trust to be honest not only liked it, but had discussions among themselves about it. Of course, that didn't mean it would work for any particular periodical. It was frustrating.

I groused about this fact on Baen's Bar, where I'd been holding lengthy debates on the history of weapons and the logistics around them. I was always careful to spell and punctuate properly. It's what I do, and this was a publisher's site. I didn't want to make the people who use the language for a living cringe with my errors.

So I complained about all these rejections of, "Alas, we can't use it at this time." "Alas, it doesn't quite grab us."

"Alas, it doesn't fit our current needs."

They were saying, "Dear aspirant: Sorry, try again." Why pretty it up with archaic wordage?

Jim Baen replied, "Perhaps they're trying to be alliterative. Alack, alas, alay . . ." He wrote a whole paragraph of alliterative A-words, which ended with, "That said, send me one. single. chapter. of something you're working on and I'll take a look at it."

After a brief adrenaline shock I shooed my wife from the office (er, kitchen), and I emailed him "One. Single. Chapter. Of *Freehold*."

He replied, "I. Have. Read. It," and offered some small advice, which of course I took. He suggested I add a bit on a page about a departure from Earth, describing the shuttle in detail. I didn't see the point. It was a plot device more than anything, connecting two scenes. But, Mister Baen had been doing this as long as I'd been alive. I took his advice under consideration, and yes, it turned a break into a segue. An astute editor, that Mister Baen, which is of course why I'd been trying to court his attention.

He then asked for another chapter. A week later, he asked for another. He was politely unhappy with some rambling parts, which I fixed. We went on. Finally, he said, "Just send me the rest of the book," and told me to politely remind him once a month. Six months after that, I got a late night email that said, "Mike, let's call it a deal. I'll take *Freehold* for (respectable sum of money for someone desperately broke at that time), and have Marla send you our boilerplate contract."

I did consult with my friend Dave Drake to make sure I understood all the ramifications of said contract. But I said yes.

I still only have one TV in the house, and it's used more for movies and games than TV. I got cable when it was necessary for Olympic coverage. My son plays the games. If it weren't for the computer (no games here, either) I wouldn't need a screen at all, really. I spend most of the time writing, ranting and creating. I do fewer events than I used to, but still quite a few. Some are large for promotion and profit. Some are small for promotion and to hang out with friends. I still forge blades and do repairs, but it's a money-making hobby, not really a job. I also do product reviews to provide feedback to manufacturers, and to then promote the stuff that holds up well. I've reviewed tactical lights, cameras, guns, backpacks, survival rations, training videos, any number of items relevant to disaster preparedness.

So here I am, doing what I love doing, getting paid for it, and telling you about it.

It's been a hell of a ride so far.

TOUR OF DUTY: STORIES

★★★

The Humans Call it Duty
★★★

The story that triggered my rant on Baen's Bar, that got me recognized and published in major media, is this one, even though it wasn't published until several years afterward. This is not a great story, even for a new writer. Asimov's "Nightfall," for example, written long ago by a then younger man, is a great story. Still, I'm not unhappy with this one. As I said, it engenders a lot of discussion among my fans, which is a clear sign that the story works.

It was rejected by pretty much every major SF magazine, because it's not the type of thing they want to publish. That's no criticism of them. We each have our market.

However, one foreign magazine sent back a form checklist letter, complete to a hand-added addendum that "This is a simple tale of revenge and killing and is not science fiction," and conspicuously did not check the "Please send us your next work" box.

Indeed.

I have to wonder if they skimmed it and didn't catch that

the character isn't human. It's also possible they wanted the purist SF where there's no story without specific science elements, though I'd argue that nonhuman intelligence is a key science point.

The coda of that was that their government-subsidized magazine failed the next year, while Joe Haldeman and Martin Harry Greenberg thought it was a good enough story—for a beginner—to be included in "Future Weapons of War" a couple of years after that.

★★★

CAP SLIPPED through the undergrowth. He was stealthy, for there were things that would kill him if they found him, men and animals both. He surprised rabbits and bouncers and other prey as he appeared like ghosts through the leaves, and they scattered before him, but he was not hunting now.

The sound of Guns had alerted him from his patrol. They came from somewhere near his friend, and he hurried to investigate. Guns were an indication of hunting, and David was alone, with many enemies in the dark woods. He increased his pace, mouth wide to reduce the rasp of his breath, and squeezed between two boles, then under the dead, rotten log he'd passed on the way out. His patrol had only been half done, and he hoped David would understand.

He drew up short. The scents in his nose sorted themselves. That one was Gun smell, and not from David or another friend. That was smell from David's Gun. That was the smell of David, and the smell of blood. Cap dropped flat on the forest floor and eased his way under a brushbush. He gazed deeply into the dappled murk, and widened his ears and nose. The Enemy was not nearby.

He moved quickly, striding forward, dreading what he would find. There was a dip in the ground, leaves hastily tossed to cover it. A few scrapes revealed a hand, then an arm. The sweet-sour smell told him already, but he kept digging until he saw the face, then more. It was David, dead. Cold flowed through him as he stared at the body, ragged holes blown through it by Guns. All David's harness and gear was missing. The thing he called a Comm was gone, and Cap knew that was bad. If an enemy had the Comm, he had to get it back or destroy it. He didn't know why, but that had been one of the things drilled into him from an early age. A Duty, it was called.

He whimpered in pain, for David had been his friend his entire life. Somehow, he had to do what must be done, and return to the fenced Home where David and he lived. He wasn't sure what happened after that, but he knew what he'd been taught, and knew he had to do it. First, he reburied David's body, sad and wishing other humans were here. They knew what to say for the dead, and Cap couldn't say it for them.

Standing and peering around, he spotted the route taken by the Enemy. He would come to that soon enough, but first, he had to do what David called a Datadump. That tree there should work, and he trotted toward it. He scrambled aloft until the branches would barely take his weight, swaying in the late evening breeze. He pressed the broad pad on the shoulder of his harness, and sat patiently. It was a human thing, and he didn't know what it was exactly, only that he was to climb a tall tree and press the pad every day at sunset. That, too was a Duty. It beeped when it had done what it was supposed to, and he eased back down the limbs and trunk, flowing to the ground like oil.

Now to the hunt.

The path the Enemy left marked them as amateurs. David and his friends left much less sign of their passing, although he could still follow them easily enough. There were some friends, those who David called Black Ops, who were almost as adept as he, and could kill silently and quickly. He wished for their company now. They were hunters as he, even if human, and would understand his feelings. But those fellow hunters were not here, and he must tread carefully. It was his Duty to his friend to continue doing what he was trained to, and to recover the Comm. After that, it would be a pleasure to kill those who had killed David. That was his Duty to himself.

There they were. He dropped into the weeds and became invisible, watching them patiently. There was no hurry, for they could not get away from his keen hunter's skill. He sat and listened, grasping what few words he could, and waiting for the right moment.

"—odd to find one rebel out like this, along our patrol route," said one.

"They're all weird, if you ask me. They don't want law, don't want schools, and don't want support. Why anyone these days would be afraid of the government is beyond me," said another. He felt like a leader, and Cap guessed him to be the Sergeant. There were eight of them, so this was what David called a Squad, and Sergeant was the Squad Leader. They were enemies. He was sure, because the clothing was wrong, they smelled wrong, and David's people had Squads of twenty.

"It is their planet. Was," said another. He carried a large Gun, the kind for support fire. He was another primary target. "I guess they were happy, but a strange bunch of characters," he agreed.

"Well, we've got a prize, and a confirmed kill, so that should make Huff happy." He was turning the Comm around in his hands. He made a gesture and handed it to another, who stuffed it into his harness. Cap made note of that one's look and smell as Sergeant continued, "He wanted to prove that initiating lethal force was a good idea, and this should help. We'll sweep another few klicks tonight, then pick up again tomorrow. Jansen, take point," Sergeant said.

"Sure thing, Phil," said the first one.

The Squad rose to their feet and trudged away. They might imagine they were stealthy, compared to city people, but Cap easily heard them move out, three person-lengths apart, Jansen first, then Gunner, then Sergeant, then the rest. Cap rose out of hiding, and followed them, ten person-lengths back. He stayed to the side, under the growth, and avoided the direct path they were taking. The Squad had Guns, and he did not, but he had all the weapons he needed, if he could get close enough.

It was only a short time until one said, "I'll catch up. Pee break."

"Shoulda gone before we left, geek," Sergeant said.

"Sorry. I'll only be a few seconds."

Cap watched as the Enemy stood to the side and relieved himself. He jogged sideways along their path, hidden by leafy undergrowth, and waited until the last man passed by his chosen target. He crouched, braced, and as the man fumbled with his pants, threw himself forward. His victim heard him, and his head snapped up in terror. He was wearing the Goggles people wore to let them see in the dark, but it was too late. Cap swept over him before he could scream, unsheathed, cut, and landed rolling. The body gurgled, dropped, twitched and was still.

One.

Cap slipped quickly away, through more brushbushes, and carefully climbed a tree. He wanted to be high enough to observe, but low enough to use the limbs to escape if he had to. He peered through the woods, eyes seeing by the moonlight, and waited for the Enemy to respond.

They weren't a very good enemy, he thought. They hadn't noticed yet. That was good, he supposed, although a part of him was insulted at the poor competition. He dropped lightly back to the ground and moved back to the kill. Sniffing and listening carefully, he made sure no one was nearby, then hoisted the body up and dragged it carefully off. He buried it under a deadfall, where the ants and flies would take care of it, and erased any sign of his passing. There was no time to rest, but he'd taken a few bites before burying the body. He could go on.

The Enemy had finally figured out that one of theirs was missing. In pairs, they stumbled noisily through the brush, whispering the missing one's name, "Misha!" They weren't talking into their magic Comms yet—the things that could reach people through the air. They might soon call for others, however, and that made Cap consider things more urgently. From his perch high in a graybark tree, he kept watch over the Enemy's movements. That pair was closer, and separated from the others by a slight ridge. He eased back down and concealed himself under a tangler, where he was unlikely to be noticed. They could see heat, but they would not see him. Even faced with Goggles he could be invisible.

They were heading off to the east. Cap followed along behind at a safe distance. Could he take two? Perhaps he should wait. But there was little time, and the Comm had to be found. It had to. He edged closer.

One paused, pulled off his . . . no, *her*, he smelled . . . Helmet, and drank from a Bottle, leaning against a tree. There was risk from the other, not far away, but Cap took the chance and jumped.

A bite, twist and roll, and her neck was broken. That injury not even people could often fix, and not out here. He heard a yell and the cough of a Gun firing, and heaved himself up and away, bounding into the heavy darkness, the growth a whisper alongside him as he slipped his feet surely into gaps. No noise from the hunter. That was the way.

"Phil! Guys!" the other yelled. "It's an animal! It got Lisa!"

Two.

Cap shot away under the weeds, found a tree and raced aloft. He could barely see through the tangle of leaves, and was worried about their Goggles. He was hot now, and they had seen him. Did they know what he was?

They were distressed. He knew it from the increasing loudness, the shakes in the voices, the reek of fear from them and their indecision. He would win this yet. He didn't know all of what he heard, but he knew the harness was recording it, and he caught some words he *did* know.

"—call for evac!" said one.

"We can't!" said Sergeant. "The rebels know we are out here, that's why we walked all this way. We are supposed to find those roving missile teams."

"I'm aware of why we're here, goddammit! But that thing killed Lisa and Misha!" one argued.

Sergeant replied, "You're going to call in and abort because of an animal? Any idea how that will sound? And evac is for the *wounded.*"

"It's still out there!"

"So now we know. We shoot it when it comes back, add it to the count," Sergeant said.

"I don't think—"

"I don't care what you think!" Sergeant interrupted. "We'll bivouac here, take a look in daylight if we can, and continue from there. Shoot anything that isn't human. Var, you and Jaime take first watch."

"S-sure, Phil," "Uh-huh," the two replied, not sounding happy. In a short while, the other four tucked cloaks around themselves and leaned against trees. Var and Jaime walked around the clearing, eyeing each other and the blackness. Cap dropped to the ground and crouched. He meant to kill Jaime if he could, then drag him off.

Jaime had the Comm.

It was halfway until dawn before the chance came. Cap didn't sleep, simply watched and waited, though the day had been draining and disturbing. Patience was a tool of the hunter. The Enemies tossed restlessly before slipping into disturbed slumber. At the darkest, coolest time of night, Var muttered something to Jaime, then sat against a tree, took off his Goggles and rubbed his eyes. That made him almost blind. Cap moved without hesitation.

He leaped over a log, dropped into a slight dip, and exploded out of it. Here is where it was dangerous, if Var was looking. He wasn't.

Jaime was just turning, not from suspicion, but from fear of the woods. Cap caught him on the back of the neck and bit, hard. A swiping pawful of claws tore Jaime's throat out and quieted him to a wet, breathy sound, and Cap dragged the body up the slope and into the dip.

A shout, the cough of a Gun, and a Bullet cracked past his ear, like a rotten bluemaple branch snapping. Cap knew what Bullets were, and flinched. He ran as fast as he could, hampered by the limp weight of his kill, and felt a sting in his tail. There were other shouts and shots, but none came close, and he ran until his legs and lungs were on fire. He crawled under a featherfern and pulled the corpse in with him, then opened his mouth wide to quiet his heaving breaths and listened for pursuit.

Three.

The Enemy was shouting now, scared. They hadn't followed him because they were consumed with their own fear, their fear of him. Cap knew what pleasure was, and that was pleasure. He took a look at his tail, and found some short length had been shot away by the stray Bullet. It stung badly, and throbbed. He would accept it. He had the Comm, and had done what his friends wanted.

"Jaime has the rebel comm!" one Enemy shouted.

"You make it sound like it chose him on purpose. We'll find it during the day. We have a sensorpack," Sergeant replied.

"I tell you that cat thing is hunting us, and knows *exactly* what it's doing!" was the response.

"And I tell you it's a dumb animal. It's been hit, look. Here's a blood trail. Grab your gear and we'll follow it."

"Are you insane?"

The voices became confused. Cap didn't understand the words, but the fear was clear. They would look for him, but not yet. Not until it was light. Very well. He could hunt in light, too. Rising, he dragged the body farther away. They might follow this trail, and he had to confuse it.

The creek was refreshing and cool, and he followed it upstream for some distance, splashing softly in the rippling pebbled shallows. He dragged his burden up a rocky shelf, back into the woods, and found a good spot, near some firethorns. No one went near firethorns. They would spring and sting their prey with a painful bite. He checked again to make sure the Comm was still in Jaime's harness. It was. The fabric was too tough for him to tear, but he yanked at the straps with his fangs until he was able to wiggle it out. He paused, turned to the body and ate noisily and quickly, until he knew to stop. If he filled up, he would be unable to hunt. He tore out a final warm, quivering mouthful of flesh, shredded it with his teeth and tongue, and swallowed. Salty and rich, and he savored it. The taste of his Enemy's death. The rest of the body went into the firethorn bed, where it could fertilize them, and the Comm went several hundred paces away with him. He bit hard, until the case—and a tooth—cracked, then bashed it against a rock until it was open. It had to be destroyed, and he wasn't sure how good the enemy's tools were at finding it. He urinated in the open case, and buried it as deep as he could in a damp depression that was overgrown with weeds.

He was done. The Comm was safe, and he could rest, then transmit his last Datadump and work his weary way back to Home. Hunger and fatigue gnawed at him to do that very thing, but another part was still awake. That part was sad, angry, and mean. It meant to avenge David's death, and it did not want to be ignored.

And there were only five of them left. Rest could wait. The Datadump could wait if need be. Some Duties were more pressing than others.

Dawn was breaking, and Cap was near the Enemy again. They looked ragged, drained, and fearful. He would help them feel that even more. They'd found no sign of either him or the Comm with their tools, and that meant Cap had done well. He felt pleasure, and a hint of satisfaction. They had killed David and taken the Comm, but he had killed three of them already and destroyed it. But it would not bring David back. He whimpered in loneliness.

They were trudging back the way they'd come, and he followed them behind and above, slinking from limb to limb on the overhead path they had yet to suspect. He detoured where the trees thinned, but kept the Enemy always in sight. It was an old game that he knew from instinct and training. When Leopards had been taken from their Old Home to this New Home, they brought their skills with them. The Ripper of the forest might be stronger and faster, but Leopards were better trackers. And Cap, or Capstick, as David had called him since he was paired, was one of the best Leopards in the Military.

Below, Sergeant said, "Look, it's daylight, we should be fine. We'll set mines there," he pointed, "and there. You watch, Cynd, and wake us in two hours. We'll move again, then rest again, okay?"

"I think so," the female, Cynd, said. Cap watched as the Squad shuffled about the area. They were placing the small boxes he recognized as explosives. He'd seen those in training. They were smaller and different shaped than his people's, but he knew what they were. He paid rapt attention to the placement.

Then the Squad lay down to sleep again, leaving Cynd to stand watch. And she did stand, not sit, and he wasn't sure of his chances.

He watched as she moved around, alert and careful. There was a smell of not-quite-fear. Eagerness. *Worry*, that was it. Cap knew how to do this. First, he must move away and out of sight.

Slipping through the growth, padding slowly and cautiously so as not to rustle, he edged around their clearing. There was one box, at the base of a tree, standing on its legs. It took only a moment to bite it gingerly between fangs and turn it the other way. And it was so thoughtful of them to paint the back side yellow.

Another patient turn brought him to two more boxes. The last of the three was stuck in a tree on a spike. It took some figuring on what to do, as it was wedged in tightly. But it shifted a little when he gripped it, and he was able to rotate it around its mount.

After that, it was no trick to get back in the trees, on the high branches. They would take his weight, and afforded him a path to the edge of the clearing. Lower he slipped, quickly and quietly, until he was following a long run over a graybark limb that overhung the area. He crouched on the perch and waited. Whenever she faced away he slipped a few steps closer. Cynd was walking back and forth, and sooner or later would pass under him. The others snored, their alertness dulled by fatigue. He would have a few seconds. That would be enough.

Cynd was walking toward him. She would pass underneath . . . now. Reaching down like a stretching spring, Cap got as low as he could. His paws were bare meters above her Helmet visor, unseen in her restricted vision. He let go with his rear claws and dropped, feeling weight pull him down.

She wore Armor and her Helmet, but her face was exposed, and her legs. He knocked her flat under his weight, felt the breath *whuff* out of her, and locked his jaws over her face. She gasped for air, and he knew she was trying to scream in his mouth, as a yearling would. Her hands scrabbled for a weapon, but he pinned her arms down with his paws, letting the claws sink into the flesh and holding them tightly. As her gyrations increased, he unsheathed his rear claws and gouged deeply into her thighs. Hot wetness splashed, and the body underneath thrashed and thumped. He was intent on the kill, but his awareness was still with him, and he heard another voiceless scream of distress and the sound of gear.

With no hesitation, he rolled off Cynd and charged away, legs pumping and lungs heaving as he plunged around the trees in long bounds. Bullets came after him, and he dodged back and forth, stumbling over a rotten stick, rolling through a patch of ground ivy, and away.

Shouts were followed by loud *bang*s as someone detonated the mines. The explosions tugged at him, wind snapping at the leaves. But if they were bad for him . . .

His ears were ringing slightly, but he could hear shrieks and shouts, swearing and confusion. The heavy growth would have stopped most of the metal stings from the mines, but they had to have been disorienting. And frightening. That was what he wanted. He wanted them afraid, wanted them to know, to understand and regret.

This was not their home. This was his. And he would protect it.

There was the sound of pursuit. He listened, head turning, to localize the noise. There was one, that way. He stretched out his hearing again.

Only one, shooting blindly and crying gibberish under his breath. Taken by panic, Cap thought, and the smell agreed. He was coming this way, but only from luck, and there were no others.

Cap could handle one.

As the Enemy came over the hummock, Cap sprang out of the leaf bed, his deathsnarl tearing the air and terrifying the animals. The Enemy stopped, wide-eyed and the color draining from his face. Smell told Cap that Enemy had voided himself and, as he tried to swing his Gun around, Cap took him.

First, he crushed the wrist that held the Gun with his jaws, while scratching for the face to distract him. Bones splintered, the Gun fell, Enemy screamed, and Capstick turned his attention elsewhere. The other hand was bringing up a Knife, and Cap rolled off, pivoted, and leapt back. The blade tore his lip as he hit, but he shattered that arm, also. The Enemy was sheathed in Armor and a Helmet and Boots, but the thighs and the groin were exposed, and Cap sunk his fangs deep into soft, warm flesh. Enemy howled in agony and thrashed, cried and shook, whimpered and twitched, and was still. Cap ate a few more bites to keep his strength up, and trotted off in a circle around the area, ears alert for voices.

Four.

"She has to have a trauma team! Phil! *Abort the goddamn mission!*" Gunner screamed.

"Yes!" Sergeant agreed. "Hold on, okay?" A moment later he continued, "White Mountain, this is Silver Three. Abort! Abort! Abort! Require immediate extraction and medevac." There was another pause, and Cap knew the message was being turned into a squeal before the Comm sent it on into the magic squeals only other Comms could hear. If he'd only been able to find friends, all these would be dead. Now they would get away. That saddened him. But he might get another yet.

Sergeant spoke again. "Understood, White Mountain. We can make exfil point in thirty minutes." Click. "Okay, let's destroy the excess gear and weapons and bury them . . . Guys, where's Jansen?"

They worked themselves into another panic, and Cap again knew pleasure.

People had good ways to deal with wounds, and Cynd was strapped to a Litter they built. She moaned, and was still alive, but Cap knew he could fix that in a moment's time. All that were left now were Gunner and Sergeant and one called Wes. Wes and Sergeant carried Cynd, and Gunner led the way. They were heading north again, and Cap used the arboreal highway to follow them. Sometimes he led them. He knew where they would go, for a Vertol could best reach them on the Bald Hill.

The three Enemy were jogging quickly through the forest. Cap slipped into the lower branches, flowing along them like an elemental force, silent and determined. They were sweating and gasping for breath, and had taken off their Helmets to get better vision and cooling. That was good. He could see Gunner curve to the right up ahead, and eyes wary, he tensed for action . . . now!

A leap, a tuck, and Wes's head was in his teeth. He somersaulted over, the world twisting, gripped as tight as he could, and felt the neck snap. Sergeant screamed, and Gunner tried to fire, but Sergeant was in the way. He moved to the side, and Cap dodged the other way as Sergeant dropped his end of the litter and tugged at his Gun. Cap tasted brains and sprang away, rolling off the path and into the soft, leafy fronds of a downweed patch, which hid him as he descended the hill and slid over the edge of the ravine, roots and tendrils snagging him. Guns sounded again, and he winced at pain in his side. He had been hit, but it wasn't bad. Nor would it matter if it *had* been bad. He was hunting. He had an Enemy to bring down.

Five.

He circled again, listening.

"—can't leave her here!" Sergeant said.

"Do you want to try getting to a weapon before that

thing rips your throat out? Mother of God, have they bioengineered those things?"

"I'll carry the back, weapon slung, you do the same up front. Drop her if we have to. At least she'll have a chance!" Sergeant said.

"You didn't hear me, Phil, *I'm not carrying anything!* I'm making that rendezvous, and they are never sending me back without a full platoon. You file any paperwork you want. I'd rather spend the war in jail than have that thing rip me to death. I liked Cynd, but she's not going to make it."

There was the click of a Gun being readied. Sergeant spoke, "Sergeant Second Class Willen Rogers, pick up that litter or I'll shoot you right here!"

"You really are insane, you know that?" Silence. "All right. Sorry. Nerves. Let's get the hell out of here." The sound of their feet indicated they were carrying the Litter, and Cap felt pleasure again. He would finish this, despite the wound. He might die as he killed them, but David would be avenged.

They were still heading north, and Cap kept back a bit. Sergeant was watching the trees. He was the tricky one, and Cap would save him for last. He wouldn't die quickly, and Gunner might shoot him while he fought with Sergeant.

Ahead was the upper branch of the creek. They would have to cross there, and that's where he'd kill them.

His side hurt severely, and he licked at it, tongue rasping through the fur. It tasted of blood, and the bitter tang of other damage. But he wasn't dead yet, and there were still things that must be done.

He rose and moved. His motion was tight and slower than before, but he ignored the pain and glided along the boughs.

Bald Hill, as the humans called it, was not the highest point around. It wasn't really a hill, just a jutting end of a smooth ridge. The creek flowed past it from the highlands, and Cap would have to be ready, as once they crossed the water they'd be where they could be found, and would have clear space to protect them. He urged himself forward, breath gurgling slightly. The wound in his side had hurt his ribs. No matter. He sprang nimbly from tree to tree, skirting the two Enemy and their burden.

This was good, he thought. They must cross here, with the Litter, as the ground sloped instead of dropping off. He would wait . . . there.

The Enemy was close now. He could hear them muttering to reassure each other, and hear their tortured breaths. They would have few more of those. He waited under the cut bank of the creek, just upstream from the crossing. Their voices resolved through the chuckling sound of the creek.

"—get across and we can rest," Sergeant said.

"Thank God," Gunner heaved out between strangled gasps. His voice was unclear yet. "We'll need . . . ready . . . for when evac arrives. How do we . . . what happened?"

"We tell them exactly what happened," Sergeant said. "There's enough evidence in the monitors."

They stopped at the beach and prepared to cross, and Cap took the moment to swim closer. A projection covered him, and he waited for them to splash into the chill water, the same water that tore painfully at the wound in his side.

Now. Their Guns were slung, they were knee-deep in water, and they couldn't move as quickly as he did. He clambered up the bank, unheard over the water, and sprang, muscles releasing like a tensed spring.

He was on Gunner, and clawed his throat out. Six! Sergeant dropped his end of the Litter, and Cynd tumbled into the water to drown, next to the worms of red leaking up from Gunner's wounds. Seven! Cap turned, and saw Sergeant raising his Gun. He ducked and leapt, using Gunner as a base and felt the burn of a Bullet through his shoulder. It spoiled his attack, but he clawed Sergeant savagely with his right paw, tearing his arm and chest. He tried to force him under water, and Sergeant fired again with his other hand. He missed.

Cap sprang lightly back to his feet in the rocky shallows, sending agony through his side and shoulder. Sergeant was scrabbling for purchase, and wasn't looking as Cap pounced again. He shoved the man's head under water in the deeper pool, and leaned on it to hold it there. Gurgling sounds came, and he knew death would follow soon. He ignored the pain in his ribs, and the new pains as his Enemy cut him with a Knife. He shrieked, but pressed lower, closing with the blade until it could cut no more.

He fed on the pain, and pressed the attack. He could feel his foe weakening, and knew it would not be long now. Exhaustion was taking a toll, though, and he lacked the strength to attack again. Blood loss was making him weak, and spots before his eyes told him he was fading. But his Enemy was faring no better. He slipped under the water again, and emerged coughing, before falling back once more. Cap crept closer, begging strength from his tortured body.

They clashed again, Cap desperate to finish this, his Enemy desperate to survive. As they wrestled, he felt death hovering nearby. Or was that the sound of a Vertol?

It was a Vertol. Cap snarled in outraged frustration. The Gunners aboard wouldn't shoot yet, but he had to leave or die. He drew back, dragging the limp, almost dead Enemy with him, keeping the man between him and potential Bullets. He slipped under water and headed for a moss-spattered rock, needing to get behind cover. Bullets like a deadly hail stirred the water, and he sank as he'd been taught. There was the cut in the bank, and there was the rocky shelf he'd used as a path on his way in.

Another burst shredded the growth as he fled. He burned with rage at not killing Sergeant. He could not dwell on that now. He had to escape to make his Datadump and survive to fight again. Let the Enemy keep Sergeant and Cynd alive. They could tell the others how the fight would go. Not only the soldiers, but the human settlers and their dogs and even the Leopards would fight.

Cap waited under a featherfern, eyes narrowed to cold slits, and held motionless as the Vertol passed over, then again, then a third time. They knew he was there, but couldn't see him. Cap had played this game before, even though it wasn't a game now. Despite their tools, people couldn't find Leopards. Not one time in a hundred.

The Vertol flew over again, even lower, then the sound of it echoed away across the hills. In moments, the normal sounds of the northern forest returned, and Cap raised himself, all cuts and aches and bruises, to end his mission. It was nearly sunset, and he still had to hurry.

High in a tree, Capstick spent some time recovering from the exertion, feeling his heart thump, sensing his blood boil, hearing his thoughts roar. His injured shoulder was an agony that he would have to accept for now. At Home, it would need Surgery. His ribs might, also, and the wounds to his skin and tail. Then there was the pain within. He was weak, ill, and hot, but he would rest to recoup his strength and press on. The human doctors could heal him, as they had before. People were good at such things. His thoughts were interrupted as his harness clicked and began its Datadump, and he heaved a deep sigh. He knew better than to roar in anger, pain, frustration.

David was dead. He knew other people, but David had been his friend his entire life. He could not yet think of existence without him. Loss . . . emptiness . . . he had no symbols to describe it properly.

Cap still had a purpose, however, and that would give him strength. But fatigue and exertion and his wounds called to him to rest. He would do that now. Tomorrow he would travel gingerly and painfully back to Home. There, he would be paired with a new friend, and he and that friend would hunt the invaders remorselessly. Perhaps the manhunters from Black Ops would join them. If not, he would teach his new friend what loyalty meant and they would hunt as a pair.

The humans called it Duty. To him it was simply the way things were.

Time in The Freehold Universe
★ ★ ★

ONE OF THE ISSUES I'm stuck with is that in *Freehold*, I developed a local clock and calendar. It's easy to use, but dissimilar from our own. Of course, for later books, I didn't always have a chance to reference this in story context—people rarely sit down and talk about the math of clocks, time and dates.

So I often used "Earth" time in reference, for readers' ease, or because it was relevant to the story. I'd mention time in seconds. Workarounds are usually possible.

However, for some of the Freehold universe shorts, it's not feasible to do either. Characters are going to discuss schedule, using their native clock. So to that end, here it is:

Grainne's rotation is 28 hours, 12 minutes, 12.9888 seconds

So:

1 Freehold second = 1.0153 Earth seconds
100 seconds = 1 seg
100 segs = 1 div
10 divs = 1 day

The year is 504.2103 local days, which is 592.52291 Earth days.

There are five weeks per month, of ten days each. There are ten months per year. Each new year, at Solstice, there are four festival days, with a day added on leap years every five years, but not every fiftieth year.

The Brute Force Approach
★★★

Sometimes, appearances in my books are auctioned off for charity. Sometimes, a friend or colleague tickles me in a certain way, and I ask if I can use them as a character.

My friend Robert "Zig" Hensley appears in here as a hull specialist. Zig was a former Navy diver supporting the SEAL teams (he was always very careful to insist he wasn't a SEAL himself). After a couple of injuries at depth, he was medically retired, and devoted his life to gunsmithing, good cigars and riding bikes. We never actually met in person, this being the twenty-first century. We talked at length by phone and online about rifles, revolvers, military issues, shooting. We'd make plans to meet at various three-gun matches, but didn't quite manage to get our schedules to work.

Then came the news that on his way back from a ride in Stone Mountain, Georgia, someone had changed lanes in a panic and knocked him under a semi. It was two days after this story was published. Given the nature of the story, I almost wish I could rewrite part of it to give him an heroic death.

However, he did read and comment on the story, a few days before I submitted the final draft for upload. I'm glad he didn't miss it entirely.

This story takes place contemporaneously with the early part of Freehold.

★★★

"MAYDAY! Mayday! Mayday! *FSS Mammy Blue* calling *Rescue* or any ship!"

Lieutenant Rick Stadter jerked in his couch at the sound of a real call. That would break up the monotony, and probably by a bit too much.

Across the bubble from him, Astrogator Robin Vela was already replying. "Orbital Rescue acknowledging *FSS Mammy Blue*. Dispatching rescue boat, please describe the nature of your mayday."

Stadter nodded, checked the grid and synched the blip to the ship's computer. Three seconds later the computer hit the grapple release. *Auburn* slipped off the station's waist, using the centrifugal force as delta V. He brought engines up smoothly, and pushed them from free fall to 2 G standard. The couch gripped him through the acceleration.

The panicky, uneven voice replied, "Everything! I'm not a flight officer, I'm a purser. The flight crew are probably dead. Engines are boosting *hard*, we have at least one breach, and I'm hearing structural noises."

Vela still had the call. "Understood, *Mammy Blue*. We have a cutter en route. Stand by for further information. Do you need a talk-through on shutting down boost?"

"Rescue, I don't think I can! There was a loud explosion from aft. The whole boat bucked and all the alarms triggered. I mean *all* of them. Even stuff I can see is working is flashing at me. We responded and the co-captain went aft. A bit later we had a breach. The captain is back there now. Do you need me to find the time tick?"

Vela shook her head as she said, "Negative, *Mammy Blue*, just give me all the info you have—break—all craft, all craft, mayday mayday *FSS Mammy Blue*. Salvage and rescue. I show one-nine-seven passengers, one-nine-seven passengers and one-nine crew. Any craft able to assist, respond on Rescue Channel Two—break—" She shouted over her shoulder, "Budd, get Channel Two, I'm handling damage report live on One. Purser, continue, describe all damage you can confirm."

"Rescue, I'm squirting full status. I can do that much. Stand by."

Astronautics Systems Senior Sergeant Peter Budd held all the non-Astrogation tasks, everything from life support to communication repair, and docking control. He also handled tracking for Astrogation, and logistics management. Budd knew his work well, and bent his big frame and smooth head over his controls. "They're at one point seven standard G," he said. "Runaway reactors, from the flux."

Stadter winced and turned to his console. It took effort in 2 Gs. He wanted information on his own screens. Two hundred and sixteen people, minus any who were dead already. From the sound of it, most of the officers were dead or incapacitated. The couch under him was itchy-damp with sweat, and it wasn't just the acceleration causing it.

Emergency calls happened every couple of days. Every couple of weeks one was significant: an engine failure, a navigation failure, a medical emergency onboard. The cutter was crammed with medical gear and spare parts, and crewed by a pilot, an astrogator, astronautics tech, an engine tech and a medic. Their suits could handle short EVA, and Medic Lowther's was meant for extended use.

This time, there were a possible two hundred and sixteen casualties and a large and substantially valuable ship. It was absolutely impossible for them to conduct a rescue of that magnitude with their boat. They had rescue balls for fifty, but any response assumed some kind of resources aboard the distressed vessel, or a failure so catastrophic none were needed.

Most of these people were going to die if they hadn't already. If they could reach lifeboats aboard their damaged ship, they'd have a chance. Otherwise . . .

"Vela, what are you working on?" he asked. Her hands flew across her screens. She was graceful despite her lankiness, and practiced, but tense under stress and acceleration.

"I'm trying to determine cause of failure. The engine damage could pose serious threats."

He'd suspected as much.

"That's important, but first is massive response."

"Sir, if we don't know what caused it—"

"Massive response," he repeated. "Then we revise details underway, and we'll also have more data to work with as ships get closer."

"Understood, sir," she agreed. "I'll scare up everything I can."

"Budd, keep me informed. You're taking sensors on those engines."

Budd replied, "Boost is erratic, averaging one point five G standard at a guess. It's hard to tell at this distance, but she looks *bent* ahead of the engines. Some struts must have failed. She's describing a complicated arc due to the varying thrust and increasing mass alignment shift."

Stadter wasn't going to ask what could happen next. He figured he'd find out.

Vela muttered, "Goddess, the kindest thing might be for it to explode."

"Quiet, please," he said politely but with some snap. She might be right, but they were not paid to hope for that.

"Understood, sir."

Budd said, "It's worse, sir."

As expected, he thought. "Tell me."

"Some of them have abandoned ship. I'm getting response on several lifeboats. However, I have fewer blips than I had launches, and two are already pinging as critical on oh two."

Stadter was Bahá'í. He wasn't sure how many religions he offended when he said, "We thank thee, God, for this disaster, accepting that it is not the disaster we would choose, but that it is better than no disaster at all." He drew in a deep breath after that.

Vela looked at him across the control bubble.

He said, "My phrasing was more diplomatic."

She shrugged, smirked, opened her channel and said, "Purser, what's your name?"

"Ben Doherty, ma'am."

"Mister Doherty, we're scrambling everything we have,

military and civilian. If you can keep any information coming, please do. I'll need you to report when craft get close. If you need to don a suit, please do. Take care of your crew and yourself first, then respond to us as you can or need to. I will leave this channel open and will hear you at once."

He sounded perhaps five percent relieved.

"Thank you, ma'am. I hope they hurry."

"We are. If you need to just talk for reassurance, do so. I'll answer as I can. If I don't answer, it means I'm sending ships."

"I suppose that's a good thing. Yes, I'm terrified, dammit . . . " She switched the signal so only she could hear it, and pulled a hush screen from her headset. A moment later she pulled it aside.

She asked, "Sir, should we transfer command and control to the military side? Is this that bad?"

He considered that for half a second. "Possibly. Make sure they're copied on everything in case. However, we're already in motion, which means shorter response, and we'll have eyes on site. Budd, can you manage command and control while we try to do rescue as well?"

The man shrugged with an accepting grin, visible through gaps between control screens now opaque with data and images. "I guess I have to."

Medical Sergeant Brandon Lowther took that moment to stick his head up from the bay underneath. That was a safety violation under boost, but he knew the boat well enough not to overload the inertial compensators, and he had work to do. Stadter didn't mention it.

Lowther said, "Sir, got my gear, and I've got spare oxy, if we can get aboard."

"What do you think, Garwell?" he called down to the engineer directly below him with a mesh deck between. When he first came aboard, it was odd to hear voices through both headset and live, but one got used to it and expected it. It did clarify things sometimes.

"I suppose if we have to match, we do, but I'd rather shave my nads with a cheese grater." Garwell had a very cultured voice. Comments like that clashed with it.

"Budd, what do you have?"

"Not much concrete, sir. Their engine controls are destroyed. Power is suboptimal, efficiency is under forty percent, leakage in all directions and it's gammas and fuel. Some of the fuel is still fusing as it leaks. The plasma stinger's half melted. I'd say someone planted a bomb, except we've got that report on lifeboats and parallel systems. It looks like complete neglect. I have no idea how it's boosting that hard."

Garwell said, "The feeds on that model are capable of three G. It's a converted LockGen cargo boat. They must be wide open, though they're supposed to fail closed."

Stadter asked, "When was the last overhaul, and inspection?"

Budd said, "According to this, last year, but . . . it was by Vandlian."

Stadter said, "I see," and everyone stared at him. For him, that was profanity.

"Yes, I get it," he said. Vandlian Assurance Inspections was a subsidiary of Resident Service Labs. RSL were in the midst of punitive proceedings for massive fraud on quality ratings. This was probably one of those. Eventually it would get added into the numerous suits and billions of credits in settlement. For now, though, lives mattered.

"Vela, what do we have on response?"

"I've got every boat, ship and robot engine within range offering, and starting to match trajectories. But that by itself won't be enough. We're going to have to have EVA capability to get to the passengers, and enough rescue gear to get them out. Our boat is not intended for an operation that size. We need some serious backup."

"Timeframe?"

She continued, "There's a streak racer that will be there in six segs. He can take four. They'll have to get to him, though. He's got professional video and sensor gear, so he's offered to be recon if we can tell him what we need shot. Delta vee will last him twenty segs. Then he has to break off."

"How far can he push it if we send recovery after him?"

"I already assumed that, sir. He'll be near dry, except for life support."

"Well done, then."

She nodded, "Yeah, they're that far out already. He's boosting at seven G standard."

A priority chime pinged from Stadter's console. He turned to a screen to see Station Commander Captain Vincent. He'd obviously been asleep. He was rough hewn at the best of times. He looked like a warmed-over corpse now.

"Do you need a brief, sir?" he asked.

"No. I have the gist. What do you need from the military?"

"Everything."

Vincent nodded. "I already put the call out, after we heard Warrant Vela's All Hands."

Stadter said, "Response is one thing. The main problem is, it's falling apart now, and getting worse. Rescue will be operating in a hot environment and we have no idea when it will catastrophically fail."

"Yes, I caught that." Vincent nodded. "So we need to get in faster. But without killing everyone doing it."

"Right. How?"

Vincent tiredly shook his head. "That's not my field of expertise. But we've got a team coming from the *Black Watch* who do things like that."

"They better damned well hurry."

"I think you can depend on that."

Right then, Budd said, "Well, I've got a *transponder* on a military vessel. Support boat, three zero four tons, named the *Black Watch*." The information was straightforward, but Budd sounded confused.

"Something unusual with that, Tracks?" Stadter asked.

"Yeah. It just blinked on a few seconds ago. No sensor image. Radar, passive, optical, all blank, and then bam! Transponder. Whatever it is, it's stealthed stupid. Anyway, got it, got a Novaja Rossia freighter just left Gealach orbit. They're empty, so they're pulling significant G. Hope it's enough. Two more pleasure vessels offering."

"We'll take it," Stadter said. He pondered a moment. "We might . . . will . . . need to have a second recovery stage that involves getting fuel and oxy to all these little craft, before they exhaust delta V and go to dead drift. I'll start a chart for that."

"I'll do it, sir," said Vela. She looked very serious. Her

usual sarcastic smirk had disappeared since the reports started piling in. "If Budd can feed me numbers, I can chart them and give them trajectories."

"Do it," Stadter nodded. Vela was perfect for the job. Obsessive on details, an asocial geek with figures to crunch, and very organized when it came to other people's stuff. Her own stuff . . . well, she'd have to work on that to get promoted. But right now . . . "Fuel, oxy, docking for transfer, rescue balls and inflatables for the mining craft and carriers." He turned and said, "Tracks, anything you decide can't make the initial rendezvous but has legs enough for the second stage, send to Warrant Vela." Back again, "Vela, stack them and pack them, ready to dispatch as soon as a primary is full. We might need to make a third wave, and that'll reduce transit time."

"On it, sir," she nodded.

Budd said, "Sir, I have military priority from *Black Watch*. They want all intel and a quick face-to-face."

"Give them the data, I'll take it here. Lieutenant Stadter," he said as the image flashed in front of him.

"Warrant Leader Bowden, Fourth Special Warfare Regiment Blazer Team," his opposite said. Young, but with a wisdom to him. No cockiness. The man was lean as a snake and perfectly poised. "If you approve, we're going to try to board *Mammy Blue*. We'll pull out anyone we can, and give you realtime video and analysis of the structure."

"Well . . . " Stadter replied, " . . . the problem is she's falling apart as she boosts. Literally. Chunks are falling free, it was never designed for sustained thrust, the thrust is beyond current operating parameters, and I strongly suspect she's *never* had maintenance."

"That's our assessment, yes," Bowden nodded. He had a helmet under his arm and gear strapped to his suit. "But no one will be shooting at us." It was delivered deadpan, but had to be humor.

"If you think you can do it, I'll trust your expertise. You've boarded craft under acceleration before?"

"No, but we have boarded craft in space. Though not quite like this. One other significant difference."

"What's that?"

"Cutting our way in we've got lots of practice with. Keeping the occupants alive is something Combat Rescue does. That's not normally part of our mission. But we can do it."

Adrenaline shock rippled up Stadter's spine and prickled his scalp. *God, I've got* Blazers *about to blast their way into a derelict under boost with live passengers inside.* This had passed ridiculous to flat out insane. "Assure me you'll bring them out alive."

"That's the plan."

"Go. Please keep us informed on your schedule."

"I'll tell the pilot. Bowden out."

"Stadter out."

He sighed and tried to untense his body in the high G thrust. Two hundred and sixteen victims, and it was virtually impossible they'd all survive. Several were almost certainly dead already. They had to save as many as they could, fast.

"Tracks, what's our ETA?"

"We'll be there in forty-seven segs and some change."

Four thousand, seven hundred seconds of boost, while the ship itself fled at high acceleration.

"Vela, what do you have for second echelon?"

"I have the cutter *Holden* out of Gealach orbit moving in, a military patrol boat from L-Four moving back, and Skywhip commandeered a freight load of oxygen. Someone will have to intercept it, but it'll be there about the same time the rest of us are."

"Tracks, what's our situation on arrival?"

"Reactor power will be adequate, fuel low, oxygen good. We can take fifteen ourselves if we have to. They'll be stacked like cargo."

"Assume we'll have to."

"Understood. *Mammy Blue* is increasing acceleration. It's a combination of less fuel mass, less structural mass as parts fall off, along with the departed lifeboats, and probably leaking atmosphere is making a slight difference. The reactor may be running away. No sign of critical levels yet, but that's possible, too."

"A fusing reactor would just make this so much more interesting."

"Otherwise it may just fail and lose all power, then tumble and leak."

"The bearer of bad news . . ."

"Yes, sir. I'll give you what good I have. But look at this, since you asked."

He looked at the image that popped up, and looked away fast. The ship was, in fact bent, and therefore boosting asymmetrically. The resolution wasn't great, but it was clear some hull panels near the reactors had peeled off. The structural failure had cracked and warped two long areas of the hull. It was a wonder anyone was alive, and he wasn't sure anyone would be when they got there, if they got there. The asymmetric trajectory was bad.

Vela said, "Sir, there's a mining tug from the inner Halo, *Rodney Six*, offering help. They're in Gealach orbit, freshly refitted and loaded. They can take fifty-three casualties with no margin, but will need help locking them through. They have big engines."

"Outstanding. Thank them and say yes."

"I already did. Also two more race boats. Apparently, they were doing early practice for something next month."

He said, "The Lagging to Leading Loop-de-Loop Rampage. They go from L-Five, orbit Gealach, whip around to L-Four and get points for speed and precision."

"That sounds like fun. They lack capacity, but can take two each short term, and both have an experienced EVA operator to help docking."

"Great. Do we have enough?"

She nodded. "It'll be very tight, but yes, and lots of boats are going to be critical after recovery. I have enough second echelon to fix that, but then we have to get everyone to the station, then we'll have to moor lots of them because there aren't going to be that many free and matching locks."

"Fair enough. What's your plan?"

"I have them scheduled by arrival time, number of victims, timeframe they need for secondary recovery, and I'm charting skillset. We want the military—*Black Watch*—and us there first or it's largely a waste, unless someone else wants to try cutting in. I ordered them not to."

"Yes, we need to minimize coordination issues. Given the Blazers have done this before, I'm planning to let them do the EVA and entrance, we'll coordinate. It would be boast bait to talk about our heroics, but I suspect we'd be in the way."

Budd said, "Sir, much as I'd love to brag of being hands on, I think I'd spend more time gibbering than working."

"They also serve who only stuff the crate."

Lowther said, "If I can get over, I'll go."

"Of course," Stadter agreed. That's what combat medics did. They were their own brand of crazy. Lowther would never wish anyone harm, but he'd eagerly pile on to help if it happened.

Vela said, "One of the lifeboats is failing. Crewman aboard reports power dropping, using backup oxygen. Their transponder is for crap, too. I've got their trajectory tagged." She waved her screens. "At emergency max we could just reach them within a seg of oh two exhaustion, but we'd have to get aboard and pop our own bottles, and we'd need backup within twenty segs."

Another flush rushed through his neck and brain. Emergency maximum meant they might get aboard a boat of panicky, hypoxic passengers, and might release enough O2 to keep them alive until someone else might arrive . . . in the meantime, people they definitely could recover would die.

He ordered, "Tag any small vessel with spare oxy to check them out if they're still hanging on at that time. Circumstances may change." His stomach roiled. He couldn't pray for them to die, but if it happened, it would make the practical and moral decisions about everything else a lot easier.

"Understood, sir," she said, in an emotionless monotone. Triage was part of reality, but that didn't make it pleasant.

Sergeant Lowther said, "Sir, I realize this may not be the best time, but it is in fact a good idea to eat something and drink a little. We're past mealtime and won't have time later."

He shuddered. "The thought of food makes me ill, but you're right. What's easy?"

"Chicken broth and orange electrolytes."

"Yes, I can muscle that down. Some for everyone. Hot, please."

Warrant Leader Rem Bowden felt a curious mix of thrill and fear. Every mission had an element of risk, and this one was passable for now, but would be high aboard that boosting bomb. At the same time, this was a real world mission. It beat the hell out of endless training.

"We get to earn our pay, boys and girls." His voice shook slightly, from the faint rumble as the boat torqued and increased boost. He and his five Blazers lay on a broad couch on a bulkhead, staring up at the hatch to the tiny bridge.

Black Watch's Intelligence Specialist, Melanie Sarendy, said, "And ours." She had her own couch, to starboard as the boat was laid out, thought it didn't matter in micro G. It mattered now.

"Yes, I expect our noble steed and crew to perform as well. What do you have for me?"

The boat commander, Warrant Leader Ulan answered, "Well, Rescue has a crazy-sounding Warrant Vela who seems to know what she's about on coordinating vessels. We're inbound, you sled over, their medic will join you. Once in they'll tell you when to toss casualties out, and someone will net them out of space."

"Simple, really," he said. "Has anyone ever done this before?"

Sarendy said, "No. Nothing like it, ever."

"I would really like to cut the target's boost," he said. "Micro G would be ideal. But any reduction helps, or it's like mountain climbing with a roaring forest fire underneath."

From her couch on the other side, Special Projects Sergeant Becky Diaken said, "You have done that."

"And I don't want to do it again. Sarendy, is there a remote way to hack into their engine controls?"

"I already tried that," the lithe woman said, turning front into her couch and arched backward. It made his spine hurt to watch, but she could talk face to face without twisting her neck, by peering over the head rest. "It acknowledged the signal, but nothing happened. The controls are separated from the telemetry."

"Well," he sighed, "that just adds another level of interesting. How long?"

Sarendy said, "Seventeen segs. We'll beat *Auburn* by three segs."

"Who actually runs this boat?" he asked, half seriously.

"Warrant Ulan runs it at your direction. I just know all."

Ulan took that moment to offer, "If you can get him aboard, Engineer Milton wants to try shutting off thrust physically."

"He's fucking insane."

"We've established that. Can you take him?"

"I can double up on a sled, yes."

Diaken twisted her neck to face him. "What about on several sleds?" There was no way someone with her figure would turn backward in the couch. She was sturdy, but fit.

"You're all insane. I shall file with my union for job interference. However, I can do it." He reflected that he had said the whole crew would be involved. He just hadn't considered they'd be involved in this manner. "I will only take people who have EVA experience, though."

"And who have suits," Milton said as he strained up the ladder from aft, now below. He carried a suit, and had removed his trademark shades.

Bowden said, "Well, don them now if you can. We'll sled as soon as we're close. Though I don't think anyone's ever locked out under boost before." He hadn't thought of that. The maneuvering sleds just didn't carry that much delta-V even if they could use it that fast.

Milton said, "You're locking out ahead in orbit, the plan being to meet at relative zero velocity. Diaken and I came up with ugly but workable grapples." He held one up to illustrate. It was a harpoon with barbs all over, pointing both ways. "You latch on, try to avoid smacking into the side, and work your way up. Of course, you'll be under acceleration then."

Bowden squinted. "The only way I can think of to do that is to climb the line while the sled smashes into the hull."

"Exactly. There are two side-lines you can grab, and swing in on a shorter arc. It's still going to be a hard landing."

"I think I'm glad I have a short team of six, not a squad of twenty, but with five of you nuts along as well . . . "

"Let me hack this rope off," Diaken said, pulling the

long braid she wore into view above her headrest. "It won't work well in a helmet."

"Ah, the sacrifices you make," he said.

"Ever seen a double back flip, sir?" she asked, and made two rude gestures.

Stadter looked at the proposed schedule and said, "Sergeant Lowther, time for you to kit up. We'll line you over."

"I've been ready," the man said. He was suited, kitted and decked with gear, most of it conformal and close-fitting. He stood gripping a stanchion next to the recovery lock.

"You're going to be three hundred meters out the line."

"Understood. I have a beacon if needed. Harness checks. Say the word."

The man really sounded confident. Either he was, or he was reassuring Stadter. Either way, it helped.

Vela said, "*Black Watch* reports they're commencing. We need to drop Lowther and clear the way."

"That's my cue," the medic said.

"Good luck."

He locked out, and his voice came over the net via wire.

"Ready to belay."

Vela said, "The controls are yours. I'm backup, listening."

"Roger. Extending."

Stadter kept his attention on course. They were barely ahead of *Mammy Blue*, barely off her ecliptic outside. Lowther had about eighty seconds of thrust in his harness to keep him at an oblique angle. After that, they'd have to cast off and reel him back fast to avoid irradiating him. Usually they docked with the calling craft. If not, he lined over while both ships were in free flight. Doing it under thrust was known to be dangerous and done only in theory before now.

It was nothing, though, on what the extremists from the Blazer Regiment were doing.

The insertion was terrifying.

Rem Bowden had done several boarding exercises in space, on vessels in orbit. Even from a distance, a vessel in orbit was relatively stationary. This one was under boost and unstable, shedding parts, changing thrust. There was no room for error, and he had little control over those potential errors.

The lock on a stealth boat took one man and one maneuvering sled at a time. Outside, he hooked onto a mounting carefully designed to be flush when not in use. He eased the line to full extension in the current 2 G acceleration, and hung as if off a cliff in open space. He then composed himself in patience, or as close as he could force himself, until the others made their way out. It would be eleven troops on six sleds, because the boat crew were not trained for it, and there were no spare sleds.

Sarendy was next out, even more shapely in a skinsuit. She was also lightly built and had a distinctive lope to her climb. She loosened her tensioner, zipped down, sending a hum through the line, braked, and then climbed over him. After latching onto the sled with two clips, she snaked a hand up and waved.

"Testing," he said.

"Ready," she agreed.

The primary crew, save the engineer, all remained aboard to manage recovery. That also left more room in the boat for casualties, though securing some of the more sensitive equipment was going to be a chore. It also meant he and the boarding party would be diverted elsewhere until all the boats could swap around in dock afterward.

That, however, was minor compared to the near-suicide they were about to embark on.

Far aft and out of view, *Mammy Blue* charged on her desperate flight into oblivion. If he could look, he might catch a reflection or a bare glow of her plasma stinger. Space was black with a few dots, when the polarizing helmet didn't blot them out.

"Boarding Party, report when ready."

"Ready," he said simply, eschewing any comments. For a real mission, commo silence would prevail. It would take effort to counter that training.

"Detaching in three, two, one . . . "

Acceleration stopped and they were in free orbit. *Black Watch* simultaneously cut thrust so they'd not be exposed to her radiation. If the trajectory was correct, they'd be close to *Mammy Blue* in two segs, at similar velocity, assuming her acceleration was reasonably consistent. Then they'd try to board. If it went wrong, they were all lined together and would light a beacon for recovery, though that could take a day. He wasn't sure what emotional shape the crew would be in after that.

Actually, he wasn't sure what emotional shape he'd be in, even without having to keep them calm. This was not an exercise with excess manpower standing by for recovery.

None of the team or the crew said anything. He wasn't sure if it was discipline or fear, but he wanted to minimize the latter.

"Count off again, just so I know you're awake," he said. It was as much for his reassurance as theirs.

The team rattled off numbers fast. The crew called their names, some sounding a bit quavery. They all responded, though. "Milton." "Sarendy." "Diaken." "D'Arcy." "Aufang."

The projection on his visor said they were close to *Mammy Blue*. Now they had to find it and board. He took his bearings from Iota Persei and his nav system, and faced in the right general direction.

He saw nothing, and instinctively checked his O2 level. Fifteen divs, plus the emergency bottle. They'd be fine. No, it was nothing like an exercise, but they'd be fine. He lowered the ratio slightly. He didn't want to hyperventilate.

A reflected splash of light indicated Engineer Milton's searchlight had caught the derelict. Then he saw the faint glow of the plasma stinger. He used the active sensor retrofitted to his sled to tag the target, and knew Hensley was, too, as was Sarendy. They couldn't miss.

"I have it, firing grapnel," he said. He reached up and armed the canister. Once back behind it, he swiveled the gun until the reticle lit, and fired.

They were actually very close; no more than two hundred meters. The question then was how well had they matched velocities?

He found out as the grapnel contacted and stuck and the line started spooling out with a thrumming vibration he could feel right through the sled and his suit. The drum friction brake engaged, and acceleration built quickly; blood rushed from his head to his feet.

In theory they were to string out in line, one behind the other. In practice, lines got tangled and they wound up in a clump.

Sarendy tried to grip the side line with a second, hand-held drum, but something didn't work. He cursed twice, then said, "We're going to impact. Everyone turn best you can and brace."

He said it just in time for them to smack into the side of the ship hard enough to bend some hardware and knock the breath out. He gasped and struggled for air, as gear and people buried him. Someone clutched at him, his right leg was pinned painfully at the thigh between two sleds, and he heard grunts, pants and whimpers over the air. It felt like hanging off a mountain, in darkness, while the mountain shook from a low grade earthquake.

Hensley said, "I have a second lock. We're secure."

Bowden firmly said, "No one do anything until told. First, I want at least two personal lines on padeyes, if anyone can reach. Four or five would be better." They were putting a hell of a strain on that harpoon, and it could fail, or the hull could, at any time.

"Linked." "On line." "Connected." "On line."

"Should I cut loose lines sir?"

"No cutting!" Gods, no. Cut the wrong one and they'd have a Dutchman.

They hung in a tangled mess of suits and sleds, lines all over. It took three concerted segs to weave in and out, disconnect and reconnect one careful line at a time, and ease the sleds aft. Eventually, they had two groups standing off the hull, hanging by line at what felt like 1.5 G. The crew had one attached bundle of their gear, the team another.

Milton asked, "Do you need us to wait on engine shutdown?"

"No, go ahead and do it. Sooner is better, just keep me in the loop. We need to go forward five frames and around two hundred mils."

"Good luck."

Just then, Diaken shouted, "Look out!" It wasn't a practical warning. It did alert everyone to take a look around. Another section was separating, pulling back and ripping free. It appeared to be just a skin plate of sheet polymer and metal, tumbling lazily in the Iolight as it fluttered delicately away. Of course, it was in orbit and might eventually collide with some other ship. The repercussions of this disaster would linger for years.

"And we're moving," Bowden said. "Time is short."

Once free of the sleds, the tangle of lines and the crew, their progress went quickly, even with the subjectively lateral G load. They lined together, swung around in bounds while linking to padeyes as they went. He insisted on at least three padeyes at a time, since he didn't trust this flying scrapyard.

That should save them against anything except another chunk of hull breaking loose with them on it, or half on it. Which, he tried not to dwell on, was entirely possible.

"Warrant Bowden, this is Sergeant Lowther. I am aboard, over our proposed entry point."

"Lowther, good to have you," he replied. It was. More professional help was welcome, as was knowing that area wasn't in the process of breaking up at this moment.

"Just so you know, I have a relayed message through *Auburn*. Apparently, the owner wants us to avoid excess damage."

Bowden finally felt emotion other than fear.

"He knowingly operated a bomb; he can suffer. Likely he's going to die in a duel with one of the victims anyway."

"Or a victim's next of kin."

"Screw that. They're entitled to take justice out on this sewerweasel personally. I intend to see they all get that chance." His scowl was dark.

"Just so you know," Lowther repeated. He didn't sound particularly concerned about the owner's plight. "I'm ready when you are, and have marked five padeyes I think are strong enough to hold us."

"Excellent. We'll be around in a few seconds."

A helmet appeared as they swung over the curve of the hull. That had to be Lowther.

He said, "I'm over a lounge that's designated priority for rescue."

Bowden said, "Okay. Are the passengers centralized?"

"Some of them. It's full of kids."

"Kids?" Bowden asked.

"Yeah, daycare center. Or kids' lounge. Something."

"Triff. How are they going to respond to us busting in in gear?" It was largely a rhetorical question, but necessary.

"Either thrilled or terrified. And they're already terrified."

"Right. No adults in there?"

"Maybe. The crewman relaying the info wasn't sure, and the locks have all sealed."

"We need some phones on the bulkhead so we can talk."

Blazer Arvil said, "Will do."

While he did that, Bowden introduced his team. They each waved as he tagged them. "This is our medic, Sergeant Marchetti. Structural tech, Hensley. Arvil on life support and systems. Lemke on flight controls if we need that. Bulgov on everything else. He's Combat Air Control, but we don't need that at the moment."

"Pleased to meet you. I've got all the medical gear we had and fifteen rescue balls." That explained the bulky pack over his tank.

The acceleration was high and irregular. But it was ceaseless, which was putting a strain on an increasingly damaged craft, and it was a massive inconvenience outside the hull. Inside it might actually prove useful. But they weren't inside yet. They hung on their harnesses and waited, shifting to keep circulation moving and to minimize pressure numbness in the acceleration.

"Hensley, what's your take on the structure?"

Hensley was qualified on surface, air and space craft. "Holding for now. I think we can open it here without damaging struts, but any loss of material weakens the whole, and will affect mass ratio and tension under load. I can't guarantee it won't shatter what's left of it."

"Well, we're getting farther away fast, so let's work faster. In, out, done."

Stadter didn't believe what he was hearing.

"Exposed?"

The *Black Watch*'s engineer, Milton said, "Yes, the feed lines are exposed, as are some of the valves."

"How's the radiation level? Those aren't made for adjustment in flight."

"Correct. We're lowering people by line and cut the line once they reach exposure limits."

That was too insane for words. Stadter felt nauseated himself, and not just because they were now shifting G to match the derelict.

He said, "They'll fall through the wash, and be lost as well."

"Yes, they'll need to kick off, then cut the line."

"I can't order anyone to do that. It's double suicide."

Milton said, "We volunteered."

"Of course you did. I can't see a logical argument against the shutdown, and it's less dangerous than doing nothing, may God help us all. Do it."

"Can you coordinate pickup?"

"Yes." That was part of the mission profile. However, juggling them aboard ships that could immediately have rad treatment available if needed would be harder. "Vela," he began.

"I'm looking for boats that will have at least emergency rad treatment," she said.

"Excellent."

"Okay," Bowden announced, "we're going to place cutting charges here and there." He splashed the hull with an intensely bright light. It could be a weapon if aimed at eyes, but here it served to illuminate for cameras. "Small for entry. Then we're going in in fireteam stacks just like a compartment clearing operation. Each troop will carry as many rescue balls as they can manage. Grab the kids, stuff them in, inflate them and bring them out. We blow the entire hull section for that. If you have to stun them or slap them to get compliance, do it. But we'd rather you took some bruising than the kids. Anyone worried about a few scratches?"

"Can't be worse than my bitch of a little sister," Arvil said. "Sharp nails."

"Good. But then we've got to clear the rest of the compartments, and do so *fast*. You can see the damage so far. Blowing those holes shouldn't hurt structural struts, but who knows what else is wrong with this piece of garbage. We can expect pressure cracks at least. There are bound to be more casualties, sorry, *passengers*, elsewhere, and they'll be going into anoxia fast. Open every hatch, clear every cubby, hit them with oxy and get them out."

Lemke said, "With active oh two depletion, brain damage starts in under eighty seconds."

"Correct. The longer they're in zero pressure, even if they have an oxy mask, the more risk of damage there is, right before death. Hopefully that won't be a problem." Even if they all knew it, it was good to go over the details. Every training exercise was a mission, and every mission a training exercise.

"I have phones up," said Arvil. "Talk away." He handed over a plugged wire.

Bowden clicked the plug to the patch on his helmet. He paused a moment to decide what to say.

"Hello onboard. This is Warrant Leader Bowden, Blazer Regiment. We are here to rescue you. Let me speak to someone in charge."

There was some shouting and crying, but not a lot. A

teen voice, probably male, said, "There is no one in charge. They went to get help when the explosion happened. Do you want the oldest?"

"That will be fine. Anyone who can follow directions while we get you out."

"That's me, I guess. Gordon Rodriguez. What do you need?"

"Gordon, I need an accurate count of everyone in that compartment, and I need to know about anyone else in that air space, if you know what that means. That's first, more afterwards."

"Okay, hold on."

The crying and calling went on, distant sounding, but plaintive. Small kids were unhappy, slightly older ones were being bossy and scared, a few were trying to offer advice, and Rodriguez was counting out loud. "Twelve, thirteen, dammit, *stop*! The soldier wants me to count you, let me do it! One, two . . . " His voice faded with distance or pressure, then finally came back with, "Seventeen, officer. Can you hear me?"

"Seventeen, one-seven understood. Stand by."

"Yes, sir."

Stadter was glad he couldn't actually watch the engine shutdown procedure. On the far side of the hull from the Blazers, their boat crew proved themselves equally gutsy, or equally mad. He listened in as they began, and set a screen to track IDs. He didn't know how they'd do this without modern commo. He could tag one way or two way for anyone involved, or go through the chain, or listen in, and it would transcribe and tell him who each speaker was.

"Milton on winch."

Aufang: "Winch on."

Milton: "Four zero. Five zero. Six zero. Seven zero. Slow to one meter per second."

Aufang: "Slowing to one meter per second."

Milton: "Eight zero . . . nine zero. Slow to point five meters per second."

Aufang: "Slowing to point five meters per second. You have four-seven seconds safe exposure."

Milton: "Nine two . . . nine three . . . nine four . . . stop."

Aufang: "Stop. Four-two safe."

Milton: "Adjust down one zero centimeters."

Aufang: "One zero down. Three-nine safe."

Milton: "Set payout length. Images and data transmitting." Pause.

Aufang: "Received. Three-two seconds. Length set."

A rich alto voice said, "Sarendy now on winch."

Aufang: "Winch on."

Milton: "Three-five millimeter connection at seven zero newton-meters torque."

Aufang: "Recorded. Two-five seconds."

Milton: "Sarendy will need to reach inside far left at once to have time to adjust Feed Number Two."

Aufang: "Recorded. One-eight seconds."

Milton: "Released locking clamp on Feed Number One. Expect gee boost before reduction."

Aufang: "Noted. One-two seconds."

Milton: "Two-three turns for full closure. Commencing."

Aufang: "Eight seconds . . . seven seconds . . . six seconds . . . five seconds . . ."

Milton: "Achieved four turns. Secure and clear of frame."

Aufang: "Kick and cut. Two seconds."

Milton: "Kicking. Cut. Clear. Dutchman, Dutchman, Dutchman!"

Whoever the man was, he'd voluntarily taken a lifetime safe dose of radiation, and cut himself free into space, trusting in others for pickup.

The female voice said, "Sarendy on station. Inside, far left. Will release locking clamp. Advise at one-five seconds."

A young male voice sounded. "D'Arcy on winch."

Aufang: "Winch on—Break—Sarendy, your exposure is increased inside hull. You are at two-zero seconds, one-nine, one-eight, one-seven, one-six, one-five."

Sarendy said, "Clamp released. Withdrawing. Stuck. Unstuck. Outside hull." She sounded mechanical, emotionless.

"Six seconds. Kick and cut."

Her voice was sharp as she said, "Kicking. Cut. Clear. Dutchman, Dutchman, Dutchman!"

"D'arcy on station."

Then it was, "Aufang on winch."

Diaken: "Winch on."

They were so calm it almost sounded like an exercise.

Vela cut in with, "Don't worry, sir, I have them both. Their own boat is intercepting, and will shadow for the others. Three of the *Mammy Blue* lifeboats are in tow. One was depressurized, and the one I mentioned earlier ran dry. There was no way to reach it in time. Twelve passengers in one, sixteen in the other. Fourteen survivors in process, some with anoxic brain damage. Third boat has fifteen alive."

"Understood. I trust you on this, just let me know if you need help." The endless tally of casualties, rad levels, elapsed times and coordinates were a blur he couldn't track. Perhaps those with brain damage could get reconstruction and save some function and memory. If not, it might have been kinder if they'd died. He shifted to relieve pressure on his spine. A wrinkle in his suit was irritating his shoulder, too.

"You won't like this. One was nothing but cabin crew and what passed for first class. They abandoned ship first."

Stadter felt conflicting emotions.

"Well, I guess the crew knew how crappy it was and bailed. They also probably aren't up to date on proper response. Nor can I believe the owner paid for good people."

"Most of them are dead."

He said, "That's something I'm not going to pass judgment on for now." He locked that down and concentrated on managing the disaster. Dead could be lashed outside, towed or buried in space worst case. That eliminated some capacity and O2 problems, leaving only some reaction mass problems.

On the hull over the youth lounge, Lowther said, "They're going to panic. I can't imagine they won't."

Bowden nodded. "Likely." His harness was tight under boost. His circulation suffered from the constriction. He wiggled to ease things.

"Any suggestions?"

Marchetti said, "Well, I was in Combat Rescue last assignment. I have one suggestion. You won't like it."

"I like it."

"One of the canisters in the standard boarding kit is SV Three. If we can vent it in there before we blow, they'll all be pretty well relaxed or even blotto."

That was unorthodox. "I like it."

Marchetti continued, "The side effects include some panic as they go under, and nausea. Good chance they'll puke all over the place, as we can't control the dose and it's made for adult combat troops, not youth."

"I still like it." Puke on a space suit wasn't bad. Puke in a space suit was bad.

"In that case we need a shipfitter and vacuum welding gear, fast."

"That would be Hensley."

From aft, Sergeant Hensley replied, "I heard. I have my gear. Roping that way now. I know where we keep it."

The ship vibrated again, and rolled a fraction. Everyone clutched lines and padeyes.

Arvil said, "I'm loose! Hull separation at radius two one zero, frame four zero. Dutchman, Dutchman, Dutchman!"

"Understood, Arvil. Got your transponder. Relaying to recovery ops. Ops, do you have him?" Bowden tapped IDs into the comm on his left forearm, hoping not to lose a good man.

Stadter said, "We have him. He's in range of something. I'll have whoever that something is grab him in about ten segs, if he can last that long." He sounded giddy with exhaustion.

"Yes." Yeah, ten segs wasn't a problem, assuming they

did get him. There were lots of craft, so the odds were very good. Still.

"Good luck, Blazers, we'll do what we can."

Hensley said, "Approaching. I could use a line transfer to speed things up."

Bowden bent over, snapped another line in place and tossed the bag at Hensley as he came over the horizon of the ship's skin. Hensley caught it, pulled the free eye out, and clipped it to his harness. He popped the old one free and let it dangle, then fall in the acceleration. The lines cost better than Cr500 each, but they could gather them afterward, if time permitted. Even then, most were only proofed for one hard yank or one abrasion. Space was not the place for corner-cutting.

"Thanks much. Where do you need me?" the fitter asked as he climbed the metal cliff.

The ship shifted violently and they all grabbed lines, but it was a reduction in acceleration. Perhaps 1.2, close to surface normal for Grainne.

Bowden said, "Anywhere here you can make a hole and pass gas."

"One dutch oven coming up," Hensley joked. "Is that a bypass valve next to the emergency panel? When was this piece of crap built?"

Bowden looked where Hensley's light splashed. Yes, that was an archaic emergency fill pipe. Ancient, but convenient, if it was intact.

"It's forty-eight Earth years old, thirty-three of ours."

"Gods, this thing should have been lashed up as a museum or broken for scrap. Okay, I need five segs."

"Make it three."

"Five it is," Hensley agreed.

Bowden nodded to himself. Sometimes reality didn't bend. Hensley leaned forward and took a bend in the line to hold himself steady. He pulled out a grinder, then contact fluid, then his portable inductor, and hermetically welded the hose fitting to the valve.

One of the trailing lines slackened and Marchetti sprang into view. He let his legs collapse and soak up momentum from the landing, while tightening a retainer. The man had enough experience he didn't even hop, but simply stood from the skin, maneuver complete.

"That should be enough gas to disorient them. I'm worried about brain damage or other ill effects, though."

Lowther pinged in and said, "I checked with the station medical officer. He said he couldn't hear my transmission and suggested we discuss hypothetical research questions after the fact."

Bowden felt a bit nervous, on top of the shaky and nauseated and icy and wired and adrenaline-soaked. He didn't think anyone would blame him for the attempt, but if anything exacerbated the disaster, he could wave his career a hearty goodbye. If he pulled it off, however . . .

He choked all that down. This was about saving a hull full of kids.

He heard an override chime, and Stadter cut in.

"Bowden, I need to know your timeline, and what you'll be doing with rescue balls."

"That depends on how these ships are going to catch them. We'll lash them together and can tow them or drop them. Otherwise, someone has to get close enough to line them over."

"Just keep them out of the engine wash. Record. Cluster of three. Cluster of four. Cluster of four. Cluster of five. One single. Give them enough drift to clear the engines, and minimize other momentum. I'll tag ships to match departing velocity and recover, but Bowden . . . "

"Recorded, sir. Go ahead."

"We're rapidly reaching the point where all these ships will need secondary rescue on fuel, power and oh two."

Hensley took that moment to say, "Ready."

Bowden said, "Ops, we'll be flinging them in two hundred seconds, I hope. Stand by."

"Understood. Also, the ongoing loss of structure and mass is affecting trajectory and acceleration."

"Damn. I thought it felt a bit brisker again. Understood.—Break—Lemke, are you ready on charges?"

"Ready."

"Marchetti, ready on gas?"

"Ready. I need twenty-six seconds, per the medical officer, who advises against doing this." He waited at the gas bottle, with a metal shield they'd use to avoid sharp edges on the entry.

"Do it. My order." He tensed at that. God and Goddess, it better work. "Listen on the hull phones, and stand by to cut and breach." He clicked through to the hull phone again. "Gordon, I need everyone to hold still and relax. The atmosphere is going to change, and we're about to come in. Stay clear of the hull."

"Understood, sir. We're on the far side."

"Ready." "Ready." "Ready." "Ready." "Ready," echoed through his helmet. Five was correct. He hoped Arvil was okay. Lemke stood with his detonation controls, waiting.

Marchetti said, "Twenty-two, twenty-three, twenty-four, twenty-five, twenty-si—"

Lemke thumbed a pad, a nimbus of boiling debris, expansion-chilled vapors and particles illuminated by a searing flash erupted from the hull, and faded to glitters of gray.

Marchetti took the number-one spot, lifting his feet and letting the acceleration slide the ship under him. He bent and twisted like a gymnast, planted his shield against the aft side of the breach, and swung in. Lowther followed quickly and smoothly, then Bulgov. Bowden twisted and threw himself down, glad of the near normal G after the torture of 3 G. The hull was two thin plates perhaps six centimeters apart, and he glimpsed crumbled faramesh as he went past. One good solar flare might have done this beast in, too.

Then he was inside, as Hensley followed, and Lemke came last. Bowden made sure he wasn't going to crush anyone, and settled on the effective deck, the rear bulkhead. It was a deck under boost. However, that boost eased off enough to make his ears spin. Less than 1.0 G, he guessed.

The reduced gees helped, but the craft's motion was very irregular, shuddering and rumbling. Still, the kids were unconscious on the boost deck, rear bulkhead, from gas and hypoxia. Some of them had puked, and all looked rather wrung out.

Lemke slapped a balloon patch over the breach, and Lowther punched the emergency O2 canister. That, at least, worked. He then punched the one they'd brought with them. The pressure wouldn't be great, but it should be enough to prevent major brain damage, hopefully. This assumed any airtight doors in this section remained functional. You did what you could, and sometimes it worked.

The bulkhead shifted as if in an earthquake, but the acceleration dropped again. He recovered from his two seconds of thought and got to work.

The smallest kids were at greatest risk, and easiest to handle. They were first, when there was a choice. He scooped up a girl perhaps two years old, a delicate little thing, and slid her into a ball. He zipped and yanked and it inflated. Then he saw he'd missed her stuffed critter of some kind. He grabbed it and stuck it into his harness as he shook out another ball and reached for the boy next to her.

By the time he reached the next, the rest were all ready to go, bundled and with transponders already lit. The last one he handled was a teenage girl, and it felt somewhat obscene, the way he had to shove her legs and butt into the sack.

"Seventeen?" he asked.

"Seventeen."

"Is that confirmed from manifest?"

"No. Bulgov is searching aft."

Bowden considered. He didn't want to leave anyone behind. If need be, they could split into elements. But the ship was failing, time was running out, and the risk increased for the rest of them the longer they delayed.

The kids started waking up.

The teenagers figured it out quickly, except for the one girl, who was apparently a claustrophobe. She thrashed and kicked, realized intellectually the problem with that, and curled up to hug herself, sobbing and trembling.

Some of the small kids, however, did not like the enclosures, nor the disorientation of waking up from the gas, nor being away from their friends. Some of them put up a healthy tantrum.

Luckily, the balls were designed not to be torn. Panic response was one of the design criteria.

One little boy found the emergency lanyard, designed for escape in case of some bizarre circumstance where one had entered by accident, closed up and needed out before the onboard O2 supply failed. He yanked it, peeled out fast, then started gaping like a fish in the very thin atmosphere, which now had several more holes to leak from. He sprawled in the direction of one cabinet. Lowther grabbed him by the collar, got face to mask as the kid faded, stuffed him back into a new ball from his kit, and in a dive, grabbed an armful of assorted stuffed toys and threw them in with the child. Hopefully one was his, and the rest could be sorted out afterward. Bowden sighed. Such things were essential support items for kids, but a pain to deal with.

Bulgov called from aft, "Someone was clever and locked themselves in an airlock between sections. The safety is working and it won't open."

Lemke said, "Arriving," and dropped down the passage. A few second later, a rumble and bang indicated a breach of the door mechanism, shallow shrieks sounded just as Bowden glanced down, to see two disheveled teens, one male, one female, letting themselves gratefully be stuffed into rescue balls. They got limper as the rare atmosphere affected them.

As soon as he had green pings on his helmet readout

from everyone, he ordered, "Hensley, we're done. Pull the plug."

They'd been inside the ship seventy-three seconds.

Hensley jabbed a sharp knife into the plug and sliced. It deflated, sucked through and stuck on a torn piece of hull, vibrating in an increasingly shallow flutter as the remaining atmosphere blew past. Then Lemke waved for attention and thumbed his detonator again.

Half the compartment hull disappeared in a flashing swirl, blowing out, peeling back, and ripping off into space. Some tatters blew in and tumbled down the companionway aft.

Stadter wished he could do more than listen and coordinate. His medic was over them pulling kids out. His two flight crew were coordinating sequences of ships to recover people floating in space, and the technicians from the Special Warfare boat were diddling the engines. Management was important, but he wished mightily for hands on.

"Rescue, this is Diaken."

"Go ahead."

"Got it down to zero point six G. How's the structure looking?"

They'd done all they could, and it might have bought enough seconds to save a few people.

He said, "Bad. Complete spine failure is imminent. It's still visibly deflecting."

"I'm last on the line. I'll see what I can do. Can you monitor my vitals?"

Vela said, "I have you."

His screen flashed the tag DIAKEN as she said, "On winch. Winch on. Descending."

Vela said, "Rad levels are reduced. Looks like you have eight-seven seconds outside the access."

Diaken: "Well, it'll be less, because I'll be inside. I might have to break things."

Vela did have a good voice for reassuring people. "We've got your readings. Good luck."

Diaken: "Thanks. We'll see if it matters."

With the hull open like a cave, it was time. Bowden made the call.

"Rescue, this is Bowden. Ready to pitch on your order."

"Outstanding. Stand by in five, four, three, two, one, throw."

"Thrown," he confirmed, as Bulgov and Lemke tossed a lashed bundle of three balls out into space. God and Goddess help the kids. Then he realized they had two extras.

"Rescue, we found two extra, where do you want them?"

"Crap. Last. Three, two, one, throw."

"Thrown," he reported, as another bundle went out.

The two larger bundles took effort, the troops grunting as they heaved the masses out, being so very careful not to rip one open on the torn section of hull.

Bulgov said, "I'm hit! Suit tear on the edge. Bleeding, level two. Pressure tight, but damn, bleeding."

"Understood. Step out, apply aid. The rest of you finish throwing."

Stadter said, "Bowden, your last three tosses are delayed. Stand by."

"Holding," he said, and gritted his teeth. He pointed at Lowther, who nodded and climbed over to help Bulgov apply a pressure bandage. They wore skintight constriction suits, so there was no risk of suffocation unless the helmet was cracked, but vacuum drew body fluids out, too. Speaking of which, he found a safe direction, popped a valve and let loose a liter, to boil away into nothing. That felt better. The gees dropped again, as did the noise and vibration.

Stadter said, "Bundle that last pair together."

Lemke grabbed a short elastic cord, wove it through the grips and thumbed up.

"Ready."

"Ready in five, four, three, two, one . . . "

The last bundle rolled out and dropped aft into space.

"Rescue, that's them all. Proceeding aft and forward for other casualties."

"Good luck, Bowden. Thrust steady at zero point six gee, but structure increasingly compromised. Estimate five hundred seconds max."

"Is it really that close, or is that your safety margin, over?" He was moving as he asked, with a wave to the rest.

"I say four hundred, I figure you can handle five hundred."

"Understood."

"Rescue, I need a count," he called over Rescue channel.

"Current count is one four seven."

"There are theoretically seven zero people left aboard."

"Correct."

"Shit."

He left it at that, and led the way forward as Lemke and Bulgov went rear. It was much easier at .6 G, but only relatively. The wreck was a mess. Struts were bent and bending, panels buckling, and leaks increasing. It was hard to see through a haze of condensation in the dropping pressure. Lacking pressure, some areas of the hull were collapsing in. Others bowed out, lacking the structural tension to hold them. The first lock they came to was jammed closed, until Hensley slapped a ready charge on it and cracked the latch. Bowden moved through, and the override on the other side worked. Apparently, the lock had been holding atmosphere within. That seemed to run in this ship. Had the pressure switches ever been tested since it was built?

He swung the lock and jumped in startlement. A figure in an emergency mask stood just inside. He could see the man talking, but there was no atmosphere. In a moment, the man switched to pointing. Staterooms. He pointed at his mask with both hands, simulating donning it, and pointed at the compartments again.

Bowden nodded, and ordered, "Check the staterooms, have masks and balls ready."

The three men swarmed around him and the crewman, used demolition bars on the hatch-doors, and ripped into the staterooms.

Sharp thinking. They held partial pressure of atmosphere, and overpressure of bodies. Three staterooms had forty-three people, with their emergency masks, taking turns connecting to the emergency bottles. They hadn't fought each other in a panic over oxy, but from the relief on their faces, they would have soon.

"Bowden, this is Lemke. Aft is . . . bad. It's mostly evacuated, physically and radioactively hot, and structurally a mess. There are holes everywhere. I'm prepared to go by compartment on your order."

He checked time on his visor. There was no way to get everyone out in the allowed time. So they'd have to hope to beat the odds, because there was no way they could leave anyone behind. The nausea and heat came back, and he increased his oxy level. He needed it now.

"Lemke, copy Rescue, what do you see of the lifeboats?"

Lemke said, "They seem to be gone from this side."

Stadter said, "There are two not accounted for, but their bays are far back near the reactor. My call is not to go there."

Bowden said, "Agreed."

Stadter added, "You'll be glad to know there are some relieved parents. The engineering crew cleared the casino and lounge and forced them into the lifeboats. Tough call, but the right one."

"Good news. Lemke, Bulgov, come forward."

"Yes, sir."

"Rescue, this is Bowden. Four-three mobile casualties in masks. We can put some in balls. Is there any way to dock or catch?"

"Bowden, this is Rescue. Your team has planted charges on the reactor feeds. They plan to cut the lines the hard way and brenschluss that way." His voice sounded tight.

"Understood. Will that be soon?" Bowden asked. Stadter did not sound happy.

"If you consent, I do."

"Do it." That would take the strain off the structure. He

felt relief and guilt. If they'd been able to do that sooner
. . . but he'd definitely live.

A moment later a bang and a rumble shook the creaky
vessel, but thrust dissipated at once, to nothing.

"Bowden, this is Rescue, we can dock at Frame One
Zero, Radius Two Zero Zero."

"Do that, and we'll shuffle people in one at a time."

"We can take the worst one-five, absolute max. The rest
will have to egress for recovery."

"Understood."

This was going to mean a fight.

Stadter didn't want to tell Bowden how the feeds had
been cut. Sergeant Diaken was dying from massive
radiation exposure, from hand-placing charges inside the
danger radius. The other four were adrift in the dark
awaiting pickup from amateurs in craft not equipped for
rescue, along with Arvil. Bowden and his team were cutting
their way through the inside . . .

"Rescue, this is *Barley Mow*. We have an extra
recovery."

Budd said, "*Barley Mow*, this is Rescue, elaborate,
please."

"Sergeant Arvil. He slapped against the hull. We got a
line on him. He's got some impact trauma, but his suit
armor took it, and he's alive if bruised."

Budd, Vela and Stadter stared at each other for a
second.

Stadter said, "*Barley Mow*, that's ludicrous, but thank
you."

★ ★ ★

Bowden wished they'd opened the staterooms one at a time. While the three crew had done a fine job herding people in, they'd reach panic level soon. Nor could he use command voice, there was almost no pressure in the forward end.

He used his map projector on the bulkhead, and Lowther and Marchetti matched him in the other rooms.

CHILREN ARE ALIVE, he flashed. YOU WILL EVAC THROUGH FORWARD LOCK. SHIP WILL DOCK FOR WORST NEED. OTHERS WILL BE TOWED.

They nodded in worried understanding, but their confidence seemed a bit higher. He wasn't going to tell them how they'd be towed.

There was a pregnant woman, two more children, three people with minor but painful injuries—sprains and bruises from the runaway G—and seven people who, in his opinion, were near breaking point.

The schedule suffered again when Hensley had to spend long segs welding cracks in the airlock. To be fair, they seemed to be recent, but it was all part of the same utter failure. The owner didn't even deserve a duel. They'd found several patches aboard that were purely cosmetic. He'd known this wreck was subpar.

Lemke and Bulgov crawled up through the wreckage from below, looking fatigued, but functional.

With one troop in each room managing the oxygen, and three spare bottles from elsewhere, calm prevailed. That left him and Lemke to push forward.

The bridge lock was sealed from inside, and he rang the chime. He waited, and rang it again. The purser should be in there. He was about to call Rescue for relay when the latch moved.

The purser swung it open and the expression on his face was tragic.

Bowden gripped him and pressed helmets for conduction. "Mr. Doherty, we're here for you."

Doherty maintained some composure. He spoke into his mic, probably to Rescue, then pulled the lead from his helmet. Inside his suit the man shivered. He let himself be led.

"Bowden, this is Rescue."

"Go ahead."

"Lowther and we came up with a plan. Take the passengers out singly. Stuff them into balls, toss them out. They'll be immediately available for pickup now that we're in free flight. All primary vessels are converging."

"That works. We can start now." The pregnant woman was already aboard *Auburn*. The kids were lined up and ready, and after that it was just a case of moving fast enough with O2 running low. Of course, the lack of lights, gravity and heat was going to be a problem. He welcomed it to the alternative.

There was an attempt at chivalry, with some men hanging back while the women were moved. A couple of quite cute ones shivered in goosebumps, underdressed for an evacuated ship. He handled them professionally, but it was hard to move someone under these conditions without grabbing their ass and shoving.

"That's fifteen," Lowther said.

"Balls," he replied.

The next woman came up the line, looked at the ball,

and clenched in fear. She didn't resist as they stuffed her in, but she wasn't helpful.

Then it became clear that some people were hanging back out of fear, letting others precede them. That meant the end would be interesting.

It was a good thing the engines were completely down. It took a lot longer than five hundred seconds to transfer everyone. More than half would have died on that schedule.

They passed people out, stuffed them into balls, and handled them through the wedged-wide lock, where Lowther and Marchetti lashed them to *Auburn*. The passengers could see out the tiny windows, and they all looked frightened or frozen. It was going to be traumatic for them, but, Bowden observed, not as traumatic as dying. One by one, the medics played out sections of line, looped and lashed them, and occasionally peeked in a window to smile and give someone a thumb's up.

The last woman and last man clung to the stanchion next to the O2 supply. He was middle aged, in good shape, even athletic, but shivered like a lapdog. She was completely numb with a thousand meter stare. Both had to have their fingers pried loose, and be towed to the lock.

And that was that. After the earlier excitement, the ending was somewhat anticlimactic.

Lowther shook hands, swung back out, clipped and unclipped lines and monkey-crawled around his charges, letting them see that he was outside with them. He would ride that way until another craft matched course to take them off.

"We're clear. We'll mount. Transponders on, awaiting

pickup sometime in the next four divs." He felt an odd mix of elated, satisfied, nervous, frightened and lethargic. They'd done it.

"Understood, and your sled transponders are still live. Tracking already."

"Thanks, Rescue." It would be divs before they were recovered, days before they filtered from ship to ship and back to their own craft, and then probably down for debriefing. One thing about real world missions; they beat the hell out of exercises for both value and intensity.

He'd say he never wanted to do it again, but he felt more alive than he ever had. Some people never knew if they mattered. Blazers didn't have that problem.

He checked his harness and prepared to line aft, leaving *Mammy Blue* cold and dead in space.

Stadter's guts flipped at the current exchange, but he had to do it.

"Rescue to Sergeant Diaken."

Her voice was raspy and ill-sounding. "Go ahead, Rescue."

"One-eight-six recovered. Four-three after you cut feeds."

"Glad to hear it. Thanks for all your efforts. Diaken out." The transmission ended in an odd fade.

"Rescue out," he said, needlessly. There was no way she'd live to reach the station after that dose, much less anywhere that could hope to do anything. It wasn't even safe to recover her body. That hiss had been her helmet unsealing to vacuum. There were no good ways to die, but that seemed so cold.

He turned his attention back to Bowden.

"Bowden, this is Rescue. I have an interim AAR if I can relay the good and bad."

"Rescue, go ahead. I can take it."

"Bowden, one eight six of two one seven recovered and expected to live. Those extra two you caught had to be towed outside and transferred to another ship. They're pretty shaken. I think most of the survivors are well-tranked."

He paused and continued, "One lost on recovery, we'll need to check your cameras to determine who. Bundle of five tumbled, one separated and caught in engine wash. I'm sorry."

There was momentary silence, then Bowden said, "Continue."

"Regret to relay that Special Projects Sergeant Diaken absorbed lethal dose, by choice, to effect shutdown on the feeds. She bought you the additional time."

"Then she saved at least forty lives. She was a good woman." The man sounded steely, but Stadter figured he'd be torn up as soon as his mic was closed.

"That's it for your watch. Other casualties due to lifeboat failing and no crew aboard to assist with backup O2. The bottle worked, they just couldn't figure it out in time. Some of the crew died aboard, and twelve passengers."

"On the whole, then, I guess we all did an amazing job. Thank you, Lieutenant, and your staff, for coordination."

"And you, Bowden. Stadter out, listening." He figured to leave the man to deal with his troops and his frustration, for the next half day.

Bowden would be the last man out of a powerless

derelict, in free flight in space, awaiting pickup in the darkness. That took insane amounts of courage.

They spent a full day passing the passengers in the balls outside to other ships, swapping fuel and oxy, coordinating others. They breathed canned air, ate plastic-wrapped food bars and were grateful for both. The rescued passengers were stuffed into the two cabins of the small craft, making any movement a pain. Luckily, the pregnant woman wasn't close to labor. They all stank of fear, the filters couldn't keep up, and even the latrine was overloaded, despite venting to space twice. Garwell had to pretty well sit on top of them. Two were billeted under his couch and controls.

Eventually, they maneuvered into their cradle and docked. Stadter hit the switches to cut power, dumped a reload request for supplies expended, and crawled out the hatch into the station. The alternate crew had lined up to cheer them, in both tribute and jealousy. A mission like this happened once in a career, though, he reflected, once was enough.

He shook hands with his opposite, Captain Brown, and said, "I need to debrief and rest. Thank you," he turned to the rest, "and thank you all. We'll catch up later."

He near staggered on his way to Station Control.

Captain Vincent looked worn, satisfied and angry. It was an odd combination of expressions.

"Lieutenant Stadter. You're just in time."

"Yes, sir?" He didn't think there was a problem at his end, and Vincent wasn't one to string things out.

"Things are very good. I want to make sure you know that. Exceptional work all around. Among your crew,

Warrant Vela is to be commended for outstanding traffic control."

"Thank you, sir."

"Just thought you'd like to know I have the ship's owner on another screen."

"That's interesting," Stadter said. He didn't want to make any assumptions about that. He was too edgy and likely to snap.

Vincent turned, lit the screen and looked into it.

"Mister Etzl, Lieutenant Stadter was in charge of the rescue effort."

Etzl didn't look like a cheap bastard, nor was he oily. However, he didn't waste any time.

"I'd like to thank you for recovering my passengers, sir."

"You're welcome. We all did the best we could. I directed a lot of professionals and dedicated volunteers."

"I'd like to discuss recovering my ship, and compensation."

Adminwork, the bane of existence, he thought. Though to a man like this, reports were everything. He saw figures. Statder saw people.

"If you are asking for a report for your insurance, it will come to you in time, after it works through our system."

Etzl shook his head. "I'm not worried about that. But there's cargo and gear and supplies aboard. I understand it's in free flight. This wouldn't count as rescue, but recovery, and of course you're entitled to a share as salvage. But will you be able to get back out on that shortly? The sunk costs increase the further out it gets." He seemed agitated.

Stadter was too numb from the mission to get angry. It

was just too surreal. Etzl needed to worry more about what would happen when charges started piling on him, and challenges to duel. If he was lucky, he'd only be indentured for life.

On the one hand, it would be nice if the passengers recovered any items of personal value. There was even a chance the cargo contained things that couldn't be replaced by money alone. At the same time, they'd already lost too many people, injured several, and one had volunteered to die to help save others and reduce the burden this scumbag faced. He really should be enraged. He should challenge the man himself, Bahá'i rules on dueling be damned.

He was just too wired, tired and overloaded to deal with it right now. He was giddy with fatigue, disoriented, and this didn't feel real. There was a policy that applied here, though. He went with that.

"Sir, you may contract whoever you wish for salvage. Neither I nor my crew are available. Your ship represents a hazard to traffic as is, so I recommend you move quickly on any recovery. I will officially recommend that the military use it for target practice if it's not dealt with in a week. This matter is closed. Good day to you."

He nodded to Vincent, who nodded back with a faint smirk. Then he turned and headed for his cabin. He could pick up the anger later, if there weren't better things to do.

AFTERWORD
★★★

I READ A LOT.

This house has several thousand books, mostly nonfiction, on a plethora of subjects. Somewhere in the section on ships is a story about a ferry in New York Harbor sometime in the 1890s, I recall. There are three events online that might be the specific one I found in the book, but they're all of a similar vein.

This small vessel, in winter, was full of people traveling from island to island or mainland. Most of them were immigrant laborers.

This boat did have a boiler explode, rupturing one side, causing it to founder and sink. There were lifeboats, bought cast-off from some better vessel, not seaworthy. There were kapok life jackets, but the rubber had dry-rotted, the kapok mildewed, and they weren't in usable condition even if the water wasn't barely warmer than the freezing air.

Every craft in the harbor did respond, in a frenzy not seen again until Flight 1549 landed in the Hudson River more than a century later. I can't recall how many survived, but most did. The owner was held in very poor regard, and if I recall correctly, sued into poverty, as he should be.

From there, I wondered how such a story would work in the Freehold universe, which, despite some parties alleging it to be a "utopia," bears several significant resemblances to the era of robber barons and exploitative management.

There are many things done better by the free market. However, some things actually do require government infrastructure to effect properly. Whether or not quality standards for spaceship inspections are among the latter probably depends in part on who's arguing the point, and if they intend to be aboard. Even if one can settle up economically afterward, duel or seek vengeance, it's probably better to have the intact ship in the first place.

Of course, the Deepwater Horizon oil spill incident in the Gulf of Mexico took place despite government inspections and approval, so it may not matter either way.

The Price
★★★

This was a bad story in 2000. In its original version, it rightfully got rejected because it was long, turgid and tried to be far too complex. I'm still learning how to write shorts. This was an attempt to cram a novel into 12,000 words.

When John Ringo told me he expected a story from me for the Citizens *anthology—a collection in which all the authors are veterans, though the stories aren't necessarily military—I wondered if this one would work. He agreed to my query, so I dusted it off. I pretty much gutted and rewrote it thirty-five percent shorter, cut scenes, tightened some stuff up, and made it work. The concept was sound. The execution had been awful.*

Both he and Baen editor Jim Minz were complimentary over it, and I got good feedback from quite a few veterans. I'll just keep working on the concept of short fiction until I get better.

★★★

FOUR JEMMA Two Three, Freehold of Grainne Military

Forces, (J Frame Craft, Reconnaissance, Stealth), was a tired boat with a tired crew.

After two local years—three Earth years—of war with the United Nations of Earth and Space, that was no small accomplishment. Most of her sister vessels had been destroyed. That *4J23* was intact, functional, and only slightly ragged with a few "character traits" spoke well of her remarkable crew.

"I have a message, and I can't decode it with my comm," Warrant Leader Derek Costlow announced. The crew turned to him. This could be a welcome break from the monotony of maintenance. Jan Marsich and his sister Meka, both from Special Warfare and passengers stuck aboard since the war started, paid particular attention. Any chance of finding a real mission or transport back to Grainne proper was of interest to them.

"Want me to have a whack at it, Warrant?" asked Sergeant Melanie Sarendy, head of the intelligence mission crew.

"If you would, Mel," he nodded. "I'll forward the data to your system."

Sarendy dropped her game control, which was hardwired and shielded rather than wireless. Intel boats radiated almost no signature. The handheld floated where it was until disturbed by the eddies of her passage.

Jan asked, "Why do we have a message when we're tethered to the Rock? From who?"

Meka wrinkled her brow.

"That's an interesting series of questions," she commented.

"The Rock" was a field-expedient facility with no official

name other than a catalog number of use only for communication logs. The engineers who carved and blasted it from a planetoid, the boat crews who used it, the worn and chronically short-handed maintenance personnel aboard had had little time to waste on trivialities such as names. There were other such facilities throughout the system, but few of the surviving vessels strayed far enough from their own bases to consort with other stations. "The Rock" sufficed.

They were both attentive again as Sarendy returned. She looked around at the eyes on her, and said, "Sorry. Whatever it is, I don't have a key for it."

Meka quivered alert. "Mind if I try?" she asked.

"Sure," Costlow replied.

She grabbed her comm and plugged it into a port as everyone waited silently. She identified herself through several layers of security and the machine conceded that perhaps it might have heard of that code. A few more jumped hoops and it flashed a translation on her screen.

The silence grew even more palpable when she looked up, her eyes blurred with tears. "Warrant," she said, voice cracking, and locked eyes with him.

Costlow glanced around the cabin, and in seconds everyone departed for their duty stations or favorite hideyholes, leaving the two of them and Jan in relative privacy. Jan was family, and Costlow let him stay. In response to the worried looks from the two of them, Meka turned her screen to face them.

The message was brief and said simply, "YOU ARE ORDERED TO DESTROY AS MANY OF THE FOLLOWING PRIORITIZED TARGETS AS POSSIBLE.

ANY AND ALL ASSETS AND RESOURCES ARE TO BE UTILIZED TO ACCOMPLISH THIS MISSION. SIGNED, NAUMANN, COLONEL COMMANDING, PROVISIONAL FREEHOLD MILITARY FORCES. VERIFICATION X247." Attached was a list of targets and a timeframe. All the targets were in a radius around Jump Point Three, within about a day of their current location.

"I don't understand," Jan said. "Intel boats don't carry heavy weapons. How do they expect us to do this?"

"It was addressed to me, not the boat," Meka replied. "He wants me to take out these targets, using any means necessary."

That didn't need translating. There was a silence, broken by Costlow asking, "Are you sure that's a legit order? It looks pointless. Why would they have you attack stuff way out here in the Halo?"

Meka replied, "We know what the enemy has insystem. We know where most of their infrastructure is. If Naumann wants it taken out, it means he's preparing an offensive."

"But this is insane!" Jan protested. "The Aardvarks will have any target replaced in days!"

"No," Meka replied, shaking her head. "It's a legit order. All those targets are intel or command and control."

Costlow said, "So he wants the command infrastructure taken out to prevent them from responding quickly. Then he hits them with physical force."

"Okay, but why not just bomb them or use rocks in fast trajectories?" Jan asked.

Costlow said, "It would take too long to set that many rocks in orbit. Nor could we get them moving fast enough. Maneuvering thrusters and standard meteor watch would take care of them. As to bombing them, they all have defensive grids, and we're a recon boat."

Jan paused and nodded. "Yeah, I know. And there aren't many real gunboats left. I'd just like a safer method." He asked Meka, "So how could you get in?"

"UN stations have sensor holes to ignore vacsuits and toolkits. Ships can't get in, but a single person can."

Costlow looked confused. "Why'd they leave a hole like that?" he asked.

"Partly to prevent accidents with EVA and rescue, partly laziness. They lost a couple of people, and that's just not socially acceptable on Earth," she said. "It's the Blazer's greatest asset to penetrating security. Systems only work if they are used. Backdoors and human stupidity are some of our best tools."

"Didn't they think anyone would do what you're discussing?" Jan asked. That was dangerous. It would push EVA gear to the edge.

"No," she said, shaking her head. "They would never give such an order. The political bureaucracy of the UNPF requires all missions be planned with no loss of life. Not minimal, but zero. Yes, it's ridiculous, but that's how they do things."

Jan asked, "So you EVA in, and then back out?"

"How would I find a stealthed boat from a suit? How would you find me? It's not as if there's enough power to just loiter, and doing so would show on any scan." Her expression was flushed, nauseous and half grinning. It was creepy.

" . . . But even if you get through, they can still get new forces here in short order," Jan said. He didn't want his sister to die, because that's what this was; a literal suicide mission. His own guts churned.

"No," Meka replied. "Or, not fast enough to matter, I should say." She tapped tactical calculus algorithms into her comm while mumbling, "Minimum twenty hours to get a message relayed to Sol . . . flight time through Jump Point Two . . ."

Jan had forgotten that. Jump Point One came straight from Sol, but it no longer existed. Professor Meacham and his wife had taken their hyperdrive research ship into it, then activated phase drive. The result of two intersecting stardrive fields was hard to describe mathematically, but the practical, strategic result was that the point collapsed. No jump drive vessel could transit directly from Sol to Grainne anymore, and the UN didn't yet have any phase drive vessels that they knew of.

Meka finished mumbling, looked up, and said, "Median estimate of forty-three days to get sufficient force here. They could have command and control back theoretically in forty hours, median two eighty-six, but that doesn't help them if they are overrun. It's risky, but we don't have any other option."

Costlow said, "That may be true, but they *can* send more force. It's a short term tactical gain, but not a strategic win."

"I know Naumann," Meka replied firmly. "He has something planned."

"Unless it's desperation," Costlow said.

Shaking her head, her body unconsciously twisting to compensate, she said, "No. He never throws his people away, and he has very low casualty counts. If he wants me to do this, then he has a valid plan."

"Trusting him with your life is dangerous, especially since you don't even know that's him," Jan said. They'd almost died three times now. She'd almost died a couple more. This one was for real.

"We're trusting him with more than that," she said. "And that's definitely him. Security protocols aside, no one else would have the balls to give an order like that and just assume it would be followed. Besides, it authenticates."

"Okay," Costlow reluctantly agreed. "Which target are you taking?"

She pointed as she spoke, "Well, the command ship *London* is the first choice, but I don't think I can get near a ship. This crewed platform is second, but I'd have to blast or fight my way in. If I fail, I still die, and accomplish nothing. I suppose I have to chicken out and take the automatic commo station."

"Odd way to chicken out," Jan commented in a murmur.

"Are you sure of these priorities?" Costlow asked. His teeth were grinding and he looked very bothered.

"Yes," she replied. "If I had more resources, I'd take *London*, too. We don't have any offensive missiles, though."

"We have one," the older man softly replied. They looked at him silently. "If you're sure that's a good order," he said. His face turned from tan to ashen as he spoke.

"I am," she said.

"Then I'll drop you on the way. Just think of this as an intelligent stealth missile," he said, and tried to smile. It looked like a rictus.

"Are you sure?" she asked.

"No," he admitted. "But if it's what we have to do to win . . ."

There was silence for a few moments. Hating himself for not speaking already, hating the others even though it wasn't their fault, Jan said, "I'll take the automatic station." Saying it was more concrete than thinking it. His guts began twisting and roiling, and cold sweat burst from his body. He felt shock and adrenaline course through him. "That takes it out of the equation, and you can fight your way into the crewed one."

Costlow said, "It's appreciated, Jan, but you're tech branch. I think you'd be of more help here."

It was a perfect escape, and Meka's expression said she wasn't going to tell his secret if he wanted to stop there. He was a Special Projects technician, who built custom gear for others, usually in close support, but too valuable to be directly combatant save in emergencies. The act of volunteering was more than enough for most people, and he could gracefully bow out. He felt himself talking, brain whirling as he did. "I do EVA as a hobby. I'm not as good as Meka, but I can manage, given the gear." There. *Now* he was committed.

"You don't have to, Jan," Meka said. "There are other Blazers. We'll get enough targets."

"Meka, I'm not doing this out of inadequacy or false bravery." Actually, he was. There was another factor, too. When she looked at him, he continued, "I *can't* face Mom and Dad and tell them you did this. No way. I'm doing this so I don't have to face them. And because I guess it has to be done."

After a long wait, staring at each other, conversation resumed. The three made a basic schedule, hid all data and undogged the cabin. They each sought their own private spaces to think and come to grips, and the rest of the crew were left to speculate. The normal schedule resumed, and would remain in force until the planned zero time, five days away.

The three were reserved in manner during the PT sparring match that evening. The crew each picked a corner or a hatch to watch from in the day cabin, a five-meter cylinder ten meters long, and cheered and critiqued as they took turns tying each other in knots. Sarendy was small but vicious, her lithe and slender limbs striking like those of a praying mantis. Jan and Meka were tall and rangy. Costlow was older and stubborn. Each one had his or her own method of fighting. They were all about as effective.

Jan was strong, determined, and made a point of staying current on unarmed combat, partly due to a lack of demand for his services. He and Costlow twirled and kicked and grappled for several minutes, sweating and gasping from exertion, until Jan finally pinned the older man in a corner with a forearm wedged against his throat. "Yours," Costlow acknowledged.

Jan and Meka faced off from opposite ends, both lean and pantherlike. They studied each other carefully for seconds, then flew at each other, twisting and reaching, and met in a flurry of long limbs. Meka slapped him into a spin, twisted his ankles around, locked a foot under his jaw and let her momentum carry them against the aft hatch, where her other knee settled in the small of his back, pinning him helplessly as she grabbed the edge. Her kinesthetic sense and coordination never ceased to amaze the rest of them.

Passive Sensor Specialist Riechard gamely threw himself into the bout. He advanced and made a feint with one hand, orienting to keep a foot where he could get leverage off the bulkhead. He moved in fast and hard and scored a strike against Meka's shoulder, gripped her arm, and began to apply leverage. She countered by pivoting and kicking for his head.

Riechard spun and flinched. "Shoot, Meka, watch it!" he snapped.

"Sorry," she replied. Nerves had her frazzled, and she'd overreacted, her kick almost tearing his ear off. "I better take a break. Default yours."

The crew knew something was up. Costlow and the Marsichs were on edge, irritable, and terse. The session broke down without comment, and everyone drifted in separate directions.

Jan signed out and headed into The Rock the next morning. The scenery was no more exciting, being carved stone walls with sealed hatches, but at least it wasn't the boat. The air seemed somehow fresher, and it was good not to see the same faces. It wasn't his choice for a last liberty, but there wasn't any alternative. It was either the ship or The Rock.

Throughout the station, soldiers and spacers moved around in sullen quiet. The reserved faces made it obvious that other boats and ships had similar instructions. Jan had to smile at the irony that everyone had the same orders, and no one could talk about it. Then he remembered what was to happen, and became more withdrawn himself.

He'd wanted Mel Sarendy for two years, but crew were

off-limits, and it grew more frustrating as time went on. Their society had no taboos against casual nudity, and the spartan supplies and close quarters aboard boat encouraged it. He'd spent hours staring at her toned body, surreally shaped in microgravity. Her ancestry, like her name, was Earth Cambodian, diluted perhaps with a trace of Russian. That he occasionally caught what he though was a hint of reciprocation in her speech and actions made it almost torture.

He didn't want to drink, in case he crawled into the bottle. He settled for a small cubicle where he could just sit in silence and alone, a luxury unavailable aboard the boat.

Costlow was excited when he returned. Jan recognized cheerfulness when he saw it, and was impatient to find out what had changed.

Some time later, the three gathered on the command deck and sealed it off. "Talk to me, Warrant," Meka demanded.

"There's enough guidance systems to set a dozen charges. We can do this by remote," he said.

"No, we can't," Meka stated flatly.

"Shut up and wait," he snapped. "We program them to loiter outside sensor range, then do a high-velocity approach on schedule."

"Thereby running into sensor range and right into a defensive battery. I suppose you could hide a charge in a suit, but I doubt it would maneuver properly, and you couldn't program it to steer itself. We aren't using us to deliver from lack of resources, it's because we can get through and a drone can't. If you want to try to program them for a fourth target, do so. It can't hurt, unless of course you need them as decoys later."

Jan breathed deeply and slowly, feeling sick to his stomach. Crap, this was the worst experience of his life. Were they going to do this or not?

Costlow looked sheepish. "I thought I had it there. Sorry," he said.

"Don't apologize, sir," she replied. "The fact that you missed that means the Earthies think they are solid and can't be taken. This will work."

A depressed silence settled over them, but then Jan had a different thought. He cleared his throat.

"There's another factor," he said. "The crewed station might have viable oxy or escape pods. After Meka takes it out, she can hunker down and await rescue . . . there's a chance you could survive, Sis."

"Well, good!" Costlow said.

Meka flushed red. "Yes, but that's hardly fair to you two."

He shrugged. "What's fair? We do what we have to. After that, who can say?"

She looked at Jan. He smiled, of course, because he was glad of the possibility. He was also furious, nauseated, frightened, and there was nothing to say, except, "Good luck, then."

It was wholly inadequate. They were all lying, they all knew it, and it was just one more cold lump in the guts.

Two tediously painful days later, the two soldiers and the pilot gathered in the crew cabin once more. They checked off lists of essentials that had been requisitioned or borrowed, finalized the schedule, and prepared to start. The equipment made it fairly obvious what they planned.

"First order of business, clear the ship," Costlow said. He sounded the intercom for all hands, and everyone boiled in. When they were clumped around him, he said, "We have a mission for which we must reduce mass and resources, so the rest of you are being temporarily put on The Rock. Grab what you need, but you need to be off by morning."

The crew and techs looked around at each other, at the three who would remain, and it was seconds only before Pilot Sereno said, "How much mass are you stripping?"

Costlow replied, "None yet. We'll be doing that later in the mission."

More looks crossed the cabin, thoughts being telegraphed. After an interminable time, Sereno said, "Yes, Warrant," and headed away. The others silently followed his lead.

Yeah, he knows, Jan thought.

Over the rest of the day, they returned, one by one, to make their cases. Every single member of the crew was determined to accompany the boat on its last mission. Death was to be feared, but staying behind was unbearable.

Sereno spent some time arguing with his superior that he was more expendable. While true, Costlow was the better pilot. He left dejected and angry.

Boat Engineer Jacqueline Jemayel had more success. She simply handed over a comm with her checklist, and said, "No one else has the years of training and familiarity to handle your hardware in combat. If you think you can handle that while flying, I'll leave." Costlow twitched and stalled, but relented to her logic and determination. They'd been friends and crew for a long time, and he was glad to have her along.

Engine Specialist Kurashima and Analyst Corporal Jackson got nowhere. Neither was needed for this. They might be needed on another vessel. Costlow wasn't taking anyone except Jemayel, and only because she did have a valid case. A good boat engineer was essential generally, and for this especially. He listened briefly to each of the others, wished them well and sent them packing. He was proud that his crew were so dedicated and determined, and he left recommendations for decorations in his final log file.

It was mere hours before departure time when the hatch beeped an authorized entry. They looked over as Melanie Sarendy swam in, followed by Sergeant Frank Otte, the equipment technician for the intelligence crew.

Costlow was annoyed, and snapped, "Sarendy, Otte, I ordered you to—"

She interrupted with a stern face, "Warrant, the *London* has Mod Six upgrades to its sensor suite. If you want to get close, then you need offensive systems as well as sensors. This is a recon boat, not a gunboat. I'm the best tech you're going to get, I can get you in there, and I'm coming along. Sergeant Otte is here to build a station for me on the flight deck, and modifications for offensive transmissions, then he's leaving." She moved to swim past them toward her station. How she'd found out the details was a mystery. No one had told her. Costlow blocked her. She looked determined and exasperated, until he held a hand out. "Welcome aboard, Sergeant," he acknowledged.

★ ★ ★

It took Otte, Jemayel, and Jan to build the devices necessary. Sarendy's requested station wasn't a standard item for a recon boat, and there were few spare parts aboard The Rock. Judicious cannibalization and improvisation yielded an effective, albeit ugly setup. Additional gear was used to build an offensive electronic suite, and some of it had obviously been stolen from other ships. As promised, Otte left, but not before trying desperately to convince them he was as necessary as Jemayel. He failed, but not for lack of determination.

4J23 departed immediately. The time left was useful for rehearsal and training, and those were best done without distractions. The short crew strapped in as Costlow cleared with Station Control, detached the umbilical, thereby cutting them off from communication, the boat being under transmission silence, and powered away.

It would avoid awkward goodbyes, also.

Meka began laying out gear for herself and Jan. They each would take their duty weapons. Jan had a demolition charge large enough for the structure in question. She took extra explosives and ammo. Both would carry their short swords, not so much from need but because it was traditional. They both required oxy bottles. He'd wear her maneuvering harness, she had a sled designed for clandestine missions. They had enough oxy mix, barely, to last them two days. That was tantalizingly close to enough oxy for a pickup, but still short. A boat might conceivably get into the vicinity in time, but rescue operations took time. If they could run this mission in the open . . . but of course, they couldn't.

★ ★ ★

Costlow spent the time getting trajectories from the navigation system. He needed to pass by two stations whose locations were approximate, get near the *London*, which was in a powered station orbit around the jump point, observe, plan an approach, execute the approach to stay unseen, and arrive at a precise point at an exact time with sufficient fuel for terminal maneuvers. Very terminal. He consulted with Sarendy as to detection equipment ranges and apertures to help plot his path. Jemayel tended the engines, life support, and astronautics. None of them spoke much.

Jan had little to do until his departure. He spent it moping, getting angry, and finally beating on the combat practice dummy for hours, twisting in microgravity. When Meka called him over to explain the gear, he was more than eager to just get things over with.

She showed him the mass of gear and began to go through it. He checked everything off with her. Weapons and gear needed little explanation. He was familiar with the technical details of her maneuvering harness and the munitions fuzes even though he'd never used them. The briefing would be far too short a distraction.

"We'll synch our chronos," Meka said.

"Goddess, don't give me a clock," Jan begged, shaking his head. "If I have to watch it count down, I'll be a basket case. Just put me there with some stuff to read and let me go." He spoke loudly, eyes wide, because the stress was getting to him.

"You need one in case the auto system fails," Meka said. "You're getting a triple load of ammo. It seems unlikely, but if anyone shows up to stop you—"

"Then I hold them off as long as I can."

"Right," Meka agreed.

Costlow showed the plotted course in a 3D, and asked, "We let you off here. Are you sure you can maneuver well enough for that distance?"

Shrugging, Jan replied, "End result is the same for me either way, but I'm sure. I do a lot of EVA. Unlike some people, I like it."

"Bite me, Bro," Meka replied and laughed, too loud from stress. She had always *hated* long EVA, and that's what this was. She was assembling a pile of gear including her powered sled, two oxy bottles, the basic demolition blocks from everyone's standard gear plus her own larger pack, weapons and stuff the others wouldn't recognize. Her actions were trained, expert, and only a little shaky from tension. She'd done long trips in the dark before, and survived, but that didn't make it fun. She had her sled for this one, Jan was making a far shorter infiltration, and the boat wasn't her concern. She prepped everything, had Jan and Jemayel double check, and went through exercises to calm herself. Those didn't work for Jan.

With less than four hours until his departure, Jan sat staring at the bulkhead of the day cabin. His bunk was folded, and his few effects sealed in a locker. He'd recorded a message and written instructions, all of which made things rather final. He didn't feel thoroughly terrified yet, but did feel rather numb. Rest was impossible. He nodded briefly to Sarendy as she swam in, and tried not to dwell on her. It was all too easy to think of justifications to break the fraternization ban. He didn't need rejection or complications now, and the sympathy ploy was the only approach he could think of. It wouldn't work, as she was in the same boat as he, quite literally.

"Come back here," she said, gesturing with a hand. She turned and swam for her intel bay.

As he followed her in, she closed the hatch and dogged it. The bay was dimly lit by one emergency lamp, there being no need for its use at this time, and there was just enough room for the two of them inside the radius of couches and terminals set against the shell. While his brain tried to shift gears, she grabbed him by the shoulders and mashed her mouth against his while reaching to open her shipsuit. Both their hands fumbled for a few seconds, then his stopped and drew back while hers continued questing.

"Mehlnee," he muttered around her kiss. She drew her full lips back a bare few millimeters, and he continued, "I appreciate this . . . but it won't help me deal with . . . this."

"It helps me," she replied, voice breathy, and wrapped herself more tightly around him. Her lips danced over his throat and he decided not to argue with her logic. His hands were on the sinuous curves of her golden-skinned hips, and long-held fantasies solidified into reality. Frantic, unrequited lust made thought impossible, and that was a good thing right then.

Jan was first out. He doffed his shipsuit and donned his hard vacsuit, intended for short duration EVA maintenance and not the best for this mission. It was what he had, though. Meka's assault harness fit snugly over it and would provide thrust. Three bottles rode his back, two oxy-helium, one nitrogen for the harness. His rifle and clips were along the right bottle, and his comm on his wrist, programmed with everything he needed. Strapped to his chest was a large, bulky pack with over twenty kilos of modern military hyperexplosive. It would be more than enough for the station in question.

Melanie and Meka checked him over and helped him into the bay. The other two were busy on the flight deck. Ignoring his sister's presence, Melanie kissed him hard and deeply. He kissed back, shaking, wanting to leave before the whole situation caused him to go insane. Meka waited until Sarendy was done, then clutched him briefly. "Good luck," she said.

"Good hunting," he replied.

Behind him he heard, "Oh, I will," as the hatch closed.

Jan stared out the open bay into cold black space with cold, bright pinpoints of light. "God and Goddess, I don't want to do this," he muttered. His stomach boiled and churned, and he wished he'd filled his water bottle with straight alcohol. Even the double dose of tranquilizers was not enough to keep him calm.

A light winked once, twice, then a third time, and he jumped out briskly, feeling the harness shove him in a braking maneuver. He was immediately thankful for the suit's plumbing, and his brain went numb. *I'm dead now*, was all he could think.

The station Jan was attacking would note the passage of the anomaly that was the boat as well as it could, and report later. Meka's target was more complicated. It was crewed, and they would react if they saw her. She'd have to ride her sled for some distance and most of a day, and try to time it for a covert approach. That might be the hardest part of this mission.

In the maintenance bay, she strapped herself to her sled and had Jemayel check her over. With a final thumbs up and a lingering hug, she turned to her controls and counted seconds down to her launch.

The boat passed through the volume as stealthed as possible, oriented so the bay opened away from the station's sensors. There were no emissions, only the operating radiation and a bare hint of the powerplant. Her braking thrust was hidden by the mass of the boat, and should be almost invisible at this distance. That should put her right on top of the station at Earth clock 1130 the next day, when the crew would hopefully be at lunch.

Once the vibration and heavy gees tapered off, she checked her instruments and took a trank. It would be a long wait, and very eerie in complete silence and blackness.

And now I'm dead, she thought.

Sarendy reported when they were outside the known range of the station, and Costlow waited a planned extra hour before bringing up the plant and engines. He wanted to be lost in background noise.

The thrust built steadily in a rumbling hiss through the frame. Most of the impulse would be used now, with only enough left for margin and maneuvers. That would simplify the approach by minimizing emissions then. The velocity increased to a level the boat had rarely used, and he nodded to his remaining crew as they completed the maneuver. Now they had to wait.

"Anyone for a game of Chess?" he asked.

★ ★ ★

Jan watched for the station. It was a black mass against black space, and he was glad to see it occult stars. He'd been afraid the intel was wrong and he was sailing off into space for nothing. Odd to feel relieved to see the approaching cause of one's death, he thought. It had been a three-hour trip, and he was hungry. He would stay that way for the next day and a half, because his suit was intended for maintenance EVAs only, not infiltration, and had no way to supply food. So much for the condemned's last meal. Then, there was the irony that his boat had IDed this particular piece of equipment, which is why it was on the list, and why he was here.

The occultation grew, and he got ready to maneuver for docking, landing, whatever it was called in this case. He switched on the astrogation controls, adjusted his flight toward it, then braked relative. He was tense, lest the reports be inaccurate and the station blast him with a defense array, but nothing happened. He didn't overshoot, but did approach obliquely and had to correct for touchdown.

There was no one and nothing nearby, which was as expected. He snapped a contact patch out, slapped it to the surface, and attached his line. There were no regular padeyes on the unit.

A short orientation revealed where the power cell was. He planted the standoff over it and slapped it down with another contact patch. When it triggered, the blast would turn a plate of metal beneath it into plasma and punch it through the shell into the power cell. He armed it, and all he had left to do was defend it against what appeared to be nothing, wait until it detonated and die with it. Simple on file. Doing it didn't seem quite that by the numbers.

At first, he was terrified of being near the charge. He realized it was silly, as it would kill him anyway, and if it didn't, suffocation would. He compromised between fear and practicality by hiding over the horizon of the small, angled object. It was a bare three meters across, five meters long, and almost featureless except for a docking clamp inset at one end. Its signals were all burst through a translucent one-way window. He longed to tear into it for the sheer joy of discovering if the intel briefs were correct about this model, but that might give him away. He'd sit and wait.

He did have emgee, and a suit, and a tether. He decided to rest floating free. The technique had helped him before when stressed. He stared out at the stars and the distant pointy glare of Iota Persei, their star, and fell into a deep sleep, disturbed by odd dreams.

Meka approached the station gradually. She'd have to leave her sled behind and finish the trip in just her suit to avoid detection. While a bedecked suit would register as maintenance or a refugee with the sensors, the sled would trigger alarms as an approaching threat even if the enemy didn't have knowledge of the precise design. She made one last correction to her orbit, set the autopilot, pulled the releases, and drifted loose from the frame. Her minuscule lateral velocity should be of negligible effect.

The sled burped gently away on gas jets rather than engines, and would hopefully never be detectable to the station. It was near 0800 by Earth clock, and another three hours should bring her quite close. That's when it would become tricky.

First, she'd have to maneuver with an improvised thruster. Jan had her harness, she had only a nitrogen bottle and a momentary valve. He'd—hopefully—made his approach with power but no navigation. She had the navigation gear in her helmet, but improvised power. The risks they were taking would cause a safety officer to run gibbering in insanity. On the other hand, they were dead either way.

There was also the substantial risk of the station noting her approach to its crew. They might await her, or send someone to investigate, or shoot her outright. She was betting against the last, but it was just that—a bet. If they met her, it meant a fight. She would win one on one against anybody she faced, but the station might have up to twenty crew. It was effectively a large recon boat with maneuvering engines, and she didn't relish a fight within.

Unlike her previous long EVAs, she was relaxed and calm. Perhaps it was experience. Maybe it was the complexity of the task and the associated thought that kept her too busy to worry. Perhaps it was fatalism. As she neared her target, more issues interfered and she dropped all those thoughts.

There were no obvious signs of disturbance as she approached. That meant that if they did see her for what she was, they were at least holding their fire. She checked her weapon again by touch, and began readying her muscles for a fight. If someone met her, she'd go along peacefully to the airlock, then start smashing things and killing on her way inside.

Nothing happened. Either the station's sensors didn't see her, or they assumed she was performing maintenance and ignored her. It was good to see the intel was accurate, but it still felt odd that her presence wasn't even reported. Perhaps it was and they were waiting for her. Dammit, no second guessing.

She was close enough to think about maneuvering now, and there were still no signs of enemy notice. The nitrogen bottle beside her breathing bottle was plumbed into a veritable snakepit of piping Jan had built for her, that ended front and back at shoulders and hips, much like a proper emgee harness. She hoped the improvised controls worked so she wouldn't have to attempt it by hand. Her record on manual approaches was less than perfect.

She vented a pulse of gas and the harness worked as planned. Two more short ones brought her to a bare drift. She sent more thoughts of thanks after her brother, who had turned out to be essential to almost every mission she'd fought in this war. His technical skill in every field was simply genius.

She managed a gentle touchdown on the station hull, letting her legs bend and soak up momentum. She caught her breath, got her bearings, and went straight to work. She had no idea how long she could go unnoticed.

She placed the prebuilt charges with a rapidity born of years of practice. Each charge was designed to punch a hole into a compartment, hopefully voiding them all and killing the occupants instantly. She danced softly across the hull to avoid noise inside that might give her away, swapping tethers as she went, and planted them precisely with the aid of thoughtfully provided frame numbers.

Magnetic boots would have made it easier . . . if the shell had been an iron alloy and if clanking noises didn't matter.

She caught movement out of the corner of her eye. She pivoted to see a UN spacer in gear, staring at her in surprise.

Her combat reflexes took over. He was unarmed, meaning he was conducting routine maintenance or inspections. It was possible he wore a camera that was observable inside on a monitor, and he would definitely report her as soon as he recovered from the oddity of the situation. She twisted her right arm to unsling, then pointed her rifle and shot him through the faceplate.

The eruption of atmosphere and vaporized blood indicated he was dead. She put two more bullets through him to make sure, the effect eerie in the silence. The recoil of the weapon was mild, but with no gravity or atmosphere it started her tumbling. She steadied out with a grasp of her tether, and brought herself back the half meter to the shell. Now what?

Her pulse hammered and her breath rasped. Despite the massive damage and casualties she'd caused in her career, it was only the second time she'd killed someone directly and up close. She forced her emotions into quiescence and considered the situation. If he'd reported her, she had seconds to deal with it. If not, she had a little longer before he was missed. If she killed the crew early, they might miss a scheduled report and the secrecy of her mission would be compromised. If she waited, they could report her presence. She didn't see much of a choice.

Her fingers activated the system through her comm, she paused a second to confirm the readings, and then detonated the charges.

If the atmosphere gushing from her enemy's helmet had been impressive, this was awe-inspiring. Brilliant bursts of white were swallowed by fountains of spewing air and debris. The station shook beneath her feet as the hull adjusted to lost pressure. Anyone not in a suit should be dead. Now to hope no report was expected before her mission zero time. It was a long shot, but all she had. And it was unlikely that the omission would be considered more than a minor problem at first.

Costlow was a first class pilot, but this would strain even his capabilities. The astronautics would take over for evasive maneuvers only. The approach would be manual.

While there was a timed window for attacks, the closer together they were the better. Any hint of action would alert the enemy and reduce the odds of success for others. He wanted to time this to the second, as much as possible. To avoid detection, he had to rely on passive sensors operated by Sarendy across from him. Passive sensors didn't give as accurate a picture as active ones, which meant he'd have to correct the timing in flight. As he would approach at a velocity near the maximum physics and Jemayel's bypassed safeties would allow, that left little time for corrections. He wanted to get inside their weapons' envelope and right against the skin before they deduced what he was. That also increased the risk of their particle watch picking him up, assuming him to be an incoming passive threat, and shooting preemptively.

They were only a few hours from target, and he'd already brought them around in a long loop behind the *London*'s engines. The emissions from them would mask their approach in ionized scatter. He wondered again just how hard this would have been without Sarendy, Jan and Otte. Sarendy was pulling all her intel from the sensors up to the flight deck and using it to assist in astrogation, and was preparing a counterintel system for use when they were detected, and would utilize the active sensor antennas as offensive transmitters. He hadn't realized that was even possible, but Sarendy was a witch with sensors, Jan an expert on improvising hardware, and Otte had kept up with both of their orders and put the system together. Amazing. If a crew had ever earned its decorations, this one had.

"Your turn, Warrant," Sarendy reminded him.

Right. Chess. "Um . . . " He moved his queen, looked at the board with satisfaction, and leaned back. Her rook's capture of his queen and declaration of checkmate stunned him.

"Perhaps we should stop now," he suggested. "I didn't see that coming and I have no idea what you did. And both my bishops are on white."

"They are?" she asked. "So they are. Let's call it a game."

Meka swam through the main corridor, counting bodies with faces reminiscent of dead fish, and checked that every compartment was open to vacuum. Nodding to herself, ignoring the grisly scenes, she made her way to the powerplant and unlimbered the large charge on her chest. In seconds it was armed, placed, and she swam back out to face the outer hatch. Little to do now but wait.

She wondered how other troops and units had done. Was anyone trying to retake the captured Freehold facilities? Or to destroy them outright? Would the attacks be successful, and allow the presumed counter to work? Would they win?

She'd never know. She could only wish them luck.

Jan awoke with a start. Guilt flooded over the adrenaline, as he realized he'd slept past when he was supposed to be on guard. He shrugged and decided it didn't matter, as the chance of anyone interfering was incredibly remote. It still bothered him.

It was close to deadline, and he realized he didn't even know what this operation was called, only that it probably involved the entire system, aimed for infrastructure, and was suicidal. That was probably enough.

He still had a couple of hours of oxy.

Hypoxia/anoxia would be pretty painless. A little struggle for breath . . . he could take those two hours. It wasn't impossible a rescue vessel might show up. It just took a hell of a lot of zeros to make the odds. Two extra hours of life, though.

He decided he didn't have whatever it took to let himself die slowly. He was already shivering in shock; the tranks were wearing off.

He snagged the tether and dragged himself hand over hand to the station. He hooked to the contact patch near the charge. The only thing worse than being blown to dust, he thought, would be to be injured by it and linger for hours in pain. He wished Meka luck, aching to know if she'd make it. That hurt as much as anything else. There were fewer zeros on her odds, but they were still ludicrously remote. Their mission was to smash enemy infrastructure, not occupy and set up housekeeping.

There was nothing left. He settled down to read, gave up because he couldn't focus, and turned on music to break the eerie silence. If he had to die, he wanted it to be painless and instantaneous.

When the charge underneath him detonated, he got his final wish.

Costlow sweated, with aching joints and gritty eyeballs from sitting far too long at the controls. He watched the display in his helmet, trying to ignore the way the helmet abraded behind his left ear, and made another minute flight correction. He had minutes left to live.

4J23 was close behind the *London*, and undiscovered as far as they knew. Sarendy screwed with their emissions, inverted incoming scans, sent out bursts low enough in energy to pass as typical, powerful enough to keep them hidden and the gods only knew what else. He wished there were some way to record her competence. She was a fifteen year-old kid, and likely knew more about her job than all her instructors combined. Add in her bravery, and she deserved ten medals.

No, he thought, she deserved to live. Rage filled him again.

He forced the thoughts back to his mission. He was hungry and thirsty, but he daren't pause to do either. This could all come down to a fractional second's attention. Especially now that they were so close.

He brought *4J23* in in a tight, twisting curve from the blind spot behind the drives, and aimed along the approaching superstructure. *London*'s defenses found him, and a launch warning flashed in his visor. It missed because

Sarendy switched to active jamming and burned its sensors out with a beam that should have been impossible from a recon boat, and would almost fry an asteroid to vapor. The brute force approach was an indication that all her tricks were exhausted, and it was doubtful they could avoid another attack. He flinched as the missile flashed past, even though it was detectable only as an icon in his visor, and heard a cry of sheer terror start quietly and build. He realized it was his voice. He'd wet himself, and was embarrassed, even though he understood the process. He could hear Sarendy panting for breath, hyperventilating behind him, and wondered what Jemayel was doing in the stern. His eyes flicked to the count in his visor—

Now.

Alongside the *London*, within meters of her hull and at closest approach to her command center, a small powerplant overloaded and detonated. It was enough to overwhelm her forcescreens, vaporize her forward half, and shatter the rest in a moment so brief as to be incomprehensible. One hundred UN spacers were turned into incandescent plasma by the blast, along with the three Freeholders.

Meka watched the seconds tick away in her visor. She dropped her left hand and grasped the manual trigger, set it, and held on. It would blow if she let go, or on schedule, and her work was almost done. The count worked down, and she closed her eyes, faced "up" and took a deep breath to steady herself. She opened them again to see it count 3 . . . 2 . . . 1—

Whether her thumb released or the timer acted first was

irrelevant. The blast damaged the station's fusion plant, which shut down automatically, even as it vented to space. She felt the cracking and rumbling of the structure through her body, fading away to nothing. It would take a dockyard to repair that, and they'd have to remove the wreckage first. She moved back toward the powerplant, navigating by touch in the dust, and dragged herself around several supports twisted by the blast. She entered the engineering module and waited. The particles cleared very slowly, as there was neither airflow nor gravity. It all depended on static charges and surface tension to draw things out of vacuum, and Meka stayed stock still until she could get a good look through her faceplate, cycling through visible, enhanced and IR to build a good picture. She nodded in approval of the damage. The blast and fusion bottle failure had slagged half the module.

Her task was now done, but she had no desire to die immediately. She could have embraced the charge on the reactor and gone with it. Her rationale had been that she should be certain, although the charge had been three times larger than she'd calculated as necessary. The truth was, she couldn't bring herself to do it. Death might be inevitable, but she still feared it.

She studied the life support system whimsically. Without a proper deckplan, she'd just vented every compartment from outside to be sure. Her charge over this one had punched into the makeup tank. There was a functional air recycling plant, but no oxygen. A meter in any direction . . .

There were no escape bubbles. This was a station, not a ship. If damaged, the crew would seal as needed and call for help. She'd fixed that when she vented atmosphere. There were extra suit oxy bottles, but the fittings didn't match. Even if they did, there was no heat, and her suit powerpack was nearing depletion. Jan would easily have cobbled something together, or tacked a patch over the hole in life support and used the suit bottles, but even if she could do so before her own gas ran out, it still meant waiting and hoping for a rescue that would likely never come. There was no commo capability, of course. That had been her prime target. No one knew to look for her. The remote possibility of rescue they'd discussed had been for Jan's benefit, to let him hope she might survive. He'd probably figured out the lie by now.

With time and nothing better to do, she planted charges on every hatch, every port, every system. She fired bullets liberally to smash controls and equipment; wedged the airlocks with grenades to shatter the seals and render them useless. Even the spare parts inventory was either destroyed or blown into space.

Finally, she sat outside on the ruined shell, watching her oxy gauge trickle toward empty. Her weapons were scattered around her, some lazily drifting free in the emgee, each rendered inoperable and unsalvageable, all save one. She really had harbored an unrealistic hope that there'd be some way out of this, and cried in loneliness. There was no one to see her, and it wasn't the first time she'd cried on a mission. Blazers didn't look down on tears and fear, only on failure. She had not failed.

The stillness and silence was palpable and eerie. She brought up her system and cycled through her music choices. Yes, that would do nicely. *La Villa Strangiato*. The coordination and sheer skill impressed her, and the energy in the performance was powerful and moving. It filled the last five-hundred seconds and faded out. Silence returned.

A warning flashed in her visor and sounded in her ears, becoming more and more tinny as oxygen was depleted. She'd black out in about a hundred seconds.

One thing she'd always wondered was how far her courage went. People died all the time. Soldiers died when ordered to fight and the odds ran out. Sick people died because life was not worth living.

But, could she die by choice? Her courage had been tested throughout her career, and this last year to an extreme. But did she have the strength to pull that switch herself?

After prolonging the inevitable this long, it was rather moot, but her life wouldn't be complete without the experiment. She armed the grenade, stared at it as her body burned from hypoxia, and tried to force her hand to open. Lungs empty now, she gritted her teeth, pursed her lips, and threw every nerve into the effort. Her wrist shook, thumb moving bit by bit. Willpower or self-preservation?

She was still conscious, though groggy, as her thumb came free and the fuse caught. Three seconds. Hypoxia segued to anoxia and her thoughts began to fade. The last one caused a triumphant smile to cross her face, even as tears pooled in her eyes.

Willpower.

On slabs of green and black marble in Freedom Park are the names of two hundred and sixteen soldiers who accepted orders they could not understand and knew meant their deaths. Words were said, prayers offered, and torches and guards of honor stand eternal watch over them. Their families received pensions, salutes and bright metal decorations on plain green ribbons, presented in inlaid wooden boxes.

One family received two.

Desert Blues
★ ★ ★

I deployed twice to the Middle East, both relatively short deployments. In 1999 I was at Ahmed al Jaber Airbase in Kuwait, doing some construction for Operation Desert Fox/Southern Watch/Guarded Skies. We had one threat warning that wasn't a big deal, except at that moment I was in a truck on the far side of the flightline on a road with UXO (UneXploded Ordnance) markers on either side of the road, and nowhere to take cover. Luckily, it was a false alarm. Good times, good times.

In 2008 I was at an Undisclosed Airbase in the Middle East (well, two, actually), which is how the USAF identifies every base unless there's some need to specify. I was armed with a brand new GUU5P carbine, the USAF version of the M4, with standard sights and a happy switch—full auto instead of burst, and body armor, etc. though most of the time the battle gear was rolled up under my bunk or cot. I never needed it, really.

But everyone has a different war. I'd stayed in well past twenty years in part to make sure I did deploy. I wanted *more action. Some people couldn't handle even stateside callups away from their families and had issues. I know some infantry guys who went six tours, and our powerplant boss was a reservist who did eleven tours—six months over, six at home, repeat.*

Regardless of why anyone chose to be there—it's an all volunteer military, and by 2008, everyone had enlisted or reenlisted after the events of 2001-2003—we chose to be there. It's a very different environment than anywhere in the U.S., with different people. Part of me is in the Middle East, and part of it is in me. In fact, I have asthma and other lung damage from sand, debris and assorted contaminants. I'll never forget that place.

But it's also part of what makes me who I am, and it shows up in my writing. I still have a story in my head that won't quite resolve the way I need it to. I'll write it down eventually. In the meantime, there's this:

A DEPLOYMENT to the Middle East is like Groundhog Day with sand. Every day, hot, dry, dusty, winds from the north-northwest at twenty-five kilometers per hour. Same people. Same duty. Same crappy music on Freedom Radio. Occasionally someone does something stupid or takes a shot at you, then it goes right back to the way it was. If you're lucky enough to be there in winter it gets cold and muddy. I was not lucky. I walked through an oven. At least it wasn't windy, or it would feel like a hairdryer combined with a sandblaster. I had a clean PT uniform, a towel, a kit and a rifle. Just the bare necessities.

One of the very few conveniences (I won't say "pleasures") is that after a shower, you dry off in seconds just from the low humidity. I'd taken a shower, was dry and clean and would be until the first breeze blew sand onto me, and was on my way back to my tent when I heard the guitar.

There's always a person or ten with enough talent to play, but this guy was good. Somewhere a few tents over, he had an electric and a small amp and I heard Clapton's "Layla." It was a pretty good wail. He could sing, too. *"You got me on my kneeeeees . . . "*

One of the sucky things was that I was at this remote hole in the middle of the desert to back up the Army. The Army does a lot of things very well. What they don't do is infrastructure. These poor saps had a growing Contingency Operating Base and couldn't get enough "big" generators in to power things. That's because a lot of Army units consider a 25kW generator to be "big," especially those units that get sent forward.

So, twenty of us Air Force engineers showed up with Christine and Lucille, each 1.25 megawatts of diesel-powered bitch, and a few Environmental Control Units for extra air conditioning, or in some cases, just air conditioning. In that part of the world, it's pretty much a necessity if you don't want to die.

Fortunately, their officers knew to slide the orders into the hooch, back out carefully, and let us get to work. We had our own sleeping tent, our own operations tent, and when not taking care of immediate tasks spent the time customizing and comfortizing the amenities.

We all had iPods and such, but good live music was

always welcome. The guitarist was better than most of the professional bands who occasionally played for an hour on some USO gig.

He trailed off "Layla" and started some Stevie Ray. Now, this was just too good. I took a detour on my way to the tent to make sure I kept it in hearing.

I just reached the north end of camp where we live when behind me I heard a whoosh and a *Bang!* Everything shook and flapped, air slapped at me, and I changed direction toward the nearest bunker, which was about twenty feet away.

A lot of people get fatalistic about attacks and just ride them out. I'm older and more cynical. The odds of getting hit are low, but who wants to win the lottery? I slowed quickly as I neared it, used the gravel under my flip flops to brake and steer sideways under the concrete overhead. Just then, someone at the Plant killed the outside lights. Good. Why make targeting easy for the insurgents?

There were bodies already here. I flashed my weapon light on the ground for a half second and in the reflected glare caught two soldiers mostly untangled. The back of her PT uniform was dusty, and so were his knees and forearms. She was pulling her shirt down and blushing thoroughly. Sorry, kids. I wasn't going to blame them for it, but they were done for tonight.

"Move to the middle," I said. I heard them scooting across gravel in the dark. I recognized a silhouetted body coming in as my buddy from Utah Air Guard, Paul. Others came in both ends as a second *Bang*! shook things. It was a pretty good sized one, too.

"I was just going to take a shower," I heard Lieutenant

Smith, the Army Engineer officer we worked through grouse from the other end. "Report," he said.

"Not much yet, sir," I said. "No casualties in here, and I was just coming from a shower."

Pretty much everyone who was going to take cover probably had by now. There were a dozen people in this sandbag-covered pipe, getting as comfortable as possible with gravel under ass, concrete behind back, assorted sharp things, crushed plastic bottles and feet and knees in the way. I folded my towel up and sat on it to cut the jabs from the rocks.

The guitarist was still playing. I heard him singing and riffing. "*The sky is crying . . .* " Cute.

"Shouldn't someone go get him and anyone else left, sir?" The question came from Senior Master Sergeant Richards. I privately called him the Big Dick. He wanted every letter of every regulation and Air Force Instruction followed, even those that contradicted each other. Then he also wanted Army regs followed, including the ones he wasn't sure about. Of course, he neglected them for himself. He might complain about someone wearing the wrong glasses, wrong hat, dogtags in boots and not around neck, but he usually needed a haircut and left his pockets unbuttoned. I was just glad we were on opposite shifts.

"Nah, I don't think so," LT Smith said. He was young but I liked him. Good head on his shoulders for a kid of twenty-two.

"But, sir, SOP is for everyone to shelter in place." Richards was just like that. Insistent. Was he going to get out and go get people? Had he done so? Nope, but he'd be happy to have someone else order some other someone else to do so.

"He's fine," the LT insisted. He sounded bored and annoyed.

I could tell from the shifting that Richards was agitated. He wasn't going to say anything now, though.

BANG!

That one was close enough to punch my ears, tug at the air in our little tube and there were gasps and whimpers. Not me. I'd laid these sandbags and trusted them, and knew if I heard it I was still alive. I also felt obligated to set a good example for the young troops, kids really, and for the honor of the Air Force. I didn't flinch that anyone could tell in the dark. I did pucker up my eyes and my ass, though.

The young woman was sobbing. I could hear mutters and shifting. We were all going to be . . . well, I don't know what word to use, but there'd be a bond after this.

Someone, either one of our SPs or an Army MP thought they had a target, and opened up with a .50. *BaBaBa-BaBaBaBANG! BaBaBANG! BaBaBaBaBaBaBANG!* hammering and drumming through the night air.

And that was when the guitarist cranked up the volume and distortion. Three chords blared out, and I had a WTF? moment.

I knew those chords.

Dire Straits' "Money for Nothing." Raunchy, cheerful, rude.

Then he started singing, loudly.

"Listen to them assholes, that ain't how you do it . . ."

And a wave of laughter and cheers just burst out of us.

> " . . . *mortars for nothin', IEDs for free.*
> *Now that ain't workin, that ain't how you do it.*
> *Let me tell you, them guys are dumb.*
> *We might get some shrapnel in our little fingers.*
> *They might get a fifty up their bum . . . "*

More small arms fire drowned him out, but I could sense applause from other bunkers, and from the diehards who'd stayed in their tents. It was just the ultimate middle finger to these frothing nutjobs. Whoever he was, he just plain rocked.

> " . . . *who's got to move these generators?*
> *Who's got to move these uparmored humveeeeeees?"*

I was just chuckling over that when—
Bang!
Everything bounced and shook, and the air slapped me. Holy crap.

The music stopped.

I heard the young woman say, "Oh, no!"

My ears were ringing, but after two decades of working with this gear I could troubleshoot by ear.

"PDP is down. Power Distribution Panel."

Sure enough, a few seconds later there was a loud click, a buzz that lasted long enough for someone to walk back into a tent, and . . .

"*I want my, I want my, I want my IEDs . . . "* and we all cheered again.

"We're all clear," the LT said. "Someone bagged the bad guys."

One of the things I appreciated was that he never called them "Hajjis." I have Muslim friends and try not to toss generic epithets around. RIF—Rabid Islamic Fu . . . Fundamentalist—is fine. It's a little more specific.

The compound lights came back up, casting a glow into the bunker. I stretched and waited. There were at least three people between me and outside, and I was in no hurry. Once people were out of the way, I rose carefully, watching my head on the roof, since I had left my Kevlar and body armor in the tent. Unless I had to work under fire it could stay there, too.

Paul was waiting outside.

"You want to check the Alphas and I'll check Bravo?" he suggested, referring to two blocks of tents. Those were the electrician's job, but we'd help out anyway, and the four Mechanical guys might need help swapping out some ECUs. Something was probably broken. If not from this, from "normal wear and tear" which happened every few hours. Fucking Arabia. I hated it.

"Sure, let me drop this crap off," I said, holding up my now sandy towel and kit.

"Alright." Paul nodded and headed toward Bravo section. He had a multimeter and a screwdriver with him, all he needed. He was a nerdy little guy, and should have been at least an E6 instead of an E5. He was a wizard with equipment, always calm and collected. I loved arguing my science versus his Creationism. I didn't have to agree with someone to think of them as a friend.

I banged my feet off on the pallet in our vestibule, not

that it would get rid of sand, but it might at least slow it down. I reached through my poncho/privacy screen/light curtain and tossed my stuff on my cot and the towel on the floor. There should be a couple of Motoralas around here somewhere. Yup, there was one left of four, in a charger at the front. I grabbed it, turned the knob until it beeped, and went back out, slinging my carbine and carrying another high-lumen flashlight. Those things got ubiquitous in a hurry.

The guitarist wasn't singing, but he was playing something long and galloping, a rock/blues solo that just went on and on. I wanted to hear it up close, but duty first.

Across the way, I wove my way down over the tangle of cables and commo wire, slipping in the sand, listening for problems with the ECUs—buzzing contactors, compressors rattling, flapping V-belts, anything and everything that might, would go wrong. I looked for impacts that would have blown cables or connectors, or frag that might have sliced them, or blasts that could have tumbled stuff over or otherwise damaged it. Nothing. As usual, the insurgents made up for their lack of competence with their lack of courage, had fired a few badly aimed shots and split.

The guitarist was in Charlie or Delta section. I could hear him.

The check done, I reported that fact.

"Scorpion, this is Scorpion Three."

"Go ahead, Scorpion Three."

"Alpha Section, operational and secure."

"Roger that."

We don't bother with overs, outs, paraphrases or all that stuff we're supposed to. Brief is good.

That done, I was damned well going to catch the show. I followed the sound toward Charlie section of the tents.

I found people gathered around Charlie Four and Five, and on the other side at Eight and Nine. So the back of one of these four tents of twelve in Charlie section was where the show was.

I couldn't tell which tent he was in. A couple of people tried to walk back, but the guy ropes and stakes were pretty tangled, and there was some stray wire. Anyway, what was the point? It sounded just great from out here.

The LT was here, and Paul, and others I knew from either our unit or Army troops we worked with regularly. The Big Dick wasn't, of course. He was likely at the Plant on his knees reading AFI 36 and praying for guidance.

I saw one kid take a step toward C5, figuring to go inside.

"Don't," the LT said with a headshake.

He was right. No one else had taken a step and didn't want to, because if we went in that tent and interrupted him, *he might stop playing.* It was just too unique, too good and too much of a relief for anyone to want it to stop.

The kid stepped back.

The guy could *play.* Jazz mixed with blues and he just went on and on, silky and then snappy on the strings, playing his own fills and rhythm. It's one thing on stage or in the studio with racks of gear and a mixing board, but he had a guitar and an amp.

The notes faded out as he dialed the volume down, and we all strained to hear it as long as possible. The dull roar of generators, ECUs and the remaining ringing from mortars meant we probably missed quite a bit. Still, it was what we had.

Then a strummed chord brought it all back to life with one of the greatest songs of all time.

> *"You get all sweaty in the dark,*
> *there's a sandstorm in the park, but meantime*
> *South of the Tigris you stop and you hold everything."*

I've tried playing Sultans of Swing. It really takes two guitars and a bass to get that groove. It can be done on one guitar, if the guitarist is just amazingly good.

This guy was that good and then some.

He played this syncopated, peppy rhythm, with this odd bluesy, jazzy, Arabian melody. It fit the mood, the environment and the time, and I knew I'd never hear anything like it, ever again. Not that I'd come back to Iraq even for a performance like this, of course . . . though I just might.

We just stood there and soaked it up, rapt or smiling, amazed or just oblivious.

> *". . . Way on down south.*
> *Way on down south, Baghdad town . . ."*

No one moved, no one twitched. The oven-dry heat covered us, and my feet sweated from the still sun-hot sand, but I was not going to move. He sang and played and it was wistful and rich and American, even though Knopfler's Scottish. This version, though, was pure American spirit.

> *"Goodnight, now it's time to go home.*
> *Let me make it fast with one more thing.*
> *I am the Sultan . . .*
> *I am the Sultan of swing."*

I had no doubt he was.

He tapped and pulled that outro solo, and I wanted him to go on for hours, days, forever, but he faded out.

We stood there, feeling the reluctantly waning heat, holding our breath and waiting. Then we heard the thump as he shut the amp off, and there was a collective sigh, followed by a smatter of applause.

Some wandered off at once. I stuck around. I can't say why I didn't run into the tent right then and talk to him personally, except that it seemed rude. I also hoped he might play something else. I had five-hundred or so songs on my iPod, but it wasn't the same.

I gave up after five minutes, though a few troops stuck around longer. But heck, it had been great, he was done and I had to get some sleep. To that end, the music had helped. The RIFs had thrown rockets at us, and we'd thrown back a defiant blast of blues and rock guitar, with the percussion played on a fifty caliber machine gun. It was our score, our win, and I don't think anyone doubted we were and would be the victors. Sometimes you get points just for sheer balls, and this had been exactly that. I was relaxed, unwound from the incoming fire and went to sleep warm and smiling.

We never did figure out who he was. There were a dozen decent guitarists on site, and several of them had axes and amps, but no one admitted it, and none of them sounded like him. I'll never know who this guy was, and we never met, but despite that, for a half hour we shared something wonderful in a remote COB in a desolate wasteland in Iraq, and he's my friend.

I'll raise a beer to him when I get back stateside.

One Night in Baghdad
(to the tune of One Night in Bangkok)

Bad puns will be the death of me. That is all

THE SERGEANT:

Baghdad, Middle Eastern setting
And the locals don't know that the city is getting
The creme de la creme of the arms world in a
Show with everything but Peter O'Toole.

Time flies, doesn't seem a minute
Since the Perfume Palace had the Husseins in it
All change—don't you know that when you
Fight MOUT it's no ordinary venue.

It's Stalingrad—or the Philippines—or
Hue—or—or this place!

SOLDIERS:

One night in Baghdad, threats in each direction
The bars are empty but the drinks ain't free
You'll find a bomb in every intersection
If you're unlucky then the threat's a she
Hope there's an angel watching over me.

THE SERGEANT:

One town's very like another
When your head's down over your M4, brother.

SOLDIERS:

It bites, it sucks, it's really such a pity
To be looking for insurgents, not looking at the city.

THE SERGEANT:

Whaddya mean? Ya seen one war-torn, polluted, third
world town . . .

SOLDIERS:

Tea girls, warm and sweet
Some are set up in the Qusay suite.

THE SERGEANT:

At ease! You're talking to a soldier
Whose every move's among the bolder.
I take my shots in drinking form, buddy.

SOLDIERS:

One night in Baghdad makes a hard man humble
Not much there between despair and ecstasy
One night in Baghdad and the mortars rumble
Can't be too careful with your company
I can feel the devil walking next to me.

THE SERGEANT:

Iraq's gonna be the witness
To the ultimate test of military fitness
This grips me more than would that
Muddy old river or crumbling ziggurat.

Thank God I'm only fighting the war,
Not marketing it.

I don't see you guys rating
The kind of blast I'm contemplating
I'd let you watch, I would invite you
But the fireworks we use would not excite you.

So you better go back to your tea rooms, your
mosques, your bomb factories . . .

SOLDIERS:

One night in Baghdad, threats in each direction
The bars are empty but the drinks ain't free
You'll find a bomb in every intersection

A little frag, a little IED
I can hear a gunship flying over me.

One night in Baghdad and the world's all backwards
You stay sober and the bar gets bombed
One night in Baghdad as you were told by Hackworth
There's bound to be a threat among the dun debris
I can feel a sniper behind every tree.

Port Call

★★★

Some years ago we got the word that Poul Anderson had died. I'd been a fan of his stuff since age twelve, and almost met him at a convention once. Almost. Some ugly personal silliness got in the way.

Then he was gone, of cancer, and he had no more stories to tell.

At 2300 that night an image came to me, of a decent ending I hoped he'd appreciate, and then I recalled some of the other giants—lots of the Golden Age writers, and others, all were in the same generation, and we lost so many of them in so short a time. A great many were veterans, all were inspirational, and all deserved tribute.

I did what I could, and the imagery flowed until 0300.

THE SHIP DRIFTED in from the pearly mist, long and lean and talking in the language of canvas and wood. She sighed and moaned, rustled and groaned, with the occasional splash from her bows. The shape defined itself, as of a ghost materializing from the netherworld, and sheeted sails, taut ropes, and elegantly turned timber rails took form. She slowed as she flew, easing across the break from chop to harbor-calmed waters, and sought haven.

"*Ho, the docks!*" a voice called, male and firm and sure. His waving arm indicated who he was, and the dockhands waggled in return. He heaved the coiled rope, watching it lazily tumble and twist, seeming almost alive as it settled over an age-blackened iron cleat.

A burly docker looped it and took up slack, waiting for the ship to bump against the boards. He raised his brows in surprise and pleasure as the maneuver was completed; the crew were masters. The vessel seemed to slow of her own accord, and barely nudged the pads. Ships of this size normally stayed in the harbor and sent boats ashore. To bring a sloop up to even this long a pier was a challenge.

The man at the prow called to the helm, "Nicely done, Robert, as always." He turned back to the jetty and lowered a plank.

"Thanks, Lynn," came the reply from astern. The tall, balding steersman came walking along the side, feet skilled as only a seasoned sailor's feet can be, and undisturbed by the still rocking motion of the wavelets under the dock pilings. He paused at a side door and rapped, opened it, and assisted two ladies over the step and to the deck. Other crew or passengers, impossible to tell apart as they all acted as if they were both, came around and helped with chores.

The dockers had seen all types over the years, yet this encounter was strange by any comparison. It was an odd crew. They were mostly old, sixty or better, but with young eyes. They fitted no particular style or body shape. Slender, heavy, elfin, and blocky builds were all represented. Yet despite the obviously unseamanlike physiques, there was a radiance, a power to all their gazes and presences.

It was an odd ship. It seemed to be a luxury sloop for a wealthy man, yet boasted five twelve pound guns per side. It also had roomy holds. It resembled the small coasters that made their living running odd jobs between the ports of the west coast, but was far larger.

A representative from the harbor master's office came by and noted the name, *Long Voyage*, recorded the names of her owner of record and captain, and the mate signed the form with a flourishing hand. The rep glanced over the scene, and asked, "Taking on cargo or supplies?"

"No cargo. Just a passenger," replied the mate. His beard was neat and gray, and he alone of the crew wore a blue blazer and officer's hat. The others were dressed as civilians, but in the most bizarre garb. One of them wore, of all things, a skunkskin cap.

"Who's the passenger?" asked the bureaucrat, looking around in confusion. Others were on the pier, but none this far out and none with the look of travelers.

"He's not here yet. Perhaps tomorrow," was the reply. "We're in no hurry."

Evening, blustery and threatening and darker than the hour would indicate. A storm howled from the west, thrumming the ropes and whistling over the eaves of the cabin. Within the cabin, a different battle raged.

"John, stop editing my log!" the other John demanded. His perfect Oxford accent was strained with irritation.

"You wrote it as if those petty pirates were an actual

threat," the first said reasonably, knowing to which exact entry the other referred. "Everyone rational knows that we always have the upper hand over those miserable second-raters."

"You pulled that manifest destiny stuff for years, but it won't fly here. I write the log, and if I see fit to embellish for sake of a better story, that's my prerogative!"

"Fritz and Gordy were more than men enough for that rabble! And it's not as if three quarters of the crew aren't aching to man the guns and draw steel at any sign of a threat. Besides, Murray negotiated their surrender quite easily."

"Gentlemen," the captain said. His voice didn't rise, and didn't need to. They both faced him. "You may be owner," he said to the first, "but we've had this discussion before. The log belongs to the captain. As captain, I've seen fit to delegate that task. Besides, Professor John is as good as they come. Trust him."

Nods and mutters indicated settlement, and everyone relaxed again.

"Why the hurry, Robert?" the gunner asked in mock bother. "No time for bets and I didn't get to crack heads!"

"Gordy, you shameless land lubber, polish your brass cannon and wait for the enemy. You know I like a taut ship." The captain grinned as he delivered the admonishment. He stretched down a hand to caress the ears of the tomcat that had appeared as if through the bulkhead and was stropping his legs, as he reached for his steaming bowl of Ipsy Wipsy stew with the other.

A heavy gust slapped the ship, rocking them sideways. Creaks from the timbers created an eerie atmosphere, made creepier by the guttering of the lamp flames. Quiet clumping footsteps from aft and below presaged the arrival of another, and a woman stepped into the cabin. Ever the gallant, the captain rose to greet her.

"Captain," she spoke, "While I know you enjoy the vitality of a storm, and Frank likes his meteorological studies, I find I cannot sleep. May I?"

Bowing, he replied, "As you desire, lady Marion."

"Thank you, sir," she nodded back. She turned and reached the door, staggering over another sway from the waves. She pulled it open too easily in the buffeting winds, stepped through and reached the rail in another jerky step. The deluge sheeted down but seemed to clear her as if deflected by an invisible umbrella.

Many who work energies require preparation and ritual. The elderly lady was quite beyond such trifles, and simply raised her right hand over the sea. In seconds, the rain had subsided, the wind slackened to a slightly gusty breeze, and the sky calmed to a distant flash and rumble, clear of the ship and the harbor. She watched for a while, then returned inside, thanking the captain again as she headed below. A bark from the ship's mascot startled her momentarily, and a crewman said, "Peaslake thanks you also, Marion."

Turning, she knelt and scritched his ears as the huge, shaggy mutt padded over. "You're welcome, faithful offog," she smiled.

A burly man with thick sideburns and a halo of gray hair hurried past her and above with a telescope clutched in his hands. He didn't acknowledge the change in weather, instead muttering about coincidence and mythical beliefs and the superiority of science as he set the device on its tripod and began to scan the heavens. He called over his shoulder, "Edgar! Doc! Mars is up!"

"Right there!"

"Coming, Isaac!"

"So when is this passenger of yours arriving?" asked the pier master. The strange ship had been here a week. While he wasn't anxious to see them off, interesting and well-behaved as they were, he was perplexed by their claim of only waiting for a sole passenger.

"Soon," the mate replied with a nod and a glance at his watch. It was full dark now, the Moon rising over the eastern mountains. "Soon," he repeated, and dropped the timepiece back into his pocket.

Midnight. It was cold and damp, the air thick and heavy across the still city and harbor, as it always was this time of year. Two figures strode along the dock, feet clattering on the aged gray and splintered timbers. They were far out from the shore and near the end of the stained pilings where the sloop waited. One man was tall and square, dressed in dark clothes and pea coat, left hand gripping a worn leather bag, sword held firmly under his arm. His lanky, narrow-chinned escort wore a black cloak and a suit, with three Chinese characters embroidered on his tie.

"Is this it, then?" the taller man asked of his guide. He wasn't sure where he was or why, or who this strange robed person was who had called him from his house at this late hour, body racked with pain as always, with a suitcase and his sword. His memory was quite hazy at the moment, but he was unafraid. He was somehow sure it would all make sense shortly. And the man was familiar, in a way.

"Right here, sir," was the agreeable reply, with a gesture. "Please come aboard."

Nodding, he stepped onto the plank, placing his feet cautiously. Perhaps not cautiously, but thoughtfully. His stride was one of familiarity; he'd done this some years before, but not recently.

He headed for the cabin, preceding his guide. He paused to stare at the proud, tall masts, sheeted sails lashed smartly to the yardarms, ropes tight and sturdy. It was a good new ship, its apparent age an illusion. He approved of what he saw, and resumed his pace.

His body betrayed curiosity, but no concern. As the cabin door was opened, he saw and smelled the oily glow of the lamps. He stepped through and descended the treads. They were firm, didn't creak, and were another hint as to expert care of the vessel.

The crew waited below, some dozens of them. Many wore swords, a few pistols, others carried assorted apparatus, a handful wore the robes of those who worked spiritual or planar power. The nearest were clearly visible, the others fading into the warm gloom.

"Ladies," he said, "gentlemen. It appears I'm expected." He looked at the faces gathered around him. There was no answer immediately, but there was a tense eagerness behind the polite stares. "I see," he said, nodding thoughtfully. The faces were familiar, as was his guide's, now. "I know where I am, then," he said at last, smiling gently.

"Welcome!" they chorused. Hugs and handshakes and

cheerful greetings broke the solemnity, and not a few tears flowed.

The tears were followed at once by steaming mugs of grog, whisky, ale, mead, and Irish coffee. Music was struck, and the tableau and silence disappeared in the mounting roar of what was almost a wake.

Almost.

It dawned a clear, crisp morning, promising a fine, breezy day. Gleaming cumulus lazed across the azure dome of sky. All hands gathered on deck as the planks were pulled, the ropes cast loose, and the dockers shoved the ship clear. Eschewing the offer of a tow out, the captain shouted orders and crew swarmed to hang royals and topsails. He watched them, reminiscent of so many spiders, and turned to the newest crewman. "So how's your health?" he asked, imperiously but with a grin that gave lie to the attitude.

"Quite excellent, actually," was the response. The tall man breathed deeply of the salt air, revitalized and surprised by it. The pain had vanished as if it never existed.

"Then man the sails!" came the order.

"Aye aye, Captain!" was the immediate reply, with a huge grin.

He turned as the captain called again, "And Poul?"

"Yes, Robert?"

"Welcome aboard again. Now let's get out to sea where we belong," he said. Turning, he bellowed, "Lynn, plot us a course for Hawaii. I need some warm nights to shake off the Frisco cold!"

"Can do. Doug, what's the least likely direction to take?"

The *Long Voyage* turned eagerly at her master's touch, seeking again the deep water, deep skies, and solitude she was built for. As she cleared the harbor mouth, the new crewman yanked loose the ropes on her forward mainsail, and it tumbled billowing into place, the motto sewn to it in bright gold thread, "TANSTAAFL," challenging the wind.

Naught But Duty
★★★

Mercedes Lackey e-mailed one day and asked if I'd like to write in her Valdemar universe. I've read a few of the many novels and liked them. She has a style that's an unusual combination of spare and visual.

The problem is I'm not a huge fan of the universe, and don't know the myriad intricacies of the Heralds and Companions. She suggested I move south on the main continent and develop some of that.

I had an interesting image of how a mercenary might protest without breaching contract. She told me to write it.

★★★

THE AFTERMATH of a battle was always confusing and ugly. Arden rode through the fractured pockets of suffering, surveying everything with trained eyes. His concern was practical, casualties and effect; there was little pleasure in this aspect.

Pleasure came from a well-planned and executed attack, a lightning raid against a larger force that inflicted casualties while keeping his own troops whole, a good maneuver around the flank of a worthy foe, or a feint that misdirected an enemy so the Toughs cracked his shield wall or line of battle.

The burning huts, the moaning, writhing bodies and the indignities and rape weren't pleasurable to any but the crass, the coward or the pervert. A common soldier could be forgiven a few hours' brutality in the aftermath, his partner's blood still splashed on his tunic. But pain inflicted against helpless civilians as a punitive measure was the mark of a scared weakling.

Crass, coward, pervert, scared weakling. Those words well described the Toughs' current employer, Lord Miklamar. Jobs had been few and far between, and it had been necessary to move farther south to find employ. But the quality of the ruler varied greatly, and Arden had little time to sound out prospects. His concern had been for good and reliable pay with enough action to keep his troops interested, not enough to wipe out them or his reputation. Here in Acabarrin, the petty lords paid well enough, and the action was steady. But with the king dead, the squabbling princes and heirs, vassal-lords and slavering, power-mad seekers were carving the corpse of the kingdom to nothing. He'd known nothing of Miklamar's reputation when he accepted the contract. He despised the man now that he did.

Arden's reputation, and that of the Toughs, was still safe. Barring an occasional looted trinket and scavenged arms and armor, *his* soldiers had left the village alone, and were drawn back up in formation awaiting his orders. The colors of a household unit they had not, but discipline, pride and the poise of professionals they did.

Arden grimaced a bare fraction of an inch, watching six of Miklamar's troops stretch a young woman, girl really, out on the ground. She screamed as they tore at her silken clothes. No mere peasant, she, but more likely the daughter of the chief or mayor, whatever he would be called around this land. Arden watched, acting as witness. Little he could do, other than remember the event. Nearby, others hacked a young man to pieces for the crime of having dared protect his house with a pruning hook.

Fire and blood tinged the air, turning the fresh breeze sickly sweet and metallic. Such a sunset was an ill omen for others. Arden turned his mount and headed out from the village, back past the lines of the allied force.

Ahead was the mounted figure he'd have to deal with, no matter how much it disgusted him. Shakis, the regional deputy to Miklamar, and the mind behind this battle. If "battle" could be applied to a bloody, one-sided slaughter and the present butchery.

He nodded in salute as he drew up. It was respect for the rank of the man who had bought his services, and nothing more. The gesture was not returned, which was as he expected.

"Lord Shakis, I see no point in brutalizing such peasants as these. It hardly seems worth the effort." It was a hint, and far more diplomatic than he wanted to phrase it. "There are other enemies we could seek."

Shakis gazed at him. The sneering contempt he had for the "mercenary" was concealed, but cut through to the surface anyway, flickering firelight from a blazing roof making it an even uglier caricature.

"It serves many purposes. The peasants will spread the word, that resistance brings only woe. It improves the take and the pay for my men. And it allows them some release, to take vengeance on enemy scum. It ensures they will have the right mindset for next time."

My men, Arden thought. Only male soldiers here. Arden would say *my troops*, because one in twenty was a woman. That had been part of the contract negotiations, too, as had swearing fealty to their employer's god. Arden had conceded on a temporary allegiance to their god, whose name he'd already forgotten, but had demanded his women warriors be kept. He would have cancelled the bargain otherwise. All his soldiers were worthy, and he wouldn't allow any suggestion otherwise.

The right mindset, he thought. That of the bully and the coward and the robber. His own sneering contempt was locked down deep. It was not something he would share. No successful mercenary did.

"After the evening's Triumph, will there be another movement?" he asked evenly.

Shakis missed the sarcasm, or ignored it, and said, "There will. Two more towns along this front require attention. Each will be a harder fight. Are your men up to it?"

"My troops are," he agreed. "If you are done with us for now, my troops and I will encamp for the night, about a mile south. We are in need of rest and to care for our gear and horses."

"As you wish, though the revelry will last all night."

Shakis chuckled and licked his lips slightly. The man was handsome enough physically, but his demeanor would strike fear into any civilian wench unlucky enough to meet him.

Arden wished he'd known of that ahead of time.

"Rest, and care of our gear and horses," he repeated. "We have our own revels planned." With ale they'd brought and hired wenches who were part of the entourage. Women who didn't require a fight and wouldn't slice your throat if you passed out. Ale that wasn't poisoned at the last minute, or badly brewed and rotten. Though the vengeance and poison were part of Shakis' calculations, most certainly, so that he could exact a price in response. Unprofessional. A professional took pride in his work, but didn't needlessly create more.

Another day, another battle. The town of Kiri. Arden scarcely remembered which were which anymore. It was easy to remember the towns where tough, honorable battles were fought. Likewise the ones where they'd rescued an employer's forces. The little villages, however, were never memorable, which made him uncomfortable. They were people, too.

The price of honor, he thought. The stock in trade of a mercenary company was its competence and reliability. The ragged bands of sword fodder never amounted to much, nor earned much. Only the best units did.

Which made those best the equal of any state or nation's army in quality and outlook. Which offended said "official" armies and earned sneers. Sneers the Toughs and the few outfits like them knew were part jealousy and part ignorance. And once you knew you were morally above the people you worked for . . .

It was rough work, and a conscience was both necessary and a hindrance. The Toughs owed allegiance to each other only. They protected each other at work, and in the taverns and camps afterwards. They thought not too hard about their opponents of the moment, who would shortly be defeated or dead as part of a cold deal and a week's pay and food.

So Arden, as Kenchen before him, Ryala before Kenchen and Thoral who'd founded the Toughs tried for only the best contracts. Supporting a proud state at its border or chasing bandits were the choicest tasks. Caravan escort was boring but honorable, as was guard duty at a border town or trading center. But there were few such jobs, and between starvation and ethics was a gray line.

Once again the Toughs cracked the defenses of the town that stood in the way of Miklamar's plan for expansion or peace or world conquest or whatever his motivation was. Were Arden a strategic planner for a nation, he'd find that information and use it. As a mercenary commander, he stuck to the closer, more local concerns of food, support and pay. Thinking too much made working for such people harder.

Once again, the rape, pillage, arson and looting began, the cowardly local troops reflecting the manner of their leader, as was always the case.

Arden wheeled his mount away from the spectacle, assured his own wounded and dead were being cared for by their serjeants, rode through the healthy ranks and nodded in salute. He always recognized his troops for doing well.

Shakis was waiting at the rear, as always. "Arden, you have done well again, for mercenaries," he said as Arden entered his tent.

Such a greeting. "Well for mercenaries." As if sword wounds felt different to the vanquished, depending on the colors worn by the soldier thrusting it home.

"I thank you," he said.

"The campaign proceeds. We will keep your men another month, as we asked."

"As long as they are paid, they will remain loyal to the contract," he hinted.

Shakis barely scowled and with a nod one of his lackeys dropped a sack of coin in front of Arden. Arden took the time to count it. Those two acts summed up the relationship perfectly. Arden didn't trust his employer, and the man was fervent enough in his religion to imagine that people should *want* to risk their lives for it.

Not for the first time, Arden pitied the towns falling to this excuse for a man.

Then it was out to ride patrol. Everyone took turns at the duties of camp and skirmish, even the squadron leaders and Arden himself. No good commander could understand the working soldiers without sharing in the menial tasks. Occasionally, he exercised his privilege not to, but it was good practice and good inspiration, so he dealt with the muck and tedium and did it most of the time.

He met up with Balyat and two newer riders. Balyat and he were the scouts for the ride, the others backup and messengers if needed, and would gain experience in the skill.

Patrol gave him the chance to explore the area

consciously, and to get a feel for it inside. It allowed part of his mind to relax and tour the terrain—rolling hills and copses of trees with small, growing streams. It let him ponder the job they had contracted.

The work was "good" in a sense. It was honest fighting at their end, the pay decent, and they had the benefits of a real army nearby. All the mercenaries were in the pay of one lord, meaning they weren't killing other professionals. Of course, they were killing innocent people and leaving the survivors to suffer at the hands of that lord.

Fausan, Mirdu, Askauk, Shelin . . . tiny hamlets, nothing but farmers and hunters with a few basic crafters. Why it was necessary to fight them was beyond Arden. He would have simply bypassed them, taken control of a large city, say, Maujujir, and let the traders spread the word that there was a new ruler. The peasants never cared, as long as the taxes weren't extreme and they were left to their lives.

Of course, that required a leader with self-confidence and who was secure in his power. Miklamar was not, and therefore wasteful. He'd been pacifying a very small province for years, proving to be a petty lord in every meaning of the word.

Riders ahead! The message came from a small part of Arden's brain that never slept. He didn't react at once, but let his mind go over what he'd seen.

Caravan, small. Not uncommon around an engagement area. It was foolish and inadvisable to fight, though both groups would report the presence of the other. To clash four on two wagons and a carriage would mean certain death for at least one rider, possibly all. Nor was Arden, as a hired sword, expected to fight outside of his contract. The train was not a massive provisioning effort, so it was not a threat to the war.

Still, a challenge and meeting were necessary, to determine the intent of the others, and their origin. Arden reined back and slowed slightly, watching to see that the others did. They were ahead to the left, crossing obliquely. One of their number took the lead, presumably the troop commander.

Shortly, the groups were drawn up facing each other, a safe twenty feet apart; too far for an immediate strike, too close for a charge.

"Arden, High Rider of the Toughs," he introduced himself. "Patrolling my unit's line."

"Count Namhar, of the Anasauk Confederacy, escorting a Lord," the other leader agreed. He wore striking blue and black colors, and had a slim lance with a small pennant. His horse was armored with light hardened leather and a few small plates that were more a status symbol than protection. Of the four others with him, two shared his colors and two were in a similar blue, black and grey, marking them as belonging to some side branch of the family.

"You are mercenaries. Who do you ride for?" Namhar asked.

"We are on contract to Miklamar, through his deputy Shakis." Arden wouldn't lie anyway, and the truth was best. Dissemblance could be seen as a sign of espionage.

One of the others, quite young, snapped, "You are the butchers of Kiri!" He reined his horse and clutched reactively at his sword. His partner extended a hand and caught him.

"Steady," the youth was told.

"Chal had friends in Kiri. He is still in mourning," Namhar said.

"I understand," Arden replied. "No threat offered, I take no offense."

"You're still a butchering scum!" the young man yelled.

"In Kiri," Arden said. "All we did was crack the defenses."

"You lie! I saw the desecrated corpses! The torn . . . " for a moment Chal was incoherent with rage.

"Shakis' men," Arden said. "We broke the line, as we were paid to, and he took what he calls 'retribution' on peasants too poor and weak to resist." Thereby showing the sum of his courage.

For a moment, there was silence. Emotion swirled in the air, all of them negative.

At once, Namhar dismounted. Arden nodded and did likewise. His two junior troops stepped down, leaving Balyat mounted, tall, bearlike and imposing, but wise enough to be a good lookout. One of Namhar's men stayed astride his beast, too.

The soldiers faced each other on the ground, the tension lessened. A mounted man was much taller and more imposing, a greater threat. With the horses held and the men afoot, it would be harder to start trouble.

The shouts had brought the other travelers out. The teamsters dropped from their wagons and the passengers in the carriage hurried over. The young man's outrage was contagious, and in moments the shouts of, "Butcher!" and "Violator!" were ringing.

Arden and his troops stood calmly and firmly, though the younger of the two trembled. Balyat sat solidly on his horse and refused to move. Namhar waved his arms and got control. The others acquiesced to his voice and presence, and the trouble downgraded to hard breaths and angry looks.

"I had a cousin in Kiri," Chal said.

Balyat spoke, his voice deep and sonorous. "My thoughts are with you," he said. "We fight only armed men. Shakis slaughtered the peasants. He left none if he could help it. He thought to show the kind of man he was."

"And you let him?" Chal said, glancing between the two mercenaries.

Arden said, "The Toughs are hired to bear the brunt against the peasants. Against larger forces, we are skirmishers and outriders. If you know of our name, we fight as we are ordered, but the pillage and rapine are not the work of my soldiers. I would not hire on to such, nor is it worthy of my troops."

Namhar nodded, recognizing the words as being the strongest condemnation the mercenary would utter.

"How can you fight for such animals? Is money so precious?" The man asking was a well-dressed merchant turned statesman. An honorable man, but not one to grasp the mercenary viewpoint.

Arden said nothing. He looked around evenly, finding only one pair of eyes showing understanding. Namhar nodded imperceptibly, but in empathy. He alone knew the conflict Arden faced, and why he could not unbind his contract. He wondered now, though, if Miklamar or Shakis were trying to ruin the Toughs' reputation, to tie them here for lesser wages. Probably not. That would be subtle, and subtlety wasn't something he'd seen much evidence of.

"It is the employment we have, until released, perhaps at month's end."

"Release now! There are worthier employers around." The merchant tugged at a purse to emphasize the point.

"That is not possible," Arden replied with a shake of his head. "We have troubled you enough. Good travel to you. I must resume my patrol. I will report this encounter with my other notes, after I return and care for my horse."

"Bastard!" Chal growled.

"Quiet, Chal," Namhar snapped. "High Rider, we thank you for the courtesy."

Arden nodded as he swung up into the saddle. It would be as easy to report the incident at once, but there was no threat here, and he had no orders to do so. He wasn't about to offer a grace before eating without pay or orders.

"If you do find your contract at an end soon, I can offer the pay of my lord for good skirmishers."

"I will remember that, Namhar," Arden replied. "Offers of support are always welcome."

Shakis appeared outraged when the message was relayed hours later.

"You spoke to what amounts to an enemy patrol, and not only didn't stop them; you report it to me after a leisurely dinner!"

"They were merely a lord's retinue. Surely you wouldn't wish me to attack possible allies?"

"Allies? There are no allies! Lord Miklamar will be the undisputed ruler, as is his right!"

"Then you need to deal with such things, not have me be your envoy, yes?" Arden asked with a cruel smile.

It took a moment for the petty underling to grasp the verbal spar. "Watch your tongue, mercenary," Shakis rasped.

Shaking his head, he continued, "There has been more rebellion along the border. Lessons must be taught. I expect this entire village put to sword." He pointed at a map, and to the south. "Manjeuk. Only another days' march."

A lesson of slaughtered peasants. Yes, Arden thought. That would surely teach other peasants not to try to live their lives. If he were planning, he would kill the village militia, then wait with baleful eye for the rest to flee. It was harsh, but it was war. It wasn't as dangerous, tactically foolish or obscenely cruel as wanton butchery.

He reflected that Shakis was acting professionally by his own vulgar standards. He wasn't sparing the town for looting, burning and rapine.

Though not every occupant would be dead after the attack. Those left would be subject to the most vile humiliations this twisted troll could devise, he was sure.

"Wouldn't it be more efficient to simply kill the armed men and drive off the rest? Why waste good steel on starving, rag-clothed peasants?"

It was a reasonable question. So he thought.

"Rider Arden," Shakis said, caressing a jeweled dagger before him, with a blade that would turn on canvas, never mind leather or iron, "the plans are made here. You and your mercenaries," that with a sniff, "are merely one small part of many in an engagement planned many hundreds of miles away. All we ask, all we are paying for, is your men to swing their swords where we tell them to, and to not think too much."

That decided Arden. He knew what course to take.

"As you command," he said with a nod, and turned to his own camp. That order he would give. That exact order.

Before dusk, his troops were ready, aligned and poised for inspection. The ranks were dead straight, the product of proud, expert riders. He felt a ripple of excitement. His troops, those of the unassailable repute. There was Ty'kara, the Shinai'an woman, tall and quick and almost as strong as some men. Bukli, skilled at sending signals with flags, hands or fires, and almost as handy with a sword. Balyat, tall and broad and powerful as an ox, with a cool, mature head. His troops, the best one could pay for.

His troops, under pay of a cretin.

Duty.

He turned through each rank, examining each raised arm, sword or spear, to see that they fit his orders. All were clean, well cared for and ready. All his troops quivered in eagerness and a little fear. The brave could admit fear. Fear was part of being human. Only the coward and the fool denied fear.

Every soldier, every weapon, fit and ready as he had demanded. And now to follow the orders of the cretin.

He passed behind the last rank, then turned between two troops. They flinched not a bit, nor did their horses shy, as he urged his mount, Fury, to a fair gallop.

Then he was through the front rank, and behind him came the snorts of horses and the "Yaaah!" of riders. Thunder rose from the ground, thunder that he commanded, thunder that shattered armies.

Far ahead, brave and fearful peasants in sorry, untrained

formation prepared to die for their homes. They trembled in fear, armed with hooks and forks and an occasional spear. A handful with bows were arrayed in rear. He respected them far more than the scum he worked for this night. But he did work for them.

Duty.

And he would see that duty done.

Perhaps five hundred yards, and the flickering lights of torches melded with a blood red sunset to set the mood for the work ahead. Manjeuk was the name of a quiet town in a forest meadow. Tonight, however, it was a dark-tinged collection of rude huts with little prettiness.

A hundred yards, and he could see faces, grubby and fearful and shifting in grimaces. That was just enough time to brace shield and lower sword . . .

He hit the defensive line and burst through the front rank. These poor peasants were no match in any fashion for professional soldiers. He chopped down and connected with a skull, feeling the crack through his arm. He let the impact swing his arm back, then brought it into a thrust that knocked another man to his feet. He brought the tip up as he swung his shield out on the other side. Two men sprawled, one of them nudged by Fury's left forehoof.

Then he was through. That dismal line of men with inadequate stakes and pits had been the defense. They'd lasted not five seconds.

Urging Fury to a charge, he cleared the deadly, empty space ahead. Four good gallops did it, and no arrow came close. Few arrows came anywhere.

Then he was inside the town. A crone with a pitchfork thrust at him, and he dodged, slashing at her chest. She went down. Behind her was a cowering girl of perhaps twelve, who had dropped her stick and was whimpering. A slight poke was sufficient for her. A boy of fifteen or so wouldn't succumb to a single blow, and had to be hit three times. Stupid of him not to stay down once hit, but that wasn't Arden's concern. He reined back, turned and galloped on.

An old man in a doorway didn't have time to raise his ancient, rust-caked sword. Two younger men drew out a rope. Arden cursed and ducked, snatching at it and twisting. The shock pulled them to the ground. Behind him, Ty'kara whacked one, dogged over and twisted, jabbed the other and recovered.

Then they were through the town and done. Few casualties, but no loot or anything positive to show for it. He sniffed in disgust as he waved his arm for the Toughs to form up.

Duty done.

Now to encamp again. They circled wide around the now flaming town. What was left was Shakis' concern. And Arden found that most amusing.

The Tough's camp was as it had been, patrols far out, pickets at the outskirts, the wounded and support armed and still a threat to intruders, even if not the heavy combatants the "regulars" were. Only half the Toughs were involved in any given battle. The rest, including recruits and their serjeants, supported them.

The regimental fire was huge, the heat palpable many feet away. Farther out, squadrons and smaller elements had their own blazes, then there were those for the watch.

Toughs' Camp was a ring of fire, ever brighter toward the center, where Arden sat with his troop leaders.

Arden took a healthy slug of his ale. It was a good, rich brew that quenched and refreshed him. The bread had been baked that morning, with a chewy crust and nutty flavor. The cheese was dry, crumbly and sharp. He dug in with gusto. Once Mirke had finished roasting that yearling stag, he would enjoy the flavor of it, the flavor that was already wafting through his nose and taking form.

Regardless of their orders, it had been a good night's work, and he was proud of it. Pride and prowess in duty. It was the only really valuable thing he had. He cherished it. A faint warmth and tingle from the ale made it sweet.

Then Shakis, that damned foppish envoy arrived, his horse clattering with ridiculous flashy accoutrements. Arden wasn't surprised, and knew exactly what his complaint was to be before the worm opened his mouth.

"High Rider Arden! Lord Miklamar is most displeased with your performance, if it can be called that, in Manjeuk!"

"We did as we were ordered," he replied, stonefaced. "As we swore to."

"You were ordered to put the village to the sword and spear!"

"And so we did," he replied. He refused to get upset with the likes of this. It would not be honorable. Emotion he reserved for those worthy, who might be allied or enemy, but whom he would count as men. This was not a man.

"I expected you would take your swords *out* of your scabbards before striking with them! And use the sharp ends of your spears!"

"Then perhaps you should have so specified in your orders," Arden said, smiling faintly. Behind him were snickers. No doubt everyone in Manjeuk had been confused to have the fiercest riders of the South gallop through, swatting and poking them with scabbarded swords. No doubt they were all bruised and broken from it. But none had been stabbed or cut. The orders had not specified that. And *had* specified the mercenaries were not to think too hard.

"Because of your cowardice," Shakis said, and Balyat and Ty'kara growled with flinty gazes. Arden laid out a palm to hold them. It was all he needed to command them, despite the mortal insult. "Because of your cowardice, our men took near twenty deaths."

"I lost a man, too," Arden replied. "Bukli, my best messenger."

"You have my pity, sell-sword," Shakis replied. He was reaching a frothing level within, Arden could see. "No matter. The town *was* taken, and now our men show them what it means to lose." The expression on his face was a combination of excitement and lust that was simply obscene.

It would have been better, Arden realized, to have killed the poor bastards quickly. He'd done them no favors as it was.

The grumbling around him rose to a barely audible level as Shakis rode out. Arden's troops were no happier than he.

For a week the Toughs were kept in camp as other units fought. It was an insult, and a further waste of resources.

Arden concealed his contempt, but his troops were not so reticent. They'd fought for harsh men before, and torture and agony were not unfamiliar sights to any of them, but any professional soldier had his limits. The Toughs were barely tolerating Miklamar's strategy and the toady who relayed his wishes.

Something had to be done.

After nine days, Arden was called to a strategy meeting. He'd been shunned from the planning sessions even though he was merely an observer. That banishment couldn't help his survival or plans, and his inclusion now, being "ordered to present" himself was yet another slap. He had expected it, of course. He'd hoped his disgusted protest in the last battle would have led to the contract being let, but either Miklamar or Shakis was too stupid or petty for that. They wasted pay to keep the Toughs doing nothing.

Arden arrived and was ignored. Movements were planned, orders given, messengers and commanders sent. Silence reigned around Arden, with no word or acknowledgment given him by anyone. Commanders of units he'd fought alongside, and who mutually respected him, gave him only a glance then studiously avoided further interaction. For two hours, Arden sat in cold drafts at the wall of the tent, watching the flickering lamp flames in meditation. He refused to get angry, for that was what Shakis wanted.

When orders came at last, while Shakis loudly chewed a pork shank at his table, spitting and getting grease on his maps, they were insultingly direct.

"Arden, you have a chance before you to redeem

yourself. This afternoon, we destroy the last vestiges of the old Kingdom in this district. You will strike in the van, and attack the village. That means, with your weapons in hand, with the sharp ends, fight as hard as you can. I will countenance no clever ploys this time, or I will have your men and yourself used for target practice by my archer regiment. You will fight any who oppose you, you will lay waste as your reputation demands, and once we are done you will be sent on your way, since you are reluctant to help the rise of a strong empire. But I hold you to your contract yet."

"Yes, Shakis. I will do as you command."

There being no point in further discussion, Arden dismissed himself. Shakis was aware of his departure, but made no sign of noticing.

The orders created a conflict of moral outrage in Arden. He couldn't obey an order to slaughter innocents. It was unprofessional, cowardly and unmilitary. Nor could he break his sworn oath and contract.

As he always did when troubled, he rode patrol. His thoughts drifted, and distance from Shakis made him feel cleaner. He'd had disputes with employers before, even if this scraped the hoof for lowness. He rode ahead of the three troops with him, just so he could feel more alone.

It was a cool night, slightly misty, and fires could be seen behind the town, of a small force preparing to support the town once attacked. Miklamar's only good strategy was to use his larger army to spread the threat of his neighbors. Though that might be accidental rather than strategic planning.

Count Namhar showed far better sense, with his army

high in the defense, prepared to rush in on a force bogged down even briefly in the town below. He knew he couldn't save the village, so he'd use it as an anvil to hammer Shakis's force against. He'd do far more damage that way, including to the Toughs.

Arden wondered if he could arrange to be where the counterattack would happen, so as to have an honorable fight against a decent enemy.

Something crept up through his mind and coalesced into a thought.

Yes. He just might be able to do that. It would take courage, risk his life and save his oath. That made it worth doing.

He wheeled Fury about and galloped back to camp, leaving the other three soldiers to catch up while they wondered what their commander was doing.

Count Namhar watched the unfolding battle from a hilltop. Part of him craved to be down below with his brave men, doing what could be done to restrain a horror. A horror that not only outnumbered them, but had hired crack mercenaries.

He was thankful that the leadership used both mercenaries and indigenous forces poorly.

His presence on the hill was for tactical advantage. He had a small device from the mages that could potentially change the course of a battle, if used well.

The tube was a magic Eye. Its rippling patterns, almost oily, resolved to crystal clarity when stared through. He could see events far across the field and send swift messengers to maneuver his forces.

The Eye only let him see things larger. It couldn't see things beyond obstacles, but did enhance anything within line of sight. And the mercenaries were just within that line.

It took only a moment's glance to cause him to grin. A surge ran through him, of respect for a mercenary who embodied every virtue a soldier should have. There was loyalty, and then there was honor. Above those was courage, and it took tremendous courage to do what Arden's troop was doing now.

Somewhere, they must have been ordered to attack the village. And that's what they were doing. Arden was a genius, and brave beyond words to offer such a tactic. Exploiting it would cost lives. But the tactic was suicidally foolish, and Namhar could exploit that at once. He could wipe out the Toughs to the last troop. Though to do so would be a shame.

Then the true nature of it hit him.

"Send Rorsy's force down to take them," he ordered the nearest of his aides.

"At once. At the charge, or dismounted?"

"No, take them alive," Namhar said. This had to be done just right. A man with a sword was still dangerous, and if he knew Arden as he felt he did, the man wouldn't simply surrender.

"My lord? I am confused," his aide said.

"I will explain, but quickly. We have little time."

And indeed, there was a risk. If Arden was what he seemed, it could be handled rather quietly. But the flash of steel could turn it into the bloodbath it had looked to be from the beginning.

★ ★ ★

"Attack the town," Shakis had ordered. "Town" had two meanings; either the population and resources of the small settlement, or the physical structure of it. It was that way Arden had chosen to obey the order, and his troops had agreed, with hesitation and fear, but in support of their commander and in rebellion against the detestable creature who'd hired them and debased them. Their honor was their coin in trade. They would fight as hard to protect it as to earn it.

Arden kept his face impassive and hacked again, the daubed withes of the wall powdering under his onslaught. Yards away, Balyat crushed small beams with swings of his axe. The Toughs were arrayed along a front perhaps two hundred yards wide, surrounding the rude buildings and smashing them. To the south, Shakis's other forces were slaughtering the helpless. Arden had killed one dweller who'd faced him with a staff. The others had run. Some had seen the mercenaries senselessly beating buildings and taken the opportunity to run away, or to the battle farther south. One didn't question an enemy's error.

Behind Arden there were men approaching, in colors that made them allies of Lord Namhar. Each swing of his head let him see their approach. They were moving to flank him and were unarmed.

So they were civilians, not a threat, he told himself, clarifying the strategy in his mind. He was playing games with his orders, and the risk was great. He probably wouldn't die at this point, though both revenge and charges of atrocity could lead that way. He might destroy a company that had a decades-long reputation for honest fighting. If this worked, he would indeed have employ, and stories told for generations. But the chance for death or disgrace as an oathbreaker hung on the other side of the balance.

But some lords were beneath any contempt. Duty bound him to a contract. Only honor could make him respect a man.

The two burly "civilians" closed on him, and he pointedly ignored them. They were dressed in battle leather and well-scarred. Professionals themselves. They had orders, and perhaps they understood those orders. If they didn't raise weapons, he was under no compunction to fight them under any oath he or the Toughs had ever sworn. "We fight only armed men." But if they did, he would perforce respond in kind. All his troops had their orders, all would obey . . . but a panicky moment could lead to a close quarters bloodbath with horrific results for all.

All three of them knew how it must play out, and the scene would replay across the front. Arden could not decline to engage, could not offer to surrender to unarmed men. If asked, he'd have to refuse.

As he drew back for another blow, one of the two lunged at him. He spun, shifted, and made to take a swing. His trained reflexes prepared to strike a blow that would cleave a man.

Then the ground shifted and he tumbled, cracking his head against his helmet as he crashed. His sword arm flew above his head, and bashing fists broke his grip. He kicked, snapping his right foot in a blow that elicited a pained grunt. The fists rained down on his chest, driving the breath from him.

"Mercenary, you are disarmed! Will you now surrender to Lord Namhar's courtesy?"

"I will," he said.

There was no dishonor in surrender once unable to fight, and he'd followed his orders exactly. His employer— former employer—had been the lowest filth imaginable. To be captured thusly should make him feel proud. It didn't.

Surrender. The Toughs didn't surrender. A wrenching pain that wasn't physical tore at him. Certainly, the fight had been honorable, but it was a defeat in the employ of a weakling. That cost dearly in reputation, in pride, in self-respect. Not to mention the hundreds of townsfolk who had been killed.

"I am to offer you employ with Lord Namhar, at Guild scale and with a bonus of one fifth. Or else you may have free passage to our northern border."

He heard the words, but there was no pleasure in him. He'd won this battle for his honor by losing the battle in the field. Even though he'd planned it that way, it was dizzying, shocking.

Slowly, he rose to his feet. One of the two had rushed to join a group of fellows beating Balyat to the ground. The bulky warrior needed six of them to restrain him before he finally acceded. Arden couldn't help but grin. It restored some small breath of life to the unit that even disarmed they fought so hard.

His remaining escort was panting for breath and bleeding from nose and lip. Arden had acquitted himself well enough, though he would have a hard time convincing himself.

"I am Captain Onri," his captor said. "If you will give your word of honor to be peaceable, I will escort you to Count Namhar."

"My word you have, Captain," Arden said, feeling a slight rise from the depths his soul had sunk to. He walked away from the village, smiling. He had lived through his oath to a coward. He had lost by his oath to a good man.

The Sword Dancer
★★★

The Valdemar stories have become an annual tradition. I continued with the same geographic area, and brought in some Vikings, though not quite Vikings, to be merchants, traders and warriors. This one was too long of a short—I was still fighting the urge to write short novels instead of short stories. It took a lot of editing, and this is the mostly original version that had to be cut to fit word count for the book. I prefer this version.

★★★

RIGA GUNDESDATI, called Sworddancer, swigged from her bottle and pushed her helmet back on. Tendrils of flaxen hair floated near her eyes until she pushed them under the sweat-soaked leather padding.

Her new opponent, Ruti, was wide-eyed under his own iron. She'd put two of four previous competitors down with healthy, well-placed cracks of her wooden practice sword.

She was glad to make a good showing. Swordmistress Morle was watching, and some visitor from far Valdemar stood at the Yorl's spot, studying them.

"Fight!" called the judge. Seeing Ruti's trepidation, she charged.

"Yaaaaaah!" she shouted at his upraised sword, and he hesitated. She swung her own stick and dropped her wrist, aiming for his thigh. He blocked and leapt, but he was on the defensive, cautious and timid. This fight was already over, even if he didn't know it.

A twist of her hips and shoulder brought her shield up against his swing. His blow was firm enough, but without heart. She swung again to press him. His next strike was surer and a bit better placed, but he hadn't yet figured out that her presented stance—sword foot forward instead of shield foot—gave her several additional inches of reach beyond what her height did.

There was his third swing, and she had the rhythm and the dance of her name. She shot her arm forward, pivoted at the hip, swung, snapped her wrist and laid timber right above his shoulder, just at the lip of the helmet. A loud *crack* indicated a scoring hit, what would be a killing strike in battle, and she had her arm cocked for a followup before he registered the blow and acknowledged it. He fell under his shield and waited for the judge to tap him out.

Taking a breath to steady herself, she bowed to him and stepped out of the rope-edged *vollar*.

Her father was waiting, and she smiled. He took her in a huge hug. She remembered how she'd complain about him squashing her, and he'd bellow, "I like squashing you!" He was getting on in years, but still tough and muscular. Running the hus and managing their business saw to that.

He stepped back and kept hold of her shoulders.

"I already saw Erki. I'm called for a scout ride. I should be back in a week. Meanwhile, take care of Erki and ask the Swordmistress if you need help."

She didn't like that latter caution, with the unspoken idea that he might not be back. Whatever was happening was huge. She kept the sob she felt to a sigh and hugged him close, hampered by leather and iron.

"Yes, Father," she said.

"Good luck, girl. I'm going to watch one bout. Show me your form."

She nodded and hugged him again, then redonned her helmet and got in line.

Ten youths in her age bracket were here today, having finished their letters and numbers. All the children were expected to learn to fight, even if they might go from here to pursuits like counting, textiles or motherhood. The Kossaki were sea and riverborne tradespeople, and might always have to fight attackers.

She wrapped up her musing because she was next. At a wave, she entered the *vollar* and awaited her opponent. It was Snorru, two years her elder, just now a man, big and proud, but he sometimes hesitated to avoid looking less than perfect.

"Sworddancer and Strongarm. Honor having been given, *fight!*"

"Go, Riga!" her father shouted, then was silent. Coaching from the rope was not allowed, and he never had. He gave her her own mind and she loved him for it.

This time Riga strode straight across the *vollar*, shield up and sword ready. Snorru swung, and it was accurate and strong. She deflected it with her shield but staggered and dropped. His followup blow cracked on her shield and skinned her helmet.

Then she was up, using her shield for concealment as she brought her sword up in front. She snapped her arm, and the tip slapped the pommel of Snorru's stick and his wrist. His hand bounced open and his weapon fell, as she swung up and around, cracked him in the back of the helmet, over and into front quarter of it, over and into his kidneys, over and into his chest, over and into the back of his thigh. The sword moved *fast* in her strong wrist and joints trained to impart all their energy in a moment. He staggered down under the rain of blows.

"You could hit harder," he said as he rose, breathing hard, "but I grant you style."

"Harder is better only so it breaks armor," she replied. "Undirected force is a waste." She offered a hand to him and he took it.

She turned to find her father's smile . . . but he was gone. He'd known she'd be occupied with the bout, and left before she could tell him how much she worried. She sighed. He was an honest but shrewd merchant, and that was so like him.

"He saw you," her friend Karlinu said from the rope.

"Kari?"

"He left just moments ago. He saw your bout, and grinned to split his face. That was great, girl! But you need to keep your tip higher when in guard."

She knew that was a problem with her form, but pushed Kari aside, hoping for a glimpse of Father.

"He's gone. I'm sorry. And the Swordmistress wants to see you at once."

She glanced at the youth *vollar* to see Erki working on his form. He was too eager, brave but incautious at times. Good with a sword, but his shield tended to drop.

She doffed her helmet, shimmied from her mail and left it in a neat pile near her cloak. Her real sword came with her, slung and ready. It wasn't something she thought about. No warrior was without a weapon. She held the bronze-tipped scabbard as she jogged. It was chased, had a falcon-eye jewel and a silver appliqué of a cat with tiny ruby eyes, its tail knotted about it. The sword within was steel fitted with unadorned bronze around a chatoyant wood grip. A fighting sword, not a showpiece. She and Erki had two of the finest blades among the youth. She tried to be worthy of hers.

Riga entered the Swordmistress's tent at the field edge. She always felt nervous facing her teacher, as if there was something she would be chastised for. Nothing came to mind as an infraction, so she put it aside. The other idea . . . that wasn't pleasant, either. Her sweaty gambeson didn't help her feelings.

Not only Swordmistress Morle, but the visiting "Herald" was within. She bowed first to her Mistress, then to the guest. She faced Lady Morle but turned so she could study the Herald. He was tall, handsome and very well dressed. His outfit was plain with just a touch of piping, but well-fitted and spotless. He looked like something from a royal court.

Heralds were highly regarded despite their scarcity, or so she gathered, having only heard mentions of them. This one had arrived a few days before, escorting a High Priest of some temple. It wasn't one for any of the Kossaki gods, so he'd been made welcome as a guest.

Riga had no idea what had come about. The elders, and her father, seemed aware of these Heralds and the priest and unbothered. Now, though, her father had ridden off, as had most of the men and some of the women, all those trained for war not needed to run hus or business.

"Sworddancer, you must lead a ride," the Swordmistress said.

"I am honored," she replied at once. Honored, and scared. At sixteen years, she was a capable fighter and skilled, but lacked the wiles and polish of her elders. She grew hotter than she already was from training, then chill.

"You hide your nerves well," Morle said with a grin. She continued more seriously. "I don't ask this lightly. A great many people need us."

"I'll do what I can," she agreed. This would be a test worthy of adulthood, she thought.

"Then look at this map."

Morle unrolled the scraped vellum across her table and pointed.

"We're here," Riga indicated. "Little Town is there."

"Yes. And there are refugees down here." Morle indicated the south. "The villages south of Paust Lake are being sacked and destroyed by Miklamar and his thugs."

Riga understood. "They're fleeing. We can't support them in our lands, and we must hurry them through in case we need to defend our own borders. We also don't want the attention of having them move through, nor to encourage them."

"Very perceptive," the Herald spoke at last. "I am impressed."

"Thank you, my lord," she replied, meeting his eyes and trying not to be shy, "but I have studied since I was four years. A map and a supply count tell me all I need to know about that aspect.

"I will lead youths, I presume?" she asked of Morle. "I can't imagine I'm to lead senior warriors."

"A youth," Morle replied, and Riga gulped. "This is scouting, not fighting. There are so many refugees, and we are not a large outpost."

They weren't even truly an outpost, Riga groused to herself. Gangibrog was a glorified camp, as its name implied. "Walking town." Little to it besides docks. Nor would the local resources permit it to become much larger. They were a trading waystop of the simplest kind. River freighters came from the coast, cargo went from there to lake and river barges inland. Her father had retired here to raise a family after fighting and trading in the far south. They were a coast people originally, from the Fury Sea.

"May I take my brother?" she asked. "He is strong and sharp, when he listens."

"And you are loud and bossy when he doesn't," Morle chuckled. "Why else him?"

"Because if he has to go with someone, he'll feel safer with me, and he'll make me feel better if not safer."

"Ordinarily I wouldn't allow it. But you are right. I've allowed each party five coins in supplies. You'll have to take any others from your own hus. I wish I had good news. There are thousands of refugees, though."

"As long as my father didn't strip it, I'll manage. Who will watch our hus?"

"Someone will, be sure of it. I know you have no mother or sister, Riga. Hurry to Arwen and leave as soon as you can. She has your directions. They speak Accabar. I know you know it well enough."

"Yes, mistress." She bowed her way out.

It was thrilling, exciting and scary. Leading an escort wasn't as great as far trading or fighting in war, but it was safer. However, two youths in hostile territory was enough to make her guts twist. She might be trained as a warrior, but everyone understood that women guarded the hus and raised the family. They were defenders, not campaigners, except in emergencies.

Erki was waiting, his gear a jumbled heap as usual.

"Erki, neaten that up and get your helm up before someone steps in it!" she commanded. Not only that, but the metal would rust if left on the damp ground.

"I forgot!" he said. "Did you see me beat Sammi?" He grabbed at his stuff quickly.

"No, but good. He's a stone larger than you. Did Father see you?"

"Yes, he's off on a ride."

"We're going, too, by ourselves. You have to do as I say."

"I'll try! Where are we going?" He almost jumped in glee. The boy could never hold still.

"We're guiding refugees and I'm not sure yet. You'll do more than try, too. This is real."

"I'll pack Trausti, then," he said.

"Excellent idea. Keep a list."

"Yes, Riga." He took off at a solid sprint. She headed for the river.

He'd do that well, she knew. He was bright if impetuous, very much "boy."

The floating dock swayed under her feet as she trudged down it. Most of the laborers were officially day hires, though regulars. She greeted Kopang.

"Hello, Lady Riga," he said between heaves of cargo. Dried fish in tubs was coming north, from a packetboat to a lake barge a yard shallower.

"Hello. Has my father been by?"

"He has. We also will be riding as soon as we're done here." Another tub slammed over the gunwale onto the thwarts of the lower boat.

"I wanted to make sure everything was covered."

"It is, and my wife will watch your hus."

"Oh, good," Riga said. She'd be sure to secure the silver. Brika was honest, but it wasn't good to put temptation out. They took care of their workers, but the traders were always better off than the laborers. "I will leave, then. Morle and Arwen are watching, too," she said, partly in warning, mostly as an offer of support. Kopang had five children to feed.

"Be safe and hurry back," he said.

"I will," she replied. Really, she could trust them. Now she'd go stash the silver.

At their hus, she decided the fire was low enough not to worry about, then fastened the place down for a trip or storm. Window shutters, back door, hang everything on hooks or shelves away from walls and floor, silver and valuables into a chest in a stone hole under a bench. Then pack, heavy on gear, light on excess. Blessi was a small horse and wouldn't take more than Riga's weight in cargo. Eir would manage a bit more, since Erki was smaller. Trausti would have only supplies.

Erki could pack well, sometimes too well. She caught him as he tried to stuff extra clothes into the pack saddle.

"Good idea, but too much weight," she said. "One change is all. We'll have to hope to air out."

"I already checked and oiled their hooves," he said.

"Good," she agreed. "I'll be back. Get finished, please."

She hurried down the planked timber street to Arwen's warehouse. "Auntie" Arwen was good to all of them. She usually found a way to sneak some treats to the children.

"Auntie Arwen, I'm here for supplies," she said as she walked through the open door. The store was built of planks, and the inside nothing but shelves, neat stacks and crates. Traders weren't impressed by pretty presentations.

"And how is our sword dancer today?"

"Tired from a morning dance, and leading a party."

"You, too? All our fighters are called. Any who have learned Scout and Sword. It worries me."

"I need some supplies. Is there spare?"

"Not much. The Corl came first, then others in descending rank. The Swordmistress is in charge and it seems all who will be left are children, the old, some craftspeople. And even the smiths and tanners have their armor and bows out. Anyone not attached is riding." She pointed at her own panoply. Her blades and armor were well-worn and patinaed with decades of use. Her age had slowed her a lot, but few could cross swords with her. Riga barely had once. Arwen had spanked her with the flat in response, just to prove to her it was luck.

"That's why I am called, then," Riga decided. It wasn't quite as flattering to be needed rather than wanted. At least not like this.

"Please check me. I have spare garb and overdress, four pairs of clean footwraps, cloaks, gloves, hats, water bottles, weapons, mail and shield, shelter, rope, our horses, buckets for the horses, personal kit for us and the horses, a map, a char stick and book, tools and parts and whetstone, bandages, some silver and bronze, a firesteel and tinder."

"Do you have your stuffed bear?" Arwen asked with a faint smile.

Riga blushed, because she did. Her mother had made it for her long ago. She tried to say nothing.

"Oh, child, take the toy. It weighs little, and if it offers comfort to have a mascot, it hurts nothing. You can't take a cat or dog."

"I would like to take signal birds."

"So would everyone. I have two left, and both are young and not the best."

"They will fit right in, then," Riga said in self-deprecating humor.

"You plan better than half the men in camp, girl. A dozen I saw without gloves. 'Just a couple of days' they said. Aye, and it will be cool those days, and colder at night."

"I will need extra travel rations, in case of delay. We won't have time for hunting."

"That I have. Dried broth, thrice-baked biscuits, hard cheese, honeyed nuts and smoked meat. It will bind up your guts but you won't be hungry. Or rather, you'll have to be to eat it." Bundles of such were already packed. Arwen dragged two of them over.

"I'm told I'm too picky about my food, anyway. This might help my reputation."

She chuckled, "Only so long as you don't come back half-starved."

"That would be my brother." Erki was finicky beyond belief. Meat and bread were all he would eat, given the chance.

"Ah, let me talk to him before you leave. I'll fix that."

"Do you have any shooting stars?" she asked.

"Only one per party. Your colors are purple and green, yes?" she turned and mixed the powders and stalk, tamped the end and sealed it with wax. "Though it will only help if there's someone nearby."

Preparation went faster than she expected. Trausti had a pack with food, the birds and shooting star, extra arrows, three large water jugs, the sundries. Their riding horses were trimmed to move fast. If it came to that, poor Trausti was in trouble.

She wore her sword high on her side; a brace of javelins and a spear rode up behind her at an angle, with her bowcase of incised leather and a capped quiver of arrows. She wore a large knife at her belt, a small one in her boot. A broad round shield, iron bossed, covered the pack over Blessi's rump, the edges of her mail and bedding peeked out, with her helm mounted atop.

Her fighting clothes were masculine, a thigh-length tunic and trews. The heavy cloth was a luxuriant weave that was very comfortable but would stop the whipping wind. Her family might have money, but they didn't waste it, so the clothes were repaired and patched, multiply over knees and elbows. Her boots were calf-high and well-worn, hard enough for riding, soft enough for walking or fighting. She hoped the dull fabric made her look a bit worn and experienced.

Erki only looked like a boy. He carried a sword with bone and wood fittings, the scabbard carved with beasts and tipped in bronze. He had no spear, just a bow, and had only the one knife. His garb, like hers, was fine but well-worn. Eir was a pony at best, but Erki handled him surely.

An hour later they were riding, leading Trausti behind them at a fast walk. They each had a pannier of oats to supplement forage. The horses weren't the massive chargers of warrior lords, but were sturdy beasts well used to skirmish and short rations, not to mention shipboard travel.

Riga kept glancing at her map. It wouldn't make things move faster, but it was a nervous habit. She'd never gotten lost, though, so she didn't plan to change the habit.

"We're heading southwest toward Acabarrin," Erki said, peering over.

"Yes. The refugees are fleeing from there."

"Why can't they stay in their towns?"

She sighed. She wasn't sure of the politics herself, certainly not enough to explain them to another child. She hated the subject, but her father was the town teacher. He insisted that relations between countries and groups was the key to trade, war, even happiness. He had to be exaggerating on the latter.

"You've heard of Miklamar. He wants their land."

"Why doesn't he just trade? He has a peninsula with

ships coming from the Black Kingdoms, all over the seas. Why waste money on a long campaign?"

She sighed. The boy was right. He was wiser than some adults.

"He doesn't think that way," she said. "No, I don't know why," she added, before he could ask. "He wants everything."

"The way I used to take all the biscuits and make you come and get them? Because I was afraid of running out?"

"That could be," she agreed. It very well could be. "That would make him as mature as a five year old." With some of the things she'd heard, even the more gruesome ones, that also made sense. It wasn't comfortable to think of adults being so immature.

They stopped talking, except to coax the horses through puddles in the terrain, still ice-skinned from the chill night. Anyone without gloves and hood was going to regret it. It was cold and getting colder. Brisk gusts of wind punctuated the air.

On the way back they'd not take this route, she decided. Too late to change now, but she'd mark it in ink when they stopped. Improving the map was the duty of every Kossaki. She marked larger copses of trees, deep gullies, and bare rocky tops and streamcourses that would work as landmarks.

They stopped at dusk, wanting enough time to pitch a proper camp on a slight rise, but below the crest, with a nearby copse as a windbreak. She found what she needed easily enough in this rolling terrain.

"Here, Erki," she said. "You trample grass."

The boy was enthusiastic about the task, stomping and

jumping. As he did so she made a quick sweep around the hill. Nothing and no one in sight. That was good, but also unnerving. It was as if they were the only people in the world.

Erki had the grass flat. She ran a line from a stake she drove into the ground with her heel. Erki laid a tarpaulin over it, then she drove a spearbutt into the ground, grabbed the rope and pulled. Erki jammed two pegs in at the outspread corners, as she ran the line around the spear's wings and down to another stake. Erki threw his smaller tarp within and grabbed the blankets. A few moment's digging with a trowel to shape sleeping hollows, and they were done. Riga grabbed hobbles so the horses could graze without straying. The plowpoint shelter opened downwind, and she dug a firepit before grabbing food.

"Beef and honey-nuts, Erki," she said, holding a bag aloft.

She was amused to see the boy tumble grinning toward her with an armful of fuel, dropping and recovering it as he came, just as if he had too many biscuits. They had been born fair-skinned Northerners, though tanned now from the plains, and Erki had sky-blue eyes and straw hair that in a few years would have the girls lining up to be courted, especially when matched with that grin. They grew taller and more robust than the plains natives, too.

It was close to freezing by the time she backed into the tent and rolled under the blankets with her fleece and linen bear. She hugged up tight to Erki, who was cuddly but getting bony as he sprouted up. He put out a lot of heat. He also kicked and tossed even when asleep. The fire burned its small sticks and moss quickly, offering little heat. She took a long time to get to sleep, starting at every howl, flutter and gust of wind. They were safe, she told herself. They'd seen no sign of anyone, and the horses would alert them to trouble, not to mention kick a wolf.

She woke stiff and groggy in the chill silver-gray dawn. Actually, it was the fourth or fifth time she woke, due to Erki's incessant twitching and kicking and stealing of covers. Kari would have been a better choice to camp with, but she had her own route.

Riga chewed on her tooth bristle as she struck the tent with its feathery fungus of frost. Oh, she ached. At home, she had a four-posted bed, like any town-bred girl of means. She could sleep on the ground when she had to, but even bundled warm was not the same when cold fog rolled past. It seemed she'd been fine until she stood, then her spine and neck protested.

There was nothing to do but ride across the dips and rises. They chewed hard biscuits, hard cheese and dried meat, all of it cold. She longed for an apple.

Half the morning and rest, lunch and unsaddle, resaddle and ride, half the afternoon and rest. Blessi was doing great for such a long trip. The two signal birds in their cages on Trausti's back were not so calm. They twittered.

Dinner was also a saddle meal. They should be getting close, she thought. They were in from the coast, and she thought she could catch occasional glimpses the Acabarrin border hills south of here. She'd know in the morning.

"I see them," Erki said. She squinted.

There was movement in the dusk ahead of them and west, a small caravan seen from the side. The wagons were not plainsworthy, clearly meant for local use in farmland. The rough, rolling ground would disable them in short order. Some walked on foot alongside. The horses and mules were old but healthy. One wagon was drawn by oxen. Chickens, children and caged rabbits filled out the swaying load.

"Good job," she said. "Look sharp and we'll ride up."

She called softly, not wanting to send echoes through the night. "Ho!" They heard and faced her, but she was far too close for them to have done anything against even a band of robbers. A few of them might know enough fighting to hold off brigands, if they had enough numbers. None of them were warriors.

She trotted to the front, watching them watch her. No one gave any indication of status, so she chose the man driving the lead wagon.

"I am Riga Gundesdati called Sworddancer, Scout Archer of Gangibrog of the Kossaki. This is my brother Erki. We will escort you to Lake Diaska."

"We will meet with your war party there?" Clearly, he didn't know where he was on the map.

"No, but that is your next stop, out of Acabarrin and past our lands," she said firmly.

"But we are pursued! And you are two youths." He eyed Erki with disdain, and her with a look that admired her, but probably not for her martial bearing.

"Many are pursued, and we are not a large town. We are dispersed widely across the plain to help you. You need not worry. Two Kossaki are more than enough ratio for a caravan of thirty." She almost smiled in pride.

"We are at least headed in the right direction." A man

commented from the second wagon. "I am Walten, the smith."

"Greetings," she said. "Yes, near enough the right direction. It's time to stop, though."

"We should travel through the night to make distance," the first driver said.

"You should stop now before losing a wheel or a horse in the holes and dips hereabouts."

"That's wise, Jack," Walten said. Jack clearly wanted to argue, but acceded.

Riga didn't believe her own tale. She was quite sure she could fight most adult men, certainly peasant levies. However, some of the pursuing forces were professionals. She put that aside. Fight the battle you have, not that you might have, good or bad.

The drivers stopped their wagons, and she dismounted.

"You will need three pickets," she said, taking charge. "Front and rear and to the steerboard. We will take port."

"Yes, I'm familiar with traveling," Jack said.

She bit her lip. While she might have come across a bit presumptuously, she was what passed for the local, the guide and the warrior here. His presentation and gear marked him as a trained village militiaman, no more.

Still, he was doing the right thing. She let them maneuver and get sorted, then chose a slight hummock to camp on.

Remembering that Erki had been nodding in the saddle, she ordered him into the tent to start sleeping. She'd need him alert tomorrow. She inspected their pickets herself, and forced herself to say nothing. They were strictly for show, not worth anything. She'd sleep with her sword in her blanket and her bow strung. She warned against a fire. For one, there was little enough to use as fuel, unless they wanted to burn animal dung, which was not only unsavory but would be smelled for miles. Straw, dried reeds or a few twigs from spare trees weren't worth the effort. For another, time and discretion ruled over comfort.

This night was worse than the last, with restless Erki and squawling babies outside. They might be uncomfortable, but they made more noise than a seasick Kossaki whelp. Clearly, they were not a traveling people. Riga awoke about dawn, still groggy but unable to sleep, and crawled out. Her cloak had been atop the bedding as another blanket. Now it was a tangled heap next to Erki. She grabbed it, wrapped and looked around. She'd dislodged her bear, which was outside. She was seen when she grabbed it. It wouldn't be fair to pretend it was Erki's either. She blushed and stuffed it into a sack.

A glance told her the caravan was readying to move. They had no trouble fleeing, and seemed adequate in their care and preparations, but gods, they made a racket and left a trail a noseblind hound could follow.

She understood their fear and eagerness, but they were already mounted and inching forward, as if they planned to leave their guides. She prodded her brother with her toe and said, "Erki, strike us quick." She walked briskly to the front of the wagons.

"I didn't get your name last night, driver," she said to the gruff man.

"Jack," he said.

"I'm impressed to see your speed in striking camp," she said. "We can make good time today."

"Guide us west, then," he said. He still didn't look at her.

"West is into Rissim and Kossaki territory. I'm to take you to Little Town on Lake Diaska."

"It's too far," he said.

"Our territory is too close, can't support that many people, and makes us a target. My orders are to take you to Little Town," she repeated. He was probably frustrated from a long trip, but he had only vague notions of where he was going. "We go north, slightly east."

"North northwest takes us to the lake," he said. Blast the man for having to argue every point.

"North northwest takes you through hummocks that will tear off a wheel. I won't even take a horse through there."

"I'm sure when you have as much experience as I do, you'll be able to."

Riga boiled and had to pause before replying.

"Have you more experience with this steppe?" she said.

He ignored her and reined forward, toward the west. The trailing drivers shouted to their teams to follow.

She sprinted back to Blessi and mounted fast. "Erki, mount now!" A squeeze of her heels and a quick gallop and she was in front.

"Have you?" she asked Jack again.

He ignored her completely, offering not even a glance.

"Get down off your wagon and face me like a man!" she demanded, quietly but with force.

Jack snorted and turned away.

If he wanted to rouse her ire, he was going at it the right way.

So she slid over her horse, stood off-stirrup, and stepped

over to his seat. He looked up surprised just in time to catch her slap full across his face.

She realized it was a mistake. She'd hit him either too hard, or not nearly hard enough. He shoved her in the middle and she bounded off. Almost catching her stirrup and bridle, she wound up on the ground, wincing at a twisted ankle and gritting her teeth as she remounted. This was not a good way to lead.

She looked at her brother and saw him fingering his hilt, a dark look on his face.

"Erki," she commanded, and pointed. He nodded at once and trotted forward to block the route, trying to look mean and only looking like a boy playing. She sighed. Jack attempted to steer around, and she interposed with his draft mules. They all bound up in a knot and stopped.

She fought down the anger. If she and Erki were reversed—him the teen, he'd probably be accepted, and she a cute mascot. As it was, he was seen as a mere boy, not a warrior in training, and she as nothing but a flighty girl. She was angry with herself over the bear, too.

"Girl, I will spank you if you don't move," Jack growled. His eyes hinted he'd enjoy it, too.

Well, that put it in terms she understood as a fighter. She looked him over. Wiry. About her height. Shorter legs.

"My father would spank me for allowing it," she replied, and swung to the ground. "But you are welcome to try."

His first move was to detour again. He thought better of it, apparently realized he had to take the challenge or look foolish. Growing red in the face and tight-jawed, he stepped down from his seat.

He'd look foolish spanking her, too. One way or another, he'd lost, but Riga had not yet won.

This could be dangerous in several ways, she realized, not the least of which he might carry through with a spanking or beating. At that, while her father wouldn't spank her, she would certainly lose face and status if she returned without her charges. Erki would probably let the story slip. By accident, of course, but it would be just as shameful.

Luckily, Jack was so contemptuous he didn't even consider she might actually know how to fight. He simply grabbed her wrist and pulled to bend her over his knee. She locked up his elbow with a methodical yank, caught his wrist in her own hand as she broke the hold, then kicked his calf until he was on his knees. He grunted as he went down. It would take but a moment to follow through and stand on his neck, but she decided this time she should hold back.

"I ask that you trust me," she said, loud enough to keep it public and diplomatic. "I do know these plains, and they are not just empty fields. I will speed you to your gathering point and keep eye out for threats, animal or man."

Walten, driving the second wagon, said back, "I call to follow her. We'd look silly stuck in a bog or crevice." Riga wondered why he wasn't in charge. He was much more mature and thoughtful. Politics.

Jack was clearly incensed, embarrassed and offended, but he seemed to grasp he was outmaneuvered. He nodded, and clambered silently up to his wagon.

"So lead us," he said with a grin. He thought to be clever and was going to leave the entire problem in Riga's lap.

Perfect.

She smiled, mounted and led the way. She pointed north and slightly east.

Then she had to rush to help Erki gather their camping gear and Trausti. It detracted from her warrior presentation.

She didn't try to talk to Jack, and cautioned Erki with hand signs to keep quiet. She couldn't have them sounding like children, and nothing was going to warm this man up until she accomplished something.

Of course, when one needed everything to go right, it would invariably go wrong. Shortly, a party became visible ahead. They were on tall horses with no wagons. A patrol.

She'd gain nothing by withholding the information, and it was unlikely they'd suddenly turn east and clear the way.

"Party ahead," she said clearly and simply.

"I wonder if it's too late to turn west," Jack said loudly. "Men, arm up!"

"Wait!" she called. "I will go and treat with them. Erki, take this," she said, handing him the map satchel.

She galloped ahead, both to avoid the tension of two armed parties meeting, and to get away from Jack's derisive laughter. He sounded a bit scared, too, but she didn't find that pleasant.

She slowed once she had space, but kept at a canter. She watched the soldiers to see how they reacted. They faced her and kept moving, at a walk. That was encouraging so far. She slowed to that pace herself. No need to rush to meet death.

Gulping and sweating, she reminded herself of her

position here. She might be barely a woman, but she was the warrior. Her duty was to protect these people. With that in mind, she sat tall in the saddle and approached, doing her best to look casually proud and secure in her status. They were not in livery, but that meant nothing. Her own people didn't wear set colors.

She brushed her bow with her fingertips. She might have to draw, shoot and drop it before reverting to steel. She wished for one of the short, laminated bows of the plains people. Hers was a longbow of two horns with a center grip, stronger but awkward from horseback. She was a foot warrior, not a plains rider. She wished she had time to don her mail.

Her opposite number was a bearlike man she knew she could never beat in any fight. She might cripple him, but even that was a long roll of the dice. Once inside bow range she had nothing but projection and attitude. Still, his bearded face and shaven head were visible because his helm was on his harness. That was a helpful sign. His three compatriots were following his lead.

"I am Riga of the Kossaki," she said simply. No need for rankings here. They'd just sound silly. "I am guide and escort for these refugees." She wondered if they spoke her language.

"Balyat of the Toughs," the man said. "What is your destination?" He spoke broken Danik. She could comprehend.

"I won't discuss that," she replied. "It is north, as you see, and away from here. That's enough for you." Had she delivered that properly? She wanted to sound firm but not arrogant.

"If you continue that way, we will not regard you as hostile," he said. "But we cannot speak for our employer."

"Good to know we might only be killed for money, not for care, mercenary," she said. Four of them, and she might take the smallest down before she died, if she were quick. She held the shiver to a bare twitch.

"Keep moving," Balyat advised. "Our report will take some hours. You are safe until then."

"Fair enough," she said, and meant it. With luck and speed, a few hours would have them safe. If not, at least they would suffer a quick, clean death from professional warriors, not the nauseating horrors of the Empire's troops.

"I hope not to meet again, Kossaki," Balyat said and turned his mount.

As she turned Blessi she smiled slightly to herself. A renowned troop of mercenaries seemed to accept her as warrior, even though inferior.

Civilians were harder to persuade, though. They always wanted to tell you how to conduct a fight, while not fighting themselves.

The look on Jack's face as she returned was interesting. It wasn't one of trust, but it might have a glimmer of respect.

"Who were they?" he asked.

"Oh, just some mercenaries," she smiled. "I told them who I was and they agreed to let us pass." No need for details, and it wouldn't have worked with most of the hired thugs on the peninsula, nor fealted troops. No need to share that, though.

Erki looked ready to burst out with something that would wreck it. "Erki, take the rear for a bit, and keep watch," she said to interrupt him. He nodded and trotted back.

She kept them driving until late, and turned further north. She ran them until full dark. Jack argued to keep going, but his own wife spoke up, and others. They were so exhausted the walkers staggered, and the riders could barely stand.

It wasn't any warmer that night, though the ground was somewhat flatter and the grass thick enough to offer some padding. They still didn't dare risk a fire. They were a few miles from where the mercenaries had patrolled. A fire could mean the difference between being passed by a few hundred yards away or being seen from miles.

Up, and move. This distance had taken under two days for Erki and her. It was taking three for the caravan, and that was at a speed that strained human endurance.

Toward afternoon, they saw movement to the west, paralleling them. It took most of an hour to discern it was a group of wagons and carts with outriders. Then a messenger bird swooped in, lit on Erki's shoulder, to his delight and nervousness, and twittered, "Helloooo from Karlinooo," as it stretched out a claw with a tiny note bound to it.

It was a rough map with a list of family groups. Riga read them off loudly. "Fenk the Smith, Nardin the Banwriht . . . boneworker? It's your language in our letters. Rager the Fitter." She hadn't talked much to the caravan members, but they muttered and exclaimed in relief that some of their friends and acquaintances were accounted for.

As they closed, it was clear the other caravan was large. It must be a dozen families, perhaps an entire village. One of the half dozen escorts shouted and broke off. Riga shouted back, a warbling shriek, and reined back.

"Kari!" "Riga!" Her friend galloped up and they hugged from horseback, sweaty and dusty and warm to the touch.

"Gentles, this is my friend Karlinu called Swordspinner, Scout Spear."

Jack just grunted. Walten nodded and smiled. "Hello," he said. The others offered greetings.

Karlinu said, "Herald Bellan wants a tally. Another Herald is in Gangibrog, and Bellan is with us."

Riga gestured with her head and moved a bit forward. Kari nodded and paced her.

Once out of earshot, Riga said, "I've barely heard of these Heralds before. Why are they so influential? Our entire town has stopped working." She didn't want to be presumptuous. Well, actually, she did. She had a vested interested as part owner of her father's dock and transfer business. Their safety was also her concern, with all this attention.

"Talk later," Kari said. "Tally?"

"Twenty-seven. And how is your mother the Swordmistress?" She changed subjects, since she apparently wasn't going to get an answer.

"Frazzled and harried and snapping as if we're at drill, even for mundane matters. It's not just us. Knutsford is about, and the Ugri. We are to meet with the Morit as well."

"This sounds like a gathering. That will be fun. I wonder if Brandur . . . " She stopped talking and blushed.

Karlinu laughed. "I expect your suitor will be there. But is it wise to be with a man you can easily best with sword and spear?"

"I don't care. I like him. He's handsome and not much poorer than we."

"I must report. The Yarl himself is to meet us. This is important!" The other woman reached into the horse's pack and drew out the bird cage. It took her only a few moments to inscribe a note, without dismounting, then to whisper another message while she attached the written parchment to the carrier on its leg. "Fly home, fly home!" she said and tossed the bird skyward.

"Fly hoooome!" it agreed, circling and heading west northwest.

Within the hour, the Herald came up personally. He wore riding clothes, but they, too, were white. His mount was a white stallion with vivid blue eyes. Riga hadn't seen it closely before. Looking at it now, it seemed to stare at her and delve into her thoughts.

"You seem to be doing well, Riga," he greeted.

She increased her pace and gave him a bare twitch of a rein finger. He made a very slow nod and moved to pace her. She waited until she had distance to speak.

"They treat me as a girl," she said, "except when things go bad. Every problem is mine. Either my advice is bad, or I'm naïve . . ."

"They are villagers of a farming culture," Bellan said. "You are a woman of a trading culture that grew from warriors and now live among others. I knew this would be a problem, which is why I hurried to gather you all. You've done well, no matter how it feels."

"Now they'll just feel you've taken over," she groused. She wasn't sure why she was sharing so much with this stranger. He exuded trustworthiness, though.

"Of course," he nodded. "But more importantly, they will be safe for now, and your people won't be burdened with noncombatant refugees as you prepare. I can't fight for you, but I can clear the field for you."

Riga didn't like the sound of that. It made sense that Miklamar was heading their way, but still . . .

"Wouldn't it make sense for your people to join us and fight here, before it reaches your lands?" she asked.

He laughed. "Oh, Riga, Valdemar is weeks away even by road, even as fast as my Companion can travel." He patted the horse's flank. "I'll do what I can to help, but Miklamar is no threat to my nation. Not even if he were a neighbor. Our rulers are busy with things close to home. Things far less important than an empire-building butcher, but far more immediate. It's one of the tragedies of the world that disasters are all over. They must be dealt with as best you can. Still, I'm glad we were in the area and can offer some help."

He paused for a moment, as if listening to the air, or his horse. Riga took the time to consider his words.

No, she didn't think her remote town, nor even their small nation, were important worldwide, though when they had been called the Rust, not many decades before, they were known all over.

"There is a war band ahead," Bellan said.

"Is it the mercenaries?" she asked, half in hope, half in dread.

"They're on foot, in formation, crossing us, probably from the coast road. We can outride them, but the refugees can't." Their wagons managed a walking pace at best in this terrain. The children and elders wouldn't be able to keep up on foot.

"Not the Toughs I met, then."

"Behind them may be more. We can't detour that way. We also can't wait. We'll have to go through, then ride fast and through the night." He seemed to shift back to the present. "Will you come with me? We need to plan this."

"Yes, certainly," she agreed. "Erki! Take point."

Riga nodded to the others as she approached. No one here looked at her as if she were only a girl. They'd seen her fight, and most had felt her blows. Kari, Snorru, Rabal and his uncle Lar, three other men and two women, plus the Grogansen boys.

A dozen Kossaki, half of them youths and women, and the Herald. The army ahead was hopefully less than eight times that size, but might be the van of a far larger force.

"What would you do, Sworddancer?" Lar asked. She realized things were being hashed out and she'd missed some of the talk.

She breathed deeply and stared at nothing. It was a problem to be solved, and she entered her realm of calm and thought.

"I'd shoot arrows from distance, and continue until closing. We should dismount close to cause maximum surprise and hopefully break their ranks with fear of the horses."

"Not bad. We need wranglers. Nor do we want a long fight with their infantry. We must hurt them and retreat, with minimal losses, then look prepared to repeat it. Those levies won't have the heart for a long fight against professionals, and the mercenaries aren't around."

"We are to look like professionals?"

"Worse," Kari grinned. "We're *girls*."

Girls with twelve years of training in horse, sword, bow, map, languages and business, Riga thought, and grinned back. It was an odd thought. No Kossaki would underestimate a youth. They were fighters, traders and travelers from the time they could walk.

She said, "Erki should wrangle horses and recover bows and glean points, but he'll complain I'm being protective." Of course, she was, but it made sense for him as youngest to hold back. He could also ride fastest if need be, to carry another message.

"I'll tell him," Bellan said.

"Also, we should fire off a shooting star."

"What good will that do?" Snorru asked. "Our nearest element is hours away."

"They don't know that. We act as if we expect overwhelming backup, and hit them hard in the meantime. As Kari says, they won't stomach a long fight."

"And best we scare them now," Bellan said. "Soon enough Miklamar will want your port, too, if he's not stopped."

"It might alert an enemy patrol, too," Rabal said.

"It might. What do you think of that risk against its advantages?"

"Yes, it's risky," Lar said. "But the mercenaries must have reported by now. That's probably why this force is crossing bare steppe toward the caravan."

"Yes," Riga agreed.

"Do it."

Riga and Bellan rode back to the caravan, now one line of the combined party, four lines across.

"We'll be fighting, then cutting across fast and continuing," Bellan said.

"We will arm up, then," Walten said, looking old but sounding firm.

"No, you should move fast and protect your families if it comes to that."

Jack nodded, and Riga steamed. He didn't question Bellan. Had she given the same advice, she knew he'd have argued.

Bellan said, "Northwest, and fast. There are towns. Don't stop for anything but feed and water, and be sure they know. Once you reach the rivers, follow them north to the lake."

"Start that way now," Riga said. "We will catch up and guide you later."

Then she turned, not wanting to know what they thought, and trying not to care. She saw a shooting star scream up, blue and yellow were Snorru's colors. It crackled and burst, visible for miles. She grabbed for her mail, and shimmied in. After that, she helped Erki with his quilted staghide. It was loose on his frame, but wouldn't be for long. Handsome boy, she sighed. She was more worried for him than herself.

One in seven, she thought. Wound or kill one in seven, and all but the most dedicated force would retreat. There were seventy-two troops, eight across and nine deep, with two mounted officers. They had bills and spears for the most part, with shields, and leather armor. They were not elite, but were definitely professional, even if levied.

If they each got one, that would do it, as long as they

didn't lose many in the process. If they lost two . . . though they were dedicated because of their desperation.

The troops looked nervous as they approached. A good start, she thought. A small force full of youths approaching with weapons drawn. Either they were insane, or expected massive backup in addition to the hundred men in the caravan. The shooting star suggested backup. Where was it, though? Riga watched them cast glances about and ripple their neat formation.

Bellan quietly said, "First line, dismount and shoot, on my order. Second line, prepare to charge." He wore gorgeous mail with iron joints, and a polished helm.

She swung down from the saddle, drew an arrow, and stood next to her horse.

"Shoot. Charge."

She nocked, drew and loosed, and shot again. She had three arrows in the air before he called, "Hold!"

Their timing and discipline was good. The other half of their force and Bellan had galloped ahead, and were dismounting right in the faces of the enemy, hurling javelins as they did so.

The troops moved their shields in response. A couple at least grunted from wounds. A score of arrows and a half dozen javelins used for that. It was amazing how quickly things ran out.

Riga dropped her bow and sprinted forward, unslinging her shield and drawing steel. She saw Erki gathering reins and backing, cajoling the horses. They were holding up well in the fight, and he was earnest in his task. She saw all that live steel and her knees went weak. Sparring with wood or blunt steel in the *vollar* was nothing like ugly strangers who wanted you dead. Her helmet was loose, but there was no time to adjust it now.

The enemy were spreading out for envelopment and slaughter, and Bellan pointed to the left. She moved over that way, between Kari and Snorru. Lar tossed a javelin right past her, to break their line into clumps. One flinched as it caught on his shield, and made the mistake of reaching over to unstick it. She reached him right then, snapped out her sword and took a chunk from his arm. He staggered back howling and got in the way of his mates.

The troops had numbers, yes, and they were trained in rudimentary tactics. They had discipline, but not the years of precision and skill she'd learned. Half were polemen, the rest mixed spears and swords. She deflected a raised pole and got in close for another thrust at anything exposed. The three nearest all turned to face her and started jabbing. It turned into a deadly dance.

This was how she'd earned her name. Her shield and sword never stopped moving. Father had taught her from the beginning, if you were blocking you should also be attacking, if attacking, also moving. One foot should be on the ground for balance, one shifting, and both arms doing something. The shield boss could also bash, its binding could smash, its broadness could conceal your movement from your opponent. The sword could threaten as well as strike. Silence and noise could both be intimidating. Use them. Moving targets were harder to hit. She hadn't inflicted any lethal blows yet, but her opponents, four so far, were cut and bleeding. A gimp sword arm took a warrior out of the fight, and was easier to score. If they wanted to stick them out, she'd readily slash them. She was smaller, but lithe and agile and used to fighting one to one as well as en masse.

"One, back!" Bellan called, and Kari and Snorru turned and whipped away. She gulped and tingled in fear. Knowing it was planned didn't make it easier to be left in front, face to face with angry strangers. They pushed forward, seeing the Kossaki retreat and believing they had won.

"Two, back!" Bellan shouted.

She turned and ran, keeping low so javelins could fly over her. Then she saw Erki. He was off to the side, dismounted to recover a bow, and one stray fighter from the brawl was closing on him.

Her first thought was that it made no sense. The man had exposed himself needlessly and was chasing a target of little value. She wondered if his plan was to take a hostage, or chase the horses off, but he was waving his polecleaver vigorously.

Then raw pain and nausea flooded through her mind. *He was going to kill her little brother.*

Tactics said she should stick with the element and not break ranks. She'd only make the disparity of numbers worse. Tactics be damned. *"Erki, your left!"* she shouted to alert him, and dodged past Bellan's mount. Erki turned to her, but grabbed for his weapons.

"Go, Riga!" Bellan said, acknowledging her, but she didn't care. The first swing of that long weapon tore and splintered Erki's shield to the boss. He stumbled back and raised his sword in a block. The cleaver fell, met the sword in a dull clang. He dropped his weapon and howled, face contorted in agony, but he hadn't been opened up yet.

Then the Acabarran realized he was being flanked and turned. He had no time to swing so he thrust. Riga caught the tip straight into the tough leather and wood of her shield, twisted into it. He made the mistake of trying to hold onto the haft, and wound up sideways to her.

Her first swing hit his thigh but too hard. She felt the blade bite and stick, and had to fight it loose as he fell, kicking and screaming. Real battle was tremendously noisier and dirtier than the *vollar*, she thought as she followed up with a thrust to his torso, and the fight was over.

She retained enough presence of mind to make a sweep around herself. Nothing immediate. Some officer had drawn the force back into a bristling defensive formation. Kossaki javelins chunked into shields but rarely found a mark, and one of the Grogansens had recovered his bow. She was safe for the present.

For a moment she thought Erki had lost an arm. He shrieked and squirmed and was painted with blood. A fresh bout of nausea started, and she grabbed for a bandage from her belt. It was only his thumb, though, or part of it. The blade had not been sharp and had mangled it. He might retain some use.

She dropped her sword flat in front of her, slapped his helmet to draw his attention back to the world and shouted, "Use this!" as she thrust the bandage at him. He gasped in surprise and nodded, before she reached under his hips and heaved him back across his saddle and the added pain of moving set him screaming again. She bent, grabbed her sword, made another sweep, then grabbed his blade and Snorru's bow. It was heavier than hers, but she'd draw it if she had to. She said, "Off hand!" and flipped Erki's sword up to him as he tumbled upright. Then she turned back to the fight, clutching at her quiver. Her hands were sticky.

Her first arrow wobbled. The heavier bow needed heavier arrows than hers, but the point here was to keep them disoriented. She wondered where the brilliant flash of flame came from, then realized four shooting stars had been fired horizontally. Half the front rank clutched at their eyes and dropped their guard, during which Snorru, Lar and Kari charged in and speared any handy flesh, then rammed the points into shields and left them stuck as they dove and rolled away. Those troops had to drop their shields, and she shot an arrow straight into the revealed mass. Two javelins followed.

She put her third arrow into the mounted officer bearing down on them. It was a lucky shot. She'd been aiming for the torso and caught him in the throat, right under the helmet and through the edge of his mail. No one could see luck, though, only a hit.

He tumbled from his horse and the fight was over, the foot troops retreating in ragged order, glancing back but with no heart to fight. They carried and dragged their wounded. Only two dead yet, four lame and being carried, perhaps twenty wounded, but infection would take others, unless their leaders were the type to waste healing magic on arrow fodder. She suspected not.

Still, the caravan would have to move faster, even if it meant losing a wagon and any contents that couldn't be shared in a hurry. Where those troops came from there would be others. There wasn't time to properly loot, only to grab pouches, weapons and the occasional helmet, and recover a few bows and javelins.

Snorru, mounted, led Erki by his left hand. The boy looked faint from pain and shock. They reached the caravan and Snorru helped Erki down as Riga jumped from her saddle.

Bellan caught up, grabbed Erki, inspected his hand in a moment, and shoved him down on the gate of a wagon.

"Let's do this fast. Riga, can you hold him? And Kari."

"I can," she said, voice cracking and tears blinding her. She grabbed his arm, pinned it down and leaned her weight on. Kari did the same on the left, as Erki panicked and started thrashing. Only his feet could move, drumming and kicking on the wagon deck. She closed her eyes and wished she could close her ears and nose. Snorru ran up and shoved a leather rein between his teeth for him to bite on. Riga heard his cries, and under them, the sound and smell of battlefield surgery. His screams hit a crescendo as Bellan said, "That's it. Only one joint. You'll still be able to work and fight. Drink this." He handed over a leather bottle as he turned to help bandage Lar's arm. There were several moderate wounds.

Erki was too dazed to handle the bottle, and Riga helped him drink. He guzzled five times and she pulled the bottle back. He needed help with the pain, but not enough to get sick. Then she took three burning swallows herself. Kari did, too, then Snorru. They swapped looks that combined compassion, fear, horror and the bond that came only with shared battle.

After helping Erki into his saddle and easing him forward so he could rest, they rode another five miles before Bellan called a halt, well after dark. Everyone slept on wagons or the ground under them, ready to fly if another troop came. Walten offered his wagon to the Kossaki youth, and slept underneath.

Erki cried and cried. He'd quiet down, drift fitfully to sobbing sleep, then some tortured nerve would jolt him awake to writhe and scream again. The herbs were supposed to lessen the pain and prevent infection, but hand injuries are among the most painful.

Riga cried, holding him tight in the damp cold amid dust and tools, trying to comfort him. They were children, not warriors. They shouldn't have to fight yet, certainly not Erki. He was barely lettered and just big enough to ride. She cursed Miklamar and his troops, the mercenaries, Jack and his helpless bumtwits, the Swordmistress, the Herald. Couldn't they fight their own battle and leave her out of it? She clutched her bear and didn't care if anyone saw.

She realized part of her distress was fear of losing Erki, had the blow been better aimed. Or her father. Or herself. A warrior should be willing to risk such things, but she wasn't sure she was.

It was only a thumb! People lost worse in grindstones, forges, sometimes in looms. Bjark had lost a couple of joints of fingers just last year. It could have been worse.

But this was Erki, and it had been in war. That made it different.

And it could have been worse.

In the morning, pressups and sword drill did nothing to loosen the knot in her shoulder or the ache on the side of her head. Erki looked groggy from shock and fatigue, but he'd stopped crying. He let nothing get close to his hand, though.

It took all day, but by dusk Lake Diaska was visible, the sun glittering off its windblown waves. Gangibrog was at the south point, Little Town, their main trade partner, now part of the Kingdom of Crane, to the north. They pushed on, sore and stiff in the saddle, but with a huge burden lifted.

They stopped, late and exhausted to staggers. The refugees rolled up in blankets where they sat or sprawled, and made snide but quiet comments about the Kossaki setting camp. Riga finished pitching the shelter quickly, despite working alone, tightlipped to their snickers. Tonight would be cold. They'd have to learn if they kept moving north.

Erki looked unhappy, being able to do nothing but hold a javelin while she drove spikes and dug them in. She shooed him in and crawled in alongside, with an extra blanket against the chill.

In the morning, the elders were locked in conference. They didn't break for long minutes while the mist and dew burned off. Riga secured the gear and handed Erki a bowl of hard cheese and nuts.

"Thank you," he said, staring at his bandaged thumb.

"I'm sorry."

"I wonder what it feels like to die?" he asked.

That was the type of question children asked parents. She wasn't ready for it yet.

Bellan finally came over with a wave for attention.

"We'll have to split up. Erki will come with us back to Gangibrog. He'll be fine. These people still need you as Scout. Head northwest for the road just south of Little Town."

She took a deep breath and forced calm. "How many scouts does it take for a caravan?" she asked. It wasn't fair to do this to her, not after all this. She'd spent all night nerving up to continue, and now she was being replaced, just a girl again. She did want to go home, badly. She also wanted to finish the job. She'd completely forgotten that she and Brandur might meet, and that chance was also gone.

"They must split up again. One large caravan moves too slowly, eats too much, and is too easy a target. Several small ones are not worth the individual effort."

"I understand," was all she could say.

"You're named well, Sworddancer," he said with a reassuring smile. "Morle was right to select you. You'll do fine."

"I'll be home soon, Erki," she said, turning and trying not to blubber. He couldn't see her tears while her head was over his shoulder. Yes, he'd be fine. She wasn't sure about herself, though. He hugged her tightly and wouldn't let go.

The two days that followed were uneventful, and she hated them. The nights were bitter cold and she stayed stiff. The days dusty, full of pollen and jagged sawgrass, burning sun, rationed water and squawling children, with a few family fights thrown in she had to shout down. Several times a day she had to take a deep breath, meditate and pray, to take the pressure off her clenched teeth and to avoid screaming.

That, and it was clear a war was coming. She couldn't decide which she feared worse, the cold, professional mercenaries and the quick death they'd bring, or the Empire troops she could match for a while, before dying in ugly ways.

What she feared most was that she'd see her father and brother killed. Nor would Father listen to a suggestion of using one of his trade boats to leave. Stubborn, he was, and loyal to his people.

She was still grappling with it when the sun flashed off Lake Diaska again. By evening they were skirting the north shore to the road to Little Town. She considered using some silver to buy boat passage, but that would mean following the refugees to town. She didn't want to do that.

"Here's road," she said, pointing ahead. It was her first utterance since, "Let's move," first thing that morning.

She turned aside and let the rickety wagons clatter past onto the packed earth and gravel.

As he passed, Jack reined back, looked straight at her and said, "Thank you for guiding us, and for fighting for us, Riga Sworddancer." The grudging way he said it wasn't insulting. He was just taciturn by nature. He was impressed and meant to compliment her. "I wish you well, and your brother and friends."

Riga found she didn't care. She took his hand briefly, nodded at the others, then rode ahead, seeking a route home. She didn't see Walten salute with his rein hand.

Riding back was a relief, with Kari and the Grogansens for company. Even Snorru, who'd always been a bit self-absorbed, treated Erki almost like his own brother. They made good time toward Gangibrog and saw lake barges towed by sail tugs. They passed occasional traffic at a run.

Once in town, she could see things returning to normal. The hus was open, too. Father was home!

They galloped alongside the planked road, heedless of the splattering muck, and she dismounted as Father came out the door.

"Riga!" he shouted, grinning and arms wide. She charged up and leapt at him.

A moment later she said, "You're squashing me."

"I like squashing you," he said, very softly. She started crying.

The fire was going, and he'd made a large pot of stew. It was so like being home, and so like being a girl again. She ate and warmed herself, peeling off layers. Meanwhile, Father looked at Erki's thumb.

"Arwen has fresh herbs, not like the dried ones for the field. And it's not much of a wound. You'll get used to it and be able to work just fine. Remember this?" He showed one of his own injuries, a smashed fingertip.

Riga moved away, not wanting to see it again. She hung her clothes, mounted her mail and helm on their stand, and set about cleaning her sword.

Before she took over the ledgers, she might have to be a warrior. She'd trained for it all her life, but she'd never thought to actually use it, beyond a tavern brawl or a mob of thieves at quayside, the occasional bandits or brigands. It was a cold thought.

Meanwhile, she was home with her family, a soft bed, her toys and crafts, and a chance to be a girl again, for the little time she could.

Wounded Bird
★★★

I liked "Sword Dancer" enough to do a second one, quite a bit shorter and constructed better. It's also colored quite a bit by my 2008 deployment to the Middle East. I wrote some of this, and some of my novel Contact with Chaos, *while deployed. Some of the stress and boredom and other aggravations crept in there.*

Women wore only dresses in Mirr. Riga had compromised with a knee-length tunic of wine silk with crimson and silver embroidery and beading over her trews. It stuck out in vivid contrast to the somber blacks and whites of the natives. She acceded somewhat to their law and wore a kerchief over her flaxen hair but her warrior's braid hung below, rather than loose under a long headdress like the locals.

Not that it mattered to anyone but her. Father and Erki knew her, and the locals would never regard her as anything other than a girl. She saw how the locals treated women; as servants.

Jesrin, for example, serving her minted tea, was lean and healthy looking, and seemed rather bright. She'd never develop as anything here, though. She was unnumbered and unlettered and probably not much of a cook, just a serving girl. Riga would have liked to talk to her at least, but she'd have to go to the kitchen to do so. Women didn't talk in front of men. Even if Riga might, Jesrin certainly wouldn't. Riga thought about the kitchen, but that was a concession she didn't want to make. She was not a servant. She was a trader and a warrior.

Jesrin moved on with more tea for the amar, the local trading lord. She hesitated around his gesticulating arms, then moved to pour. He changed his motion just in time to catch the spout of the samovar and deliver a big splash of liquid to the lush woolen rug the men sat on.

"Clumsy wench!"

Riga twitched as Amar Rabas backhanded Jesrin. The blow was hard enough to stagger her, but she flailed through contortions to avoid dropping the silver tea set. Riga could only imagine the penalty if the girl did that.

A moment later she wasn't sure she could imagine. The slight girl shrieked as her ankle twisted, but laid the tray down carefully on the marble flagstones behind her. Not a drop spilled.

However, Rabas drew a heavy cord from somewhere, and laid into her, the knotted end thunking heavily right through her thick clothes. The girl writhed and twitched, but let out only whimpers. Presumably crying was punishable, too.

Father gave Riga a warning glance, and she nodded once, her face blank, while inside she burned with rage. It was not their business to interfere, though he obviously didn't like it either. Riga's brother Erki fought to keep his own temper. He was three years younger, though, only fourteen. What a lesson on foreign cultures this was for him.

It was worse, because Riga was a trained warrior. Had the amar swung at her like that, she'd have broken his arm, and then sliced his throat. And, of course, been beaten to death or hanged for her trouble. It just drove home that fighting was not always the answer.

It also drove home that she despised this southern city and its culture. In the week they'd been here, the amar had escalated his hospitality, gifts and praise every day. He'd also escalated his brutality and rudeness to his servants and his own hires.

She knew she had to calm down, so she looked around their setting again. The walls were faced in gleaming marble. Wrought iron and bronze rails, hooks and mountings adorned the stairs and walls. The doors, posts and lintels were carved elaborately, some of them with scenes that made her blush. Apparently, denied other outlets for their energy, it went into suggestive figures.

While the small drove of five ships—both of theirs and three others belonging to distant cousins—were being packed with valuable spices, silk and teas, Riga really wasn't sure it was morally worth it. Mirr was pretty. Mirr was also a filthy dump as far as attitudes, decency and anything beyond decadently carved stone and flowers.

"Amar Rabas," Father interrupted diplomatically. When the man looked up from his flogging, he continued, "We are grateful for your hospitality. It is time to retire to our inn for the day. I hope to see you again tomorrow, as we prepare to leave."

The amar rose, and the girl crawled to her knees and bowed low. He glanced at her, snapped, "Get to the kitchen," then turned back to his guests. "Of course, Gunde. May I host you for dinner tomorrow? A feast in farewell before you eat ship rations?"

"My son and I would be honored," Father said. Of course, Riga was only a daughter and was not mentioned here, anymore than a dog would be.

They bowed all around, and departed, as the girl scurried limping away, taking the tray and towel with her.

Once outside and out of earshot, Riga muttered, "I think I'd prefer ship biscuits and salted meat to hospitality such as his."

"They are not a nice people," Father agreed. "But we need the trading stop. If we could only transport across the lake back home and stay solvent, I'd do that. We need proper trading voyages now and then, though. It's also good learning for you two."

"We need to learn that some people are pure evil?" Erki asked.

"The amar is brutal even by our warrior standards," Father said, "but he is not evil. At least their trade is honest, and tariffs fair. They've held off Miklamar's encroachments so far. If you want evil, you remember the refugees fleeing that murderous thug."

"I do," Erki said as he rubbed his stubby thumb. So did Riga. She vividly remembered him losing half that thumb when the two youths had had to be warriors and guides for those refugees.

"Tonight is our last night in the inn," Father said. "We'll remain aboard ship, under tent, until we leave."

"Oh, good," Riga said. "I prefer our tent to their opulence. It's friendlier." Nothing about this city was friendly, except the other traders and embassies. Of course, they weren't of this city. Riga wore heavy clothes despite the mild weather, and no sword. Erki and Father carried swords. They were her protectors. Her status: none. At home she wore her cat-jeweled sword, and no one would be silly enough to ask if she knew its use.

The feast was not a happy event. It could have been, but . . .

Riga had no complaints about the food. She didn't like being behind a curtain at a second, remote table set up for women, where she ate with the wives and servants. She didn't like getting what were basically the leavings from the men. The entertainment would be better if she could actually see it, rather than just hear hints of it past the curtain. The food was wonderful, though, redolent with spices and rich and savory. The manner took getting used to. One formed rice into balls, or tore pieces of bread, and just reached in to scoop up the saucy mess.

Even at the women's table, there was a hierarchy. The senior wife sat at the far end. Her two junior wives flanked her, and the wives and concubines of two other guests sat down from there. Riga guessed her position at a table end was of some status, and two daughters flanked her. Between were the servants.

A warm, sweet smell seemed to indicate dessert, or at

least a dessert. There'd been two so far. Jesrin served the men, then came through to serve the women.

As she leaned past Riga to place a platter of pastry down, her layered gown slipped, revealing some shoulder.

Riga almost recoiled in horror at what she glimpsed. That delicate shoulder was a mass of blood blisters, bruises and welts. Their color indicated they were healing, but he'd laid into this girl horribly.

Steeling herself, she said nothing, made no acknowledgement—servants weren't people here—and ate quietly. The food was good. It would have been twice as good if she'd been granted the courtesy of eating with the men. She reminded herself that her own people regarded her a warrior. No insults here could change that.

Of course, Father had asked that she diplomatically not discuss any of her "manly" skills. While she knew weaving, and a little of spinning, she knew much more of boatkeeping and lading, numbers, letters, horse care and maneuver. The women chatted amiably about textiles and art, and Riga just nodded and smiled.

Jesrin slipped back through a few minutes later, came over, and discreetly handed Riga a slip of parchment, which Riga just as discreetly opened in her lap and read.

"We are staying here tonight. Your room will be across the hall from mine—GundeFather."

If there was one thing Riga didn't want to do, it was stay here, beneath her status. She momentarily raged inside.

It wasn't just being treated as an inferior. It was that it didn't matter what her status was, didn't matter her skills. She could run the business herself if need be. She lacked Father's decades, but she had a grounding in all the basics and plenty of her own travels and deals, and war. But here, just being born female meant that she was beneath a horse, even beneath a dog, and wouldn't even be treated with contempt. She just wouldn't be treated with at all. The offered hospitality was for Father and Erki, not her. Her room was a mere courtesy to Father, otherwise they'd stick her in a hole with the servants, she was sure.

After that, she withdrew completely from the conversation, and just steamed silently, until Jesrin led her up the marble stairs, long after the men had retreated, and to a frilly, dainty, girly room. It was very lavish, of course. See how well the amar treats even a daughter of a trader?

"If you need," Jesrin said, "That cord will ring a bell below. I'll hurry right up."

"You won't sleep yourself?" Riga asked.

Jesrin seemed confused by Riga's accent, or perhaps the question itself.

"Of course I'll wake up. It's my duty to serve. If I'm not available, then Aysa will come."

"Thank you, though I'll be fine. You've been so gracious."

Jesrin replied with a demure bow. "Thank you, all I do is on behalf of my lord."

Riga couldn't wait, so asked, "Jesrin, would you like me to look at your shoulder? I may have a salve that will help."

"Oh, Miss Riga, you are gracious, no. The housemistress is taking care of it. I will be fine." The poor girl seemed embarrassed and ashamed just to discuss it.

Girl. Jesrin was easily a year older than Riga's seventeen. Yet Riga was a woman among her people, able to run her household, sign contracts, travel freely or as mistress of a mission. Jesrin seemed younger, frailer, helpless. She could manage any number of chores, but had no voice, was illiterate and a glorified pet. Riga could give orders to laborers and warriors. Jesrin wouldn't know how even if she could.

With nothing else to offer, Riga said, "Then I shall retire. I hope to see you in the morning, and please rest. You've made me most comfortable, thank you."

"A blessing on you." Jesrin bowed and withdrew with what looked like a happy smile. It made Riga shudder.

The next morning, Riga awoke to sun peeking through chiseled piercework in the shutters. The weather was wonderfully mild. The bed was silken over feathers, with a very fine cotton sheet.

Riga would gladly give it all up to keep her status.

A breakfast of fruit and pastry sat on a tray near the door. She snagged a couple of fat strawberries and a roll, partly to quiet her stomach and partly to be polite to Jesrin and the other servants. She didn't care what the amar thought and was pretty sure he wouldn't even ask how she'd fared. She rebraided her hair, threw a scarf over it to appease local customs, and opened the door.

No one was around, so she crept across and tapped on what she hoped was Father's door. She could hear his voice, and Erki's, and that brightened her mood a lot.

He swung the door open and said, "Welcome, Daughter! I'm sure you're dreading returning to the *Sea Fox*."

"Oh, yes, very much Father." *Please get me out of here now*, her mind and face said.

Once downstairs, she stood back while Father, Erki and the amar exchanged bows. She wasn't expected to participate, for which she was glad.

A few minutes later they were striding down the broad, dusty street toward the port.

Erki said, "I'll be glad to eat normal food. I got sick of the rich, fancy stuff very quickly."

"I enjoyed the food. Not the company. I wish I could have. Jesrin seems like a nice girl," she said.

"She does. He sent her to my room an hour after bed last night," Father admitted.

"Oh, Father, you *didn't*!" she exclaimed.

"Of course I didn't," he replied with a grimace and shiver. "Gods, she's barely older than you, girl. Ugh." He cringed again. "I bid her sit and talk for a while, gave her some medicine for the pain and some herbs to help heal. They don't do that here, either. Herbs are the work of the devils. She wasn't easy to convince, but I promised her I'd never mention it. Then I made her sleep on the divan. She seemed both grateful and put upon."

Riga wasn't sure she parsed that, but no matter. "Thank you," she replied.

"For what? Not bedding a child? I need no thanks for that." He sounded annoyed.

"I wish we could help her. Buy her, perhaps?"

Father leaned up and back, and met her eyes.

"I know you mean well, but no. Her looks make her highly prized."

"You could ask," she said. "I have my share to pledge against the cost."

He sighed and looked uncomfortable.

"Riga, His Beneficent Excellency was struck by your stature and eyes. He offered me a sack of saffron and your weight in gold for your hand for his son."

Riga choked and stared wide-eyed. Great gods. That was more than both their ships were worth. They might do that gross business in five years.

Feeling nervous ripples, she asked, "And you told him . . . ?"

"I said you were to be betrothed to a wealthy merchant in our lands, but his offer was most generous and thoughtful. I thanked him for the compliment he paid me as a father and merchant."

Seeing her sunken expression, he added, "Riga, she's got good food, a warm bed and shelter. Her lot as a free peasant would be no better in this desert. It would be worse. You can't save everyone. Remember the birds? And the rabbit?"

Yes, she'd tried to save injured animals when younger.

"You stewed them," she said accusingly.

"I only stewed them after you tried to save them and they died. They were meant for the pot anyway."

"I didn't appreciate it at the time," she said.

Erki said, "If a Kossaki treated a woman like that, he'd be driven from town in disgrace. It's a strange place. You should have been treated better, Riga. I'm sorry."

"It keeps me humble," she said, trying for self-deprecating humor. Few places gave women the status the Kossaki had. This place, though . . .

"Well, tonight we sleep in linen and wool and fur," Father said. "We have dried goat and fish, berries and nuts. I'll see about a stew."

Erki said, "Let me, Father? I'll be glad to make us some real food." He leaned over and added, "And I promise not to cook any stray pets you find, Riga."

She stuck her tongue out. "You cook. I have to help tally the goods, the tariffs and the port fees. Then Father can sign it and pretend I'm just a dumb girl."

"I'll pretend nothing," he said. "They can assume whatever they wish."

Under the sail-tent, Riga couldn't sleep. The contrast between the beauty and the evil just seemed to make the evil that much more horrifying.

The girl had been beaten for the slightest of errors, because it "embarrassed" her owner. Then she'd been sent to whore for a guest, while still full of welts and crippling bruises. That was considered redemption here . . . for the amar.

That thought decided it for her. Riga rolled her quilt off carefully, slipped to the deck, and felt for her boots.

In minutes, she was dressed for her mission, and in a way no woman should dare dress in this city. That made it both joyous and sobering. She could wind up dead for what she planned, even if she didn't succeed.

Erki was still and undisturbed, and she figured to leave him there. He was handsome even asleep, and she smiled. Then she realized there was one thing she needed him for, if nothing else.

She touched him on the shoulder, and his eyes snapped open.

She held a finger to her lips in a shhh! and beckoned him to join her.

He slipped his feet out and fumbled for clothes and gear. He was always twitchy and energetic, but at least he was silent about it.

He seemed excited, probably because he knew she was up to something. Would he be agreeable when he found out what, though? He matched her choice of dull fighting clothes. When she pointed, he grabbed his sword without hesitation.

A few minutes later, they shimmied over the gunwale and onto the beach. None of the crew were awake or had noticed. Some of them were still in rooms in town, in fact, and would only return in time to push off, she hoped. If they were late . . .

Erki whispered, "What are we doing?"

"We're going to rescue that servant girl, Jesrin."

"You haven't discussed this with Father, have you?" he asked at once.

Damn the boy.

"No," she admitted. "This is my plan."

"He'll thrash us both," Erki said. "How will that help her?"

"He'll thrash us because we deserve it," she said. "That girl got far more than that."

"I didn't say I wouldn't help you," he said. "But how do we keep her from being found?"

With that first part agreed, she started creeping across the beach. "She only has to keep out of sight in our ship. The drove leaves in the morning. With luck, they won't even start looking this way by then."

"If they do, Father might just give us to them. We'll be endangering everyone."

"Really. I thought we were warriors and nations quivered at our mention," she said with contemptuous sarcasm.

"Not as much as they did long past," Erki said. "Look, I'm still with you."

"Good, then stop trying to argue me out of it," she said, because he was right. What she proposed was dangerous, foolish, and could start a war.

She also knew it was the right thing to do.

"I swore my Warrior's Oath to protect the weak," she said. "And I didn't swear that it stopped at the edge of our lands."

The beach was convenient. The docks proper had activity at all hours, but just a few dozen yards away, few people were about. Only small fishing vessels, or the shallow draft Kossaki trade and warships used the beach. Even when trading, the Kossaki ported like raiders, ready to dart away in moments.

The two youths flitted through from shadow to shadow. Their boots were soft-soled leather. Their dull clothes disappeared into the night. Riga had no sword, but she did have her *seachs* knife.

She planned to not need it. That would mean their mission had failed. It was the principle, though. Besides, if she did get caught, she wanted them to know she was a warrior.

It also helped her cope with the knowledge that if discovered, she would at the least be publicly beaten with canes and heavily fined. Or rather, Father would be fined. At worst . . .

In far less time than she remembered, they were at the

outer wall of the amar's residence. The building ran around three sides of a courtyard.

"I know her room is on the left . . . " Riga said.

"Second window from the far end, down that alley."

She cocked an eyebrow.

"How do you know?"

Erki blushed even in the dark, stuttered, and then said, "She's very pretty. I watched her go there."

She had to smile.

"That's fine. Good lad." She left it at that. "Lead the way."

"Right there," he pointed.

She really hoped he was right. She also hoped that Jesrin was there. If the amar had her in his bed . . . or even if she was just doing scullery work . . . of course, either would let them return, knowing they'd tried.

Or more likely, cause me to escalate until we do have a war, Riga thought. She had no illusions of her diplomacy or temper.

The shutter opened to the fourth pea-sized pebble.

Once Jesrin understood their gestures, her eyes grew a foot wide and she shook her head in horror. They gestured again, come down, come with us. Riga even held up the spare cloak for emphasis.

It took long minutes, while occasional flickers of lamplight in other windows indicated early risers, up to bake breakfast or reach the tide, before the girl nodded assent.

Erki tossed up a coil of thin, strong silk rope, and it took more minutes to explain she should loop it around the center post of the window and run it back down.

Riga was worried if Jesrin was strong enough to slide down a rope rather than fall, but she managed well enough, though clearly stiff from some beating or other. She bumped the wall and scuffed loose some plaster, which made Riga cringe. Perhaps she was being too cautious. There was no indication anyone else had noticed. She was thankful they didn't like dogs here. Dogs would have heard and smelled them long before.

The seconds were hour-long, as Jesrin slipped down the slender rope. Her layered dress was not practical, and would be abraded to shreds before she reached the ground.

Then she slipped and fell. Erki and Riga both rushed forward and caught her, and she convulsed in agony, with their hands on her beaten back. The fall had scraped her knuckles and forehead, and she leaned over in the dust and vomited, twitched, lay still for a moment, then twitched again as she woke up. Through it all, she barely uttered a sound.

Erki snatched the rope down as Riga gingerly helped her to her feet. With the shutters ajar and the rope recovered, there was no obvious sign of departure. But it was early, and Father would awaken soon himself. They had to move.

The girl meekly donned the offered hood and tied the cloak around her neck, wincing as even that weight touched her abused flesh. She'd pass as Kossaki from a distance, but her underdress was clearly servant class, and her poise was as submissive as Riga's was challenging. Still, that shouldn't matter.

"This way," Riga said, and led the way. A moment later, Erki grabbed her shoulder and stepped in front.

Oh. Right. Male must lead. She flushed in anger, embarrassment and frustration. Still, that's why she'd asked him along, and he was doing his part well, the stout boy.

They were five streets away when a Watchman came around the corner, right into their faces.

"Who are you?" he asked. Riga could puzzle out the words, but she couldn't speak. Had Erki paid attention to their lessons?

And then she knew why she loved her brother, annoying as he could be. He stepped forward, as he did for any problem, and showed no reluctance.

"Harad of the Kossaki," he lied, "and my sisters. I return to my uncle's ship."

"It is very late." The man spoke simply for them, but his tone made it clear he wanted an explanation.

"My sister took sick and had to stay with friends. We are lucky your gods saw fit to make her healthy in time."

It was very rude to look at a woman's face here, but this man was an official. He looked as if he was considering doing so, and stared at their feet.

She's wearing sandals, not boots, Riga realized. Explain them as locally supplied? But she couldn't talk, and would Erki grasp it?

Under her cloak, Riga gripped the hilt of her *seachs*. In about five heartbeats, he was going to find out why she was called "Sworddancer," even if all she had was a knife.

He looked at Erki again, said, "A blessing on you," and turned away.

Riga exhaled. Jesrin whimpered. Erki didn't twitch at all, and led the way forward.

It was definitely near dawn, and gray, as they reached the beach.

Jesrin spoke at last. "We go on your ship?"

"Yes, quickly," Riga said, gripped her elbow carefully—it might be bruised—and hurried her along.

Some crew were about, securing the ships for sea. The tents would be down soon, then hoisted back up as sails. Luckily, no one paid much attention to three youths.

Erki bounded catlike over the gunwale, and pulled at Jesrin's hands as Riga shoved at her hips. The girl winced. Beaten there, too. But it took practice or help to board the outward curve of a *kanr*.

In the dim twilight, Father was visible at the stern, checking the steering oar and ballast. Before he turned, Riga shoved Jesrin down behind a pair of barrels.

"Erki," she said, and stood as he threw a heavy, smelly tarp atop the girl.

He stood and whispered, "Don't move at all until I say so."

Father came back, moving easily around netted crates and barrels. He didn't look or act his age, and the ship was his domain.

"Where have you been?" he demanded crossly.

"I took a last look at the tiled market to the south," she said. "It's so pretty." She tried hard to make that sound honest. It was something she might have done . . . four years before. Would Father catch that?

"You'll have cleaning duty until I say otherwise. Both of you," he replied. He looked relieved and annoyed but not angry.

"Sorry, Father," she said.

"Yes, Father," Erki agreed.

"Stow the ropes, help with the sail bindings, and get ready to depart. We have a good wind to speed us north by west."

"At once," she agreed. Good. Shortly they'd be away from this beautiful hell.

The incoming tide made the ship sway and bob, and the wind and the poles inched them down the sand. All at once they shifted, dragged, shifted again, and *Sea Fox* was back in her realm. The crew jumped to the oars and sculled for deeper water. They were free peasants, hired and paid, and Riga would bet them against any slave rowers. As free men they'd also fight for their master and their pay. Yet another reason the Kossaki traded unmolested.

The ships were just forming up in line to head out to sea, when a bright yellow harbor boat headed for them, with a crewman tooting a brass horn. They all stopped their departure, keeping station in the lapping waves to avoid beaching again.

The boat drew alongside, and some official or other in gleaming white silk accepted a hand aboard. Behind him was the Watchman from the night before, and Riga's nerves rippled cold.

"May I help you?" Father asked. "I believe our tariffs are in order." He held out a leather book with a stamped sheet from the revenue agent. He'd paid the tariff Riga had calculated, and tossed in ten percent as "a gift for the temple," which meant for the agent's pocket. All should be in order. Though Riga knew that was not the issue in question.

"My apologies for disturbing you," the man said with mock politeness. "The amar sends his regards, and his sadness at losing a fine servant girl."

"We brought no servant girl," Father said. "The only woman on my ships is my daughter. Grom has his wife and girl child aboard his ship. Ranuldr has his wife and two daughters."

Erki stood alongside Riga. They'd had the same lesson, that to stand firm was better than to cower. Here they were side by side, and would the guard know, or mention it if he did?

Erki had changed clothes, so he would not be apparent at once. Would the man recognize Riga, though? But no local man should look at a woman. He'd seen her early, but had he "seen" her? She was also in shipboard trews and tunic now, leaning on a rigging hook as if it were a spear. She stared back at him, trying to look quizzical and faintly bored. He studied her, but it was all pretense. He really hadn't noticed the women. There'd been no real reason to at the time, and he wouldn't admit so now. Riga didn't blame him, knowing how the Amar might respond.

He looked hard at Erki, but without the cloak and in light, the boy looked more a man. He also didn't show any expression at all, though she could sense the nervous shivers.

"She was with a young boy last night. What about your boys?"

"Only Erki here," Father said. "He was on watch last night. I expect your own shore patrol will remember him. There are a number of other young men, though it depends on what you mean by 'boy.'"

Was Father lying as a matter of course, to get this over with? Or did he know and was covering for them? His words were unbothered.

The Watchman looked Erki over, but didn't finger him. Good so far.

The official asked, "Which girl was sick and stayed in town?"

"Not mine," Father said. "I suppose it could have been Ranuldr's eldest girl. She's fifteen. All ours are accounted for, though, we're not missing any."

Of course they weren't missing any. Father was deliberately misunderstanding. *My people are in order. Do you believe your own are not?*

"All your women are as they should be?" They looked uncomfortable. The Kossaki ships had canvas weather shields at the rear, and little privacy. It was understood that one didn't stare or annoy a woman even bathing or changing, but that was certainly not understood here. The very subject made them nervous and shy away. Inside, Riga grinned. They were going to back off, right now.

"There are few enough that I can count to six," Father said with a grin. Riga twitched. Would he insist on seeing them all?

"I will inspect your cargo and your manifest then, as a courtesy."

Riga grimaced as Father said, "If you wish." Everyone knew something was up at this point. They were just all pretending it wasn't.

He started at the bow, peering through the nets and checking the crates for stamps and seals. All were as they should be, and of course he knew that. He moved slowly back to a pile of barrels staked down, containing figs, tea and spices. Past the mast there were bundles of sail lashed to the spar.

Father said, "I don't wish to rush you, but we have five ships, and tide to keep. We've always dealt in good faith."

"I'll just work my way back and be done, then," the official said, with a false frown.

"Be quick about it. I feel sorry for the amar, but I have my own dramas, and I don't share mine with the help."

Was Father trying to cause the man to search in detail? That comment flustered him, and he checked a barrel's number very carefully.

"You might want to check under that tarp. It's a prime place to stash an escaped servant girl. I don't find my own daughter enough trouble, so I try to pick one up in every port."

Clutching his tally board, the man strode forward again in a careful, dignified fashion, swung over into his boat, and indicated to the rowers to leave.

He turned back, looked at Father and said, "Thank you for your help."

"You are most welcome. I hope the Amar finds this girl, and that she hasn't fallen among those who would shame her or him. I cherish his hospitality and trades."

"I will tell him," the official said, beckoning the guard to join him as he sat down on a thwart. "Good travels to you, and a blessing."

"A blessing on you, and the amar and your king," Father said.

As the inspector rowed away, Father turned and ordered, "Pick up the speed. We're not earning money to row like a holiday ship." He seemed quite relaxed and good natured.

Riga wanted to run back and check under the tarp. She knew Jesrin was alive, though, and silence was a good thing. It might be night before she could come out. It might even be five days and port before she admitted the girl's presence. She had silly notions of sneaking her ashore with a few coins somewhere she could find good work, though she knew the girl, like any injured creature, would need support for a bit.

She stood her post, and helped tighten the sail as they gained room to maneuver, and the five ships spread into a longer line for travel.

They cleared the headland and entered open ocean, the deeper swells swaying *Sea Fox*, twisting and torquing her. She was designed for that, though, and surged across the waves.

Father came past, checking the rigging. "How's the servant girl?" he asked quite casually.

Riga knew better than to lie. "Alive and quiet," she said at once.

"This is the same servant girl we discussed, I assume."

"Yes, she is. Jesrin. Badly bruised in body and spirit."

Father sighed and tugged at a rope. "Damn it, Daughter, this is worse than an injured goose. You can't save every helpless creature in the world! Especially at a risk of war."

"Of course not," she said. She looked back as Erki peeled off the canvas, and helped Jesrin, blinking against the light, come forward. Father might punish them both, but it would not be for spilling tea. She reached out a hand and helped the girl keep her feet on the swaying ship.

Then she smiled at Father, a challenging smile that would yield a flogging in Mirr, and perhaps start a duel in Kossaki lands. It was the smile of a merchant and warrior among her peers.

"But I can save this one."

The Groom's Price

With Gail Sanders

My wife has a very quirky sense of humor. She's been my best friend almost as long as we've been together. I can't be blackmailed because there's nothing relevant about me she doesn't know.

She's a big fan of the Valdemar universe, has multiple copies of all the books, and knows all the details necessary for a story in the main lands.

She's also a pretty decent writer. I did some of the plotting and pacing. We split the writing. The rest is actually hers, with my edits.

HE WAS MISERABLE, absolutely miserable.

:*No, you're not.*:

I am too—how could I be anything else with all of these Outclans strangers staring at me?

:*You only think that you should be miserable, you're*

253

really having an adventure, and you feel guilty that you wanted an adventure when your Clan thought it was only your duty that made you go. Besides, if you hadn't argued so persuasively, we'd still be on your plains.:

Keth're'son shena Tale'sedrin was quiet while he thought this over. He found the gait of the companion to be smooth and enjoyable. So enjoyable that it distracted him from his train of thought for awhile.

That's Companion, not companion, he thought, finally coming back to the topic. A Companion that was sneaky enough to blend into the herds being kept for youngsters to choose and train. A Companion that had disguised herself using the magic that had been forbidden to the Clans until the Mage Storms had swept through the plains. A Companion that was slowing her pace and moving up to a palisade partly hidden by trees. With a start, he realized that it was getting dark.

:This is Bolthaven. Tell the gate guards that you're here to see Master Quenten. If they ask you who you are, tell them. They still remember Kerowyn here.:

From a platform, a sentry demanded, "Name yourself."

"Keth're'son shena Tale'sedrin, for Master Quenten."

"Hold and wait."

He waited, nervously, but the gate was opened and another watchman gestured for him to follow. He found himself ushered and escorted through a town that seemed over-busy and over-populated. No one paid the least bit of attention to him, other than a look of admiration for his mount. He wasn't sure if the presence of the guard was insulting, he was after all an adult by the Clan's standards. Surely he could have found the school on his own.

:The guard is both for your protection and for the protection of the town's folk. Very few people this far out of Valdemar know just what Companions are. With the mage students here, loud noises are common; leading me along is to prevent me from running off if I get startled. I'd prefer it if very few people knew a Companion out of Valdemar was down in the Dhorisha Plains.:

Quenten jerked from his book as his mage barriers flared a warning. After the last time a Guardian Spirit gave him the collywobbles he had decided to set up an alarm. While he had plenty of experience thinking on his feet after his time with the Skybolts, he had reached an age where he preferred at least a little notice. After carefully putting down his book, he moved over to the window that overlooked the main gate. Sure enough, there was one of those Guardian Spirits. Perched on the spirit's back was something unexpected, a Shin'a'in youngster—the leathers were unmistakable.

"May the Blessed Trine curse that woman with children." *What does Kerowyn want now? At least last time she sent a letter ahead, even if it left out more than it told.* He had decided to meet the Shin'a'in when an apprentice knocked.

"Yes?"

"Sir, a strange child on a white horse says he's here to see you. One of the gate guards is downstairs with him."

"I know. I'll go down and meet him, Cuthbert." For some reason, using the apprentice's name seemed to make him more nervous.

The voice that spoke in his head was unexpected, but didn't scare him.

:That would be because he doesn't know how much you notice the students. Look, you've got a delicate situation here; it's going to take tact and all of your experience dealing with youngsters. This boy's considered an adult by his people, if just barely. He's got a powerful gift that needs to be trained and his people have traditionally shunned magic in general and have little experience with mind-magic. I need your help to convince him to go up to Valdemar. He still thinks that I'm his horse:

Surely being able to talk to him in his mind would have told him otherwise? Quentin replied in shock at holding a conversation this way. He could see why Kerowyn had complained about the Companions' high-handed attitudes in Valdemar.

:One of his gifts is animal mind-speech; he's used to hearing animals talk in his head. He's young enough that he hasn't learned that not everyone does. I've just got a larger vocabulary.:

Quenten moved down the stairs with an undertone of caution. He wasn't young anymore, even though being a mage preserved a person. Cuthbert had taken them five at a time with the boundless energy of youth.

He emerged into twilight supplemented by the flickers of watch fires, and saw the boy leaning against the Guardian Spirit. *Companions, they're called Companions,* he reminded himself.

"Greetings to you, and to your Companion. I am Master Quenten, the head of the mage school here."

"Greetings to you," the boy replied, his Rethwellan

rather accented. "I am Keth're'son shena Tale'sedrin and this is Yssanda."

"I bid you come up. Cuthbert, please bring us dinner and ale after you see to Lady Yssanda. Our guest stables should be adequate to your needs Lady, and I will have a gate to the gardens left open for you. If you will follow me?"

Cuthbert stood waiting respectfully near Yssanda. Before she turned to go, she wickered gently and nudged him towards Quentin.

:Go on, I'll be with you.: Cuthbert led her away towards the stables. Obviously setting his chin, Keth' turned to follow Master Quenten.

The meal was dispatched with the economy of the young and perpetually hungry. While the boy ate sliced meat and cheese quickly but neatly with a belt knife, Quenten mused on what the Companion Yssanda had told him about the situation. It wasn't enough to make a decision, and with a skill he had developed as head of a mage school he extracted more of the tale from the young man.

It was the tradition of his clan to prove they were ready for adulthood by choosing and training a horse out of the Clan's herds. Keth're'son had done well, especially for his age, and his pride in his skill was present in his voice. Then when he was on his trial journey the unexpected had happened: his horse had talked back to him. His horse had the nerve to tell him that he had been chosen and not the other way around. Quenten could hear the bafflement and confusion creep in past the confidence. Then the horse had the nerve to say that he had mind-magic and real magic. He was no shaman. He didn't want to be a Hawkbrother, and he didn't want to leave the plains. What would a Shin'a'in do with magic anyway? He was going to train horses and trade them like his father and mother. It wasn't his fault that his mother's mother's mother had been Kethryveris shena Tal'sedrin.

The chance to tell his story paled before the attraction of more food and Keth' dug into the lentils. They were firm and tasty and there was rabbit as well, with some savory spices. It warmed him and renewed him. As he paused, Quenten put forth his proposal.

"I have need of your services. There is an advanced mage student wishing to study other schools. Far Valdemar has many in one town. The student is young and unfamiliar with wilderness. You, however, are an experienced traveler, and have your Companion. You'll be heading that way already, so I would ask that you act as escort."

Keth' didn't regard himself as an experienced traveler. This was his second journey on his own and he'd gone astray on his first one due to the Companion. The second comment brought him to a halt, spoon almost to his mouth.

"How did you know I would be going to Valdemar?" he asked.

He knew how, though, even as Quenten spoke.

"Keth're'son, you must develop your mind-magic and your bond with your Companion. That can only be done at the Collegium in Valdemar. I thought you would know of this." The mage frowned, suddenly looking older as he did.

Keth' scowled and put down the spoon.

"It's been suggested. It's not something I'm interested in, or able to do. I have plans for my life that do not include going to a strange land to be schooled as if I were still a child." He was betrothed to Nerea. His family had horses . . .

The mage looked gently at him. "Keth're'son, not everything in life is as we plan or wish, and sometimes events change our route."

You lied to me. If thoughts could burn with accusation his would be acid now.

:I did not. I said Quenten would have better information. It must be your choice. While you are still young, by your own people you are considered an adult. Would you leave a child to wander the plains with a lit torch? That's the potential hazard you present to your people.

Keth' sighed and said, "Who is this student?" He was not conceding the point. He needed more information, though.

Quenten nodded slightly and flicked a bell with his index finger. The tone seemed to penetrate the very walls. A moment later, the student was ushered in. She was elaborately and impractically dressed. The sheen of the fine woven fabric moved like water. It was completely unsuitable for rough travel. The dangling sleeves and the ornately upswept hair did nothing to hide the penetrating glance she gave the young Shin'a'in. With a dismissive shrug she bowed briefly to Master Quenten.

Keth're'son looked at the girl and felt unnerved. She was pretty, yes, but it was her gaze; far more mature than it should be. She stared back, disinterested except in his potential as a guide, and clearly not impressed by what she saw. He blushed.

Still, there was good pay involved, and he was going to Valdemar, at least to deliver the Companion.

Only to deliver the Companion.

Quenten said, "This is Armaeolihn and this is Keth're'son shena Tale'sedrin." His pronunciation was quite good. Keth' was impressed.

The girl bowed slightly but politely, and he raised the age he guessed her, from her figure. He returned the bow. He thought he should say something, but he wasn't sure what, so he turned to Quenten.

Quenten said, "You will travel together for safety. Keth're'son is bonded to a Companion. Armaeolihn, you have your pass, and I shall write one for Keth're'son. I will also give Keth're'son a letter to take to Herald Captain Kerowyn, his cousin. She'll see that he gets paid. If you choose to stay, she will ensure your learning and settle you."

"How much pay?" he asked. He understood this to be an escort duty, and Shin'a'in were well-sought for that.

Quenten named a sum, and Keth' opened his mouth to haggle, then kept it open in surprise. That was a goodly sum.

"Then I accept," he said, before realizing he should have asked for more anyway. Not that he needed to, but still, one should never take the first offer.

"Good. Rest well, and we'll prepare her horse and a pack beast. You can leave in the morning." *And be out of my hair*, was unspoken, but Keth're'son heard the undertone. This mind magic was problematic. He heard whispers of things that weren't spoken, and of course, no one knew how to teach him to control it . . . except in Valdemar.

Another student mage appeared and led him to a comfortable room, with a pitcher of cold, clear water, another of hot, and wine and fruit. Over his protests, his traveling clothes were whisked away, washed and the minor tears of constant travel mended, then returned. At first he was uncomfortable. It felt like an attempt to place a debt on him. Then he concluded it was just service provided to a professional.

Alone, Keth' spoke to Yssanda. *Should I do this?*

:Now you want advice. Am I suddenly of worth?:

You always have been, he protested. *You also know these people better than I.*

:The journey fits my plans. You must understand that affects my advice. However, it pays you well, it gives you experience and travel, and it gets you where you must go regardless of your choice.:

That's fair, he thought. Very fair. Yssanda hadn't actually offered advice, though, only facts.

:Often, that is the best advice of all:

He scowled. Why was everyone assuming he would be one of these Heralds?

He awoke at graylight, and followed the smells of breakfast downstairs to a common room. He was an outsider, but treated cordially enough. As he finished, one of the omnipresent mage students led him to the stable, where Yssanda was ready, groomed, in new harness, and Armaeolihn waited in comfortable traveling clothes with her own roan gelding, and a lead to a sturdy draft pony.

"Good day," he said, in Rethwellen.

She nodded politely enough, if a bit noncommittally. He got the feeling that she was unsure of his qualifications but glad to be finally going to Valdemar. It was going to be a long enough journey as it was, hopefully she wasn't going to act superior the entire way. Not that it mattered with a language barrier.

:Don't worry, for all that she's a mage she's also a young girl. She'll open up a little more as we journey. Of course, that's going to depend somewhat on you. Don't you know how to treat a girl? Or are the Shin'a'in all unlettered barbarians?:

While her tone was teasing, that was the root of this problem. He was out of his depth.

The journey through Rethwellan passed in a series of inns, where Master Quenten's letter secured them supplies and sleeping quarters, and then there were the times between the inns.

Keth' was learning Valdemaran while trying to wrap his mind around the philosophy, history and ways of that strange land. The education did pass the time, especially when delivered with the biting sarcasm of the Companion.

This time, when he laughed out loud at Yssanda's comment, he heard an exasperated sigh.

Blushing, he turned to look at his herebefore stubbornly silent traveling companion.

Noticing his glance, she scowled at him. "What are you laughing at?"

"Something that Yssanda said." It didn't occur to him to prevaricate.

"Yssanda? Who's Yssanda?"

"You've been traveling with her." He leaned forward and patted the Companion's shoulder.

Yssanda turned her head and winked at Armaeolihn. The crystal blue eye glinted briefly before resuming the dark brown color that Yssanda used for discretion.

Armaeolihn was silent again. Keth' hoped he hadn't annoyed her. She'd been more friendly of late.

During their lunch break at the side of the road, Lihn broke her silence.

"Is Yssanda some kind of Guardian Spirit, or are you a mage?" she started off accusingly.

"I don't know." Keth' scowled. "I'm supposed to have some kind of Gift—mind-magic and true-magic. But I don't want it and don't need it. Yssanda won't tell me what she is—just that she's a Companion and that they'll tell me everything in Valdemar."

"You don't want magic? How can you not want magic?" Lihn sounded absolutely shocked.

"Where I come from, only shamans and Hawkbrothers have magic. Mages meddle where they're not supposed to and are forbidden to be on the plains. At least they used to be. Things have changed since the Mage Storms."

"So what are you doing riding a spirit horse, speaking to it using mind-magic, traveling with a mage and going to Valdemar where there are many mages?"

"That's what I'd like to know."

His reply silenced her again. But this time it was a puzzled silence, rather than a hostile one.

"I would ask you the same," he said to her after they began to ride again.

"For learning."

"I was told that. What kind of learning?"

"Ah," she said, and shifted, with a breath. "I am a born mage, and have studied many disciplines. I can gather dispersed magic and build its power. Not like before the Mage Storms, but to a level suitable for serious study. Each style has its limits, though. There are more schools, more ways, in Valdemar. I will share what I know, in exchange they will let me study more."

"I see," he said. "I wish I could unlearn mine. I have no desire to improve it."

"But you must!" she said.

"Eh. Why? I don't use it." He shrugged.

"You have been using it. You say you talk to animals. You talk to this Companion. That's why you're going for training."

He flared up again. "Everyone assumes I'm getting trained."

"Magic not controlled is magic that controls the mage. It's far better that you do. Far, far better," she said, and shuddered slightly.

"I have a life," he said. "I am happy with it."

Lihn said, "Magic changes things. You can feel this."

"Shin'a'in don't use magic."

She said nothing.

They rode on, munching rations as they traveled, resting themselves and their horses every couple of hours. It was midafternoon before she spoke again.

"Imagine a campfire, in dry grassland," she said.

Yssanda had said as much. He didn't feel that was a fair comparison, but everyone else seemed to.

:You channel magic. That is what you must learn.:

I don't have to use it and don't want to. Even this is more than I care for.

The trip was long. The weather was fair enough, and they were sure of supplies without hunting; the letter from Master Quenten assuring them of food, water and lodging whenever they stopped. In between, Keth' was quite comfortable on a roll under canvas. Lihn clearly wasn't, but said nothing and put up with it, though occasionally he caught what he thought was a gesture of her hands before sleeping.

One morning after rising, he felt the ground she'd lain on. It was spongy, like moss or the ground beneath evergreens. Magic.

That is something I dislike about magic, he said. *It makes people soft.*

:Only as soft as they need or want. This is why control is important.:

I don't want to argue about that.

:Neither do I, so let us work on language. Ten more words today. You have a good basic vocabulary now.:

He preferred the language lessons to lectures on mind-magic.

He understood why he had been hired, and promised pay for this. Lihn was quite smart, but not skilled in wilderness. Keth' was the one who loaded the pack pony with dried fat and fruit for the ride through the mountains and White Foal Pass, with extra blankets of thick fleece, and waxen fire starters. It was easier than long caravans or herding, and they made good distance each day, even in the brisk chill the mountains had even in summer.

Then they were descending into glorious greenery again, until it became humid, rich and with the scent of lush life growing in between outcroppings of stone. Shortly, grassy hills stretched on before them, not his plains but refreshing after the rocky pass.

"This is the South Trade Road," she said, showing him on the map. "We are in Valdemar. Having crossed half a continent, we have merely half a country still to travel."

"Well, good," he said.

:We shall stop before dinner, Yssanda said. *:There are now Waystations and Inns for us to use.:*

"I believe we're stopping soon," he said.

"Yes," she agreed. "I can tell when Yssanda talks to you."

He scowled, because it felt intrusive for her to know that and he wasn't sure how else to respond.

They soon came to a town with a guard station. Yssanda moved up to the guard and stood still. A guard came out, eyed the Companion who was no longer disguising herself, eyed Keth', and said, "Ah, a newly chosen one are you? We'll see you right, we will."

Keth' thanked him with what he hoped was a fair accent, dismounted and led Yssanda towards the corral, stable, lodge and watchers. He presented the letter for Lihn and she dismounted as well. The guard examined it and handed it back to Keth' along with another town chit—this one said Sweetsprings—and they were waved into the inn. The staff took charge of providing them with bathing, cleaning, food and beds.

There were clearly apparent advantages to even association with a Companion. While he had been comfortable enough in the open air with the tarp overhead, he certainly appreciated the regular occurrence of sleeping pallets, hot meals and sweetened travel rations. Even the Waystations had been an improvement over sleeping on the ground. A Shin'a'in didn't need such things of course, but they sweetened his traveling companion's temper— such was always to be wished as he had received the sharp edge of her wit several times.

:There are Waystations from here on, so we shall have shelter each night.:

If we must, though I may sleep outside with the tarp and enjoy the breeze. He was even thinking in Valdemaran now, if haltingly. He was starting to grasp the language, though the attitudes and philosophy still escaped him.

He wondered what the cities ahead would be like. This area was more populated than his Plains, and it was a remote hinterland for Valdemar, he understood. The first time a small train of goods wagons came the other way, he'd stared. There would be more, though.

:I will teach you more of mind-magic as we near, so you are better prepared.:

I can accept that. I'll be sorry to turn you over to the Queen's stables. You're . . . a friend.

:We don't have to part ways.:

Yes, we do, he said firmly. It would be more than a year by the time he returned home, most of it traveling, much of it with this mage girl.

If it were possible, I'd stay with you and let you teach me.

:If it were possible, that would still not be possible. I asked for special dispensation to teach you this much. It is only to familiarize you. It could, in fact, make things worse.

Normally, only Herald trainees receive this kind of training.:

How? And why did you, then?

:Think of a wild youth, you know of them, you were one not long ago yourself. Unschooled, untrained, eager. Imagine that mischief, unintentional, with the force of magic. As to how, if you stay they'll teach you.:

You hoped I'd learn to like it and change my mind.

:Not quite. However, without familiarity that would be impossible.:

Three months ago, Keth' would have been furious. Now he was just bothered. He had a choice to make, and everyone was presuming to push him in the same direction. That made him stubborn, but, did they all know something he didn't? Wasn't he the best judge of himself?

Something else nudged at him and he put it aside. The training took years. It would divert his life. At the same time, there was a vibrancy to this place. It bespoke adventure and restlessness, which he shouldn't let sway him, except . . .

The nudge came again, firmer.

He quivered and said, "I think there are others nearby."

Lihn asked, "Possibly a patrol? Travelers?"

"A patrol maybe. They don't feel like travelers."

"Did you feel the previous travelers?"

He twitched at that. "Yes, actually I did, now that I think about it. Sort of a background distance noise like a camp. Something I was aware of but . . . this isn't that."

Not far ahead, a voice roared something almost intelligible, and both sides of the road erupted in men, dressed in threadbare uniform parts and twigs and leaves.

In the Plains he'd have seen that deception. These plants, though, he was still learning.

There were a dozen or so, and all he had was a large knife, which he drew, and urged Yssanda forward in front of Lihn, though what good it would do with them all around.

The air shook as Lihn shouted something, and the air burst in a soft thunderclap. One man went down, and two others stopped charging, to tumble sideways.

But those two were up again. Lihn couldn't fight. Yssanda had hooves. He had a knife. Here at the end of their journey, a dozen brigands were going to end it, and likely their lives.

Rage welled up, and Keth' shouted "No!" from deep inside.

He woke with someone slapping his cheek. "Son? Are you there? Son?"

He shook his head and garbled out, "I'm all right" in Shin'a'in, then Valdemaran when the man looked at him strangely.

He peered around to see the band of robbers in shackles, being herded by three men on horses. Another man dressed all in white was on a Companion and clearly talking to Yssanda.

"What happened?" he asked.

Lihn appeared above him.

"You did it," she said, looking down with a smirking grin.

"Did what?"

"You used the mind-magic you disdain so much. I knocked down three with my Storm Blast spell, and that's all I had, my power for a day or more. You shouted and they all collapsed, clutching their heads. Then you fainted. It's been half the morning."

"I did it?"

:You did.:

"Lots of power, no control," she said. "That's why you need training."

It was hard to argue.

Two weeks later, they were near Haven. The roads carried more people than Keth' had ever seen, with wagons, carriages, horses, donkeys, packs and trucks and carts. The roads had been graveled and marked but now they were paved in some strange material.

"That's the sign post we were told to seek," he said. Near it was a small group of people. They were set back from the road and observing the busy traffic, while being out of its way.

"Yes," Lihn said. "And that must be Master Arak. It is."

Another old man in a robe, only this one had aged with power in his physique, under the lines.

Next to him Keth' saw a woman who could only be Herald Captain Kerowyn. With her was one dressed completely in white and another that looked to be of the plains, complete to the fringed leathers that he hadn't seen in months.

The journey was over. At least, this part of it was.

:Have you decided what you are going to do:

I'm going to use my Shin'a'in craft and guile, he replied with a grin.

Keth're'son shena Talesdrin squared his chin and

swallowed a brief spurt of homesickness. No matter what happened, it would be many months or years before he saw his Clan, his family, his plains or Nerea again. Then he smiled. He was ready to do battle—and it would go his way, because these outlanders were no match.

:And I will help you.:

The Bride's Task
with Gail Sanders
★★★

It worked well enough we did it again.

★★★

KETH'RE'SON SHENA TALE'SEDRIN was learning weapons work: the sword. This would have been useful to know for his journey to Valdemar, but his people were warriors from horseback and with the bow—not with the sword and dagger and on foot. He stepped aside a sweep, blocked and countered, but his teacher parried that and beat back at him.

:But no knowledge is ever wasted, chosen. You won't always have a horse to hand. What if I were injured? Just because your people haven't done something before, doesn't mean that it's not a valid way to do things.:

He replied *:I know, 'there is no one true way.' It's taking some getting used to. Traditions have always played a strong role in the life of a Shin'a'in, they had to.:*

:Right now, you need to pay attention to your role here,

or the weapons master is going to give you the 'traditional' bruises.:

:You know, I would probably be doing something like this at home as well—I wonder how Nerea is doing with her lessons; she was always better with the bow than me.:

:You miss her.:

:Did you really expect that to change? We are pledged. She's why I work so hard at these 'lessons.' I only hope that she'll wait until I can return. I'm not sure she understood why I had to come up here when I wasn't sure myself.:

Yssanda was silent.

"There's a herd of horses in the Palace courtyard," one guard said.

"Why is there a herd of horses in the courtyard?" asked the other.

"I don't know, but isn't that a Shin'a'in on the back of one of them?"

"Sure looks like it. Heya, it's a girl! And look, she's getting down."

"Do you think we should tell somebody?"

Sergeant of the Guard Selwin spoke loudly behind them, "Yes, you half-wits, I think you should tell somebody! You, Rolin, go get Herald Captain Kerowyn. *At a Run!* You, Vark, suggest to the young lady that she should stay outside the Palace door."

"Yes, sir!" the two guards saluted in unison and moved with a sense of purpose.

Shaking his head, the young guard sergeant moved towards what seemed to be an escalating argument. The burly guard was having an increasingly difficult time with the slim Shin'a'in who seemed determined to simply get through that door. He'd managed so far without actually laying a hand on her, but it didn't appear that was going to last very much longer. She wasn't so much aggressive as persistent.

Moving past the string of exceptionally quiet and serene horses Selwin came within range of a contrastingly loud and agitated Shin'a'in girl.

"She doesn't speak Valdemaran, sir!"

"I'm gathering that impression. Let's see what I can do." He strained to remember a bit of the language.

In very slow and careful Shin'a'in he said, "Please hold, coming someone who speaks language."

The young girl nodded briskly and moved back to reassure her riding horse. Selwin wasn't sure who needed the reassurance more; the horse or her.

Herald Captain Kerowyn didn't take long to arrive, which was all to the better as far as Sergeant Selwin was concerned. He wasn't a diplomat and very much preferred going back to his post near the main gates. He simply briefed Kerowyn on what had happened so far, saluted, and then gestured the guards to head back to the gate.

Striding forward, Herald Captain Kerowyn gave the impression of impatience.

She didn't hide it. It might help speed this encounter.

:*What happened to Shin'a'in staying on the plains where they belonged?*:

:*What happened? The Mage Storms happened and erased the tasks the Shin'a'in had been given by their Star-eyed.*:

Kerowyn really hadn't needed the rejoinder to what had

been a rhetorical question but trust Sayvil to make sure her opinion was heard—needed or not.

"Welcome to Haven. I'm Herald Captain Kerowyn. What brings you here so far from the plains?"

"My name is Nerea shena Tale'sedrin. I'm here looking for my pledged, Keth're'son shena Tale'sedrin. The Clan Elders said that he had come up here for training in his 'Gifts.'" Her skepticism in the need for such training was obvious. "They gave me permission to bring his Clan share up here to him when the Tale'sedrin came up for the Bolton Faire. Where is he?"

"Ah." Suddenly Kerowyn understood both her animosity and her vulnerability. By giving her permission to bring Keth's Clan share up here to him, the Clan Elders were both telling him that they weren't expecting him to come back to the plains and giving him permission to stay where he was. They were also putting the responsibility of telling his pledged this, off their shoulders and onto his.

:Practical but not very kind of them. This Nerea must have been quite a nuisance.:

:Yes,: Kerowyn sighed to herself, *:And now she's our nuisance. Sayvil, please tell Dean Teren about the situation out here and ask him to bring the Shin'a'in envoy with him if possible. Have them meet us at the stables.:*

"He is here at the Collegium. But first, we need to get these horses settled and out of the way. If you'll follow me, I'll lead you around to the stables. There should be room for them there." Kerowyn knew better than to offer her any help with this. After all she'd gotten them here from Bolton. It would also keep the girl busy while Kerowyn figured out what to do. The girl followed agreeably enough, since the horses were something she cared for. She did not seem to care for local rules.

The Companion-relayed message brought Dean Teren down from his office in a rush. From another direction, the Shin'a'in Envoy Shaman Lo'isha shena Pretara'sedrin was only a minute behind. The dean arrived at the stable entrance panting. The shaman heaved one sigh and had his breath back under control.

The dean said, "A Shin'a'in invasion? That wasn't quite the message, but I gather this matter is important?"

"Not quite," Kerowyn said, hiding a smile. "However, we do have a Shin'a'in girl, far out of her area, seeking her pledged, who is one of your students." She indicated the stables.

"I see," the dean said, and seemed to grasp the import. He followed her gesture, to where the girl was taking proper care of the horses, including a quick brushing, with an economy born of lifelong experience.

When Nerea finished watering them at the trough and ensured they had a panful of oats and plenty of hay each, she turned and walked back. She seemed fully aware of the dean and shaman, but waited for Kerowyn to make the introductions. She greeted the dean with a bow, and spoke formally to the shaman.

"Nerea, there are things I must attend to, but the dean and shaman will aid you."

"Thank you for the introduction, Cousin."

"You are welcome."

With that, Kerowyn turned and left with the intention of finding out just who in Bolton let Nerea off her leash with fifteen horses and who there might be missing her.

★ ★ ★

Lo'isha shena Pretara'sedrin, Shaman and Shin'a'in Envoy, found himself in the midst of the problem. With Kerowyn gone, he was both translator for the dean, speaker for his own, and the only possible authority figure the girl might acknowledge.

Neutrally, he said, "Nerea, you are far from our lands."

"As are you, Elder. We both have our reasons," she replied, with not quite a smile.

"Yes. You are here for your pledged, I'm told."

"I am. If he is to be here, I am to be with him."

He recognized her expression now—determination, with a slight challenge.

Lo'isha translated for Teren. Teren raised his eyebrows.

"Well, first I suppose I need you to help explain about the training."

Lo'isha nodded, and translated for Teren.

Dean Teren twisted his mouth for a moment, apparently in thought, then spoke. "Nerea," he said, "mind-magic is much more than empathy for animals. I know you can work with these creatures—" he gestured towards the stables "—better than most people, and it's a natural talent for you. However, Keth' is able to do the same to people and objects; whether they want it or not, whether he wants it or not. He and his traveling companions were attacked not far from the city on their way here. His reaction caused unconsciousness for the brigands, and two never recovered properly, being mind-lame since then." He waited while Lo'isha caught up.

"Well, good," she said. "I approve of retribution to such *grek'ka'shen*."

Teren winced slightly at that.

"Perhaps, but it wasn't an intentional response. He panicked, they collapsed. This could happen to innocent people, too. Nerea, I understand this is something you had planned by you and your people for some time. You must understand that his mind-magic changes things. He needs to learn to control it, for his own safety, and yours, and that of others." Lo'isha translated.

She stared right back at Teren, then spoke to Lo'isha. "I understand that. You must understand that our pledge doesn't change due to side matters. He is alive, he is very much himself, and he is very much mine. I remain with him, and he with me. Explain that to him, please." She gave a single, firm nod. With a raised eyebrow at her firmness, Lo'isha turned and translated for Teren.

Teren said, "That is not possible." The flat tone in his voice almost did not need translating.

"For you, perhaps not. I assure you it is quite possible for me." She sounded almost haughty, certainly confident and stubborn, and yet calm. She was like a mountain in storm, while the trees swayed in distress.

The dean looked at Lo'isha in controlled exasperation. It wasn't that she didn't understand. She understood fully and was unswayed.

The shaman placed a calming hand on Teren's wrist and tried a different tack.

"It is obvious this is true. Things have not changed for you, and you are on your course. However, have they remained the same for him?" Lo'isha spoke with the authority of a shaman and brought up exactly what Nerea did not want to hear.

She flushed slightly.

"I don't know," she said. "I haven't seen him since he left our lands. That is why I am here now. This must be resolved between us." She almost stamped her foot in emphasis.

"I don't disagree. This training, though, is for safety. Consider a fire on the plains. There's a reason children are taught to tend a fire carefully. They must know how to judge fuel, to avoid a flare of flames and disaster."

Her expression was most put upon.

"I don't seek to hinder that. Only to be near him."

Inwardly Lo'isha sighed; the girl wasn't being unreasonable, just stubborn, and adamant, and unswerving in her intent. The shaman said, "Well, then please let me start by offering a place to stay and clean up from the journey, in the embassy in the Hawkbrother *ekele*."

She widened her eyes slightly.

"Thank you," she said. "I will be comfortable with our cousins."

"If you wait I will show you the way. I and the dean need to discuss how we can arrange this meeting for you."

With a frown and flick of her eyes, she said, "You have only to tell me where he is, but clearly that is too simple for this city, with its costumes and rules and gates and castes." She paused briefly, as if only then aware of her bad manners. "Forgive me. Thank you for your hospitality. I will leave you to your discussion, and I will await your direction, for now."

For now, Lo'isha thought. This wasn't over by far.

He watched her move a discreet distance away, enough

to be in another tent, were there any tents here. She paid attention to some detail of the bricks and moss, and, while not relaxed, was not intruding.

He turned to the dean.

Teren asked, "How do we get her out of here?" in a whisper. He glanced over suspiciously at her.

"I don't know that we can. It would be up to her and her pledged."

"The distance should have made this impossible, especially for one so young."

"For our people, they are man and woman grown. You mustn't mistake her for a child."

"I'm not mistaking her for a problem." The dean clutched his hands together.

"No, but you are mistaking her for your problem. I will show her to the *ekele*. Then we can talk."

"Very well, and thank you. Then we can have Keth' deal with the issue."

Teren seemed quite exasperated, and Lo'isha surmised that by "issue" he meant "sending her home."

He didn't think it would be that easy.

"I will meet with you shortly," he said. Then he turned, and to Nerea said, "Come then, and I will show you to the *ekele*."

Teren was in his office when Lo'isha returned. He gratefully put aside his writing and said, "Please, have a seat." Lo'isha sat in the one available chair in the cluttered and paper-filled office.

"Always one chair not used for storage, I see," the Shaman offered with a chuckle.

Teren shrugged and nodded and chuckled back. "It's my way. If anyone were to straighten my clutter, I'd never find anything again. But as to the other . . . Thank you for your aid in this matter. This is most awkward. Students are unaccompanied, and if not single when they commence training, are by the time they graduate. This is how it is done, and most arrive knowing it. If he's to be a Herald . . . "

"You are assuming he will complete the training, and follow your chosen path. There are at least two people assuming his fate for him. It seems to me that is a question for him to answer."

Teren startled at that. "How could he refuse to be a Herald?"

"Quite easily. Are you asking, 'Will he be the first to refuse?'"

Teren had no response. He never considered that possibility. There were traditions and cultural assumptions to the Collegium. Those weren't necessarily the traditions and assumptions of the boy, and most definitely weren't those of the girl.

By choosing him, Yssanda had thrown things into a fine tempest. Perhaps it was an amusement for her. Or, it might be a necessity. What would have possessed a Companion to go all the way to the Dhorisha Plains to choose a Shin'a'in child? What would Valdemar need him for, or was it that the Shin'a'in would need him more?

Regardless of the cause, this situation needed resolution.

"I suppose we should arrange for them to meet," he said, leaning back and stroking his chin. "After that we'll see."

"Are you going to warn the young man?"

"I'm not sure we should. He'll want to meet at once, and it will distract him. I'll arrange some time, and we'll let them meet. He can explain to her better than we."

"I'm not sure it will be that simple."

"Oh, of course he'll have second thoughts and some homesickness. However, he's a fine pupil. He's learned a lot of fundamentals quickly, and even accepted the separation. It was long in his mind. They've both grown and changed, and this will make it clear."

The next morning, Lo'isha met Nerea at the *ekele* entrance. She was staring wide-eyed at the lush and fragrant growth. It was very different from the Plains and being surrounded by the local terrain only emphasized the differences. Hearing his footfalls on the graveled path, Nerea turned and greeted the Shaman.

"Bright the day, Elder," she said cheerfully.

"Did you sleep well?"

"I did, thank you."

"How are the younger-sibs?"

"They are comfortable and getting refreshed. How much is stabling? I have little money, but I can offer work."

"Nothing is required for now. You are a guest at our invite."

"That's gracious of you."

Quite a few youths would have assumed hospitality, without even thinking. They expected adults to manage things for them. The locals had trouble grasping that, by Shin'a'in tradition, she was a woman grown. Of course she asked about debts.

"Actually, it's gracious of the dean, and of the queen," he smiled. "But it's something they plan for, so you need not mention it."

"I will do so, at least once, but I understand," she said.

He sighed, slightly. Yes, the ways here were strange, but as a guest, one should learn and abide by the local rules. She was a headstrong and inexperienced youth, well-intentioned, but fiery.

"If you are ready, then please come with me."

They walked out into a damp spring morning. It had rained during the night. It might be warm and muggy later, but was clear and fresh now.

He led her through Companion's field, along Palace garden paths and to the Collegium main hall. At a side entrance, Teren awaited, and with him Keth're'son shena Tale'sedrin.

Nerea was not so formal with Keth'. She charged forward threw her arms around him in a tackling hug, feet off the ground and looking melted in place. Lo'isha stood back and let them resolve that. Their embrace was one of innocent companionship, not of long-parted lovers, but it still held that same intensity.

Keth's mind whirled. How did Nerea get here? But she was so warm, and her grip so tight. He could smell her hair, and the scent of her leathers. He closed his eyes and hugged her closely.

When he finally bent to put her down, and her feet touched the ground, she stepped back and grinned hugely at him, her dark eyes glowing.

She said, "It is so good to see you, my pledged. I have

traveled far to keep our bond." Her voice, that language, was music to him, after months of the strange tongue and stiffer rules it used. Shin'a'in flowed from the lips as was proper, Valdemaran seemed to march backwards instead.

He remembered there were others here, and they were being watched. He kept hold of one of her hands, and said, "I am so thrilled to have you here. But I must introduce you to someone."

He tugged and she followed him, smiling, into Companion's field and away from prying eyes.

"Who did you need me to meet?" Nerea asked.

They had been walking away from the Palace and the Collegium for some minutes now, while he enjoyed her company. She'd come so far. He had so many questions and so much to say, but first, he had to introduce her to his Companion.

There she came, from a shady copse of trees, toward them. He pointed as she came close, then laid a hand on her shoulder.

He said, "This is Yssanda. She is, in part, the reason why I came here."

"She's beautiful. Good lines, broader head. How did they get the silver hooves, and does she suffer any eyesight problems with those blue eyes? Do the hooves breed true?"

:I can see as well as you do, dear, and sometimes clearer. And don't you even think about breeding me—I can pick my own mates, thank you very much!: Yssandra let him hear her comment, even though she spoke to Nerea.

Well, that certainly moved things along.

Nerea stood very still. The sensation of having someone

speaking inside her mind was disconcerting to say the least, he recalled. Having that sensation come from a horse made it even more so. While the Shin'a'in consider horses to be their younger-sibs, they didn't expect them to talk back.

"Nerea, she's not a horse," Keth' said gently "She's a Companion, a person in her own right. She's been my friend, teacher and ally while I've been in this foreign place. Even after I'm done here, she's going to have to be a part of any of our plans."

"What are those plans going to be? You've already been gone so long, am I still a part of any plan?"

Keth's heart went out to her. She seemed to shrink inside herself a little, both wanting to hear the answer and not wanting to hear. Nerea deserved his honesty, but he wasn't sure himself.

"We need to talk about that. I think that's why you're here."

Dean Teren sat in his office, yet again considering the problem that Nerea and Keth' presented him. Neither one of the youngsters was taking into account what the Collegium might have to say in the matter—they just assumed that they could order the world according to what they wanted. After all, they were young and together—who could stand against them . . .

That was exactly the reason Herald trainees were expected to be unaccompanied.

It occurred to the dean that while it was certainly possible to stand against them, it might be very problematic to do so; sufficiently so to give the bards song fodder for a long time.

Keth' wasn't precisely a disappointment. He learned very well. However, he hadn't internalized the right attitude, and didn't see a problem with Nerea remaining here. She stayed at the *ekele*, and had worked out a labor exchange for lodging. She was quite competent.

Teren realized he'd underestimated them. A Valdemaran youth of that age could be swayed through reason, emotion, or social suggestion. Not only were these two from another culture, they'd grown up much faster. They were a strange mix of adult minds in juvenile spirits and bodies. He needed to talk to the envoy again.

Keth' walked with Lo'isha, near Companion's Field, with his own concerns. There were few people he could even begin to discuss this with.

"It's aggravating," Keth' said. "All this past year, I've been told I must continue alone. I had accepted that—well, somewhat—but now she shows up here. *Here*. Halfway across the continent."

The shaman paused to study a flower. Keth' was not interested in flowers.

"It should be flattering," the Elder said.

"It is," Keth' agreed, quickly. "It's also very inconvenient."

"Not just for you."

"I understand. But I want her to stay. I want to go home with her. So does she. I also do want to continue my studies. There's so much to learn and I'm improving." He paused, unsure what to add.

"You are improving," the shaman assured him. "You also can't control this situation. Unlike mind-magic, this involves people's intent. Even if you had that power, it would be unwise and unfair to use it."

He nodded. That such might be possible was disturbing.

As to the matter at hand, he asked, "So who does control it? And what should I do?"

"We each control our own part, or we think we do. Eventually, each of us will find a path that fits the events."

"That makes sense," he agreed, and he did feel better. "I just wish it would hurry up." He realized he was pacing back and forth as the shaman strolled.

The shaman said, "It is better that it take time. As to other things, I understand Nerea is taking language lessons?" He smiled with a twinkle.

"Yes, Clan k'Leshya also have given her lodging and some small allowance in exchange for stablework. I let her have a little of my own funds," he admitted, blushing. "I do care for her." She was so stubborn. Or not stubborn, but simply unswayable.

"There is no reason you shouldn't," the shaman said.

"But they want me to become a Herald, and Herald's—"

"You are not yet a Herald, and you remain Keth're'son shena Tale'sedrin. Those are two more things that must be reconciled."

"This doesn't sound possible," he said. He'd wanted reassurance. This was making him feel more depressed. He didn't feel Shin'a'in, nor Valdemaran, nor even himself now.

"It is all possible, and we need not know how at this point. It will all resolve in time."

"Thank you, Elder, I suppose." He tried to smile. "Can you give me something more immediate and practical?"

"You are free for the day. Why not take your pledged into Haven? I'm sure she'd like to see more than stables."

Lo'isha found himself quite busy. While he couldn't fault Kerowyn for handing the problem off, and it did involve his people, it was quite an interesting one, with all that entailed.

"So, Teren, what are we to discuss today?" He took the empty chair, and noticed it was a different one. The piles of parchment had moved.

"The same as we've discussed every day, the last two weeks. Nerea."

"Yes, she's quite the item."

"A pest. Sweet, pretty, too clever for her own good, and a pest." Teren twiddled a quill in his fingers.

"The language lessons?" he guessed.

"That, and still being here, and loitering around. I suggested she stay in Bolton. I offered to pay for quarters across town, to make some distance."

"She would refuse, of course."

"She did." Yes, Teren was most agitated, and on such a fine day.

"Is she affecting his studies?"

"Not that I've noticed, and I've been watching. It is disruptive to others, though, on top of his existing differences as a foreigner."

Lo'isha kept being calm and reassuring. "Well, I should think that would be good for the other trainees. They'll have to deal with such matters in the field, after all."

"Indeed. I would just prefer their practice problems be more organized."

"You can't send her away," he pointed out.

"I know." Teren stood and looked out the window. "I'd hoped she'd get bored and leave, or he'd realize he'd grown apart from her. Something. If anything, they are reconnecting and throwing sand in everyone's shoes."

"Then perhaps now is a time to walk barefoot, and enjoy the sensation."

Teren said, "Walking barefoot also involves thorns."

"Then walk carefully." Lo'isha offered his friend with a smile. "I have a feeling these thorns will be trodden down by many feet."

"Let me show you the city," Keth' said. While it wasn't home, it was a fascinating place, and he was eager to introduce her to some of the more interesting foods.

"Whatever you like," she said with a smile. It caught him off guard.

He offered an arm, and led the way toward the horse and animal market, figuring to stop at the Compass Rose just beyond it. It wasn't the cheapest, but it didn't attract lowlifes and the usual clientele wouldn't be surprised to see a pair of Shin'a'in.

They were almost to the market when he realized why her smile had concerned him.

There was a glint.

They'd both grown in a year, and she felt like a part of him. Then he realized he felt the same way. Even if he did agree with the Collegium's rules, and he'd only admitted to understanding them, this was something he wanted more.

"The Ashkevrons do have some fine horses," Nerea said.

"We have better, but not by much, and no others I've seen come close."

"Well, they do buy ours and breed them."

"Certainly, but it takes more than stock. It takes care and raising." Her energy never faded. He'd always liked that.

There were a lot of horses here today. It must be some market day. There were wagons, carts, horses with pannier saddles, mounts for nobles and the wealthy and draft horses for farmers. Some of the wagons held oats, nuts, apples and other fare meant for the animals, and several stores had displays of combs and brushes. There were also saddles, tack and clothes for riders, and even a carpenter's display of stable making. The place smelled of fine horseflesh, and he enjoyed it.

"Some very fine creatures," she said, smiling. She was relaxed, he realized, and comfortable for now. With food, and fine weather, there was nowhere he'd rather be.

Which was odd; this place was not home. He could speak the language well enough to get by, but it still felt foreign.

Rather than ponder it, he decided to just enjoy the day. Her hand was warm as she clutched his. Her shoulder brushed him every couple of steps. He was comfortably fed and had no pressing worries for the day.

It was at that moment that the Star-eyed saw fit to give him pressing worries.

A cart-hitched horse suddenly stepped sideways, reared up, and came down in a limping gallop. His cart knocked a stall askew, spilled some contents—bags of feed—and rode over the collapsed legs of the vendor's display.

The horse was clearly hurt, right rear leg tipping the

ground as the rest clattered on the cobbles. People dove from its path, shouting and screaming. Other animals shied and whinnied, backed and sidled, until carts crashed and tangled in a huge mess. It would take hours to sort out. It had happened in moments.

The chaos spread as other horses and even smaller animals caught the whiff of panic. Their instincts fought their restraints, and the din of it all was astounding.

Then Nerea stepped into the street.

Keth' knew what she intended, and made a half step to grab her, then decided he would only make it worse. He had no doubt she knew what she was doing, but he wasn't sure the horse did.

Three people buffeted him as they darted past, urgently clearing the street and seeking somewhere out of reach of rearing hooves and twisting wagons.

Then the horse, a very handsome dapple, reached Nerea at a near-gallop still dragging the remains of the cart. She stood calmly, stepped aside just enough to avoid it, and stroked his flank with her fingers.

He slowed haltingly, and stumbled two steps forward as the tilting cart's momentum shoved at him.

Nerea walked around him, fingers tracing his muscles. After the dapple was calmed, she stepped over to a dun mare. Nerea held a hand to her muzzle, and she quieted. Then a roan stallion dropped, relaxed and stepped out of the wreckage of a pushcart yoke. The waves of calm rippled out, where waves of panic had flowed only breaths before.

Nerea turned back to the dapple, walked around, and touched his injured leg. He raised it at once, and she studied his hoof. Taking out her belt knife, she pried something long and sharp out of the frog. Releasing the foot, she patted the dapple's flank.

And Keth' smiled, because he knew what could keep her here, near him, and near the horses.

He would stay here and finish his studies, because mind-magic, and animal speaking, ran through his people. It was inevitable others would show their talents, and possibly more so. He'd be needed to teach those children of the Shin'a'in who had mind-magic and who could not or would not leave the plains. Nerea would stay here until then, and teach the Valdemarans about horses, for wisdom ran both ways.

He also understood why the day had been so sweet, even though Valdemar wasn't his home. Nor, anymore, were the plains.

Home was where Nerea was.

"So, how are our lovebirds doing? More importantly has Nerea started home yet?" Teren asked Lo'isha hopefully, after serving the shaman some tea.

Lo'isha smiled at him.

"I think that is a vain hope, my friend. She does not look as if she is leaving anytime soon. If she was easy to dissuade she would have never left the Plains in the first place."

Teren sighed and leaned against his desk. "What am I going to do with them?"

"Why do anything? They will solve their own problems and have indeed begun to do so." Lo'isha calmly sipped his tea.

"What do you mean?" asked Teren suspiciously. He had the feeling that he wasn't going to like this.

"After that incident at the horse market, Nerea has

received more offers for work and horse training than she knows what to do with. She isn't going to go anywhere," he repeated.

"What about Keth'? Has he spoken to you at all?"

Lo'isha sat back and steepled his fingers.

"Yes, he has asked me about becoming a teacher on the Plains. He believes his talents lie not with Valdemar but with his—our—people. He's not entirely wrong. Her talent, of course, is a latent power manifesting itself. There will be others. He can hardly be the only one needing trained in mind-magic. Since the Storms there is now no reason not to. My people would learn better from one who has the proper attitude; magic is not to be meddled with but controlled and tempered."

"But, he is supposed to be a Herald! Anyone a Companion chooses has to be a Herald!" Teren was agitated. He'd thought Lo'isha concurred with him.

"Why? 'There is no one true way.' It's time to change. Not every Shin'a'in with power can trek to Valdemar, and certainly they can't remain here. At some point, we must have our own schools. In the meantime, he will be an intermediary, learning here, and mentoring others. Perhaps one day he will return to the Plains."

Teren said, "That's not what he wants."

Lo'isha replied, "Nor is it what you want. Nor even what I'd want, if I had a choice. None of us do, though. The Storms have blown the slate clean for us down on the Plains."

He took a final sip of tea and placed the cup down on a clear spot amid the clutter.

"I believe they have for Valdemar as well."

Heads You Lose

Through a network of authors, I was invited to write in Janet Morris's Hell universe. I wasn't familiar with it, and am still catching up on the stories now.

One thing I found very interesting was her edits. Her grasp of proper English is better than my own, and I was raised in the UK. It seems colloquialism brushes off on one.

I had a lot of fun with this. The anthology was Lawyers in Hell. *It almost writes itself. We networked, chose characters, then went through history consigning characters to eternal damnation we devised personally for each.*

I never liked one of these characters. You may be able to guess which one.

★★★

CAPTAIN JOSEPH MCCARTHY shouted, "Ready men, this is a combat drop. Hostile territory." Over the angry buzz the C130's engines, McCarthy was hard to hear.

Lieutenant Roger Upton Howard III rolled his eyes at that. *He says that every damned time. We know it's hostile. It's hell. We're lawyers.* Some, like McCarthy, were famous. Roger was largely a nobody. There was no significance to Earthly status in Hell.

In life, Roger had never imagined he'd wind up like this. It was a joke, back on Earth: Sell the devil your soul. The lawyer asks, "'What's the catch?'"

The catch was, Hell was real, and he hadn't even signed a contract. Those vague maunderings about ethics were all it took. Was it right to defend drunk drivers and petty crooks he knew were guilty? Apparently not, since the universe had seen fit to have a drunk driver crush him. Death had been close to instantaneous. He recalled a moment of pain, and then waking here. Here, pain was part of the scenery, and it seemed eternal. He couldn't say how long he'd been here, just "a lot of days."

Then Roger stopped reminiscing, because it was time to jump. The light blinked, and McCarthy shouted "Hook up!"

It was Hell, he couldn't die permanently, and every drop was terrifying because there were endless new ways to suffer.

The Coordinating Legal Airborne Platoon (the CLAP, with all the jokes that entailed) shuffled forward toward the paratroop doors, and Roger's guts and sphincter clenched. He joined the shuffle, hit the door, and jumped out over the choking clouds of hell—or more accurately, Ashcanistan.

The ripcord tugged his canopy open. He didn't realize his leg straps were loose until they drew up and yanked his groin. He flinched and tried to separate them. By then he was directly over Henry J. Summers II, another criminal defender. He dropped scrambling through Summers' canopy as it blocked the air. They didn't quite tangle, and Roger made it into the open.

That was worse.

Now he could see that the denizens of nearby Kabum were expecting them. They didn't like lawyers in death anymore than they had in life: what price repercussions to the damned?

A rocket ripped past him with a roar of white noise and a stench of ammonia, and ripped HJS, II's canopy into flaming shreds. The elderly man plummeted faster and faster as the rushing wind fanned his chute into flames, then embers. Roger tugged a riser to slip away from those glowing sparks. He didn't want to catch on fire.

He wondered if that fire had anything to do with Henry defending arsonists on Earth.

In moments, flak started bursting around them, spit from crude but functional AA guns. All Roger could do was shiver as they dropped. Then they got in range of rifle fire, catapults, javelins and arrows. He pulled the release on his ruck and prayed to no one in particular. He'd never known how. At least he'd known how to parachute; he'd been in the 82nd. Most of these poor bastards jump-qualified the slow, painful way. Or sometimes, the quick, painful way.

The earth below was cratered landscape; Hell's Ashcanistan had been a battleground for eternity. The sky above twisted in nauseating lavender and green moirés.

Then they were landing in heaps on the rocks. Some

caught on promontories. Others bashed into cliffs and tumbled into sharp valleys. Roger was lucky. He descended smoothly into a flat-bottomed gully. Two monkeys hopped on the edge of it and threw . . . he grimaced as feces splashed across his chest and spattered his chin.

He overheard one of the gibbering primates say, "Not like that, Phil, you clumsy monkey . . . " then Roger hit the ground, landing on a sharp rock, and his knee . . .

Electric jolts shot through his leg. He heard and felt his knee pop. He collapsed to the ground, whimpering.

General S.V. Benet (not the poet, but his grandfather) hopped over to shout at him, and a poor trooper nearby whose leg was blown clean off.

"Pick up that leg and get moving, Horace!" Benet shouted, fluffing his beard with his breath. "And you, Howard, on your feet and—"

Right then a bullet grazed Benet's throat, then two more ripped his uniform coat and tore his torso. He gargled, "Bloody repeaters!" in a spray of blood as he bounced away on his pogo stick.

Roger drew the metal frame from his ruck and assembled his own pogo stick, flinching as bullets whacked past. Then he crawled over to help Carlton Horace with his. The poor man was on his first jump and from the looks of him, in horrible pain.

"Hold your leg in place," he said. "It'll reattach and heal. And hurt." He made sure the kid did that, while he assembled Horace's stick.

"Now up," he said.

How they managed, he didn't know. He never knew. In short order, though, they were astride their metal steeds and bouncing ignominiously across the rockscape, joining up with others and forming a loose column. Satan had decreed that the CLAP's ground transport would be pogo sticks only. It was undignified, inefficient, liable to make one puke, and excruciating on injuries. Every bounce sent spikes of agony through his balls and up his spine. The only positive aspect was that the bounding, irregular motion made the riders harder to hit.

He caught sight of Henry, barely recognizable, a mashed sack. He winced in fear and revulsion. Wincing hurt, too.

Just behind him, Horace said, "Sir, my leg is healing already, like you said, but it's healing crooked."

He nodded, looked over his shoulder and said, "Yeah, sooner or later it'll get shot off again and maybe it'll heal straight next time." It would heal. After all, pain would be less effective a torture if one got used to it.

He felt sorry for Horace. The poor guy had it worse than the rest. He wasn't even a lawyer. He was an accountant.

The transit to the site was worse. Whenever you felt at your lowest in hell, they found a way to make it lower. Your only option was to do nothing, sit still, and ferment. Except that didn't work well, either. Something would come along to displace you or crush you or otherwise deepen your suffering.

That was exactly their mission here: Make things worse. Hell wasn't supposed to be fair, or even unfair. There was some kind of algorithm at the head office as to how fair or unfair it was supposed to be, and when. Said algorithm probably changed regularly. Everything else did.

So the CLAP rode pogo sticks in Hell, because they caused more pain. They'd had camels once, in Sinberia. In Hellaska they'd had fast dirt bikes, but no Arctic clothing. The CLAP's missions were recorded in the scars on his body—some healed crooked, some that wouldn't heal and just oozed.

That Fucking Benet. He was as atrocious in afterlife as he'd been in life. Roger had never heard of the man. Apparently, it was his brilliant idea to have single-shot rifles at the Little Big Horn and for several other battles during the Indian Wars, insisting (despite evidence and pleading troops) that "aimed single shots" were better than repeating weapons. The locals here had AK-47s, RPGs, that Russian .50 caliber machine gun whose designation Roger could never remember. That Fucking Benet, as everyone referred to him, insisted they use .45-70 Springfield rifles, single-shot. The rifles were accurate enough, except when gravity or the laws of explosives suddenly changed, but the CLAP were routinely slaughtered by peasants with better weapons. And That Fucking Benet would never learn. "Aim better!" was his only advice.

All Benet did was tell them to aim better. McCarthy ran everything else, while constantly ranting about Communists. He was doing so at that moment, voice shifting and syncopating as he bounced along. They could hear him through the speakers in their helmets. The CLAP had the highest tech gear imaginable, sometimes. The helmets contrasted with their proper pinstripe suits and ties, and their patent shoes. You could tell what era someone was from by their style of suit.

"Remember . . . that the Commies . . . had a huge . . . operation in . . . Afghanistan . . . Probably did . . . here, too . . . Be on the lookout . . . We'll need to ask . . . that question of anyone . . . we meet."

Seemingly, the locals would never run out of ammo. However, while progress was infuriatingly slow, pogo sticks did make the CLAP harder targets.

There were ways to approach that wouldn't have seemed like an invasion. Of course, in the best traditions of armies and hell, they didn't use those. Who could one complain to, in hell? In fact, that was their task here—to ensure that unfairness escalated.

Given the idiots in charge, that was certainly the case. Roger pounded across the landscape, the pain in his knee like a red-hot rod, jabbing through the side of the knee joint. He motioned Horace slightly ahead of him, watching the poor kid grimace rhythmically in agony. It always sucked to be the new guy. Although Roger wasn't that salty himself.

He had no idea how long he'd been here. Why think about eternity? He hadn't been here long enough to get philosophical about the stabbing pain, or the stupidity. Though he wasn't sure one ever did. The discomfort changed regularly, you never got used to it.

Roger threw himself off and behind cover. It was trained reflex. He was in the air before his mind told him there was incoming fire. A moment later he realized he was about to smash into hard desert and sharp rocks.

As he crunched into the dirt, he shouted and groaned, "Contact right!" Others yelled the same warning.

Then he sought cover by rolling behind a slight rise. He

abraded a shoulder on something rough. The new pain joined that in his knee, and every movement felt like fire.

His military training came to the fore, as did his military gripes. The designer of the ALICE pack he wore should be somewhere in hell, wearing one for all eternity; and that the stupid Springfield rifle he carried was a bitch when you had to roll over on it.

He pulled its sling from around his shoulder, dragged it from underneath him, opened the breech, then fumbled for ammo. He had twenty cartridges, which That Fucking Benet determined were all one needed, if every shot counted. The man predated suppressing fire.

Unfortunately, the enemy didn't.

The locals were pouring out fire from a Russian Dushka, now that he recalled its name, and he thought he recognized AK fire.

Between bursts, Roger heard Benet shout, ". . . precise, aimed shots . . ." and gritted his teeth. In his opinion, they needed a machine gun to lay down fire, then maneuver, suppress, and riddle every enemy in sight. This aimed shots crap was not going to work—again.

He wriggled out of the pack, with the frame gouging him as he did. They had no body armor, of course. They couldn't die permanently; obliteration was a mythical fate, or at least very rare. If you did die, you were recycled through the Mortuary and usually sent right back to your unit. The CLAP wasn't issued body-armor. Why carry the extra weight? Why bother?Why bother with anything?

Then someone started screaming as he was hit.

That's why.

He slid his pack up near the ridge of this little

hummock, raised his rifle carefully, and tried not to flinch as he shot. He didn't shoot at anything in particular. He just felt better doing something instead of nothing.

Benet whacked him stingingly with a swagger stick, and shouted, "What are you shooting at, trooper?"

"A general," he snapped.

Poor Benet was condemned to try to lead lawyers, accountants and philosophers in battle, for all eternity. A more prestigious post in the regular military perpetually eluded him. That didn't make the jackass pleasant.

BA-Boom!

The massive explosion blew a huge ball of dust into a rising cloud, followed immediately by a concussive slam that shook the ground and punched his ears. Overpressure slapped him with hot gas and ammonia. The explosion would be the calling card of the Supervising Legal Airborne Group, SLAG, dropping aerial judgment on the opposition.

Then it got quiet, very quiet, and not just only he was partly deaf. There was no opposition left alive anymore.

The deafness was always temporary. Hell liked its residents to experience every sensation to the fullest, like that Britney Spears song playing incessantly at full volume for a week. He'd never get that insipid tune out of his mind.

Benet had been blown flat, and no one was disposed to help him up.

Captain McCarthy took over, with his helmet off, slicking his hair.

"We are here to provide the damned with the benefits of modern legal judgment and, I hope, to promote the American way of life. I—"

"Shut it, Taildragger Joe, America ain't no part of perdition," someone shouted.

McCarthy spun, snarled, seemed to realize there was nothing he could do about it, and gritted his teeth. His speech shifted to practical matters.

"Before we start, let's find a building and organize our files. Thurmond, go ahead, please."

Catcalls went up throughout, though they'd all known this was coming.

The crusty old sergeant bounded away with two flankers. It was hard not to respect Strom Thurmond, even if he was a stubborn old womanizer. The man had volunteered for the Airborne in WWII while in his forties, then served in the U.S. Senate until he was over a hundred.

Roger grabbed his ruck, gingerly easing it on his blistered and battered shoulders. He found his pogo stick (sadly still functional) and joined the rest of the CLAP bouncing into town. His slung rifle banged his shoulder and head with every leap, until he was in a murderous rage.

Up ahead, Sergeant Thurmond had picked a convenient building from several still standing. It was of low, thick brick, on the near edge of this once-sprawling hive of scum and villainy. Once within a hundred yards of it, Roger gave up bouncing. Holding the stick over his shoulder like a ladder, he sprinted for the designated headquarters through the jolts of pain. He tumbled through the doorway in a tangle with Horace and McCarthy, who never waited to be last.

Benet, the jackass, was at least was man enough to wait outside until they entered, counting them. His bushy beard fluffed with every word.

The bombardment and confusion seemed to have given them a hiatus. Troopers stood watch at the high windows. Medics treated casualties.

Roger waved one nurse away: he didn't need a clumsy lawyer-medic looking at his knee. The knee was intact; little would improve it; and, with no anesthetic, treatment would be agonizing.

Speaking of which, Henry Summers looked pretty bad. Half his face had been shot off. Now the remaining face was healing, crushed and twisted, with a drooling smile that exposed broken rear molars on the right side. Missing teeth and crushed bone made his jaw asymmetrical. Added to the wrinkled ruins of his leg and torso, Henry's situation was nightmarish.

Henry would adapt to it. Roger would get used to it. Eventually. But not quite yet. Roger dropped his eyes and busied himself with his gear.

Everyone was preparing for the next phase of their mission. They carried the necessary legal codes with them, in those brutal ALICE packs. Roger reached for his, safe in a lockbox with sharp corners, then bound in an accordion file, sealed with a Perdition Seal that whoofed into flames when he released it so he could access the several binders within. The acrid smoke from the seals was something he was used to. He wondered if that would change shortly.

Each of them carried two hundred pounds of documentation. All documents must be accounted for, because those were their only references: the infernalnet was, of course, unreliable, even if they could get signal out here. Pages were always out of order. Any file might contain any page, in different fonts and spacing, so it was hard to tell which followed which. It was an administrative nightmare.

Right then, McCarthy screamed like a girl, and kept screaming.

"Nooooo! Eeeaaaaeeiii!"

They all stared at him. Had McCarthy melted down again? On McCarthy's pants were telltale stains of wetness at the crotch. Wonderful.

"Sir?" someone asked. "Captain?"

McCarthy hummed or cursed to himself and nobody else spoke or moved for far too long.

Finally, Benet stepped over and lifted the cover letter from the dirt floor of the makeshift headquarters. Smoothing out the wrinkles caused by McCarthy clutching it like a doll, Benet read aloud:

"The operative legal code of the day is that of the USSR, nineteen sixty-five."

McCarthy was curled on the ground, whimpering, "Commies . . . commies . . . commies . . ."

While Benet alternated between cajoling and kicking the worthless old radical, Roger sorted his papers, leaving appropriate gaps where pages were missing.

Crooked-legged Horace and Rehnquist, the CLAP's paralegal, came around to sort, stack and box. Boxing was necessary to keep the papers in order, but the boxes were held together with duct tape that had degraded in this dusty, gritty hell of hells. Horace and Rehnquist did the best they could. Roger snuck his phone behind his raised knees. Perhaps there might be some brief infernalnet connectivity. Worth a shot. He slid out the keyboard and pulled up DisgraceBook, on the off chance of connecting.

He recognized no names. He had fifty invites for IQ tests, questionnaires, and suggestions of people to dis. He clicked on the first one of those.

The page came up on his screen, where a grizzled old man leapt naked out of a bathtub. The nude senior snagged an old Garand rifle from the corner, hurling enough invective to merit notice even in hell, and rasped, "Get off my page!"

Roger snapped the phone closed.

Quiet persisted until a relief platoon of infantry arrived to assist with insecurity. They remained outside for the most part. He avoided meeting them, but caught a glimpse of them when their lieutenant came in to talk to Benet.

Infantrymen spent the afterlife getting shot up. One—with dark, curly hair and a Greek accent—was horrifically scarred. Disfigurement was part of this hell. Roger wondered if he'd eventually end up like the Greek. He tried not to be disgusted by the poor guy and dreaded lunch.

As always this year, lunch was a stiff stick of jerky and a piece of dry bread. So was breakfast and dinner. He sighed as he chewed slowly, wondering when the menu would change, and to what. Last year they'd had only raw tuna, past its peak. One ate because nerves and habits compelled it—if you could. Some guys in hell had no stomachs; some had no anuses. Some starved to death, becoming more and more helpless and easy prey in the process. . . .

"Howard, wake up," someone snapped, too loud.

He jerked upright. He'd been napping against the wall, and now had a crick in his neck.

McCarthy glowered at him and moved on.

"Yes, sir," Roger said to his back.

Next to him, mashed-up Henry said, "Get ready." Roger knew what Henry meant. He turned away, trying not to look at Henry's twisted face. Poor bastard.

Get ready—to work. Hell might have too many lawyers, but none were in residence here. The locals wanted their grievances heard. The CLAP would hear every one, rendering injustice as best they could.

Horace limped outside on his bent leg, carrying a roster, so the locals could lodge their complaints and seek resolution.

The good part was that the shooting had stopped. The bad part was the cases ranged from sad to bizarre to disquieting.

McCarthy grabbed the first dozen and read them off. Then . . .

"Next we have a classless action lawsuit by the remaining eight lives of a hell-kitten for attempted genocide of mice; suit brought by the tabby hell-kitten (striped wings and all) called Lucky, who wanted to grow up; with a countersuit by a certain desert hell-fox, who determined that life number three was the tastiest and he had been unfairly deprived of it. Howard, can you handle this?"

"Yes, sir. I can." You knew you were in hell when you were a lawyer defending talking animals with manners no better than drunks. "Yes, sir."

McCarthy read on: "A Mohammed (. . . why is every third male in hell named Mohammed? . . .) alleges that a prostitute did not give him, and I quote, 'a poetically succulent release,' and did give him several nasty diseases. She says because in hell orgasm . . ." McCarthy hesitated over the word, ". . . is commonly unattainable, and the diseases were the weekly special, she's innocent: she only provides a service. Benedict?"

"I can do that, sir."

"A certain former presidential candidate, Democratic (presumably a Communist), insists an election wasn't run fairly. Regulations say that elections in hell are supposed to be unfair. I'll take that one."

Roger felt sorry for everyone in that case. McCarthy would rant.

Benet said, "And here're our primary mission orders."

You could hear a feather drop as he ripped open the package. These were never good. A flash and a strong whiff of sulfur attested to its authenticity.

Benet scanned them, sighed in relief, and read aloud: "We are to bring back the head of the most honest man in hell for deposition."

"It's a trap!" McCarthy scoffed. "An honest man in hell?"

Roger muttered, "*Certainly neither of you.*" Nor himself, but he was honest enough to admit it.

Horace said, "Evil and honesty don't have to go together. The only hurt I caused was some fractional percentage of shortage to the IRS. It benefited my clients. I was not very evil in that context, but I was certainly dishonest."

McCarthy asked, fairly lucidly, "Who are we going to find here who's evil but honest? Peter the Great? Julius Caesar? Those Greeks from that famous battle?"

Horace said, "I can get on the infernalnet and see who's here."

"Do that. You young kids know how that stuff works."

"Yes, sir," Horace agreed, though he was fifty at time of death. "Young" in this case meant "more current."

The next morning, in a red-painted mudbrick hall, domed and spired, Roger conducted his trial as barrister for the tabby hell-kitten named Lucky, using the legal code of the UK, 1923, complete to powdered wig. Standard procedure, most days, but today the minor demon serving as judge was glorying in his role.

"Your Dishonor, we—" Zap! Lightning singed Roger's butt. "Your Dishonor, we object—" Zap! Zap! "My Lord Judge, we propose—" Zap! Zap! Zap!

At noon, the code switched to that of King Kamehameha of Hawaii. Roger steeled himself for horrors to come. The Hawaiian death penalty was even more terrifying when you knew you couldn't die permanently from it.

Mercifully, he was able to argue the winged hell-kitten's case well enough for it to be dismissed before the Kamehameha rules kicked in. He doubted that poor little Lucky would really enjoy his victory, since after his eight more legally-mandated lives were lived, the hell-kitten faced innumerable lives with no legal protections: the restraining order against the hell-fox would lapse.

That evening, back in the CLAP's compound, now wired and sandbagged, they chewed their jerky and discussed their mission.

Benet said, "Satan wants the head of the most honest man in hell. By specifying head, should I assume he wants it *sans* body?"

"I believe we must, son," Sergeant Thurmond drawled in his scratchy voice; ancient skin wrinkled around his beady eyes. "I always take His Satanic Majesty at His word."

"The next question is: who's the most honest man in hell? Accepting that 'good,' 'honest' and even 'kind' don't necessarily overlap, who would meet the criterion of 'honest'?"

Roger thought about that. Nearly every damned soul in hell thought he was doomed unjustly to eternal torment; they sinned and died and sinned more and died again; the damned dead never learned; new sinners arrived constantly. Everybody in hell lied constantly, if only to himself. So could there even be a soul in this area of hell who was honest?

Horace said, "I have it: Ghandi."

Roger tried to smile but smirked instead. "Gandhi. Of course."

McCarthy muttered, "That swarthy little Communist bastard."

Roger didn't think Gandhi qualified as communist. The father of nonviolence as a political strategy, yes. Liberal, certainly. Pacifist, mostly. Of course, McCarthy accused everyone of being a communist.

Benet said, "I have only heard the name."

Roger said, "In India, Ghandi promoted passive disobedience against tyranny. He helped lead people to independence from the British. Nonviolent. Persuasive. Unassailably consistent in his beliefs."

Benet snorted, but said, "He certainly sounds promising. Where do we find him?"

Horace said, "I believe he's right downtown, protesting something."

Hardly surprising.

The day turned cold; its chill bit Roger's lungs. He wished for an overcoat. Benet had that wool uniform, which must be horrible in the heat—certainly it smelled that way—but would be wonderful now.

They met no resistance on their way "downtown." Factions abounded in Kabum; after their landing the day before, they were just one more clutch of damned souls from everywhere. Distant battles raged, as residents of hell fought over metaphors or territory or eye-color or infernal affiliation: men made hell familiar, and war was familiar to every soul from every era.

They walked downtown. Roger preferred the blisters from his boots to yesterday's parachuting and pogo-sticking. Streets here were convoluted and narrow, and of course their maps were wrong. So they walked in the general direction of downtown, among mudbrick facades and teetering high rises with blown-out glass, guided by eye and ear and instinct to where the damned were congregating.

They found an open plaza surrounding a parliament building: in it was a flagpole; on the pole flapped a tattered flag showing a black devil dancing on a red mountaintop: the symbol of Ashcanistan.

Only the flag was familiar. Roger wasn't familiar with Kabum. They'd not been briefed for this foray. On the whole, the town felt ancient, but then there were the gutted Soviet-style high-rises with shacks between them . . . stupidity from every age, chockablock on the streets.

A protest was ongoing, involving thousands upon thousands, old and new, in the costumes of human history. The CLAP went unremarked and unchallenged, despite weapons, as they patrolled the perimeter looking for their witness: nonviolent demonstration or not, sarrisophori and demons and bedawi and ifrits and kaffirs and modern soldiers prowled among the throng: helmets with horsehair crests and metal wings and slitted visors and horns and feathers and spikes and chinstraps and faceshields and MOPP masks turned to them and away again. Kindred souls.

"I see him," McCarthy said. "At the base of the steps. A scrawny little weasel, sanctimonious in his cowardice."

Ghandi was wearing homespun, despite the day's chill. Roger recognized some people around him as dedicated disciples. He couldn't name them, but he recalled faces from famous photos. Ahead, people squeezed toward demon guards. Closer to Gandhi, his followers were organized in ranks, climbing low stairs in formation.

"Very much like communists," McCarthy commented.

"Or soldiers," Roger threw out. McCarthy's paranoia and obsession irritated him more as time went on. He felt some sympathy for Benet, who at least acted like a leader, if misguided. McCarthy was just a narcissistic jerk.

As marchers reached the top, demons on risers flanking the podium held up pokers that flashed into orange heat, and stabbed the leading wave of demonstrators. Screaming, the damned protesters thrashed and rolled down the steps. Some got to their feet and stumbled toward the rear of the line, to repeat the process. Others crawled away.

"What the hell is this?" Benet asked.

"It's called 'passive resistance.' They seek to overwhelm the demons without fighting."

"Does that work?"

"Only against a civilized enemy."

"Isn't it rather ridiculous? You think he'd learn."

So are single-shot rifles against repeaters, you jackass. "It did work against the British in India. His proposal to use it against the Nazis was never tested."

Benet said, "So I suspect. Well, let's see if he's our man." He hooked his scabbard onto his belt and advanced.

Sobs from the nonviolent seared by pokers were strangely disturbing. The fried bologna smell of scorched flesh didn't improve Roger's mindset.

McCarthy said, "Roger, you seem to know something about this man. Introduce us, please."

"Yes, sir." Probably a good idea. Benet knew nothing about Ghandi or his time. McCarthy had the manners of a pig. Even a simple, reasonable request came out of McCarthy's mouth sounding pompous.

Surprised by his own calm, Roger led the way, politely stepping in front of Benet. He hadn't yet died in hell, though he'd suffered numerous indignities. He sighed. There was going to be a first time. Maybe today.

Nothing untoward happened, though, as Roger stolidly led the party from the CLAP forward, edging the through the edges of the throng.

"Mr. Ghandi," Roger said, "Or do you prefer *Bapu*?"

Little Ghandi was all cheerful smiles. His cohorts stood nearby but made no move to interfere.

"I answer to either. How may I help you?"

Ghandi, in the midst of this mayhem, seemed so

confident. Roger could smell roasted flesh, hear the wails, and yet the leader seemed undisturbed.

Benet asked, "Mister Ghandi, sir, is the mob going to be a problem?" The CLAP moved in, creating a wall between their target and the *danse noir* on the steps.

"The 'mob'?" Gandhi asked, still smiling. "Right must battle might, or lose all legitimacy. They are but supplicants for decency, presenting a rational request to the demons. This 'mob' is not a problem, though certainly the demons may decide to make them such, for their own purposes."

Roger said, "Well then, sir, we were sent to bring you."

"'Sent'? 'Ordered'? You do not yourselves choose to come for me?" He smiled knowingly, and Roger understood it was an attempt at debate. Among doomed screams and demonic violence, this tableau was bizarre, even for hell.

Benet looked confused and annoyed. McCarthy looked apoplectic.

Roger stifled a grin. That sight was worth enjoying. Pleasure in hell was hard to find.

Benet faced the little Indian and said, "We must bring you with us, or face pain and suffering. I personally try to avoid pain and suffering." Benet must think Gandhi didn't understand.

Gandhi said, "You could choose to endure it, however. You could choose not to participate in hell's charade. New Hell, they call this place, but nothing is new here." He waved around, indicating the marching masochists, the observers, the demons. "If people refuse to take part in Satan's games—that would be new. If all do that, the devil, by any name, becomes powerless."

That was incorrect, but inspiring. Torment didn't require assent on the part of the tormented: you liked it, you didn't; you ran, or you fought. It didn't matter either way: this wasn't a world to win by intimidation and press manipulation, by inspiration or steadfastness. Right and wrong were meaningless here.

So Ghandi didn't get it. He was doing in afterlife what had worked for him in life, like so many others. Kabum was a part of the greater underworld, in all its manifest complexity. No debater's trick or fillip of law could change that. Roger admired Ghandi, the way you'd admire a diorama. It took exceptional strength of character to behave this way in hell. Or sheer insanity. Impressive, either way.

McCarthy muttered, "Goddam commie."

Ghandi heard McCarthy, turned and responded. "Indeed not. I am not a communist, nor a capitalist, a monarchist, nor any other type of categorized statist. I am myself, and only myself. You serve another, by choice. I serve myself," he nodded, "by choice."

Realizing that Benet was confused and McCarthy about to burst a blood vessel, which in hell meant literally and messily, Roger stepped in.

"Bapu Ghandi, we have been asked to find the most honest man in hell. Your name was mentioned, and I took the liberty of presuming you might be he."

Ghandi laughed in a low resonant tenor, head back and cotton robe shifting as he raised his arms.

"Oh, young man, I can make no such claim."

Modesty, but perhaps false. All men lie. Even in hell.

"No?"

The wizened elf sighed and smiled and said, "I was once a lawyer. I lusted and lied to protect a lustful dalliance." He shook his head. "I manipulated truth for effect, for my nation. I made statements deemed racist. I do not regret any of it, even now, but I am here because I was not as honest as I was effective. And I am in New Hell, subject to Satan's will, when Naraka is in the place of torment, or proper hell, for Islamists and Hindus and Sikhs and Jains and Buddhists—Yama should be my judge, not this Father of Lies who rules in New Hell. The underworld's mistake, or my own? No matter. Here I am, among the other New Dead, liar that I am, opportunist that I am, with the flock that died believing my lies all around me." He raised an arm to indicate the moaning protesters again.

He'd stopped smiling, at last.

McCarthy asked, "Who then?"

The little man shrugged his skinny shoulders. "The princess in the minefield would be a good bet. If one wanted to bet in hell. What is there to lose?" He smiled again.

"Very well. However, we must bring you along as well, just in case."

"With respect, I refuse to comply."

McCarthy shrugged and grinned. Benet drew his saber and swung smoothly. He'd had much time to practice his technique here.

The anti-communist crusader looked down at the bruised face rolling on the ground, and said, "I should think it was obvious, and now demonstrated, what one could lose." He wore a shit-eating grin. God, Satan, whoever you wanted to invoke, what an asshole.

Ghandi smiled wanly at them, as his body vomited blood and collapsed next to his head. His eyes tracked it, and looked calm and resigned as he was was stuffed into the sack Thurmond had in his hand.

Roger felt nauseated. McCarthy had enjoyed that.

They all stared around them at Ghandi's followers, who stared back. They weren't supposed to use violence. Roger didn't trust that, in hell, armed with a slung single shot rifle, even if he had a long bayonet at his side.

Ghandi's assistant shrugged in a broad gesture and said, "Bapu will come back to us in time. We shall continue our sagratyha." He turned and walked up the steps, heedless of the writhing wounded around him. The others followed.

Benet said, "So we proceed to the minefields."

The princess in the minefields was easy to find. South of town was a large, vacant area, with craters and pocks. They pogoed past animals and pieces of them that lay scattered, crusted and fly-encrusted. Roger wondered what they'd done to deserve this fate.

Ahead, a figure in khakis with a tool belt became visible through the dusty haze. He could tell she was female, but only from the gait, despite a bad limp. She had a metal detector, chemical sniffers, a toolbelt and a shovel.

They dismounted, stacked arms—well, sticks—and approached carefully, following the existing holes and paths. They stepped over a bactrian's corpse, which squished and slid, the skin loose from the meat beneath. He winced.

She'd clearly been pretty at some point. Now, though, she had divots from her flesh, joints that had healed in lumps, lacerations and generally looked as if she'd been run over, repeatedly.

Her joints were a moment of clarity for Roger. The human body was intelligently designed, if the purpose of the design was to enable easily inflicting maximum pain and damage.

Behind and to the right, there was a muffled blast that threw a shifting shadow. Roger turned cautiously, to see someone flail in midair and die. He turned back and ignored it. It was hard not to be fatalistic in hell.

The woman stood waiting, offering nothing.

As they got close enough not to shout, Benet asked, "What are you doing, ma'am?"

"I should hope it was obvious I'm clearing mines." She sounded amused, sad, bored and annoyed.

"That could take forever."

She shrugged elegantly. "I appear to have the time."

Benet said, "Mr. Ghandi suggested we talk to you. We are seeking an honest man."

She smiled faintly. "You may be out of luck. I am not a man."

"But are you honest?"

"That's the question, isn't it? Why would a princess and victim of a tragedy be in the depths of hell pursuing her hobby in this fashion?" She gestured at the surrounding craterscape.

Roger said, "That's certainly a legal question. One we'd pursue if we had time."

"Ah, yes. The lawyers. I've heard of you," she said.

Roger offered, "Likely nothing good and likely all true."

"Yes, that would be the case here. Why would you think

I am honest? I had a very ugly, very public divorce with all kinds of audio recordings and publicity. Then a terrible accident involving alcohol."

"No conspiracy?" he asked, ashamed but curious.

She looked disgusted. "Only from the media, to make as much money from me any way possible. You might check with the famous mister Cronkite. He's here, and surprisingly candid. I wish I'd encountered more of his type of press."

Benet said, "Unfortunately, this is not a trial, nor an inquest. We're to take you back to the Pentagram, so you can be deposed there."

"How amusing," she said. "I never sat as queen, and yet I am to be deposed. I suppose you'd best take me, then."

"It's not you we are to take exactly, ma'am," Roger felt compelled to say.

"Oh?" she asked, turning to face him, and he felt disgusted by his role in this.

Benet made it one motion draw and slice, and her once-pretty face acquired a new set of injuries as it smashed nose first into the ground.

Thurmond scooped up her head, gently. She was crying, lips trembling, as he swept off debris and placed her in the sack.

"That's a shame," he muttered. "She was as sweet as she was pretty. I can't think of anything ill to say about her."

He'd lived longer than she had, and apparently had respect for her.

McCarthy asked, "Who was she, anyway?"

He really wouldn't know, Roger realized, and offered, "A tragic figure, just as she said. A lady and a princess."

McCarthy snorted. "I don't approve of royalty. Seems somewhat elitist."

"Indeed. Quite far from communism, though."

"Hmm. True."

Benet interrupted their musing. "Howard, get on that gadget of yours and find where this Bronchitis fellow is."

"Walter Cronkite. Famous reporter, and actually very well respected. I do think he's a good bet, sir."

"Well, get on with it." Benet fluffed his whiskers and pulled a handkerchief from his pocket.

For some reason, Roger had trouble manipulating his phone, with its intermittent connection, the shifting sunlight and a sack with a wiggling head in it nearby, as well as a staring, belligerent McCarthy and a confused, frustrated Benet cleaning his saber.

After a few minutes of swiping, typing and cursing, he had video. Cronkite looked good, as he had at his prime, which was about when Roger had been born.

"He's reporting live from the east side, where a battle is."

"Which battle?" McCarthy wanted to know. "A battle against commies?"

Roger calmly replied, "Who knows which battle? There are so many."

"Well, let's proceed. Back out the way we came, then a blister break."

Roger tried not to think about blisters. Blisters in hell were worse than blisters in life. They infected, oozed, scarred over. He could feel them blossoming inside his stiff leather wingtips, and along the edge of the upper. They'd pop and peel. You could ignore the burn, and the layers of skin coming off. The damage was something else.

You wanted to be first for treatment. Treatment hurt a lot, but was over quickly. The later patients got to anticipate the pain. Shrieks from each victim primed the next to expect agony. Benet always went last and, to his credit, never uttered a sound. That Fucking Benet had never commanded in battle, but he did have courage.

He was also stubborn, after a century and more, about those stupid single-shot rifles.

Roger wondered about Gandhi and his obsession with passive resistance and Benet with his single-shot rifles. Neither could help you in hell. So was hell meant to break the damned of their sinners' habits? Satan never offered explanations, never actually met with anyone—at least not to answer inconvenient questions. The CLAP handled petty cases to no useful end, for eternity; and with the endlessly shifting legal codes, botched most of them. Like that hell-kitten named Lucky.

When they stopped to lunch and to treat their feet, their shrieks and screams seemed to please the locals. Hawk-nosed men and gray-eyed women in indigo and bright scarves watched in delight as lawyers suffered.

When Roger's turn came, their company combat medic punctured Roger's festering sores and poured alcohol over them. Roger tried not to howl when the alcohol hit his liquefied flesh. He flushed and sweated; his brain spun; nausea washed over him like surf. Then he spun down a deep dark tunnel into unconsciousness.

In his nice, black comfy place, a shoe prodded him. "Howard, wake up."

He groaned, tried to rise and failed with the pack holding him back, rolled on sharp rocks and stood. His feet were numbed now, so he felt the pokes in knees and elbows all the more.

There were no showers or clean suits in hell, either, and his tie was too tight.

They bounced endlessly across the craterscape. The water in his canteen tasted like a combination of mud and urine. In coldest weather, they got moldy iced tea. In extreme heat, it was sometimes boiling Drownin' Donuts coffee with cloying sweet cream and sugar, offset with a dead mouse. He'd like water. Clean, clear water. Just once.

Without warning, sniper fire ripped from cover across the wasteland. Henry fell over, his shoulder blown apart. He uttered gurgling noises. Thurmond grabbed his shoulder and held it so it might heal reasonably straight. Three CLAPpers returned fire, and despite the single-shot nature of their rifles, the massive .45-70 rounds scared off the enemy.

They bivouacked under a shivery chill vault of sky, red like clotted blood with heaving violet and pink swirls. Not pretty like an aurora. Just disorienting and vomitous. He shivered miserably for hours on end, trying to recall black starry nights and crescent moons smiling at him.

The next morning they munched their rations and moved out. His feet were lumps of rancid meat in his shoes at this point, and his knee had stopped hurting, and stopped bending. The pogo stick caused the joint to smash with every bounce.

Far ahead, though, was a defensive line of rocks, sandbags, mortars, machine guns and other weapons, and thousands of Ashcan troops trying to protect their little piece of hell from an onslaught of Chinese and Zulu and punk kids.

"Damned commies!" McCarthy muttered deliberately loudly. "If we can find something to charge them with, I'll haul them in for hearings."

Roger really wished McCarthy would forget communism. Even communists were victims in hell. The past of a sinner paled before his netherworldly sins. The damned butchered hapless victims because they could. Because they always had. Because they always would.

Roger had never been a hero. He'd been too clever by half for that. But in hell, if could find some heroic path, he'd take it. If it could get him out of hell. But then, heroism wasn't about premeditation. Holding "hearings" of alleged communists was about premeditation.

Ahead, though, was a small civilian pickup truck bristling with gear. As they got closer, Roger identified its satellite dish and antennae. They dismounted and proceed on foot, pogo sticks under their arms. It felt strange to walk—well, limp—and to see a stationary horizon. What twist of physics let them pogo so well, without falling and exacerbating injuries more? Or was it just personalized torture for men who'd enjoyed limousines and first-class travel?

A short distance away, one man stood in front of a camera, a pop-filtered microphone trained on him, pointing to the outgoing fire. It was definitely Cronkite: handsome and dignified. He seemed in fine shape.

Then when he turned, Roger realized that Cronkite was shot to hell. His camera-loving face was perfect, unmarred. Battlefield butchery covered his body. Par for the course in

Ashcanistan, but anywhere else in hell he'd be dead and recycled by now.

Cronkite's voice was deep, resonant, familiar: "Greetings, gentlemen. Are you here with the Forces Unified for Central Kabum Emergency Resistance . . . ?"

Cronkite's next words were partly drowned out by mortar fire, and the basso whoosh of a round incoming.

Roger ducked. The round landed far behind them. He stood up, and realized no one else had twitched.

Benet nudged him. He said, "No, sir, we're lawyers."

"Ah, yes. The lawyers. The CLAP. I've heard of you. You are almost as popular as I, myself." Cronkite smiled slightly.

McCarthy stared at Cronkite wordlessly.

"You are *the* Walter Cronkite?"

"I was, yes. What I am now, I'm not sure. But that's how I think of myself."

"I'm Roger Howard, sir. I remember watching you while I was growing up."

Cronkite said, "You're making me feel old."

"Sorry, sir."

"No apologies necessary. I assume, though, that this is a professional visit? Am I being sued again? That happens more here than it ever did in life."

"No, that's not why we're here. We're here to—"

McCarthy finally said, "Cronkite . . . weren't you the understudy of Murrow?"

"I was," Cronkite nodded. "I recognize you, sir."

Roger noticed Cronkite hadn't offered McCarthy a greeting. McCarthy was still staring, too. It was creepy.

McCarthy said, "Polls said you were the most trusted man on television, Cronkite."

"I was called that. I certainly tried to be."

"So tell me the truth, now that it doesn't matter. Was Murrow a communist? A sympathizer?"

Cronkite rolled his eyes and feigned surprise: he must have heard the slur in life.

"Murrow? Not to my knowledge, no."

McCarthy shifted uncomfortably.

"You're certain?"

"Quite certain. Is this something that still matters to you, here?" Cronkite used his hand to indicate the area around them. Cronkite didn't even wince in pain until after he lowered his injured hand.

Roger could see McCarthy considering Cronkite's question. If Cronkite was honest, Cronkite's expression of certainty was genuine. If not, then Cronkite wasn't the soul they wanted. But McCarthy obviously hoped to harm Cronkite.

What a struggle must be ongoing inside McCarthy's twisted mind, between duty and vendetta.

McCarthy, you're an idiot, Roger thought.

"Are you the most trusted man in hell?" McCarthy pressed.

"I would hope not."

"In life, on television. But not in hell, on hellovision?"

Cronkite smiled sadly. "Television in life was a lie; hellovision in afterlife is the same. I condensed the events of each day in the world to a small nugget of glossed-over facts, presented for the layman. Usually the subjects I explained were beyond my own knowledge, yet I was expected to report and comment on them. I tried to be fair, but I did have opinions."

"You sound like you might be our man," McCarthy said slyly.

"You are seeking the most trusted man in hell?"

"The most honest," Roger clarified. "To depose for a trial at the Pentagram."

"I see." Cronkite sounded dismissive. "Well, I'm afraid I must decline the honor. I certainly can't claim to be the most honest man in all the hells." He turned toward his camera crew, as if the discussion was now closed.

Benet asked, "Do you know who would be, Mr. Cronkite?"

"Who would be?" Cronkite turned back to them. "No. However, in my own limited experience of the afterlife, I'd recommend Mathew Brady."

Roger had no idea who Mathew Brady might be.

Benet looked as if he'd been shot.

"The Civil War photographer? Lincoln's portraitist?"

Cronkite said, "Yes, that is he."

Roger asked, "Do you know where this Brady is?"

Cronkite pointed to the north.

"When last I spoke to him, he was just over that rise, capturing images of the aftermath of the battle between the Taliban and the Taliwhackers."

Benet nodded. "Thank you. Unfortunately, we'll still have to take you with us."

"Oh? Very well," Cronkite said, seeming rather relaxed as he motioned his crew to take a break. Roger looked at Benet and at McCarthy, and back at Thurmond and crooked-legged Summers and smash-faced Horace and the rest of the CLAP. With the camera crew right there, there was no way to take this head clandestinely.

Roger realized no one else was going to come out and say it. Sighing, he said to Cronkite, "Sir, we are supposed to bring Satan your head."

"Well," Cronkite said, deadpan, motioning his camera crew to start rolling: "That's the way it is, this day in hell."

He stared unmoving, eyes locked with Roger, as Benet's saber sliced through his neck.

McCarthy stepped back as blood spurted and the head of Cronkite bounced and rolled at their feet: "I *still* think Murrow was a Commie. Cronkite may have been smart. That doesn't mean he was informed."

McCarthy had no decency in life or afterlife, in Roger's opinion.

Thurmond had the head in the bag, and he spoke. "I found Cronkite a gentleman," he said in his scratchy Southern drawl. "He was fair, respectful. He talked to the person, not just the politician. I had good friends on both sides of the aisle, and we all respected him."

McCarthy snorted.

"So long as we have him. I'll find Murrow sometime, too. I know you never believed me, Strom, but you were a Dem yourself at the time, hugging those union cretins. You never saw the bureaucratic communistic Frankenstein that was there." McCarthy's voice trembled; he was excited.

Tiredly, Thurmond said, "You convinced people at first, Joseph. But in the end, no one saw what you saw. Either you were alone in your genius, or mistaken." Thurmond headed back to his stick.

Roger said, "Sirs, we need to move on," ducking his head and turning his back on McCarthy while, inside, he seethed.

Amid sporadic outgoing and incoming fire, they made their way across a rocky hillside. No bullets came their way. To the north, Taliban shot into the town. To the south, the Taliwhackers, Cronkite had called them, returned fire but aimed poorly. Other rebel groups fought the Chinese, the Zulus, the Mughals, and Satan only knew who else. Apart from the racket, travel was reasonably safe.

They made it over the next ridge, on foot again. Some distance down-slope, there was an American tent, Civil War vintage; farther away were encampments of other civil warriors: English, Irish, Russian, and Mexican.

They spotted Brady, all alone outside the American tent.

Benet said, "That's odd. During the War, Brady sent teams of photographers out, while he stayed in New York. Each team was three to five. It does appear Brady's by himself."

Brady was handsome. His bushy hair and Van Dyke beard framed an aristocratic face. He didn't seem to be wounded or disfigured.

Roger thought the large bellows camera mounted on a sturdy wooden tripod delightful. He imagined, though, that trying to photograph hell with it was eternal torture.

Here and there in the camp were other tripods and cameras, a tent with folding wooden doors that was probably a darkroom, a supply-wagon overflowing with boxes.

Benet stalked over to the photographer. Roger stumped along behind him.

"Mister Brady?" Benet asked.

Brady squinted, pulled his glasses back and forth a bit to adjust focus, then stared.

"General Benet, isn't it?"

"Indeed I am, sir." Benet bowed fractionally, and extended a hand.

Brady shook it and said, "You seem a bit older than I recall. I met you as a colonel. I'm glad you had a long life."

"I was sorry to hear of your passing, even though it came after my own," Benet replied.

Brady's face drooped slightly.

"I'd hoped afterlife would be better than life. Instead, it seems perpetually to show me the worst of existence. I suppose that is punishment for my photographs."

Benet said, "It may be. Though you always showed things honestly."

Brady's Van Dyke trembled.

"That I did, or tried to. War needs no exaggeration. Nor, I found, does everyday torment."

Benet said, "So it seems. For your candor, sir, we must take you to Satan himself to be deposed."

"Deposed?"

"This is the Coordinating Legal Airborne Platoon, Mr. Brady," McCarthy interrupted, puffing himself up.

"Ah," Brady said. "Yes, there are jokes one could make, but it's hardly worth doing so, is it?"

Benet nodded, without rancor or humor. "You *do* speak the truth, Mr. Brady."

"So you need me to accompany you?"

Benet said, "Actually, sir, I will be forthright with you, as a peer. We need only your head."

Brady slumped and sighed. He looked from Benet to Roger to Thurmond, to the rest of CLAP.

"May I make a final request, then? Final for now, I suppose."

"What is that?" Benet asked.

"Would someone capture a photograph of this event? Before I go? It can be delivered with the others." He indicated the leather box, with a large label gummed to it.

Benet said, "I can work the camera. I am familiar with the type. Mr. Howard, will you take my sword?"

There was nothing Roger wanted less than to take Benet's sword in hand. Death might not be permanent, but suffering was always remembered. Brady's head would be turned over to higher authorities, perhaps to Satan himself. Roger looked around, hoping one of his colleagues would volunteer to do the deed. All the CLAP knew what Roger wanted. Everyone looked at their feet.

"I regret this," he said. "But I will do it."

There was no way to fight the inevitable. Brady led Benet to the tent. Roger followed slowly.

"Let me prepare the plate and set the equipment," Brady said wistfully.

The two disappeared inside the tent, leaving Roger alone outside. In tight quarters, the two bumped canvas now and again.

Behind Roger, McCarthy came up.

"Are we ready, then?"

"Yes, sir," Roger agreed. "General Benet will take a photo of the scene as Brady's last request."

"What the hell's the point of that? Really. This is hell, if no one has noticed. It won't go anywhere, accomplish anything . . . "

"I suppose a paper somewhere might print it, sir," Roger said.

"If anyone remembers who this man is. And he'll be

back, soon enough. I live for the day when I get to meet Karl Marx face to face."

"I'm sure you do, sir." He leaned onto his good leg to ease the ache.

"What is that supposed to mean? I've been watching you for some time, Howard. Didn't you go to some fruity liberal school back east?"

"Harvard, sir."

"Harvard. A stronghold of communist ideology in the decades following my death, I understand."

"Certain professors, yes, sir."

"I never did trust that type. Nor artists. This fellow," he nodded his head toward the tent, "is one like that. Always wants to show the pathos, the tragedy, the art of misery. Next thing you know, people think the aggressor is some kind of tragic hero. Who was that little commie after I died? Made into some kind of tee-shirt icon for hippies and lowlifes?"

"Che Guevara?" Roger guessed.

"That's him."

McCarthy finally shut up as Benet and Brady brushed the canvas aside and came out of the tent. Brady took a deep breath and shivered slightly. Benet placed a comforting hand on Brady's shoulder. With the other, he drew his long, curved saber.

Roger awkwardly accepted the heavy blade from Benet; he had little experience handling real swords, and a gimp leg. That was a problem.

"Mr. Brady, I am ashamed," he said, and hesitated. "I must ask you to kneel."

Brady's eyes dampened, as he lowered himself to his knees with dignity, and bent forward.

Benet was at the camera, under the hood, fiddling.

Roger asked, "Sir, are you ready?"

"Almost. This is not quite what I trained with. However, I have focus, I think. And flash powder."

He fumbled with the glass plate, reached back under the hood, and slid stuff around. He poured a measure of powder over what looked like a long match, and held it aloft.

"You may proceed."

Brady shut his eyes and started praying. "Our Father, who art in heaven . . ."

It was both touching and ridiculous. It could do no good here.

Tears filled Roger's eyes.

Brady stopped praying when McCarthy made dismissive noises: "Great act."

Roger raised the sword. Its edge was keen. He must ensure his swing was straight. If he let his arm drop, then snapped his wrist, the blade should cut cleanly through Brady's neck.

Benet pulled the lens cap, then tugged the string that ignited the powder. The flash lit the lurid landscape, and the stench of sulfur filled the air, so familiar here.

Roger dropped his arm convulsively, making sure to keep his eyes open, and snapped his wrist.

The saber cut between the skull and the protruding vertebra at the shoulders, shearing through cleanly, and struck the rock underneath.

McCarthy snapped, "Goddam it, Howard, don't knick his sword."

Staring at the crimson fountain splashing out of Brady's neck, Roger decided he'd had enough.

He'd accept a court-martial. First, he had to earn one.

Roger turned and thrust, as he'd learned in fencing class at Harvard, long ago. The saber didn't respond like a foil, but with no opposing blade it worked well enough.

The way the smug little McCarthy grunted and convulsed as the saber pierced his guts was most satisfying. A half turn to the right caused McCarthy's eyes to bug out, and dropped the little commie-hunter to his knees.

Seeing McCarthy kneeling there was too good an opportunity to resist; it made any pending punishment worth it.

He withdrew smoothly, raised the saber, and swung a second time.

McCarthy's head tumbled onto the rocks. Roger stepped back to await further hellish torment.

Instead, Benet said, "Brilliant, Mr. Howard. What could be more honest than monomaniacal purpose? But please do me one favor."

Roger's brain spun as he tried to parse the unexpected praise. "Yes, sir?"

"Please clean my sword. Thoroughly."

A Hard Day At The Office

Once you start thinking about Hell, there's no end to the characters and torment you can arrange. This time, I picked a character I liked, and let that inspire me to create a persona. The actual Peter Hathaway Capstick was a fine writer, and I highly recommend his books.

★★★

AFRICA AT NIGHT is awesome and vital. The cloying, damp heat with scents of rot, of animal and growth punching the nose. The discordant symphony of beasts, from crickets to lustful frogs to the warning growl of leopards on the prowl. Nowhere on earth can offer the immersion of sensation one finds in the Limpopo, Okavango, Serengeti or Kalahari. They're all different and unique, constantly changing and fresh, and all part of the greatness known as Africa.

Hellfrica, on the other hand, is everything Africa is, and less.

It is just as vital. The scents are better described as stenches. The animals sound desolate, effete and bored. The heat . . .

Ah, yes, trust the Prince of Lies to make Hellfrica cold. Not all the time, of course. Hot and cold fight each other for supremacy, below the boiling sun and the scimitar curve of the moon, or at least it appears that way. What beauty Hellfrica has is illusionary. Hellish beasts aren't concerned. Damned souls suffer, but never too much. Always does it change and irritate. The tsetse flies leave welts the size of a fist.

I grew up hunting in rural New Jersey, when it was rural. A stint as a stockbroker bored me, and I turned back to hunting. Once bitten by the Africa bug, I'd never left. I had been a game officer, writer, and professional hunter, and I still was, sort of. At least I wasn't Bowlegged Bwana, the taxidermist. In life, he'd mounted animals. . . .

My client this day, at least, was worthy—or was once. I can easily understand how I made this descent, with liquor and hunting and overblown stories. "Nonfiction," the spines said. Nonfiction they were. Dramatic elaboration, however, is apparently a sin. Or it might have had something to do with that bar bet in Nairobi...

Mr. Roosevelt, of course, had done any number of things worthy of hell, politics among them. He'd also kept his Earthly persona in hell, and was still grounded in the early twentieth century, as I'm grounded in the latter half.

Given my druthers, I'd carry a good double rifle in .470 Nitro Express. I'd be perfectly comfortable with a bolt action .416 (any hellish knockoff of a Remington or Rigby), a .458 Sinchester Magnum, or even the venerable .375

Helland and Helland. What I had, though, changed randomly in the morning. Some mornings I'd awake with a .22 and wish fervently the client could shoot. I remain allergic, even after death, to being kneaded by a Jumbo's barstool-sized legs. One morning a few days ago, a .729 Redneck dislocated my shoulder. Once it had been a crossbow. I hesitate to mention a slingshot. I'm sure that's waiting.

Today I had a very marginal Lee-Enfield SMLE in .303 British. Teddy, God . . . well, somebody . . . bless him, had a late 1800s double gun in 8 gauge, the bores of which were rifled deeply enough to resemble transmission shaft splines. The cartridges within compared respectably to the largest cigars to come out of Cuba.

I just hoped it was enough for hellephant.

We crawled through crud. It would be hard to improve on the nastiness of the African swamps, and they hadn't, as far as terrain. There was a croc here somewhere, though, and those damned baboons that fought with sticks and branches chewed into spears. Every beast of my past jockeyed for a bite of my favorite hide.

Close alongside me, Teddy reeked. On Earth, he'd been a teetotaler most of his life, guzzling coffee the way a 1960s muscle-car guzzled gasoline. I could smell the coffee. I could also smell the gin, or what passed for gin in hell. Added to his sweat and mine, it was a piquant vapor to churn one's guts. I'd never been a gin drinker. I'd gladly be so now, if I could tolerate drink in hell.

"Well, Cappy Pete, I see we have sign." Teddy Roosevelt was a good tracker, but in this case it was easy. The hellephant had left a trail about like that of a motor home, with grass and small trees crushed and bent. We'd have to walk through a tangle atop the muck.

"Hopefully he's right ahead. Are you in good shape to shoot that cannon, Teddy?"

"Right as rain," he slurred as he staggered. "Point me at our worthy trophy." The muzzles swung dangerously past my face, looking like two bores of the Lincoln Tunnel.

Then I heard a rumbling rustle to our left. I swung that way and something about the way the grass moved clued me in. I shifted my aim down, fingered the trigger, and as soon as I saw that triangular mark of death, I shot, cycled and shot again. I only had seven rounds in the Smelly, but crocoviles are no easier to kill than their earthly counterparts.

I was blown off my feet, deafened and blinded: Teddy had cut loose with the shoulder cannon. Nausea gripped me, and I tumbled, got a knee beneath myself and gingerly rose up just as he snapped open the breech, the empty brass arcing over his shoulder with a *POUNK* while the sulfurous smoke wafted past to worsen my plight.

"We got him, Cappy Pete!" Teddy announced. I hate being called that. It makes me sound like a comic strip character. My surname is Capstick. It's a minor irritation, but of course, I am powerless to change it.

Looking down, I saw we had indeed got the reptile. My two bullets had removed most of its brain pan. Teddy's artillery shell had almost severed its neck. "A fine pair of boots and a nice case he'll make."

I strongly doubted it. Though the beast's skin would certainly suffice, being the size of an Austin Helly, it was unlikely the machinations of hell would permit Teddy luggage and good footwear. Then again, who knew? I was wearing a reasonably effective hell-made version of Rhodesian Army combat boots. This eon, at least, my feet suffered only wet, rot, ringworm and aches—but no blisters.

Despite having been brained and cleft, the crocovile corpse still twitched. Real crocs do that. Here, I was sure it wouldn't reanimate. At least not today. But I backed away quickly, drawing Teddy with me.

"Leave him for the bearers," I advised. "We must pursue the hellephant."

"Right you are!" Teddy snuffled through his impressive moustache and led the way.

I don't like clients to do that, but he was Roosevelt and this was my eternal damnation. What did it matter?

Leaving the wiggling corpse, we trudged along the one-lane trail left by the Hellfrican Jumbo.

The weather had shifted to hot, such as even Africa never knew. Salty sweat trickled into my eyes. My khaki collar abraded and begrimed my neck. Even more than the bourbon, I miss showers. In this eternity, I've had no bathing except in rain, usually shivery frigid.

After much trudging, Teddy slowed, extended an arm and whispered, "I do believe I see a hint of the prey just ahead."

I looked where he pointed. Indeed I did (gratefully) see a touch of gray.

"Slowly now," I whispered.

"Most certainly." He very carefully broke the action of his double, ensured it was loaded, eased it closed and slid the safety off. We advanced in the high steps so beloved of comedians and cartoonists that nevertheless reduce noise and trace. The growth had been knocked down, but it wasn't dead and would still rustle and crack.

We inched forward with a favorable breeze in the miasmic humidity. Within a few feet I could smell the animal's exudate, pungent, earthy and one of the least unpleasant things in Hellfrica.

It smelled off, though; different than usual. The management were changing things again, for any reason or no reason.

Closer. The hellephant was hidden by two scrubby trees and whipsaw grass, but I could gauge its size. It was a smaller one.

"Not quite what we're looking for," I murmured to Teddy. "Best to bypass this one and look for another, or a herd."

"I think you're right," he said. "Perhaps—"

That was when he stepped in a rut, twisted over on his ankle, and sprawled.

The brute was thirty yards away, but they don't need hearing aids. It rose up on what passed for tiptoe, turned in its own length, and charged.

Then I realized why the smell had been off. It was not a hellephant. That long, oversized spike on its snout made this clear: it was a hellefino.

Reaching with my left hand across my body, I tugged at Teddy while trying to steady the rifle over that forearm with my right. There wasn't a chance I could kill it, even if it stood still, with such an anemic caliber weapon intended for use on Indian peasants, Frenchmen and the occasional German.

The lumbering giant was charging, snorting breath like

a locomotive building up steam, legs pumping and shaking the ground with its own stampede.

"Run, lad!" Teddy shouted, fumbling his huge rifle up over his knee. I saw then that his ankle was bent at an angle rarely seen on Earth, and surmised he was about to meet the Undertaker.

"Run!" he shouted again, balancing the barrels.

I stepped back, hoping to confuse or distract the monster, and mayhap that "rear-quartering brain shot" used by Karamojo Bell might work, if I got lined up right.

Teddy touched off one barrel, which would have laid a lesser man prone. Through the pounding drum of the repercussion, I watched as he shrugged, snorted, and fired again.

The first massive lead slug battered the hellefino between the eyes, tearing a furrow in its skull but missing its squirrel-sized brain. As on Earth, the only thing that might be stupider than one of these things would be two of them.

The second round smashed through its throat with a splatting gurgle, and I'm sure I saw bone erupt as its spine was blown out the back. That made two impossible shots: from the ground, over a damaged leg, through the head and throat of a charging ungulate packing more power and less sensitivity than a Mack truck.

The brute piled up like a cross between a runner sliding into home and a wreck on Turn Three at the Indianapolis Motor Speedway. The hellefino rolled, bounced; crashed down, crushed Teddy, and made two more tumbles before it stopped in a roil of dust, shuddering in an earthquake of dead meat.

While alive, I never lost a client. In hell . . . I've had many fine conversations with Mr. Roosevelt, and they all seem to end the same.

I sighed, rose and dusted myself off, little the worse for wear, considering. I was scratched, bruised, sore, scorched and bit, but alive.

The illusionary sun was melting and dripping into the Limpoopoo. I limped toward it and the hunting camp. I'd've killed for a Land Rover or Land Cruiser, but why would the powers of hell allow me even that creaking, spine-breaking creature comfort?

I awoke in the morning feeling hung over and raw, though, of course, I'd had nothing to drink. I get all the pain and none of the pleasure. My throat was sandpapery from too many cigarettes I hadn't smoked. Breakfast sizzled on the fire, but I'd have to be much hungrier to eat it. I'd been a big fan of impala liver and scrambled ostrich egg while alive; but here, eggs are half-developed and I swear the impalas are cirrhotic. After the first thousand days or so, the dish lost its charm.

I'm a social being, so of course I have no companions in hell. My clients walk into camp. We go hunting. I hurt. They die. Repeat *ad infinitum, ad nauseam.*

My daily gun was next to me, and I picked it up to have a look. This morning, my new weapon was a French-style MAS36, France's (and possibly the world's) last military bolt action rifle, in a very odd caliber. It was in fine shape apart from some gravel indentations on one side. Probably never fired and dropped once. I opened the bolt to find four rounds stacked in the magazine with one up the spout.

The caliber is fine for shooting people, inadequate for anything larger than a medium gazelle. Its action is quite good, as is the balance.

There was coffee in the percolator, but it was awesome in its earthiness, as if it had been filtered through rags drenched in motor oil. I clutched a cup, hoping in vain the brew could counter the rock drum solo inside my skull.

Rustling in the bushes down the path presaged my client. I looked up. Then I saw what was there and climbed my chair while clutching the rifle. It was a bloody leopard.

"Oh, calm down, Peter," it said in a guttural rasp. "I'm the hunter this day, but you are not my prey."

"D-did I know you in life?" I almost squeaked, accepting a talking leopard but fearing no less my future as hamburger.

"You wrote of me," he said as he padded easily into the clearing and across the fire from me. I had a grass hut behind me that wouldn't slow him for more than a second, and in the tall scrub I'd have no chance whatsoever. He was seven feet if an inch, rippling, muscular; the feline equivalent of a wrestler. His coat had dappled spots that would make a Hollywood star debate between skinning him for a bedspread or filming a documentary.

"You're the Rudyaprayag Leopard?" I asked.

"Well and truly," he said, and half bowed, stretching his forelegs forward, paw by paw. "You may call me 'Rudy.'"

Rudy had killed about three hundred people in India whilst alive. Documented. How many more, undocumented, was unknown. Colonel Corbett had ended Rudy's reign with a lucky shot, after an entire regiment had failed. I also knew this cat could disable traps and open doors.

I thought, *Look, if the beggar rips you to shreds, you die, the Undertaker revives you, and there's a slim chance of ending up somewhere more palatable, like Hellaska. Or even Hellwai'i, while we're dreaming. . . .*

Rudy seemed rather relaxed, though, and said, "If you aren't going to have the liver, might I have a nip? My tummy is aquiver."

"Go ahead," I consented. Before me sat a poetic leopard, though not up to the standards of Rudy Kipling.

The liver disappeared as fast as a credit rating, and he sat back licking his chops.

"Thank you," he said. "Let us depart this base and on with the chase."

"What's your pleasure this morning, Rudy?" I asked.

"Lion. The Nemean Lion, to be precise."

I thought back to the mythology I'd read in high school, far back in New Jersey. "Isn't that a North African or Middle Eastern beast?"

"And where are we?"

Then I realized that the camp today was in low scrub, and drier. They'd relocated me again, to the Searingeti. That explained the heat shooting up. I could already see mirage waves in the distance. Yes, this was lion country.

Sighing at my hangover, lack of attention and general bad mood, I flicked a wave: *after you.* Might as well have the heat behind us.

The leopard padded ahead, shifting muscle under a fine hide. I'd helped quite a few clients convert leopards to rugs, and always respected the beasts. I wasn't sure of his odds against a lion, though—particularly not a mythic one of heroic stature. Leopards are more energetic and cagey, certainly more intelligent and flexible; but lions have more mass and more hide. I'd consider shooting a leopard with the 7.5X54mm cartridges I had. If I shot a lion with them, and the lion noticed, the result would not be pleasant.

"Why *this* lion?" I asked, still feeling odd, conversing with a cat. Or walking along a rutted trail with one, winding between short, scrubby trees and armpit-clumps of grass.

"Why not?" he rumbled back in a purring chortle.

I'd have questioned his sanity—except he was a talking leopard, we were in hell, and I knew in life he'd taken down buffalo. On the other hand, the lion had the same weaponry he did, only more so.

Some hellish principle prevents me asking my clients if they realize they're doomed to die. I'm blocked, for whatever reason.

"Short break," I said after an hour.

"If you wish," he replied, unruffled so far.

I had water and it was clean enough, for a wonder. I drank sparingly. Rudy stared at me and I got the hint, but there was no bowl for him to lap from.

"Can I pour you some?" I offered.

"You are gracious, for my thirst is hellacious."

"Isn't everything?" I replied.

He bent his head far back, and I poured several gurgles into his open jaw, staring at fangs that were larger than bucksaw teeth.

On we trudged, the ground turning to rolling hummocks and thicker grass. Lion country, as if there'd been any doubt.

"You know of this beast, from far to your east?" Rudy asked.

"Heracles killed him, didn't he?"

"Without sword or spear, for his skin won't tear."

Oh, Christ on a crutch in a tutu. Now I recalled. No mortal weapon could touch the Nemean lion. Rudy was on his own, because I certainly couldn't choke any lion to death.

Rudy said, "He is ahead; I smell him." He didn't try a rhyming couplet that time, which made me wonder if it were an act.

The Nemean lion appeared over a rill. It was a gorgeous beast, fur of what seemed pure gold, proud of stature, with a long, thick neck better befitting a jaguar. His mane shimmered, and he was easily twice Rudy's size.

My client wasted no time, slinking into a low sprint that any Army Ranger would trade a testicle to learn. He must have taken lessons from James Brown, the way his paws floated across the landscape. He approached in a long, darting curve, sinuous and fluid; slowing behind cover, then streaking between.

The Nemean stood taller, then splayed and coiled and sprang. He wound up a good twenty feet in the air, as Rudy emerged from a tuft of grass. That lion dropped like a mix of skydiver and pro wrestler, casting a broad shadow of foreboding.

Rudy leapt up, snapped his jaws around the lion's throat, and made that twist leopards use to snap the neck. On a lesser creature, that would have been it. On a lion, even with a neck that long, all it did was set Rudy swinging like a baboon until they crashed together into the ground. He tried to sink rear claws for a gut and front claws to sever tendons, but the Nemean batted them aside and roared like a B52.

The preferred follow-up of the leopard is to close jaws over the muzzle and suffocate the prey. Hardly. If he let go of the lion, he'd be pâté. They rolled around snarling and grunting, trying to eviscerate each other with rear claws. Rudy's were sharper. The lion's were larger and stronger. Ribbons of blood turned into Picasso-esque splashes, the two felines melting across the rocks then rising into the air.

All I could do was watch, and be grateful I'd not met this end in life, given the many chances I'd had.

Rudy was slowly choking the undeath out of the lion, but his grip was not great and the thing's neck was so huge he couldn't open wide enough: Rudy would have to be able to dislocate his jaw like a rattlesnake for that.

The Nemean meantime was crushing the leopard under his greater mass, batting him with plate-sized paws, and trying for his own bite with jaws that could easily span Rudy's neck.

The sound was nightmarish, reminiscent of chainsaws and chalkboards. I wondered if we were in India, because I could swear I saw eight limbs on each, ripping and tearing. The lion was not impervious to leopard claws: there were rips in that flawless, legendary hide. Rudy, though, was clearly the undercat. They fell apart for a moment, heaving for breath, and I tried to judge their state.

The lion had an injured paw and several tears. Rudy had a damaged shoulder and a huge flap peeled off his right haunch.

Then they were at it again, shrieking and shredding; fangs locked in an obscene kiss as each tried to tear the other's jaw. They circled and slowed and fell, then squirmed and thrashed. Even if I didn't know how it was supposed to end, I could tell Rudy was taking his number for the Undertaker.

I'd never shot at a client before, and I wondered what hellish rules there were for mercy. I'd never liked wounded animals; it was my duty as a professional to put them down. And the lion was in sad shape, too.

Then I remembered that mortal weapons wouldn't work on that magnificent creature.

But those had been ancient weapons: spears and swords and arrows. Heracles had clubbed the thing. I thought perhaps a bullet would act as a club, not penetrating, but applying 2700 foot-pounds as blunt trauma.

I raised the little MAS, fired, and caught the lion near the spine. Lucky shot. He staggered from the blow. I cycled that odd backward bolt, fired again, and grazed his neck. The third round punched through Rudy's shoulder and he snarled a keen of pain. The fourth caught the bullseye—or lion's eye. He recoiled and writhed and left my client alone for a moment. Protecting my client is my duty.

Then the lion rolled and rolled back, trying to get Rudy in a hug between us. I figured I had nothing to lose and fired the last shot.

I missed. That is, I'd aimed for the head, but hit his shoulder. However, I hit where Rudy had ripped open a chunk of skin and, without his magic hide, the bullet did what it was supposed to, smashing bone and chewing down into his thorax. He gurgled a roar with bloody, frothing bubbles and arched back in agony, then collapsed.

The lion breathed twice more in deep, laboring heaves, then went limp.

Rudy shimmied and clawed from under the corpse of his trophy, little good would it do him: His ribs were cracked, one eye swollen closed, a fang snapped off and bleeding, and his skin hung in tatters with loops of gut protruding. Part of me wished I had a round for him, if that was allowed, or if I morally could nerve myself to use one on him.

In a raspy, gasping growl he asked, "Do you know why I wraithed the night, to leave the locals in fright?"

I had to think on it, to decide that was all one question.

"No," I said, panting for breath and nervously caressing the trigger of the empty rifle.

"Four hundred and seventeen. I counted. Four hundred and seventeen humans, aged from three to eighty. The numbers are quite weighty. Cows and chickens and goats. Not once did I chance on a tiger, of stripy and orange coat."

I understood. He was so good no earthly beast he'd met had been a challenge. He'd pick school kids out of the line walking home, unseen. He left many of his kills uneaten. He'd killed for sheer pleasure, an almost human trait, and he suffered a human penalty, damnation, for his sins. Here, he'd hoped to find a fight.

His breath was fainter already. I suspected internal bleeding.

"Was it worth it?" I asked.

"That answer you know. For now, I must go."

He sighed and rolled over.

I did know. All of us who hunt feel that frisson of danger, the pushing of boundaries. We stand on the edge and dare the wind to throw us over.

Perhaps in hell itself, Rudy had found what he'd sought in life. Was his torment to endlessly stalk the most nightmarish of prey?

With the light of Paradise masquerading as the sun, staring from beneath an eyelid of clouds to taunt me, I turned to hike the miles back to a hut and dine on a dry rope of biltong.

I felt worse than usual on waking, having been up late, pondering. My shoulders felt as if some kinbaku practitioner had used them on a human sculpture. Of course, I had no woman bound in knots, and no aspirin for surcease. I tried to stretch and press, and rose from the taut canvas cot. I glanced around and took in the angle of light. Then I stopped and forgot how much pain I was in.

There was a bloody huge rifle leaning against one pole of the hut.

I wasn't sure of the brand, but that was most certainly some semiautomatic .50 BMG, a pocket cannon, if you have pockets that start at your shoulders and reach the ground. The .729 Redneck is more potent, as are a couple of other insane wildcat loads. However, almost nothing man-portable matches the destructive power of John Moses Browning's gift to the U.S. Army. The barrel was thirty inches or so; the action, a huge block with a magazine six inches long and deep and an inch wide. The muzzle had a chambered brake on it to reduce recoil by diverting some of the gas sideways.

If hell had rules, we'd be hunting hell-meerkats with that thing. In Gutswana. From Damnzania.

I blundered through the door, squinting against the

stabbing light, and saw a figure by the fire. My client had already arrived.

"Good day," he said.

I recognized that beard, that proud stature, that voice. How many times had I led him, now?

"Hello, Mr. Hemingway."

"Good morning," he said. "Would you like some coffee? I find the local grind to be rather harsh, but it settles if brewed fast with a pinch of salt. I made do with some from the lick yonder."

I accepted a cup. He was jittery and some spilled on my hand—hot, but not scalding. It also tasted somewhat better, as if free of hellephant dung.

"What is your pleasure to hunt today, Mr. Hemingway?" I asked.

"Please call me Ernie," he said. "Eternity is too long for formality."

"Ernie, then."

"I wish to test my heart against that most fearsome of monsters from Earth's nightmarish past."

He would. The bloody fool. "It's a good thing I have this fifty caliber, then, if we're to hunt Demonosaurus Rex."

I really needed a drink, if only to toast my pending demise in this iteration. The D. Rex was smarter than a hellefino by five percent or so, more massive than a Jumbo by a factor of two; fast, vicious, with jaws as strong as a car crusher. If a D. Rex caught someone (which it usually did), it would bite off whatever it reached first, which was relatively painless if the head, but much more so if a limb that it would then chew thoughtfully for a few seconds, fifteen feet over your screaming corpse-to-be, before bending down for a follow-up morsel. It regarded humans as a tasty snack food, and sought them as much as it sought any protein. It was a perfectly Hellfrican species, no matter when it had existed. Or still existed.

Not that I'd encountered one personally. All I had were reports from survivors who'd run while their second was consumed, who relayed the anecdote to me before dying themselves.

I said, "I take it we're up near Lake Victgoria then."

"Presumably, Mister Capstick," he said. "I do know I have this." He turned on his stool and bent, to bring up a Circassian-stocked double rifle with better lines than you'd see on the Rockettes. "Four-seventy nitro express."

That's my preferred big-game caliber, for Cadillacs, Mack Trucks and low-flying 747s, though I wasn't sure it would even attract the attention of a D. Rex. I was also afraid it *would* attract that attention, without actually doing significant damage.

"Well, then we'd best be to it," I decided. Better to meet it on terrain we could exploit than wait for it to come to camp. The beast always came for the client. I just had to make the most of the circumstances.

I led, and Papa followed closely behind. He moved surely and well for an older, heavyset man with a healed knee injury. Hell, he moved better than some younger men.

Other than being a fellow professional liar, I wondered, what had consigned him to hell? It could have been many things. Some doubted the stories of his knee. I'm told that walking after a knee shot is all but impossible. Exaggeration of facts might have brought Steinbeck to hell, and me; so it might hold for Hemingway, too. Or perhaps his politics?

He saw me studying him, seemed to gauge my thoughts by eye and said, "We are all here for reasons known or unknown; only the purport of our damnation remains muddy."

I nodded.

Finding the brute really wasn't difficult. This was *the* top-end predator, perhaps of all time, until man happened along. So it had no incentive to worry about noise.

I was worried about how fast D. Rex might move. Something scuffled in the wild ahead. The scuffles turned to cracking whips of bent branches and reeds, to thumps, and then . . . there it was.

D. Rex stood so tall I wondered if he regularly got nosebleeds. The ground trembled with each hop. Yes, *hop*.

When I was alive, portrayals of T. Rex resembled Godzilla, or vice versa. The reality (or hellish incarnation, or both) was bizarre.

He was feathered.

I knew some dino-related critters had been, but to see it in the fledge—eighteen feet tall with a wattle, comb and crest—was ridiculous in a terrifying way.

Nor did he trudge upright. He actually hopped like a chicken. Of course, this hopping, six-ton chicken made the ground shake.

Then he clucked. The sound was a gurgle like that of a manhole sized drain. I'd have nightmares about this for weeks.

Was that this creature's sad eternity, if that applied? To be snickered and gawked at?

I was so entranced, I started when Hemingway whispered behind me:

"What do you suggest, Peter?"

I was going to suggest a quick, quiet trot back to camp and a game of cards. There was no escaping this confrontation, though. Not now.

"My guess is the brain is between the eyes and that knob at the rear. I recall it being a tubelike thing. A shot there should ruin his day," I said.

Ernie nodded and rose carefully into a good stance. I eased sideways and down, tensing my ears for the assault. One can't go deaf in hell. Or at least I haven't. I'm sure it's possible if Satan decrees. I still get the full brutal impact of each concussion wave.

This all seemed too easy. Suspiciously so. We'd found the beast, the shot was lined up, and if Hemingway missed, I had sufficient light artillery to do major structural damage to the thing, as well as disable its legs.

Was it the D. Rex who was supposed to suffer?

Ernie was stable enough, feet balanced, that beautiful rifle nestled against his shoulder and over his hands. I split my attention and watched his finger flex, felt the muzzle blast roar and boom in basso, and looked to see the effect.

He missed. Oh, it creased the feathers and blew some fine tendrils free, but it grazed at most.

The Rex whirled, clucked in a voice like a sinking drum, lowered its jaw and hopped, then started into a run. It was fast off the blocks.

Ernie coolly fired his other barrel, and hit it in the throat. The Rex shuddered but kept coming. Hemingway calmly broke the action; the two panatela-sized empties ejected over his shoulder as he slid two more in and clicked his weapon closed.

I was a good ten feet away and crabbing sideways when I saw he wasn't going to have time for a follow-up shot. I raised that insane rifle to my shoulder, watched the muzzle waver as I pointed, then spiraled in on the tiny brain inside the huge case—and snapped the trigger.

The recoil was no worse than a 12 gauge magnum, but the blast from the muzzle brake hit the grass like jet exhaust. I suppose it was.

I hadn't missed. The bullet was the size of my thumb and punched into the target just below and behind its eye, a quartering shot. The eyeball actually popped loose from its orbit; sticky, feathery gunk blew out the far side.

I didn't know if the Rex would drop, though. There was every chance that momentum would carry its bulk right over Ernie. Or it might be stupid enough to continue to run for several seconds.

I was right and wrong on both counts.

I hadn't put it all together. Feathers. Clucking. Hopping like a monstrous bird. What is notable about birds? Their hindbrain runs far down their spine.

I'd headshot it.

The D. Rex took two steps before it fell over, almost at Ernie's feet. Once it fell over, it did the Curly Shuffle and booted him sprawling; hopped up again, fell down; kicked like a frog and went on a rampage of flopping, just as if some seven-ton chicken had been given the axe.

In lieu of skirts, I raised my gun and ran screaming for the largest bole I could find. I wanted mass between me and that Rex, and I wanted it now. Ernie was a big boy;

he'd know what to do. Besides, I owed him for being more famous a writer than I. He deserved a great story from this.

There was a mopane tree ahead of me and I got it behind me in a hurry, then got the bole in a romantic embrace so its mass could shield me in most of an arc.

The aptly named demon dino still convulsed. Ernie was nowhere to be seen. I wished him well.

Rexian convulsions turned to twitches, but those twitches threw its tail five yards in each direction. I hoped that was a safe enough level of dead and peeked out, then eased a foot out. The Rex didn't hop up again, so I stepped forward.

"Ernie?" I called softly.

I saw what looked like a foot, sticking up at a nauseating angle. The thrashing super-chicken had crushed him like a roach.

The fun wasn't over, though. A hellyena appeared through the crud, sniffing and yipping. It was followed by a brother. I moved to keep the carcass between them and me, and sidled over to see how poor Hemingway had fared.

But the two hellyenas turned into four, a dozen, a deluge of carnivorous scavengers panting and drooling and swarming over the yet-twitching meat. Others lapped at a small puddle that must be brain-covered feathers. Some eyed me.

I made it back to my lover the tree in seconds, and fairly levitated up to the ten foot level, unslung the .50 and used it as a ward, although I was more than prepared to splash one of the cursed things if need be. Jackhells and hellyenas are almost the same here as in life. There's apparently little one can do to improve on the revulsion they generate in onlookers.

I waited a long time in the baking heat and the stink of emptied dino guts (reminiscent of three hundred pounds of sulphurous bird guano), before the pack thinned out.

Then I took a long, careful survey of the area, slid down the bole and made my way cautiously over to the kill zone. The D. Rex was a pile of bones, hide and offal covered in bloody feathers and hellflies.

There was little left of Ernie but chawed bones, and I wondered how he'd be revived—remorted?—by the Undertaker. That lovely rifle had an intact action, but the wood was scratched and chewed to splintered kindling. This seemed most unkind of all. It was a fine weapon; it had done nothing wrong, but had been punished all the same.

Sighing, I checked my directions and started back toward camp. I wondered which of my heroes I'd watch die again the next day.

Misfits

With Gail Sanders

★ ★ ★

There's a half-true joke about characters talking to the author. One never admits to voices in one's head, but there are times a story explodes fully realized in my mind. For some tales, I know the characters, the history, the background and even the future just like that, and it comes out in a rush.

Other times, deadlines come looming up faster than expected. With real world matters, family, multiple pursuits and multiple stories, as well as occasional health issues from military service, I can wake up and realize there's too little time to get things done.

I often find it useful to bounce ideas off my wife, who's a big fantasy fan and occasional SF reader, and has helped me out on some previous short stories, of course. She can be very down to earth one moment, and completely round the bend another. Most of this story is mine, but she offered a few key comments that helped me find direction.

As to those deadlined stories, they still get done. It's just sometimes it feels like this:

HOW THE HELL did I wind up on the back of a *mammoth?* Phil wondered to himself.

The armor was a surprise, too, and the spear. But those were things one could get at a well-equipped store, or somewhere through the mesh. He was quite sure mammoths hadn't been cloned yet. But here he was.

The sky was a weird green color. What book cover had he ended up in this time? Someone always wanted to add some twist on what had already been done. Mix up a mammoth with a guy in armor and maybe someone would buy the book. These days it was the only way for an actor to make money. Apart from a few RL stage productions, everything had become computerized and now hologrammed.

They used to use living people as store manikins, now they were used as models for story plotting. The actors were put on set and then left to react, while the author was plugged in and writing. "Write what you know," it was said. Well, now they wrote what they could watch happen. Reality writing they called it. He was getting paid to make it interesting—best to be getting on with it.

All he could do was ride. So he rode. West.

He was supposed to be on a simulator, imagining it and posing for movement modeling. But this felt, looked, and smelled like a real mammoth. Or at least a real animal, which he'd smelled on occasion. He'd never been close to one of the cloned mammoths.

The beast seemed tractable, and responded like a well-bred horse. Though due to its height he mounted a lot higher, and it swayed. The saddle was oddly shaped, and Phil knew his thigh tendons would ache after a while. He was spread pretty wide.

"I think I'll call you 'Lumber,' if you have no objections, my friend."

The mammoth seemed almost to shrug, and trudged on. Phil swayed atop it. The landscape seemed bleak and deserted but he was wary. The armor he was wearing had to be for protection against something; it would be no use against a charging mammoth. The spear worried him too; there had to be an opponent lurking somewhere in this scene.

"Stop telling yourself it's not real. It's real for as long as you're in it. You're paid to do the job." Lumber twitched an ear at the sound of his voice and Phil realized he had actually spoken out loud. This place was too quiet. He didn't think much of the author if this was how they wrote up a scene. There were no animal sounds, no birds and no breezes either. It was about as cardboard a setting as you could get—just Phil and Lumber. It could be a travel book, except there was nowhere to be traveling that he could see. It could have been an adventure story except nothing had happened yet. Phil even found himself hoping for a cliché to happen—where was the damsel to rescue or the beast to slay? He'd be glad of a damsel for once, even if she was as cardboard as the rest of this story. Or silicone.

"I bet it's some damned bestseller trying for 'mood,'" he muttered.

He noticed he could smell. It was earthy, dusty, with a hint of vegetation. The hazy sky resolved into mackerel stratus clouds, but remained green. Wind soughed softly. No, it blew in lazy breezes. It was almost as if the stupid author's brain was in his. At least it was a real world now, though, not just a TV shot.

TV? That was an old term. Where had he come up with that?

The ground textured into hardpan with clumps of brush and grass; arid semi-desert.

He hoped the poor cover artist would have more to go on than this. It didn't offer much. It would be a shame to waste good talent on cliché blahness.

How the hell did he know it was going to be a good artist? He knew so, but how?

The author was in his brain.

In his head, he heard, "No, you damned plodder, you're in mine!" The voice was masculine, middle aged, well-modulated.

"Really? Where are you?"

"In my living room in my underwear, trying to beat a deadline."

So the author was talking to him somehow. Something in the helmet? Except it sounded like internal monologue, only it was dialogue. Swaying on a mammoth while talking to himself. Lovely.

He said, "Good luck. You're not getting there very fast like this." Trudging, landscape, nothing else.

The voice replied, "Good luck back to you. If this doesn't work by tomorrow, you're going in the trash. That'll be the end of your sad, boring little tale."

"That's not how it works. I'm an actor plugged into VR so you can throw images and let me help you model."

"What, like Disney did with Bambi back in the Thirties?"

The voice had said, "Thirties," not "Nineteen thirties."

He asked, "What the hell year is it where you are?"

"Nineteen ninety-eight."

"A hundred years ago."

He could almost hear the eyes roll. "Great. So the imaginary character talking back to me is from the future."

That sent ripples through him.

The author wasn't supposed to interact with the actor. That's what the director was for. Not only was it union rules, authors generally didn't know how to direct.

He keyed his mic and said, "Director, oversight, please."

There was no response.

He felt for the mic taped to his jaw, and couldn't find it. It should be a little rubbery spot, right there. It wasn't there. Fallen off? Except . . .

The same voice said "Director? You egotists still can't talk to the real creative mind without an intermediary?"

"'Real creative mind'?" Phil retorted. "I've got nothing to work with but a brindle-coated mammoth in a cross between an animated Old West and the Arabian desert, wearing medieval armor . . . wait, this is completely ridiculous. What are you smoking?"

"It's called 'fantasy.'"

"It still needs to make sense," he insisted. He badly wanted it to make sense. He thought of dismounting and running for the studio door, but he wasn't sure where it was, or if it was.

The author said, "It does. Or it will. This is the rough draft."

"Yeah, this isn't my first LASR gig, dude. Plotting. Planning."

"It's called 'they cut a story and I have a deadline to make.' Anyway, I work best free form."

Yes, this guy really did sound like an author. Phil tried to shake his head, but the helmet hindered him.

He said, "I can't tell it from here."

"No? Watch this."

The wind changed into buffets, then a shadow crossed overhead. He looked up and blinked.

It wasn't quite a dragon, nor a pterodactyl. For one thing, it had a beak like a toucan.

"That's pretty good," he said. "Vivid, at least. You have my attention. What does it do?"

"Yeah, I'm working on that."

"I'm curious."

"Don't be. I borrowed that," the author admitted.

The Toucanodactyl, Toucansaurus, whatever it was, hovered into an angled stoop like a seagull awaiting a piece of popcorn, from that ferry ride when he was twelve. It remained in a hover.

The author said, "I'm glad you remember that. I'd forgotten."

"Just doing my job," he said. "Okay, so I'm Phil. What do I call you?" The creature's wings blew gusts in tempo.

"I like being 'God.' Or so the joke goes. But I hate lording it over my characters. I'd rather be on good terms. Call me Joseph."

"Well, the director isn't in the loop, so let's do be on

good terms." Yes, please. This was too creepy. Friendship with the voices in his head was better than the alternative.

Joseph said, "This 'director' thing. You seem to seriously believe you're from my future, and real."

He replied, "I sure as hell hope I am. Though things are a bit hazy on getting on set. I remember my past, I see the present, but the sequence is vague."

"Try now."

Yes, there it was, gearing up, getting briefed, reviewing the basics of the script, which were still vague, then into the environment room, which . . . yes, looked like a 1990s TV studio he'd seen once online.

"Oh, shit."

"Told you," Joseph said. "It's my universe."

"And yet I remember a past that includes your era."

"Of course you do. Do you remember two thousand ten, though?"

He thought back. "Not directly. I remember some stupid protests, airborne drones being used in battle, financial crises in Europe and an America that got worse. War in the Middle East."

Joseph snorted. "That's a copout. There's always war in the Middle East. There is now. Everyone with a brain knows it's going to get worse. And do you notice you talk like me? We'll need to fix that."

His brain roiled and he almost vomited.

"Oh, gods, don't do that, I beg thee."

The Toucansaurus cawed and settled.

He felt a bit safer with that thing grounded.

He tried again. "Dammit, Joseph, don't make me talk like a cliché high fantasy warrior."

"Yeah, I'm working on that, too."

The Toucan spoke, in a voice musical and deep, a baritone.

"You think you have problems," it said, in a human voice from that monstrous beak. "I'm told my name is Buttercup."

Phil winced. "Better change that fast."

The lizardbird said, "It's better than Sam. This writer is atrocious with names."

"Yes I am," Joseph said. "Work in progress, okay?"

Phil said, "Just keep in mind that apparently our lives depend upon your work in progress. I'd like to return to my, very real to me, present, when you get done."

"I'm not used to letting characters live. But let me see what I can do."

"Please." Oh, hell, not one of those angsty, everyone-has-to-die for pathos types.

This wasn't what he signed up for, and scale plus per diem wasn't enough for it. A little shaking around in set was inevitable. Nausea, vomiting, psychic connections with the author and potential death called for a contract review.

Joseph said, "I always hated you union types, but in this case I do sympathize. But you need to get the hell out of my mind or I'll want to kill you."

At least his voice was outside Phil's head now. But it came from the sky, loudly, much like some deity. That wasn't an improvement.

"Are we separated?" he asked.

Joseph said, "Yes, at least enough to work. Okay, we need an interesting universe. Let me think what's been done."

The dust stirred, rose, and other mounted troops appeared, in garish armor on mammoths, mastodons and woolly rhinos.

"Going Paleo, are we?"

John said, "That's from some other story I'm working on for next year. It's warmup."

"And the enemy? We must be fighting something."

There was more stirring, and across from them, cowboys on Camptosauri.

A brawl between cavalry didn't suggest a good outcome.

He said, "That's some imagination there, Joseph. I can't help but notice they have revolvers."

"Yeah, but Thirty Eight Long Colt shouldn't penetrate your armor."

"'Shouldn't'?"

"As far as I know. I guess we'll find out."

"This still makes no sense. And I'm getting ill again." He wasn't sure if the nausea was related to the world change, Lumber's movement, or feeling his impending doom.

"Good. Once you get it all out you'll feel better."

Phil leaned sideways, puked hard, and splashed vomit over his armor and Lumber's coat.

"Sorry, friend," he gasped.

Lumber again seemed to shrug.

Was he doomed? He was an actor in a sim. He wasn't really in this world.

"Do I have a water bottle?" he asked.

"Sure. Inside your armor, tube next to your mouth."

He turned, and yes. He had a hydration pack. He gulped thirstily, and the water was cool and fresh . . . then warm and stale. He spit the second mouthful out.

"Why did you have to get realistic there?" he asked. "Especially as it doesn't fit the milieu anyway."

"What milieu? When did knights on mammothback ever face cowboys on dinosaurs? This is my universe, bub. Deal with it."

"Okay, okay, not to be killing the actor, please."

"Here, try again."

He carefully took another sip. It was now a cold, malty beer.

"Much better, thanks," he said.

Joseph said, "Right, well, the weapons are semi-lethal, to keep things exciting, and it's an arena type game. Sporting. We'll call it 'Strongest Warrior.' Or 'Last Grunt Standing.'"

"I think both of those were done in the Twenty-twenties."

"Really? Listen, if I can keep you here somehow, I can make a fortune."

"I think the universe, real universe, wherever it is, would frown on me doing that. Anyway, you've had influence on my mind, so the results won't be reliable." He hoped it made sense.

"No, not that, winning lottery numbers or some crap. I'd rather create genres and themes. Money is okay, but history lasts."

"As you noted, you're controlling me, at least in part. If you want to create stuff, it has to be done honestly."

"I thought I was doing pretty well."

There was another swirl, and more hodgepodge characters popped up in groups.

Phil was impressed. "But some of this stuff is real. Old

interpretations, but real, like the T-Rex and the Victorian era Romans. Some of this is nightmarish, and some just weird."

Some of it was all of that at the same time. He wanted out.

Just then, something crashed into the ground nearby, and they all flinched. It was, or had been, a planted pot—a geranium. Amidst the scattered shards and rays of soil lay the remains of several abused flowers.

Buttercup said, "Oh, no. Not again. Move to the rocks. Quickly."

Lumber gave a nod and took the advice directly, carrying Phil straight toward the nearby outcrop at an elephantine trot. Where had that come from?

"What are we waiting for?" he asked.

"Anything," Buttercup said, settling in and tucking beak under wing like some monstrous, misshapen duck.

A faint whistling turned rumbly, then something large and dark slammed into the ground. Phil had a momentary perception of a flipperlike tail, then the air was filled with dirt and chunks of sour-smelling flesh.

"Was that a whale?"

"It was. Anything might fall here. Once it was a phone booth with a crazy man inside."

"Okay, we need an actual plot, a conflict and then a resolution so I can get out of here," Phil thought. "Any idea where he's going with this?"

"He's a writer. They say that writers feel compelled to write the stories that the characters whisper in their ears—shout in some cases. Aren't you the character?"

Phil paused. He really hadn't been expecting decent

advice from a talking Toucansaurus named Buttercup. Buttercup was right however; he'd better start giving the author some input and quickly if he wanted to get out of this with a whole mind. Or maybe just get out of this at all.

Clearing his throat, he hesitated. "Joseph?" Phil noticed that while he and Buttercup had been dodging office plants and whales, another layer of realism had been added to the scene—smell. That whale was really starting to reek in this heat. John must be busy, but it was really time to get his attention.

"Uh, Joseph? Are the Roman costumed Victorians with the steam powered spiders on my side or against me?"

The God replied, "If I were you, I'd worry more about the Norwegian trolls and the AfrikaCorps."

"Okay, okay, I admit it, you have a fantastic imagination. I'm not sure what the point is, but it is impressive. Now, how do I stay alive?"

He heard the wind sigh.

"The problem is that the readers like carnage."

"But the hero survives."

"Sometimes. I'm known for . . . being mean to my characters."

"Great. That which doesn't kill us makes us stronger." He was sweating heavily now, and it wasn't just from the armor and heat. Nor was his nausea entirely from the environment. If he died here, was it permanent? It certainly seemed as if it would be.

"Well, the other option is gratuitous sex, but I don't think you'd like a Victorian orgy with Romans."

"I guess random gunfire isn't too terrible," Phil said with a shiver and a flush.

The mammoth-mounted cavalry started charging the tanks. The spiders waded into the melee, but their legs weren't strong enough to take impact from the tanks. The Romans leapt down to jab javelins and swords into the turrets, while the trolls jumped onto the mammoth riders. Then the Nazis started shooting back with machine guns and occasional barks of the turret guns. Those were loud. Painfully so. He could feel the shockwaves and hear the sizzling of transonic rounds nearby.

Then his helmet started talking to him.

"Sire, what are your orders? What do you want us to do?"

The men on the rearing mammoths were his, and they were dying. Mammoths apparently squealed in agony, and writhed with feet in the air.

"Joseph, what the hell? Do I have a radio?"

"Yes, I made you duke. The royalty sit back and aren't as exposed. You'll see the Roman legate up on the low hill, and Rommel over to the left."

"Dukes are not always royalty. They can be nobility. But whatever. That Roman should be a tribune."

"I often mix those up. I remember this one story where . . ."

"Screw that, are there more Toucanodactyls?"

"There can be. How many?"

"At least one hundred."

"It's going to take a while. The artist isn't going to like that, either. It means more work for him."

"As opposed to the work of keeping me alive. I understand your priorities are different from mine."

"I'm still having a hard time believing you're real."

"Well, believe yourself, and I'll believe me, and just write this so I come out alive."

"But what about all the other characters?"

"Are they talking to you? Do they have names?"

"Other than Rommel, who was a pansy twit anyway, no."

"Then they're not personalities, just figures."

"Right. I'll try not to talk to them."

"There we go. But I need to talk to them, and to the Toucans."

"Okay."

"Buttercup, can you and the others . . . there they are . . ." There were swarms of them, in mobs of ten or so. "Can you have them fly over the battle, then point straight up and flap as if our lives depend on it?"

"I can. But there may be a—"

"Perfect. Do it." Then he found the switch that let him transmit.

"Retreat," he ordered. "Just pull back out of the fight, and await reinforcements."

His unnamed assistant said, "Aye, sire!"

Mammoths needed distance to turn around, and it took some time, as they bumped and shoved their way clear, taking more casualties as they did. The duckbill dinosaurs darted around nimbly. The cowboys shot at Romans.

The beaked beasts were big enough to displace air into local gusts, almost like helicopters, and there were a lot of them. Dust churned into concealing clouds, and that was a good start.

Then they reached the center of the battle in concentric rings, hardly noticed amidst the wreckage below. They swept back their wings, pointed those huge beaks up, and cawed in huge gasps as they heaved their shoulders into the effort.

And just like birds, they ejected ballast as they rose. At a guess, something that size should drop about fifty kilos. In fact, if it was his world, that's what he wanted. Five tons of dinopoop, give or take.

It rained down amidst the clouds of dust, clogging mechanisms, splattering everywhere, and crushing one poor Roman bastard who took it straight to the head at speed. It flattened him much as if it were an industrial bag of soil.

One of the Nazis got clever, and lucky, and managed to get a burst of machine gun fire into one of the flyers. The tracers made streaks visible even through the dust.

Then he realized his mistake as several tons of flappy, dying lizardbird dropped straight down onto his tank, crushing him and bending the main gun forward into the dirt.

In the near distance, if he didn't know better, he'd swear the trolls were doing a Maori war dance—a Haka. Then they went in ripping Nazis and Romans apart and carrying off haunches, apparently for dinner.

It was so godawfully macabre he couldn't help but laugh, and he heard Joseph cackling maniacally overhead.

"That does it," he said. "I can work with that. This is going to be an epic tale of dead Nazis and reaving trolls, with dinosaur crap air support."

"Great, just no more whales. Now, how do I get home?"

"Oh, that. Easiest thing in the world. Writer's stupid copout number three."

"What's that?"

Overhead, a dot resolved into a growing sphere of someone's catapult stone.

No, it wasn't a stone. It was a man in armor . . . a midget . . . a cat . . . in armor . . . Japanese armor . . . with a frowning face.

"Aw, crap," he thought, and braced himself for the crack.

He had a momentary glimpse of striped fur under the helmet as the creature blotted out the sky and smacked into him.

"Phil, are you okay?"

The voice belonged to Franklin Maas, whom he'd worked with the last week.

"Wow. I'm dizzyish. Am I back?" He stared up at the lights. The aches and bruises felt real enough.

"Back? You're on an auto gurney in the green room."

"Right. So I am. How am I?"

"Physically you seem fine. What happened out there?"

He suddenly didn't want to talk about it.

"What did you see?" he asked.

Maas grinned and said, "You went boggle. It was great. The director is pissed, though. You ignored him totally. It was almost as if you were actually talking to the author yourself. He messaged in and said no one ever gave feedback like that."

"Good modeling?"

"He seems to think so. Fight movements, gallops, the works. Then you took a tumble."

"Yeah. Is my neck okay?"

"It's fine. A few days' rest and some mild regen. You've already got a medicated wrap."

"I can feel it, yes."

"You even got a kudo from the artist. He said the toucan beak makes the lizard work."

"Ah, that. Good."

He remembered to say, "We should discuss some additional contracts, then." Then his rational mind caught up and thought, *Or retirement. Right now. Because that was too goddam real.*

"I need some water."

Maas said, "You're still wearing your stage kit."

"Oh. Good," he said. He found the tube and took a pull . . . and it was full of malty beer.

The universe still made no sense, and he wasn't sure Joseph had any future as a creator of genres, though he might make a good living if he switched to screenplays for stoner films.

At least now he knew why there was a Toucansaurus on the front of the book—even if he still didn't know why it was named Buttercup.

★★★
TOUR OF DUTY: PROVOCATIONS
★★★

April Fool

★ ★ ★

At LosCon in L.A. one year, there was a rumor that Brad Linaweaver was very unhappy with me, because Freehold *was "Certain" to beat his* Anarquia *for the Prometheus Award. I wasn't so sure. (In the end, he won.) Then there was that Heinlein pastiche put together by Spider Robinson.*

Spider is a fine writer and a fine man, to be sure. I respect him, and don't fault him taking the money and writing the best story he could. However, regardless of what some promoters say, Spider is not Heinlein. Certainly good, certainly worthy, but they are not the same.

A few years later there was another "lost" Heinlein novel. I think it was lost for a reason—the same reason the first draft of my story "The Price" is lost. The author wasn't happy with it.

Once again, Spider stepped up and did a professional writing job.

However, I e-mailed Brad and mentioned that each successive story was written from less original material, and Locus Magazine's *April Fool's edition was approaching . . .*

379

He concurred with my logic, and we actually did get paid for this. I guess that was our April Fool's joke on Locus.

New Heinlein Novel To Be Written
With Brad Linaweaver
April 1, 2008, Locus Online

While going through the archives of Wilson "Bob" Tucker, writers Michael Z. Williamson and Brad Linaweaver found an as-yet unpublished Heinlein novel.

"It turns out Heinlein and Tucker were at dinner one night during MidAmeriCon," (The 1976 Worldcon in Kansas City) Linaweaver said. "Bob (Tucker) made notes of their conversation on three napkins."

The napkins are currently being analyzed for impressions and other marks, and to clarify part of the text blurred by a coffee stain.

"It looked like 'Time for the Pie,'" Williamson said. "But we knew that was wrong. My guess is that it's, 'Time for the Pie in the Sky,' based on a reference he made frequently. Brad thinks it's 'Time for the Pied Piper,' hearkening back to one of his earlier stories."

Since the notes were not in Heinlein's archives, and since Tucker had no legal claim to Heinlein's intellectual property, the ideas were free for the finding. They could be developed in any direction desired.

"As a formality, we're currently in negotiations with the

Heinlein estate," Linaweaver said. "We're looking to do something different with this valuable find, and actually write it the way Heinlein would have." Williamson said, "Spider's a fine writer, but he ticked off a lot of fans with his hippie take on Variable Star. I figure Brad's got the libertarian philosophical depth for this, and I've got the right wing militarism down cold."

Readers can expect to see a development of this lost story within two years.

Crazy Einar
★★★

The Society for Creative Anachronism (SCA) is a very loose reenactment group, whose members vary from strictly researched to farflung fantasy. I ride a line between, doing a lot of research, and trying to bend it enough to be believable, but within my own interpretation.

To that end, my persona is Crazy Einar (technically Einar the Mad), who is free with the wit, the sword and the flaming brand. I write articles for the various publications at the larger get togethers (usually for the annual Pennsic War), and try to have fun with it.

Here's my advice column.

Dear Crazy Einar: My son just turned 14. He refuses to grow his hair to a decent length, uses something called a fork to eat, sips wine from a goblet instead of guzzling from a horn, and dresses like that minstrel Marilyn Olaf. How do I keep him in line?

—Harried Mother

Dear Mother: Five words: Anchor chain, bullwhip and wet kitchen towel. After you have his attention, a few loving cuffs and boxes about the ears daily from your sturdy peasant hands should be sufficient to steer him back to a life of brigandry.

Dear Rampaging Pirate: I understand you are involved with battered children. I'm happy to see there is hope even for brutal, marauding, heathen scum like you.

—Your Local Monk

Dear Do-gooder: Dip 'em in egg, roll 'em in flour with a little pepper, and deep fry for three minutes a pound. I like children, yes I do. Battered and fried or boiled in a stew.

Dear Crazy Einar: I just met this wonderful traveling barbarian businessman (he's in sacking and looting, like you!) Can you recommend a gift that tells him I'm interested, but in a subtle way?

—Happy Lil Peasant

Dear Wench: A gift should be personal, useful, and something the recipient wouldn't get themselves. How about underwear?

★★★

Dear Crazy Einar: You heathen scum! Haven't you heard of the Code of Chivalry?   —Appalled Knight.

Dear Silly English Pig-Dog: *Of course* I've heard of it. I think chivalry is a wonderful invention. I especially like that part about not harming women. It makes raids so much safer when I strap a few to my horse. Not an arrow comes close.

★★★

Dear Crazy Einar: What do you think of Atilla the Hun?
                    —Admirer and Aspiring Barbarian

Dear Suckup: *That* bleeding heart liberal wuss? Please. Just look through history for an example of where he's heading. Genghis Khan. First he got soft, then he was history.

★★★

Dear Crazy Einar: I understand you once conducted a poll of politicians. Can you tell me about your results?
                    —Student of Statistics

Dear Over-educated, Decadent Fop: Dunno about *polling* politicians, but I have *poled* a few. They usually wiggle and weep as they slide down the spear haft, with the occasional scream to add piquancy to the crackling sounds of the campfire.

★ ★ ★

Dear Crazy Einar: Why do Vikings sack villages?
—Wants to Know

Dear Now Knows: Because it's easier than bottling them.

★ ★ ★

Dear Crazy Einar: Which is better, a galley or a knorr?
—Business Investor.

Dear Investor: A galley. It burns longer.

★ ★ ★

Dear Crazy Einar: A merchant offers to sell me pitched torches which burn for 20 minutes each and weigh 8 ounces apiece, and oiled reeds which burn for 10 minutes apiece and weigh 3 ounces, with the torches costing 1/4 pfennig each and the reeds being a dozen for a pfennig, what should I do?
—Ship's Purser

Dear Tightwad: Club him and take all of them. Stop your dawdling and woolgathering and load this sack of silverplate. Then take a turn on the port sail rope. There's a crate of fine beeswax candles if we really need additional light.

Dear Crazy Einar: My servants keep coming out of the kitchen and sassing me. It gets very embarrassing when the Jarl visits. What have I done wrong?

—Flustered Lady.

Dear Flustered: You made their chains too long.

Dear Crazy Einar: Recently, my cousins and I went on our first strandhogg. Despite the gaiety of the event, I found I got little pleasure from burning and pillaging. The whole thing made me feel a bit remorseful for those we left stripped poor and homeless. What should I do?

—Confused Young Norseman

Dear Freak of Nature: I'd check your ancestry. Sounds like some of that civilization stuff. Did one of your forefathers travel to the Mediterranean? Take a local wife? That probably explains it. Either that, or you're an adopted Dane. Don't worry; with time, you'll learn to appreciate the stark beauty of hovels lit by firelight and the whines of kicked dogs.

Dear Crazy Einar: What colors have you found most frightening on Landsknechte?

—H R Puffinslash

Dear Puffer: Is there anything unfrightening about landsknecht? It's not so much the colors as the slash and puff codpiece. Makes me want to reach for a warclub and langseax.

Dear Crazy Einar: Is it true that Vikings didn't kiss to greet each other due to the velcro effect of their manly beards?   —Goatee

Dear Fashionable: No, that was because of their permanently stiff upper lips.

Dear Crazy Einar: I engage in some unusual behavior and need your advice. Last night, I watched *The 13th Warrior* and *The Vikings* from a chair surrounded by shields, while clutching my spear, with seax by my side, wearing leather and a spangenhelm.   —Clinging

Dear Clinging: I understand your background. Please go ahead and tell me about your unusual behavior.

Dear Crazy Einar: What's an appropriate ax for 12 year old girls?   —Hunting

Dear Hunting: Depends on the size of the girls. Anything from a light hatchet to a small skeggox. However, I believe the risk of a pre-teen apocalypse is slim, and you will not be culturally popular in the event.

Crazy Einar will be happy to answer any questions on business, social etiquette, or whipping serfs into submission, provided such inquiries are in poor taste and addressed to this paper.

Crazy Einar is a eleventh century Viking (T)raider settled in northern Scotland, and those farmers were dead when he arrived. He deals in cutlery, armor, and garb, all acquired legally under his laws as overlord of Scotland and Vinland.

So You Are Going To Be Raided By Vikings

★★★

WELCOME to our introductory lesson on receiving Scandinavian visitors. If you live in the Mediterranean, coastal or riverine Europe, riverine central Asia, the British Isles, North Atlantic Isles, Greenland or North America, their world tour may be coming soon to a village near you! This free brochure will help you properly welcome these unexpected guests.

1. Have a smooth beach nearby. While the handlers are capable of landing on anything from finished timber docks to shattered cliff faces, a well-prepared beach will make their departure easier afterwards. If departure seems awkward, they may elect to stay over.

2. An ancient Scandinavian law states that anything not secured is theirs. To avoid disputes over this precept, the following simple suggestions may help:

Secure the following: Unattached women, attached women, prospective widows, gold, silver, gems, furs, spices, food, dogs, sheep, cattle, beer, mead, wine, ale, food and books.

3. Provide PLENTY of refreshments. Beer, wine, mead, ale, sweetmeats, meat, vegetables, salt, bread, and fish will all be graciously accepted. Bring all you have and lay in extra. Then stock more.

4. Entertainment is good. Bored Vikings feel obligated to provide entertainment to you, the host. Dancers, minstrels, jesters and others are a good start. Comely wenches are better. So are sporting games with swords and shields. Any martial competition will be enthusiastically joined, but be warned! They excel at these events, and the lack of referees in the traditional rules can be confusing.

5. You may be unsure of etiquette regarding the above. Relax! Vikings are informal folk, and will gladly take any of the above at any hour of the day or night. They LOVE being surprised, and will cheer loudly. They may light spontaneous fires for ambiance.

6. Rumors to the contrary, Vikings do NOT put heads on pikes. The Vikings are civilized folk. As such, all heads are put on forks.

7. Have lots of firewood and other fuel handy. Vikings are used to cold weather. Remember that these are the

people who regard the Orkneys as a summer resort...so plan accordingly. Pitch-soaked reeds and thatch are greeted with hearty approval.

8. The high point of their visit will be firelight rituals, where they may decide to adopt offspring, spouses, or livestock. You may be filled with trepidation at this idea. Relax! Despite rumors, Vikings are far more civilized than many allegedly superior cultures. They bathe regularly, take sauna, travel extensively, enjoy a high level of literacy, and pride themselves on gathering the finer things in life. Your social status may climb immensely with marital ties to them. And you'll be far safer, one way or another.

9. It is confusing to many cultures, but Vikings place women in charge of steads and villages. The extensive business travel the men engage in makes their regular presence impossible. If a woman gives you an instruction in camp, it would be in your best interests to do as she says. Trust us.

10. Once they have enjoyed your hospitality, they may elect to make your village a regular stopping point. This is a high honor, and may require you to borrow or acquire additional supplies from nearby villages. You may wish to suggest these other venues to your new friends.

One year I organized a small get-together, and did a round of promotion.

TELL US ABOUT THE VIKING RAIDING PARTY™.

The Viking Raiding Party™ is a party to celebrate our Norse heritage and to correct many of the wrong impressions about Vikings. Many people hear "Viking" and think "Murdering maurauder." But there was a lighter side to Norse culture that also enjoyed looting, pillaging, and arson.

WHAT ARE THE REQUIREMENTS TO PARTICIPATE IN THE "VIKING RAIDING PARTY"?

To participate, one must be of the proper ethnic background, or able to fake it. "Proper ethnic background" means of Norse extraction, which includes Scandinavian, Russian, Germanic, Baltic, Dutch, English, Irish, Scottish, French, North African, Turkish, Central Asian or East Indian. To fake it one must A) be blonde, or B) be a man with a beard, or C) wear trews and tunic or D) know at least three words of Old Norse, or E) know someone who does. So you can see it's very exclusive.

SERIOUSLY, THOUGH, WHAT ARE YOU GOING TO DO?

We're going to start in the merchant area, swarm down into the bog, and graciously relieve camps of all the things they'd really rather not take home, like booze, beer, food and other comestibles, and the occasional unattached wench or rogue. At least two camps have said we can storm their gates.

AND WHAT WILL YOU DO IF THE GATES WON'T YIELD?

I've got a lawyer and a two-year-old. The gates will yield.

SO WHAT SHOULD PEOPLE BRING?

Wagons and flagons, good spirits of both kinds, loud singing voices and sturdy walking shoes. But no attitudes. This is fun, not real pillage. Flaming brands and prybars won't be needed. And if you'd like your gates to be stormed, let me know and we'll arrange a special trip. The raid will leave from our camp tonight at exactly 10ish.

Random Maunderings About The Celtic Peoples

★★★

GAELIC

Ah, Gaelic! A lovely lilting lyrical language . . . or else the incoherent slurs of drunken Celts, depending on one's viewpoint. The roots of Gaelic go back thousands of years, and were refined by generations of use into its present fluid form.

Of course, such perfection of anything, especially in speech, is bound to create jealousy. It was after the Vikings in Drag, led by William the Bastard (no, no! the *other* one—1066), created a unified Anglo-Celtic-Saxon-Jute-Norman-Roman England, that they saw how much better their northern neighbors had it and declared war. Cunningly, they gave the Celts *writing*.

This dastardly plot was intended to pave the way for *spelling*, which would be the downfall for the Celts much as it was for the earlier civilizations of Europe. The Spelling Campaign of the war introduced dozens of extra consonants per word, including such dastardly concepts as the "h", which serves as a silent backspace delete. Assorted other letters, sprinkled without rhyme or reason, all failed in their intended plan, as all Celts are instinctively able to understand their native lauhngsuage.

BAGPIPES

The pipe were invented in Northern Greece by a drunken proto-Celt who grabbed a cow's stomach and blew into the numerous openings while belching. Not having an ear for fine music, and having nothing but Yanni CDs to offer in trade, the Celts took the pipes elsewhere to find an audience.

Their first demonstration was with one Joshua, at Jericho in 1394 BC—first use of sonic weapons and psychological warfare. Joshua used Method 1 of pipe warfare. This involves tuning several thousand pipes in unison, which creates a resonance that can bring down castle walls.

Method 2 involves having several thousand pipers each tune to taste or lack thereof, which creates a subharmonic dissonance that sends people, dogs and Englishmen running and screaming while clawing at their faces.

Finally, the pipes made their way to Scotland. The Scots, canny as they are, swapped the pipes to the Irish in exchange for *whisky*. Sooner or later, the Irish will sober up and realize they got the bad end of that deal.

And I still haven't been able to find a performer for my composition, "Fugue in C Sharp Suspended Minor 7th for Bagpipe, Saxophone, and Accordion."

My favorite recollection of the pipes is a gentle(?) who

was with me at a convention in a hotel, staffed by rude people. He announced, "Boy! I'm mad. I should go home and get my bagpipes."

"Oh, you play bagpipes?" I asked, interested.

"No, but I *own* bagpipes!" Shudder.

What's the range on the bagpipes?
Twenty yards if you have a good arm.

What's the difference between the bagpipes and a trampoline?
You take your shoes off to jump on a trampoline.

SCOTTISH INVENTIONS

The Scots have invented many things over the years. Sure, you know of James Watt and the steam engine, Dunlop and rubber tires, MacAdam and modern roads, but did you know: *copper wire* was invented by two Scots fighting over a penny?

The Scots invented *golf*, and introduced into the rest of the world? (By the way, we were joking!)

It was a Scottish engineer who defined the exact time for a hot-air hand dryer to dry one's hands only three quarters dry, then shut off to conserve power.

The Scots, however, did *not* invent the term "Animal Husbandry," so take your sheep jokes and ram them . . .

THE MANLY WAY
TO COOK MEAT
by Crazy Einar
★ ★ ★

The following bits of uber-macho silliness were written for one of my online hangouts—ManlyExcellence.com. The short summary of the site is that flame wars are not prohibited; they're graded. If you come in there, you better be equipped with facts, debate skills and an attitude. If that doesn't work, resort to personal insults. Just make sure they're creative.

There are some members with rather derogatory attitudes about everything from race to religion, but the free-speech atmosphere is refreshing. The whole point of free speech is to be able to make comments that others might find offensive. Though I do wish some of them were more intelligently made. Still, that's the price we pay, and I approve.

What I find amusing from my end is that crap written off the cuff for the sake of entertainment, on a site that endorses steroids, eating meat, voting Republican and shooting Mosin Nagants, gets taken so seriously, and how a few people can zero in on a phrase, twist it into their own context and pronounce me to be a "closet racist." Yeah, whatever. I've never had a problem telling people I don't like them, do so pretty openly, and don't need to hint at it. You might have read that in here somewhere. If I were a racist, there'd be nothing closeted about it.

★★★

SINCE THE DAWN OF TIME, fire has been an indication of civilization. It treated flint, steamed wood, cast bronze, smelted iron, burned out peasants for the obligatory sacking and looting, hosted leaders and their war bands before they engaged in the slaughter of squatters or savages, and cooked meat.

Today, the call of the flame is strong. Entire industries exist so that pussified office bunnies may feel its comfort, usually imprisoned behind glass and possibly with some frou-frou scented sparkly wax.

I'm here to tell you what should be obvious: That's not manly.

A microwave is acceptable for warming a cup of second-rate coffee or leftover pizza. A stove or range is okay for soup, vegetables or baking a cake. For some modern dishes, they do excel. But they are utilitarian conveniences.

There comes a time when a man must chop up meat (preferably that he killed and gutted himself with a knife, spear or bow, but a rifle or a punt gun is certainly an acceptable modern substitute) and apply it to fire, while quaffing ale and mead, insulting his foes (like that nancy-boy Mohammed chap and his boyfriends), scratching, belching and generally fuzzing the line between civilized and barbarous.

It is time, then, to retreat to the outdoors and cook like a man.

This is easy, as long as one understands the simple truths. Fire is fuel and flame. It doesn't, and shouldn't take a fortune in fancy stainless, digitally controlled hardware to produce it.

Gas grills: Gas grills are right out. If you're the kind of pansy who puts aluminum foil on the mesh of a gas grill to fry your burgers and brats, you're, well, a pansy. All you've done is move a range outdoors to fry with. You're probably cooking tofu burgers with bean sprouts. "But, Einar, the instruction say I shouldn't get grease into the carefully fabricated imitation pumice rocks above the gas flames!" you say. In other words, it's an expensive yuppie-scum wannabe grill, like those "gas fireplaces." You may as well put your testicles up there and cook them, because you're not using them.

Perhaps you cook directly over the gas flames, and imagine this is manly. I take it you either have no tastebuds, or like the taste of partially burned hydrocarbons in your food. Still, at least you have an actual fire kissing the meat. It's cooking, but it's like the difference between a methed-up stripper smoking Marlboro Lights and Arnie smoking a cigar.

Charcoal grills: Ah, now you're almost there. Charcoal grills are acceptably manly, if done properly.

First, no real man cooks with cute little "briquets" (that term just sounds phagadocious, when you say it) of ground coal dust held together with binder and soaked with glorified kerosene. If you are going to use charcoal, save money, show some class and testosterone, buy a bag of "hardwood charcoal." It looks like someone chopped up a tree and carbonized it, because that's exactly what it is. The taste and smell are superior. It's easier to light and burns better. I find twenty seconds with an oxy-acetylene torch creates a good, hot core to pile the balance of the fuel on.

Obviously, the best way to light this fire is with flint and steel, the Viking way.

But isn't it hard to strike a fire with flint and steel, you ask? Not at all. Flint is just a quartzite—a silicaceous rock. Steel is easy to find. My preferred method is to chuck a silicon carbide abrasive wheel in my half horsepower drill and run it against an old file. I get three feet of hot, red sparks.

Of course, you can make your own charcoal, but the Vikings regarded charcoal as forge fuel. Proper cooking was done over an actual fire with wood.

The way this works is to light your tinder, feed it kindling (matchstick sized pieces), then gradually work larger, to a small tepee or log cabin arrangement of sticks. They don't need to be huge. This is for cooking, not burning a village before raping the inhabitants (*always* burn first. It's so much more romantic by firelight). Thumb-thick is plenty large. For roasting or searing, just hack off some gobbets of flesh, skewer on a stick, dredge in salt or herbs, and stick into the flames until done. Alternately, skewer the whole joint or carcass, lay it across the fire on iron poles, and slice off the crispy outside as you go.

Once the fire has burned down to coals, about a foot across and an inch or so thick, the artistic cooking can commence. Beginners will want a green stick or metal grate to lay meat on, to cook with sizzles. If fat falls into the fire and creates a burst of flame, don't be a wuss and squirt it out with water. The gods are gifting you with a fiery seasoning for the meat.

Ultimately, you will want to try a Viking steak. Blow the dust off the coals and drop the meat straight on. It will douse the surface fire and the coals will act as insulation. As soon as you smell scorching, flip over and cook the other side in the same spot. It will take fractionally longer. The proper way to eat this, of course, is to slice bits off with your seax and eat them off the back of your thumb, Viking style.

Good ways to prepare the meat ahead of time include sprinkling with sea salt, crushed red chilies, pepper and/or crushed garlic. Appropriate marinades for overnight soaking include teriyaki, Worcestershire, barbecue sauce or hot sauce. Once the meat is ready, pour off the marinade and use it to sautee squash and carrots first, then mushrooms and onions, in a cast iron pan oiled with butter or olive oil. Take whole, unhusked ears of corn (this being America, the last bastion of Viking manliness), peel back one side, add a tablespoon of butter and a sprinkling of seasoning salt, close back up and toss into the coals until it smells ready. You'll know when. Squash and carrots can also be basted with the marinade and laid on the fire/grate until done. A true master has the vegetable garnish ready just as the meat comes off the fire.

Shellfish can be tossed directly in the fire. Fish should

be grilled, placed skin-on in the flames or planked onto wood and cooked by radiant heat.

A note on "desired doneness": Some purists insist a steak must be still bleeding and mooing to be manly. While it certainly is manly, it's not the only way. Medium pink is still meat, after all, and well-done is just a sacrifice to Odin, without wasting the leftovers. He will be honored to know that men are still thinking of him. Just be aware that chicken and pork MUST be cooked completely to be safe, as must sausages.

Some of the more manly choices for meat include elk, venison, antelope, ostrich, bear, kangaroo and alligator. But any animal flesh including fish retains the power and sense of our great ancestors, roasting it on the beach before or after a raid.

Afterwards is the time to toss on a knot of pine and some wrist-thick scrub to create large, manly flames, illumination for the drinking of ale, mead and whisky, carousing, cursing and boasting that must surely follow.

The Ten Manliest Firearms

by Guest Author, Crazy Einar

★★★

These next two pieces are funny. Not because they're humorous, though I'm told by many fans that they are, but because of the outrage they generate. Pretty much every gun on these lists has been scoffed at by a group of others as "not manly," while they extol the virtues of some other gun, which another group of detractors mocks. I get regular mail that by not including gun X, I can't possibly consider my list to be manly. When I rattle off from memory a dozen critical flaws in said firearm, they resort to ad hominem *argument that I can't possibly be a man if I disagree with them. They don't actually address the matter of the critical flaws.*

Of course, those flaws don't really matter, given the introductory statement. And there are some manly French guns, too. I do, however, draw the line at pearl grips and gold plating. Those are not subject to discussion.

Actually, nothing is. If you don't like my list, if you have

*a better list, I really don't care, and don't waste your time
telling me. Read the first paragraph again and heed it.*

THIS WAS A HARD PIECE to write, because guns by
definition are manly, except for Berettas, gold-plated
TEC9s, .25 caliber pistols or anything made by the French.
To simplify things, I have limited it to modern cartridge
firearms a man might, can, and should collect and shoot.
There are certainly other manly weapons, and you may
have a different list. As long as the list contains nothing
French, gold-plated, .25 or with pearl grips (which Patton
correctly observed are the mark of a New Orleans pimp),
it is a good list. *Let me repeat that*: You are encouraged to
make your own list. As long as you're shooting something,
it's all good. Now please read this intro again so you don't
embarrass yourself by arguing a point already made. Ask
for help with any big words.

★ 10: SMLE

The 10 SMLE was the other great weapon of the Modern
British Empire (The Brown Bess musket being the first).
Several MILLION Short, Magazine, Lee Enfields, in .303
caliber are still spread across the Earth, waiting to be used
to evolve the species by killing the weak.

The Smelly, as it is called by those who love it, can also
be had in .308 from the Indians at the Ishapore Arsenal.
There are still several billion rounds of .303 surplus out
there, however, and it is still loaded by modern
manufacturers. Karamojo Bell was such a testosterone

laden bastard he used to hunt *elephant* with one. Forget .470 Nitro Express and .375 Holland & Holland Magnum. This was a warrior par excellence.

The Smelly is still the fastest bolt action out there, and a trained soldier (all Brits have Viking blood in their veins, either from the Norse, or those lesser Danes, but probably both) can fire just about a round a second in volley fire, and easily a round every five seconds aimed. It's an ugly stick with a barrel on it, and a bayonet lug that mounts either a spike big enough to crucify someone, or a blade the size of a small sword. The front end of a SMLE is the bad end of a SMLE. You want to be on the good end, behind it.

It was used in WWI by Brits, Canadians, Aussies, Kiwis, some Americans and various allies. It slaughtered Turks and Germans. In WWII, it slaughtered more Germans and Italians. Okay, maybe bragging about dead Italians isn't so great, but it also killed Sicilians. And killing Germans definitely is a mark of manliness, because they also carry strong Viking genes. It was used in Burma, Malaysia and throughout the Pacific against the Imperial Japanese. It has won many wars.

Best of all, with so many still out there, the prices are quite reasonable, and spare parts are plentiful. Of course, the Smelly doesn't break down much, so you shouldn't need spare parts, except the safety lever, and why would a real warrior worry about the safety? If you shoot someone, it's because you intended to and they deserved to die. If you can't find a Smelly near you, you may also carry a Lee-Enfield #4 Mk 1 and feel just as manly, it being the final offspring of the line.

★ 9: Mosin-Nagant M91/30

Speaking of guns without safeties, here's the Mosin-Nagant from Russia. The Mosin was used by the Russians against the Finns, the Finns against the Russians, the Estonians against the Russians, the Russians against the Russians, and the Russians against the Germans. It does, in fact, have a safety, but it's quite hard to engage. But this is not a complaint one would ever voice in the Red Army. Your officer would reply, "Safety? Safety? Is gun! Meant to kill! No warrior should know he has safety on gun, because he should be killing enemies of homeland! Safety make loud click to aid enemy in locating warriors! No safety!" while pounding his fist on the table.

And the Mosin can kill enemies of homeland. The muzzle blast will vaporize green growth within a few feet of the bore, and even if you miss, the enemy will be reduced to shouting "WHAT?" to communicate. You'll need a recoil pad or shooting jacket. Ordinarily, this might be considered unmanly, but this rifle has a short stock for using while wearing several layers of wool for a Russian winter. It is acceptable to wear padding to fire a Mosin.

Of course, there are also M38, M44 and other variations of Mosin-Nagant and all are cool. All, also (except the M38), come with a bayonet. Russian doctrine held that the bayonet was mounted except while traveling in a vehicle, because the Russians understood that an empty rifle could still be a pointy stick—a Viking spear. The Russians loved to spear Turks. So, coincidentally, did the Vikings. This rifle sounds better all the time, doesn't it? The Finns used the Mosin as a sniper rifle during the Winter War, and their greatest Sniper was Simo Häyhä, who had 500 confirmed kills in 100 days. This is a man the Finns describe as "modest" and "self-effacing." It's a good thing the Russians didn't run into a Finn who was proud and arrogant. They'd have been wiped out.

It fires a 7.62X54R (for "Rimmed") cartridge, about as powerful as .30-06, which holds the distinction of being in service from 1891 to the present, longer than any other military cartridge. It is still used in Dragunovs, PKMs and other Russian weapons. It's cheap in quantity. So are the rifles, because they were built for (all variations) over 70 years, by Russia, Finland, Poland, Romania, China, even the U.S. As I write this, arsenal-new M44s are $55 to $200. At that price, you should have several, so any guests you have during the Collapse can be outfitted as they receive Enlightenment. Then they can pillage, kill, sack and loot with the rest of the men who secure a new Dark Ages to hasten the new renaissance. We have kingdoms to carve, men!

★ 8: GLOCK

The GLOCK is feared by neoliberals. It's called "plastic" and "ceramic" and "capable of going through airport metal detectors." If this were true, it would be the coolest gun on Earth. But these things are total lies, and serve to point out that neoliberals are not men, and have no honor. The GLOCK has a plastic frame molded over a kilogram of metal (84% of the weight is metal), and will in fact, show up on any metal detector. So will the dense plastic.

Yes, the correct spelling is GLOCK. GLOCK insists so. As they are men and wish to loudly announce themselves, this should always be respected, despite any personal allegations against Gaston. A man is known by his work.

But the GLOCK is tough. How tough? http://www.

theprepared.com/index.php?option=com_content&
task=view&id=90&Item. To summarize: The GLOCK in
question has not been cleaned in ten years, has been buried
in dirt, saltwater, gravel, talc, dropped from a plane, dragged
behind a car, tossed off a roof, driven over with a truck, and
it still works. Gaston Glock didn't know anything about guns,
and started from the ground up, thus not having any
preconceived notions and incorporating the best technology
available. It is an almost flawless killing machine.

GLOCKs came originally in 9mm, and have also been
made in various numbers in 10mm, .40S&W, .380, 9X21mm,
.357 Sig and .45 GAP. However, the only acceptable caliber
for a man to carry is .45 ACP. 10mm is good but hard to find,
.40S&W is a wussified 10mm that the FBI created when it
found out its agents weren't manly enough for 10mm, .357
Sig is excellent but hard to find, .45 GAP is new and untested,
.380 is only acceptable as a backup caliber, and no man would
be found dead with a 9mm. Actually, a man knows he
WOULD be found dead with a 9mm, because a 9mm is a
.45 set on stun, and real men do not believe in stun.

GLOCKs are not cheap. They are much in demand by
police and military around the world. Fascist European
pussies refuse to sell them to Israel, because they secretly
like the idea of dead Jews. The Israelis, being practical and
almost as manly as Vikings, acquire GLOCKs anyway. If
Viking king Harald Hardraada were alive today, his symbol
of power would be a GLOCK 21.

★ **7: Swiss K31 Carbine**
*"While traveling around Switzerland on Sundays,
everywhere one hears gunfire, but a peaceful gunfire: this*

is the Swiss practicing their favorite sport, their national sport. They are doing their obligatory shooting, or practicing for the regional, Cantonal or federal shooting festivals, as their ancestors did it with the musket, the arquebus or the crossbow. Everywhere, one meets urbanites and country people, rifle to the shoulder, causing foreigners to exclaim: You are having a revolution!"

—General Henri Guisan

Switzerland has not been invaded in a long time, because every man and a lot of the women are issued guns which they keep at home. Imagine a government that not only allows but *insists* its citizens keep military grade weapons. That's points right there. Even more, they hold quarterly Schützenfests, at which shooting, carousing and drinking are expected. And it's entirely possible you will have your ass handed to you by a thirteen year old girl shooting an StG90 assault rifle that she carried to the range from school, slung across her back while pedaling her bicycle. Swiss GIRLS are better men than most allegedly-male American liberals.

There is a story, possibly apocryphal but awesome nonetheless, that a ranking German (perhaps the Kaiser) was visiting and watching the Swiss military on their summer maneuvers. He asked the Swiss commander, "How big a force do you command?"

The Swiss general confidently replied, "I can mobilize one million men in twenty-four hours."

The German asked, "What would happen if I marched five million men in here tomorrow?"

The Swiss replied, "Each of my men will fire five shots and go home."

Note that Switzerland was not invaded during either World War, and still used an updated version of the same bolt action rifle from 1889 to 1959, and kept it in reserve service until 1980.

The Swiss K31 carbine is . . . well, the Swiss Watch of rifles. It is precise, sturdy, accurate, powerful and unusual in having a straight pull bolt action. It might as well be semi-auto, if a gas tube had just been added. But the Swiss are traditionalists and not afraid of it.

The K31 packs a kick. It fires a 7.5 mm Swiss round that is expensive, because it only comes from Switzerland and it's only available in match grade. There is no non-match grade Swiss Ammo. Swiss soldiers don't miss. This is why they've never had to demonstrate the fact. Invaders fear a mountain range full of snipers.

The K31 is available surplus for $275 or so in 2011, in conditions varying from "Arsenal new" to "Beaver chewed." The beaver chewed version is because the Swiss, when performing their summer drills, tend to use the rifle butts to pound TENT STAKES when they run short of mallets. It is an ugly but durable weapon, from a nation that respects the warrior spirit. As a bonus, when buying one surplus, one may find a card under the buttplate identifying the gentleman who was issued it. This is an awesome historical detail: a warrior's weapon with the warrior's mark on it. Some people have even managed to contact the soldier or his family from this information.

★ **6: AK47**

Another communist piece of trash, and I say that with the greatest respect. The Automat Kalashnikov in

7.62X39mm is simple enough for a third world peasant. It's quite robust. It is muzzle heavy and thus shoots well in full auto, though it is unlikely you can own a full auto one legally. Still, in semi, the weight helps a bit with rapid fire. The AK can be called anything except pretty and accurate, and it lacks a bolt stop to hold the action open when empty. On the other hand, you can bury it in the mud for a week and it will likely still fire after you urinate in it to sluice the mud out. You can also elect to get a variation of the newer AK74 and AK100, in 5.45X 39mm. Also look at Valmet, Finland, who makes AKs with their own name. These *are* accurate, but pricey.

The AK is one of the two most popular and common military rifles in the world today. It is a must for a warrior's armory.

★ 5: Smith & Wesson Model 29

The .44 Magnum, as carried by Dirty Harry, is the quintessential man's gun. Harry took no crap from anyone. Any cop who clutches a thug in the elevator in front of his attorney and the prosecutor, compares him to dogshit and implies impending death is doing Odin's work.

Did you know that in *The Eiger Sanction* Clint decided the stunts were too dangerous for him to ask anyone to do them for him, so he learned mountain climbing and was the last climber up the Totem Pole in Monument Valley, before climbing the Eiger? That scene with the 1000 foot drop below and he has to cut his rope? Yup. Clint did that stunt. He writes his own music (he's an accomplished jazz pianist), performs it and directs most of his movies. He ran for mayor of Carmel, then left after one term. A modest, competent man and a role model for all. He should play heavy metal to be perfect, but he was also born in 1930 (meaning he was 43 when he climbed that mountain), so we can excuse the jazz bit. At least it's not rap, country or disco.

Even without that manly vote, the Model 29 was designer Elmer Keith's triumph: A hand cannon that packs as much wallop as many mid-range rifles. It can be used to hunt fairly large game, and it will put a thug down with extreme pain. Mercifully, the pain will fade concurrently with blood loss from the gaping hole it leaves.

It's a comfortable revolver, and if .44 Magnum is too much, you can load it with .44 Special instead. It is stronger than it needs to be, quite accurate, and instantly recognizable. Carrying it in a well-made leather holster says that you are, in fact, a man and you take no crap.

★ 4: AR15

Lots of people will dispute my choice of this rifle. Those people are whiners and pussies. Let's look at the facts: The Air Police grabbed it under direction from General Curtis leMay. Upon seeing it in Vietnam, the Green Berets, SEALs, and SAS jumped on it, to be followed by the Singaporean Special Forces and the Israelis. It soon became standard. Certainly, there were problems early on, in part because the limpwristed twits in Army Logistics made changes to the weapon and ammo without consulting with the designer, Eugene Stoner. The USMC (the manliest men of the manliest military on the planet, and true Vikings—shipboard warriors who strike fear into their enemies just by existing) were called in to remedy some of those flaws with the M16A2. Some milspec guns have reached almost 30,000 rounds without maintenance.

It works well in the desert, as long as it's run dry (to blow sand out) or well-lubed (to sluice the sand out). Choose your method, and don't pussyfoot around. All myths aside, the 5.56 mm round has killed a LOT of Asian losers who thought they could screw with Americans and come out ahead. If anyone doubts it, I have a standing offer to meet them at 500 yards and we'll swap fire. I get to shoot first. At 500 yards, a 5.56mm still packs more energy than a .45 ACP does at the muzzle. That's plenty of power. And it's not a sniper rifle. You should not be engaging at that range with an assault rifle. It's made to be light, deadly and face-to-face. It's the modern equivalent of the Viking's bow and broadsword.

What can you do with this rifle? What *can't* you do with it? It can be converted to .22, 6mm, 6.8mm, .300 Fireball, 9mm, .50 Beowulf. All you have to do is press two pins and swap upper receivers. You can have anything from a 6" pistol to a 24" match rifle in a matter of minutes. It can be equipped with scopes, sights, lights, lasers, grips, slings, counterweights, pouches, compartments, underslung launchers and shotguns, bayonets and probably a kitchen sink. The USMC is impressed enough to have designed an M16A4 and plans to carry it for some time. At fifty-one years as of 2013, it holds the record for rifle service life in the U.S. military, was and still is the rifle of choice of several elite units. Third world peasants carry AK47s. Elite experts carry AR15s. It does require occasional maintenance and you must read the manual. Real men *do* read manuals, regarding instruments of death.

AR15s start at $550 and go up. Generally, the manlier, the more expensive, but over $2000 indicates you are just showing off.

★ **3: Remington 870**

Geek with a .45 says, "The pump action shotgun is sort of a Swiss Army gun." He's correct. You can hunt birds, squirrels, deer, criminals or terrorists.

The Remington 870 has been around for decades. It is easy to maintain, easy to find parts for, almost flawlessly reliable, can be outfitted with a broad variety of accessories that enhance its inherent and undisguisable lethality. I recommend a twenty inch barrel with an extended seven-round magazine, plus one in the chamber, alternating buckshot and slugs. Or you can go with all buckshot. This affords the opportunity to fire eight-rounds with nine pellets each of 000 buck, measuring approximately 9mm, in about two and a half seconds with practice. That's twice the output of an Uzi with better hit probability and more power. In other words, as guns go, it is very well hung.

For hunting, I'd recommend a twenty-four inch barrel with changeable choke tubes. You can get longer, but don't really need it.

The only real disadvantage to a shotgun is range. One hundred yards is about the limit, and less with shot. This is offset by the advantages of a reassuring "ka*clack*" as you cycle it (Reassuring to you. Gut wrenching to your target), massive firepower that can leave a man standing dead, looking down at a hole in his torso big enough to toss a dog through, versatility of ammo, simplicity and low cost. You can often get one police surplus for under $150, used, and new for under $300.

Every house needs at least one pistol, rifle and shotgun. *This* is the shotgun if you can afford it. By all means buy a more modern Benelli as well, but the 870 is still the American standard. When the revolting scum start rioting like chimps and burning cars in the streets of America, it will quickly come to a stop because of Viking-sired rednecks with Remington 870 pump action shotguns.

★ 2: Colt Model 1911A1 .45 ACP

John Moses Browning is the patron saint of shooters and weapon designers. This was a man so manly that his sole purpose in life was to create weapons to kill tasty animals and the enemies of our nation in job lots. These weapons were so successful that both sides used the Hi Power in WWII, and the U.S. Army is fixing its unmanly error of the 9mm by calling for bids on a new .45, while the Marine Recon units and certain other Special Operations units are STILL using the Model 1911A1 with a few improvements, now well over a century after it was first fielded.

There are many versions of the 1911. The patent is expired, and dozens of companies produce a version. What can you expect? Real warriors know a good gun, and this gun is the most popular for that reason. This is a pistol so manly that during WWII, it was even made by Singer Sewing Machine, and collectors prize that version for its rarity. The 1911 is *the* pistol people think of when the word is invoked. In fact, when I am World Dictator, the only pistols that will be allowed to be produced will be the 1911 and the GLOCK.

The 1911 is available in long slide, standard, short, bobbed, officer's models (slightly more compact), with dozens of accessories and custom shapes, in chrome, nickel, stainless, blued steel, Damascus, aluminum, titanium and plastics. All are good. The one caution is that some effete wimps have persuaded makers to produce some *non* .45 versions, in .38 Super, 9mm and other inferior chamberings. A real man may carry a more powerful 10mm version, but he'd better have a .45 ACP slide and barrel at home as backup.

★ 1: Barrett M82 .50 caliber rifle

Ronnie Barrett is a true modern Viking. He hunts big game. He plays with guns. One day in the late 70s, he thought to himself, "Wouldn't it be cool if there was a *rifle* that fired the same .50 BMG cartridge as Saint John Browning's Heavy Machine Gun?" So he built it. That's manly.

When the metrosexual Kalifornia wusses were wetting their pants over "assault rifles," he got dragged into the argument. You see, Ronnie sells many weapons to police departments, for use in stopping bad guys, so they claim. By "bad" guy they sometimes mean tattooed gangbanger. They also sometimes mean balding, pony-tailed, pot-smoking hippie, though. After all, this IS Cretinfornia.

But that wasn't enough for Commiefornia. They had a ban on "assault weapons" (An "assault weapon" is a semantically null political term that means "It can be used to hurt people.") As the *real* commies in Russia, who were men descended from Vikings (at least the ones in charge) would note, "Of course hurts people. Is weapon." You may as well refer to your "house home." The wussy definition of "Assault weapon" bears no resemblance to the U.S. military's definition. It comes down to, "It's black and makes us poopoo in our panties!"

So, even with a ban on "assault weapons" that included most self-loading rifles, including Barrett's M82 Light Fifty, the People's Republic of Kalifornija wanted more. They dragged one of his rifles from the L.A. SWAT armory and used it (illegal for civilians to own, mind you), as a horrible example of weapons that Must Be Banned Lest They Pollute Our Precious, Bodily Fluids.

They got their ban, because their voters are the type of trilling limpwrists one sees portrayed in movies as stereotypes . . . only in Californica they're not stereotypes, they're typical. It must suck to be a real man on the Left Coast.

Now, Ronnie is not a metrosexual wuss. Ronnie is, in fact, a real testosterone-laden Viking *man*. He warned them then, then he told them, he would oppose them in their pursuit. And Ronnie does not make idle threats. He is a man of his word.

A few weeks later, LA SWAT sent one of these rifles that they use for shooting fleeing mopeds back to Barrett for maintenance . . . and Ronnie sent it right back to them, untouched, contract cancelled, with polite instructions to stick it somewhere dark and smelly and ride it straight to hell. Not only that, he publicly and proudly announces in all his advertising that he *will not* sell to or deal with *any* government entity in communist third world Kali.

And *that*, ladies and gentleman, is a *man*. While not everyone can afford or make use of his wonderful toys, it's certainly an honor and privilege to promote a real modern Viking who understands the application of bowel-emptying terror, and how to tell friend from foe.

And there's more! After securing military contracts for antimateriel sniping (generators, vehicles, radars, etc), and facing the wrath of Sarah Brady and her Gun-Grabbing Sideshow (which wrath he snickered at, it having all the intimidation of an angry kitten and Ronnie, as we noted, being a Viking), he gave the ultimate middle finger gesture and redesigned the weapon into 25 mm, or TWICE as big. This is a man so cool even his sperm smoke unfiltered Camels. And that makes this gun the manliest gun on Earth.

Ten More Manly Firearms

The hilarious thing about the list of the ten manliest firearms was the hate mail. I must have received a hundred letters informing me that if XX firearm wasn't on the Top Ten list, I was not a man. So apparently there are 100 Top Ten firearms. Or more. As I noted up front: Make your own list. It's all good.

In fact, it's so good, I did it again.

***

PREVIOUSLY I compiled a list of the Ten Manliest Firearms. I noted that variations on the list were certainly acceptable, but still ran into a bunch of grief from non-men who were unable to read, nor to grasp that real men don't care if other real men disagree with them. Still, there are a *lot* of guns out there, so I figured it was time to compile another list. You should own all of these guns before they're illegal, then buy more until the politicians wet pants and blubber like the wusses they are. And if you don't like this list, compile your own, or wait for the next one.

★ 10 1895 Nagant Revolver

This is the revolver used to invent the game of Russian Roulette, and not that pansy one round in a cylinder version. The original version was to remove one round and play with six in the seven round cylinder. That tells you what Imperial Russians thought of the Bullshiviks. Yes, I spelled it that way on purpose. Imagine the balls it takes to raise that to your head, knowing there's almost an 86% chance (85.7%, and you gain a *slight* edge from the weight of the other cartridges tending to improve the odds of the empty chamber*) you're going to blow your brains out.

The trigger pull is also manly—seventeen pounds in double action. That's because the cylinder actually moves forward to seal the breech, making this the only revolver you can effectively silence. Not that a man should use a silencer, of course. If you kill someone, everyone should know about it. Still, that sealed breech does add a slight improvement in velocity.

The downside is that 7.62 Nagant is not the most robust of rounds. However, it is currently in production. You can also get a conversion cylinder that fires .32ACP, and a gunsmith can ream it out to fire .32 Smith and Wesson and .32 H&R magnum as well.

This gun holds the record for largest body count, having dispatched almost two million people. Granted, most of them were kneeling six inches from the muzzle.

And if you can do that calculation while spinning and pointing, you're a man among men.

★ 9 1893 Turkish Mauser

An odd choice, you might think. However, you may not

have all the facts. It fires common 8mm Mauser, the preferred German round from 1888 through the 1950s in various loadings. That's a little bigger than .30-06 and about as powerful. It served to kill Frenchmen in WWI and Commies and Frenchmen in WWII, among others. It's reliable and cheap (both the ammo and the platform).

It's also legally an antique. Weapons manufactured before 1899 (and some other categories we won't discuss) are not firearms. Yes, they shoot ammo and kill people, but due to one of the many, many, many, many, many stupid, irrelevant and cowardly gun control laws by whiny statist slime, such rifles and revolvers are not considered to be firearms. This means you can send them through the mail. Yes, really. A Federal Firearms Licensee (gun dealer) can't even enter it into his books as a firearm, because it's not. These are one of the last bastions of freedom. You should own several.

★ 8 Colt Python

There are revolvers, and then there are revolvers, and then there's the Python. One of, if not the, best fit and most accurate revolvers, and in .357 Magnum. The Python is all that, and elegant and classy as well. This is the kind of gun you wear to dinner, in a well-tooled leather holster cut to show off its lines. It's jewelry, if real men wore jewelry, which they do not. Except things like this.

★ 7 98K Mauser

The rifle used by German Bastards! as Patton called them. The 98 action was copied for the 1903 Springfield (and the poor Mauser brothers sued, won, and then had the settlement seized as part of WWI. Why? It wasn't their fault), and is still used for the best hunting rifles, either directly, or as a CZ or Winchester, among other brands. It's accurate, durable and reliable, and a neat piece of history. I have one in my collection that was used to kill Commies on the Eastern Front, then was captured by the Commies, rearsenaled and used to kill Nazis. It's twice as cool.

★ 6 FAL

The Fusil Automatique Legere is a heavy bitch. Battle rifles generally are. It was called, "The right arm of the Free World" and was NATO standard for decades. It was used by most of the former British Empire, most of South America, Japan and other nations. It's still used by a few. It manages what the M14 failed to do, which is to be a rifle and a squad weapon, and carbine. It's reliable, simple and shits all over that HundK clone of the CETME, the G3. Rainbow Six players like HundKs. Real warriors would go for the FAL.

★ 5 CZ550 in .600 Overkill

One day, an American scientist from Nevada decided to pack the biggest, most powerful cartridge possible into a Mauser action. The result was the .600 Overkill. This is not just an advertising name. This is a gun so insanely powerful it can put a solid bronze bullet *six feet* into an oak log. The bullet going through the rifling can twist the barrel right out of the shooter's hand, and recoil is "manageable" in a fourteen pound gun with three mercury recoil reducers. Sure, you could get a fancy double Eurorifle . . . if you sold your house. This is more affordable, more powerful, cruder, more atavistic . . . in short, more *American*. And manlier.

★ 4 Martini-Henry

Rorke's Drift was the British Empire's equivalent of the Alamo, except the defenders won. Balls the size of melons, stiff upper lips, Martini-Henry rifles, and yards of bayonet. This is a rifle with a point blank range exceeded by the length of barrel and steel. And what steel! It doesn't matter if you get caught reloading (The Martini-Henry is a falling block single shot. Victorian British men only needed one shot), because you have a bayonet long enough to skewer a goat, an Arab, a couple of onions and a chicken. Bring it on.

★ 3 Webley Revolvers

The Webley .455, nicknamed the Wobbly, was the British service sidearm for a long time. It's certainly not concealable, but why would you? This is a weapon you're proud to show a thug, and if you run out of bullets, you can always proceed to brain him with the thing. It breaks open, takes 6 large cartridges, and many have their cylinders shaved to take .45 ACP in moon clips.

It's manly no matter how you look at it. There's no shame in being put down by a Webley. Better men than you have been given a .455 dirt nap.

"How did he die?"

".455 Webley through the skull."

"Damn, that sucks. Manly way to die, though."

No one would say that about James Bond's .32.

★ 2 M1 Garand

I don't like the Garand. It has a legion of flaws. However, for its time, it was state of the art, and that time did coincide with WWII. A great many Nazi and Jap bastards learned to fear the Garand, with good reason. The WWII American forces were definitely manly, so their rifles were also, by definition. It fires a slightly downloaded .30-06, and was the arm of a great many MoH winners and millions of unsung heroes. In its time, General George S. Patton described it as, "The finest battle implement ever devised."

You can still buy Garands from the U.S. Government, delivered directly to your door, in order to exercise your rights and duties as a member of the militia. Contact the Civilian Marksmanship Program at odcmp.com All real men and women should do this.

It gains additional points from Clint Eastwood's use in Gran Torino, which of course you have seen. Just remember: Chuck Norris stays off Clint Eastwood's lawn.

★ 1 Browning 1919A4

There's not much manlier than a belt-fed weapon. A great many Browning .30s are available converted to semi-auto, or a man skilled with tools can build his own sideplate and have one completely legal, paperwork free and cheaper. This monster weighs thirty-one pounds, and is a "rifle." Of course, it's legal to have a crank . . .

You can also drop in conversions for 7.62 NATO and 8mm Mauser. The Brits had a .303 variant, and there's a custom 7.62X54R variant, also. The Israelis, bless them, make a metal link that fits 8mm, .30-06 and 7.62. You can also use old cloth belts. Best of all, it's Commiefornia legal, the Sniveling Wussbags not having found a way to define it as an "assault weapon," which is funnier than hell when it's one of the few weapons that might legitimately be called so.

Being able to shoot $25 worth of ammo in six seconds means you are not afraid to waste a little ammo . . . or the next zombie outbreak or post-hurricane riot. It's a serious investment in time, money, equipment and training, but it marks you as *the* neighborhood man, the one to seek protection from when mutant zombies, aliens or greeners invade.

The Mosin Nagant

THE OFFICIAL Rifle of The Hall of Manly Excellence!
The Mosin Nagant is truly a manly piece of hardware.
Let's discuss why.

★ ★ ★

1: First, the Poison Maggot is a time proven design.
Dating from 1891, all the bugs have been worked out.
This assumes there were any bugs in the first place,
which there were not. No one would dare to be less
than optimal for the Tsars and Commissars.

2: It's very simple and robust. There are very few things
that can go wrong with the Noisy Nagger. There isn't
even a bolt release — the trigger serves as that. The
springs are heavy gauge, the mechanism basic steel, and
the stock a solid piece of wood. Remember that the
Russkies and the Commies figured that the bayonet
was as important as the bullet. This means:

3: Versatility. One can argue the benefits of the spear versus the club. Guess what? The Russian Gun-Club is both! And it shoots bullets! Why compromise when you can have all three?

4: Physical fitness. The Rosined Nag is heavy. No real man would complain about this. In fact, he boasts of it. One has to be fit to carry it, and fit to aim it without shaking like a coward. Not to worry. The recoil will reseat that loose shoulder and save you the medical bills.

5: Economical. The Soviet Man Cannon is dirt cheap— $100-$200 in 2009 prices. You can typically buy ten to twenty of them for the price of a modern rifle, and the ammo is about half the price, and has been in production for more than a century. One sacrifices rate of fire and accuracy, but that's offset by the fact that an entire platoon of your friends now have guns. Besides, your friends are men, so every shot counts, right? Who needs rate of fire? And any real man can hit through force of testosterone, without bothering with sights. Just imagine your enemy is a toilet, unzip and pull the trigger . . . so to speak. Flush him straight into a grave or outhouse. Or both.

6: General manliness. The Tula Jackhammer has no prissy "ergonomics" or "delicate triggers" or other crap. It is a brutally simple tool. If you can't pull the trigger, then do some more grip exercises, you pansy. Don't like the recoil? Get a recoil pad, chew a handful of Vicodin, and see your doctor for some testosterone shots. The length of pull is too short? Wear a stout Russian overcoat and stop whining. And some earplugs, since you probably don't want to hear the rest of the Commie Chiropractor community laughing at you.

7: History. You may wind up with a Russian or a Finn rifle built on a Russian or French receiver, a Czech, Chinese, Polish, Hungarian or even one of the rare American made models, from the Russo Japanese War, WWI, the Russian Civil War, the Spanish Civil War, WWII, the Winter War, the Continuation War, Korea, Vietnam, Afghanistan... the Baltic Flamethrower has traveled the world. Be sure to check the date on the tang under the stock—it may be an antique made before 1899, which means it's a rifle, but not legally a firearm in most English speaking nations. This just makes politicians go into a tizzy.

★ ★ ★

You may hear complaints that as a non-American weapon, or worse, the weapon of our former enemies, no American should own one. But that's just a misunderstanding of the situation. The fact is, Ronald Reagan, one of our manliest presidents (after such other greats as Teddy Roosevelt), stomped the Soviet Empire into the dust with the tool of capitalism, and we are now selling that empire off on the internet for ten cents on the dollar. A Musty Nugget is not only a manly weapon, it's a political statement.

If you can only afford one rifle, this is the one to have. If you can afford several, this should be one of them.

Men, raise a glass of vodka to Sergei Mosin and Leon Nagant, men for their time, and ours!

On Reparations Generally, For The Descendents Of People Long Departed

★ ★ ★

A lot of people don't realize I'm an immigrant, and even more don't really grasp that there is bigotry against immigrants, not to mention all kinds of bureaucratic issues if you work for the government or military. I've been told that, "Immigrants shouldn't be trusted in the military" and "Immigrants shouldn't be allowed to own property" and quite a few other things. I've had a roommate in the military mock my queen to my face, with no traces of humor involved. I then had someone else tell me, "You're American now, so you're not allowed to complain."

Relatively minor, to be sure, but I am aware of prejudice and bigotry firsthand.

There is some validity to being an American before all else. I even hurl my own barbs at the UK. I also don't play the victim card. I've been poor to the point of homelessness in life, and I don't believe it's any group's fault, nor that anyone owes me anything because of it. This is probably a good thing, because some of my ancestors really took a beating.

DEAR UNITED NATIONS:

I note with approval that there's a bill before the U.S. Congress to compensate African Americans for their mistreatment in the past. However, I was talking to a Russian Jewish friend of mine, and it occurred to me that her ancestors were slaves to Nubian Africans. Should she not be compensated also?

The Jews were also repressed by the Romans, forerunners of the modern Italians. But the Romans were subjugated by the Celts in 390 BC. The Romans returned the favor, and then oppressed Christians as well, before becoming Christians themselves and forcibly converting the Pagan Celts. Later Christianized Celts were oppressed by other Christianized Romans, and the two combined, which is where we come to the African issue. However, certain Africans enslaved other Africans, so perhaps the Central African Republic should be footing part of the bill.

The Pagan Norse oppressed the Slavs, predecessors of the Russians, which brings us back to my Russian Jewish friend. On the other hand, the Germans have subjugated the Balts and Danes and Norwegians, as did the Russians, who also hurt the Finns and the Andronovan steppe people of Central Asia. Sweden claimed Finland and Norway for some length of time, and there were atrocities in Germany during the Thirty Years War by them, the Germans, the Austrians, the Scots, the English, the French and the Spanish. Then there were Norse-descended Norman French (coming back to England), who oppressed Jutes, Angles and Saxons from the German region who were in England to repress the Romano-Celts, and became English, but whose descendants were oppressed themselves under Henry II, and during the Hundred Years War by France or England, depending on whose land claims one believes. The later English oppressed the Irish, and Scots, who were Irish who earlier moved across the sea and displaced the Picts, who themselves oppressed the Celts and the Irish, as did the Phoenicians, which brings us back to the Greeks.

The French and Germans, besides the Franco-Prussian War, WWI and WWII, went at it over the African-exploiting Belgians a few times, and made their own incursions into Africa and the Far East, as did Portugal. Portugal and Spain maltreated large numbers of American people, except for those oppressed by the English, French, Russians, Old Norse and each other. On the other hand, the early Celtiberians were themselves subjugated by the Romans, so they can't entirely bear the blame. Spain also subjugated the Netherlands during the Thirty Years War mentioned previously. On yet another hand, Spain was invaded by the black Moors, who also enslaved many white African Berbers. The Barbary pirates made raids on Cornwall. The Sudan has slaves to this day. This would mean that black Africans have their own debts to pay.

The Muslims also oppressed the Jews, as did the Persians, so it seems that the Middle East and Africa are liable once again. But then there's the way Israel and the Palestinians treat each other. There's the native Kurds, who play both sides against each other, and subjugate the local people north of them. Those from the former Soviet Southern Border states were oppressed by the Russians and the Turks, who have had go rounds with the Greeks, who also oppressed the Semitic peoples. And yet, those same Southern Asians made inroads into China and Tibet. And China is now *in* Tibet, which puts me in an uncomfortable position, China being the last bulwark of the Marxist socialist utopia. And China has oppressed also Southeast Asia, Korea, Mongolia, which also oppressed them, and has been oppressed by Japan, who also mistreated the Pacific Islanders and its own Ainu people, as well as the Inuit and Alaskans and Americans in WWII, who were at that time good for fighting Nazism, but bad for nuking Japan. Then the U.S. again oppressed Southeast Asians and Pacific people and Inuit.

The English usurped power in India, who has had incursions into Pakistan, Bangladesh, Sri Lanka and Afghanistan (as did the Russians), and there were various operations against the Bengalis, the Thais and Cambodians, and on into the Indian Ocean nations as far as Madagascar, which is African, at least currently, despite having Indonesian and Indian language groups. African nations under the British also had Indian slave laborers.

I tried thinking about the Balkans, but it made my head hurt, what with them killing Nazis, helping Nazis, killing Italians who oppressed them previously who had themselves been oppressed by Alexander of Macedonia, who also oppressed Africans. Also, the Huns went through there from Central Asia, and the Muslims came north. Then, the Christians went through there during the Crusades. The Vatican should likely be treated as a direct descendant of Rome, and charged separately from Italy itself, which includes the descendants of the Etruscans. The Etruscan-descended Italians have a separate claim against Rome, I would guess. Also during WWI, the British Royal Family, the Saxe-Coburgs, were actually German but changed their name to "Windsor" to sound more British. This deception should not go unnoticed.

Back to Germanic peoples, there were the Dutch in South Africa, oppressing the Zulu and Bantu, who themselves oppressed the Bushmen and Hottentots, who harassed the Pygmy cultures. The Indonesians and Australian Aborigines and were shoved aside by the Dutch and English, however, those Dutch and "English" (including many Irish), were themselves prisoners of their own regimes and in dire straits.

This brings me to my question: I'm an immigrant to the U.S. from Canada, who before that came from Britain, where my mother is Anglican English of German and Celtic extraction, my father Norse-descended Presbyterian Scottish possibly with some Spanish ancestry from after the wreck of the Armada, and my stepmother an Irish Catholic. My wife is English and Austro-Hungarian in origin, with some Macedonian, and one eighth Cherokee. Which of us owes money to the other and why?

—**Michael Z. Williamson**

My True Encounters With The Indianapolis Police Department

These events dates from 2001, right after our house was burglarized, right before September 11, just as Jim Baen was looking at Freehold.

Part One

WHOSE SIDE ARE THEY ON, ANYWAY?

The burglary was a shock.

I was at Pennsic, Gail was home with our then three year old and six month old. Each morning, she dropped our daughter and son off with a friend, and picked her up after work. Several evenings, they offered her dinner as well.

The summary was that she was predictably gone for 10-

12 hours each day, our neighbor had a record of legal problems that had once resulted in 17 cars, a SWAT van and forty officers, and the other three sides of our property were fenced and covered in growth. Someone kicked in the back door, stole most of our few possessions, and was still there as Gail arrived home, but slipped out fast, fortunately for their own safety.

She called the police, called our friends, and they were there in 30 minutes—the friends. The police showed up a good two hours later.

The place was trashed, and that becomes important later. All our tax records, files, bills, were scattered across the kitchen/dining room/office, and we never recovered some of them. Among them were all our current bills.

The police did dust for prints, and it was about that time I made my nightly call home (Before we had cell phones), and realized my life had been stolen. The guitar she gave me as a wedding present, my custom made guitar, the knife I'd carried for 15 years of military service to that point, the coins and currency I'd collected all over the world, and a crate of collectible knives I'd put aside to sell at a future point, new in box, for income, as well as my camera. They didn't take the books. They did take quite a few of my clothes. They got two unworkable firearms that I wished worked, because as antiques they might have exploded in the face of whomever tried to shoot them, and a very interesting original M1935 Browning 9mm.

I was not only shocked, I was impotent in rage and panic. I was 400 miles away and could do absolutely nothing. The place was so trashed we didn't even have a full tally of the loss for days. I went into the post-fight reaction I get, with shivering shakes (they hit me after the fight, not during), and someone forced three ounces of medicinal bourbon into me.

When I got home two weeks later, I was able to assess the loss, and determine the crooks had left via the open side of the yard, where our troublesome neighbors had just, conveniently, moved out with a moving van, leaving a bunch of junk, and taking our nicer stuff. I even found cigarette butts (we don't smoke, nor do our friends) in our grill, indicating a certain amount of stakeout. The butts matched the brand I found in the neighbor's yard. At some point, someone had brought the cordless phone up from the basement and called out, almost as if making a shopping list.

I called the phone company, and was told I couldn't get a list of my own (non toll) outgoing calls without a court order, which seems bizarre. So I furnished all the above information to the police, who did . . . nothing.

I asked about following up on the phone, as presumably someone had called out, the cordless handset being upstairs. The detective in charge snidely asked, "Whatever would possess them to do something that stupid?"

I'm not sure, Detective. Maybe because they're barely smarter than the police?

Nothing was done.

I eventually found one of my guitars in a pawn shop, though not the Schecter that was my wedding present, nor the Korg DW8000 synth my daughter had taken a liking to, nor any of the foreign currency, which should have been readily trackable—big denominations look impressive and encourage the ignorant to take them to stores and banks to look for exchanges, only to find that 100 in some nations is .60 in the US. I called a few local places, and I suspect if the cops had made a few calls, they'd have found more leads and been able to effect an arrest. Since pawning items requires ID and a thumbprint, they could have found some lead, obviously.

I've never left a house unattended since. I even have friends or associates stay at the house to watch it and the pets when traveling. I just won't do it.

So, with nothing to do but carry on, that's what we did.

But, those scattered papers came back to haunt us. A couple of weeks later, we got a late notice on something. And of course, our already tight finances were strained by the event, and they'd been tight to begin with. Add in a summer of traveling, which often led to chaotic income schedules and payment schedules, and we had a minor problem that became major.

It was a week after that when there was a knock at the door one morning. I answered it, and it was a service rep from the power company, who wanted to confirm if I had a receipt for payment, because if not, he was turning off our power.

Well, no, I didn't, and I wouldn't have been able to locate it if I had. So he headed around back with his tools.

I beat feet through the house, out the back, and politely said, "Sir, I will have a payment made in twenty minutes. Please don't turn off the power."

He shrugged and said, "I'll just come back with the police," and turned and left.

I called Gail at work, because I was watching the kids and working evenings at the store. I couldn't leave the kids.

She departed in a hurry, checkbook in hand, and headed for the nearest bank that could take a payment for the power company.

The rep was back as I hung up the phone, in about three minutes, with two police cars.

Yes, they responded 40 times faster than they had to the burglary.

It was so bizarre I thought I was in a Monty Python movie. The cops spread out to keep my attention divided, as if there were some kind of threat, and "engaged me in conversation." Why was I stopping this man from doing his job?

I tried being clear and direct—we'd had a burglary, as they could check, the place had been trashed, and the bill and late notice buried in the mess, complicated by several weeks of running around the Midwest earning a living. I politely informed them that no threat was offered, this was a civil matter and they were not welcome on my property, unless they could show me a warrant. I voluntarily identified myself with ID.

Badge Number 2676 then said they weren't in my property, they were on public land.

Yes, he really said that.

"Sir, the yard inside the fence to the sidewalk is my property."

I asked again to see warrant or cause. I was again told they needed none, as the city owns the property. They repeated that they were to escort the man back to do his job. The officer stated he was just doing a job. Then he asked if I'd want their help if I had a problem in my store. I pointed out that they weren't in his store, they were on my property. I mentioned that an IPD officer has been in my store, in uniform, to call me satanic.

(Aside: My merchandise was cutlery. Everyone needs knives and scissors, larger ones for hunting and tactical use. Proof of age was required to purchase, and I did refuse unruly elements. The swords I sold were largely decorative, except for stage use and reenactors, who don't actually use them except as props. It was a legitimate business, in a major mall, and even if it was "Satanic," last I checked we had freedom of religion.)

The argument degraded further. Officer warned me that if I crossed the line, I'd be subject to arrest. Assured him I was being polite, called everyone sir, made no threats, repeated that this was a civil matter and I did not wish police on my property. They made no move toward me or the back, which confirms that they in fact had no authority, and couldn't actually do anything. The warning was likely a good idea for all, although unnecessary in this case. But I realized they wanted an altercation. They wanted to haul me off in cuffs, have a car show up to take my kids to foster care, utterly fuck the rest of my life, because I was an easier target than actual criminals. They were a pair of bullies, just waiting for an opening.

I made comments about how there was useful police work they could be doing, such as finding my stolen property. At this point, one officer said that "Given your attitude, I don't care if they do find your stuff." Lesson here: they're hired goons, not concerned at all about law and order.

Badge number 2676 then tried to explain to me that the city DID own my property, under "stere desis," that they could seize property for public use. I asked to see the document that showed my property had been seized. He had no answer of course. (FYI: Stare decisis has to do with the setting of precedent. This costumed clown thought to impress me with fake Latin.)

They insisted I had a signed contract with the power company about access. They insisted it was on my bill. It is not. I asked if such agreement existed, if I could see a copy. No one had one. I would have my employees carry such with them, but you already know my opinion of the morals, ethics and competence of IPL. I asked if I furnished them with a list of bad checks written at my store, if they'd collect on those checks for me as money rightly owed, or accompany me to retrieve the property by force, since they'd previously offered "Help" in my store. No answer.

I went back inside, telling them to do whatever they felt they had to do. Officer 2676 followed me closely, observed as I locked the garage door. Again, had I intended violence, he was dangerously close, his weapons secure on his belt, and in a bad tactical position. I'm not sure what the point of this was, except harassment. I had already identified myself to them, assured them I intended no violence, and been polite if loud.

At this point, my wife showed up to take checks to bank and cash to make payment. It should be obvious to all that our intent was to pay what was rightly owed, but orders are orders, and IPD takes IPL orders. They are mercenary thugs, hired on my tax dollars to oppress me in the name of corporate America. Not even whores, as whores are paid for their work.

The watch sergeant now arrived. Repeated the same

thing about doing their jobs, why was I holding this against them? Why was I holding the actions of other officers against them? Stressed that she felt she was a good cop. It's my experience that good people don't need to stress their qualities, they are apparent. Assuaging guilt with words, perhaps?

I asked again why they weren't actively pursuing the burglaries. She stated that she wasn't the detective on the case. Now, some of the stuff is very distinctive, I have photos, and it's easy to spot. But one detective is handling all these cases, part time for each one, meanwhile, three thugs can show up to not arrest me, not charge me, merely hassle me over a civil matter that's none of their business. I guess we can see what IPD's priorities are. And they were bought cheap, too.

As the technician went to disconnect our power, depriving our children (fortunately) of nothing more than TV for a couple of hours until he knew he would have to return, I insisted that the cops stay in front with me, not enter my yard, not intrude. This legal, reasonable (since, as the "threat" I was in front with them) was ignored. In fact, one of the officers put on that huge, smug grin and made a point of marching about my yard. It was obviously a petty attempt to demonstrate power.

All this could have been avoided with a pending disconnect warning (which is on the same form as the disconnect notice,) or, saving manpower, with a phone call or followup letter. Instead, IPL sends out a flunky with a van, backed up by armed thugs if necessary, removing those thugs from any real work they might do, and you and I pay the bill.

I wished them a good day as they left, and suggested loudly that perhaps IPD only tackled the tasks it had the competence for.

There has been no followup from them on my stolen property.

In fact, I found one of my guitars in a pawn shop, another on the street, (which led to the incident which follows next) and never saw a trace of anything else. The cops never followed up at the pawn shop (Indiana law requires ID and fingerprint to pawn goods). I'm sure they found a bunch of late utility bills to help collect though.

Part Two

WHICH TOOK PLACE LATER
THAT SAME NIGHT . . .

Recently, I was arrested. Why isn't important. Let's discuss the procedure and treatment a citizen receives at the hands of those who are supposed to protect and serve us.

When the police approached me, I took the wisest course I could think of. I cooperated. I did everything I was told, answered all basic questions and said I would wait for my attorney, addressed everyone clearly and directly as "Sir" and "Ma'am."

I received a merely passable response. Not a lot of questions were actually asked regarding the incident. Neither I nor the other gentleman arrested were hurt, nor disposed to make trouble, nor interested in pressing charges. With very few exceptions, no charge from a complainant is supposed to mean an arrest is impossible. That didn't seem to be relevant. There was a debate between a patrolman and a sergeant as to who would make the busts.

Patrolman said, "It's technically your area, but if you're busy with that shooting, I can do it, if the paperwork is a problem."

The same Watch Sergeant as earlier said, "Oh, hell, I'll do the paperwork for two felony arrests. That's a heck of a tally for the evening." I and the other gentleman were both to be charged with felonies.

I suddenly realized: I was not a person to this woman. I was not a suspect to this woman. I was a mere number, a notch in the belt, to this woman. Who cares what happens to me? A good bust is a good bust, and the judge can sort out the details. Why think? Why ask questions? Fill out the paperwork and take the pat on the back.

They did treat me safely and unroughly, treated my personal property with respect, and did keep me informed of what was to happen to it, so I suppose there's a mixed message here. Clearly, they want and intend to be good cops, but there's that bureaucracy thing hovering over all of it. With a shooting nearby, it would have been easy for them to overreact while hyped, and they didn't. I'll give them a seven out of ten for my treatment. It's good, but it could be better.

A tow truck was called for my vehicle, and the hairy freak who drove it couldn't even figure out how to turn the key in the ignition after repeated fumbling. He left the car in park, dragged it onto the hauler, rubber abrading from the tires, and left the headlights turned on even after repeated polite requests to, "Sir, could you please turn my headlights off?"

"Yeah, I'll take care of you, buddy," was the bored response, and the lights were still on as the car was towed away.

"Ma'am, could you please call my wife, because she has no way of knowing and no transport," I asked the sergeant.

"You can call her as soon as you get downtown," I was told.

Throughout all this, I was not treated as a person. I was

not treated as an arrestee. I was treated as a felon. Innocent until proven guilty? Surely you jest.

The van came for us, and we were recuffed with different cuffs and each searched and placed into one side of the tiny, SAE 304 Stainless steel blocks, with howling air conditioning and bright lights. A claustrophobe would turn into a gibbering nut in about ten seconds.

The drive took an interminable time, and they picked up others on the way. If you need to use the restroom, you'll be very uncomfortable or wet and filthy by the time you arrive downtown. Believing that hands behind the back is a dangerous position should there be an accident or "accident," I maneuvered my hands in front of me, by dint of athletic flexibility.

When we arrived downtown, we were marched out. I expected to be hassled about the cuffs, now in front of me, but no mention was made. So why the insistence that cuffs be behind your back? An elderly lady there for domestic violence was not cuffed due to her age, yet she obviously had been accused of violence, so why wasn't she?

We were slowly processed in, thoroughly and not uncomfortably searched, and stuffed into a holding tank. The only toilet is in clear view of everyone, male, female, prisoner, employee, whatever. My military experience made this no problem for me, but I'm sure for many it would be demeaning and embarrassing.

After being fingerprinted, we were led to another holding cell. I asked about phones and was told, "You won't see a phone for the next four to six hours."

I said that my wife had a medical condition and needed to know that I was at least alive.

This woman replied, "You should have thought of that earlier. We didn't put you in here." The utter stupidity of that statement made me laugh. They didn't put me in here? Who did, the Tooth Fairy?

The toilets in the holding cell have never been cleaned. I doubt they can be—when is it empty? There's no furniture, just concrete and block walls and shelves. It was crowded at 11:30 PM, it was elbow to nose by 6 AM. It was cold. It stank. Leftover food sacks littered the place. This was good, as the brown paper could be used as insulation to stop one from freezing to the floor. Ones with sandwiches still in and mashed flat could be used as pillows. The leftover sandwich bags made handy cups to get drinking water from the sinks over the toilets, inch thick in gray slime mold.

I recalled tricks from my military survival training, which I never thought I'd use domestically. If you pull your arms inside your shirt, you maintain body heat. Sleep as much as possible. Save small things like toilet paper for later use. Talk little, and try to help others. I gave some of my hoarded brown paper to a man with no shirt, who had to be suffering from hypothermia on that floor.

No one seemed disposed to trouble. In fact, everyone in the cell was very polite. Those who had to sit on top of the wall over the toilets because of lack of space politely would look away while you used them. Mumbled "sorry"s could be heard whenever someone bumped another as they walked. Most were quiet. After I was taken out to be identified and brought back, I was able to get my same place by the wall back without any hassle.

I was then served with an automatic and form "no

contact" order, which prohibited me from having contact with the other gentleman in the incident. As they had us in the same cell, sleeping side by side, the city violated my order for me. It also contained the same dreary language about "not possessing firearms or other weapons while under this order." This has already been found unconstitutional, is on the face of it unconstitutional—accused still have rights, until convicted, and considering what I sell for a living (cutlery) is regarded by the court as "weapons" even though under Indiana law is not, impossible to comply with. Some judge gets paid $70K a year to sign these papers all night long, without ever actually looking at the case. It could be worse—they could let this idiot sit on a bench and decide people's lives. They were just going through the motions. I signed mine, "Mickey Mouse."

At 6 AM they brought us breakfast. The guards handed it out personally to ensure that every prisoner had a meal. This must be procedure, as they clearly didn't care. Breakfast was fake ham on soggy bread with stale cheese, and a cut up apple, with a bag of sterilized, sour-tasting milk. To drink the milk, you must chew off the corner of the bag.

I saw one poor derelict, filthy and hungry, eating leftover food that had fallen around the toilets. Clearly, this man needed a hospital, not a cell. Some few had sketchy bandages from fights. One man who kept demanding his medication had apparently been there for eight hours already. He was obnoxious, either from desperation, or from needing help. Still, if he had medication, he should have been taken elsewhere. He wasn't exactly built like a boxer.

Theoretically, one has privacy while talking to the bonding commission at the side windows. In reality, the cell was so crowded that when my name was called, after eight hours in the place, there were two people sleeping under the stool, and one standing in each corner. We were all there for something, so it didn't really matter.

One man was released on his own recognizance. For some reason, he had to stay in lockup while he was "processed." Apparently, the system is so inflexible that one must go all the way in before being allowed out.

I was at last officially informed of the charges against me, one felony, one misdemeanor. I was asked for an approximation of how many times I had been arrested. "This is the first," I told the woman. Just to reiterate, from her vantage, she could see anyone using the toilet. It had to be as unpleasant for her as it was for us. I asked if she would be calling my family, and she agreed that she was, to confirm my identity.

At 10 AM, I was finally taken upstairs to the regular cell block. It had steel bunks, and we each took a thin but functional mattress in with us from a pile outside the bars. There were showers, but no towels or soap. We had sinks, still filthy and moldy, with no soap. We were also expected to get drinking water out of them. There was a TV, and more importantly, phones. I actually had no idea what time it was. There were no clocks anywhere and the guards literally would not give us the time of day.

No sooner had we got in there, however, a curse-screaming, obnoxious woman guard told us she was turning the phone off until we cleaned up the mess left by the last occupants, of whom only three were still present. I resented being held incommunicado, I resented not being asked first, then given an ultimatum—I'd be glad to clean it for the sake of cleaning it, and to have anything to do for a few minutes. Most of the rest of my cellmates felt the same way, the sole exception being a screaming, cursing twenty-two year old admitted drug dealer. We picked up the trash and swept and mopped in short order, and I recognized other military veterans from their cleaning style. The dealer spent the time calling her every unimaginative name in the book, while boasting of his prowess in acquiring stolen property. In response, the guard shouted that she was leaving the phones off to teach us a lesson.

What lesson? That this punk was an idiot? We all knew that. Was she hoping we'd attack him so she could Mace a few of us? We offered no hassle or resistance at any point. *She* initiated hostilities. More on that later.

She ignored my polite request to call my family to let them know where I was after twelve hours. I finally yelled over to another cell and had another inmate call on my behalf.

Let's note that here: he did me a favor. We all took care of the man with the artificial leg. Everyone was careful of the toilets and toilet paper, as we all knew we'd have to use them eventually. Leftover food was shared with new arrivals. The prisoners, with perhaps two exceptions of sixty, were polite, courteous, and addressed all guards as "Sir" and "Ma'am." We did not cause trouble.

The guards ignored every request, either without comment, with "I'll see," or with, "That's not my job." Taking care of prisoners? Not their job. Just signing papers. We were all there for a reason, right?

The phones came back on at 11AM, and I called home. Each call costs $3.35 collect, and is monitored, so you don't dare give details to your family in case it's used against you in court. I agree with the logic of this. It's still hard on the family.

The Bonding Commission had called home to check my identity, but hadn't really identified themselves or said where I was.

"Is this the residence of Michael Williamson? Thank you." Click.

Luckily, my wife is competent, and had already found out my whereabouts from the police. She did not have any details, and I couldn't share any. She'd been afraid I'd been in an accident. I gave her the bare bones, and list of people to call for help for her and me, and let someone else get to the phone.

At noon, they brought lunch. Fake ham on soggy bread with corn chips and nasty chocolate chip cookies. Some analog of Kool-Aid in a bag, chew off the corner to drink, just like last time. That's two sandwiches, an apple, two ounces of corn chips and twelve ounces of liquid in twelve hours. Barely enough to keep someone from curling up with pangs, especially in the cold. One experienced inmate offered to swap his sandwich for another drink. He got no takers. The sandwiches were that bad. I had to choke it down in small nibbles, and almost threw up twice.

At 1:30 PM, there was a court call. My name was called, last on the list, while I was using the toilet. I finished, ran to get my mattress (it has to leave the cell with you) while my cellmates yelled at the guard, "Sir, there's one more guy coming, please wait a moment."

He slammed the gate in my face. I said, "Sir, I'm your last person."

"I'll come back for you," he said, back to me. He didn't even have the guts to look me in the face while lying to me. He lied to me, in uniform, wearing a badge that he'd taken an oath for. As a veteran, I downgraded this guy to "scum" in my rating.

Depressed, I called home again, got an update that not much had happened yet, but bail would be waiting. Apparently, it could have been made at 8 AM, had my family known where I was. However, once court was scheduled, I had to remain until I saw the judge. Because this punk of a guard couldn't wait ten seconds of my taxpayer's time, I would have to wait perhaps another day until it was convenient for him to let me out.

Bail was set at $10,000, and several of my friends, and my inlaws had already arranged bank transfers to cover it. Upon hearing the charges, all of them said, "Mike wouldn't do that." It's when your character is called into question that you find out who your true friends are.

Court ran until four. I hoped against hope that I'd actually get called again. Every time the guard came back for someone, I'd politely ask him, "Sir, I missed my 1:30 call. Will they get me soon?"

The responses varied from totally ignoring me, to telling me "Soon," to telling me, "I don't have a file on you." Clearly, he did. He'd called my name. He was continually lying to me. As a professional, he was not.

I called home again after 4, told my wife I'd likely be there another day, and she said, "The Sheriff's Department says court runs until nine." I wasn't hopeful. It might run until 9, but the regulars were sure no one got called after 4.

More prisoners came in, and there were no more mattresses. Another exchange took place, and in perfect Nazi or Stalinist fashion, the departing prisoners were required to remove the mattresses from the cell, even though there were those inside who had none. Repeated requests of, "Sir, we need some mattresses," were met with the standard, "Soon," but no mattresses. They were left outside the bars as a taunt.

That evening, we ran into two more guards. One young man, and a slender elderly lady with curly hair. These two people deserve thanks, promotions, and praise from the city, because they acted and treated us like human beings. They were genuinely embarrassed by the petty bullies around them, kept apologizing for them, and did their best to help us.

Let me reiterate: they did their jobs as required. That was unusual and worthy of note. I won't give their names here in case their coworkers cause them trouble over it, but I will let the city know.

On missed court calls, they took our names and made inquiries. We got no answers from the system, but they did ask. A man who needed his medication, who had previously been told that the medics were "gone for the day," was scheduled for sick call. They gave us the time. They explained procedures. They got us mattresses. They were treated exactly as they treated us—politely, and every request complied with without hassle.

The entire day, I didn't see any violence. There was rudeness to the guards, after it was clear they were of no help. There was shouting and boisterousness to kill the boredom. There was a drug-dealing, fire-and-brimstone Gospel comedian who kept us laughing for half an hour, and even got cheers from the next block. But no violence. These people were human beings with problems and who were accused of mistakes that society finds unacceptable. That does not make them criminals. Only a court conviction makes one a criminal.

At 6, we were brought dinner. You guessed it—fake ham and soggy bread with stale cheese and corn chips and nasty cookies and orange juice. The man trying to exchange his sandwich for a drink had no luck again.

After 9, I called home again, to tell my wife I would be at least another day. She said, "Oh, you haven't heard!" and my stomach flipped. This couldn't be good. "All charges were dropped at 4 o'clock," she said.

Five hours previously. I was a free man. Except that I was still on the wrong side of the bars, still being treated like refuse by all except for two of my custodians.

I was to be released at midnight. I felt so much better that I relaxed a little. I'd thought I was relaxed earlier, until I'd realized my pulse was around 90. I was actually calm now.

I stayed with my form. I ate leftover chips to keep up my strength, poured a bag of water to keep myself hydrated. Nodded to conversation but said nothing. Stayed with my bunk so my mattress wouldn't be stolen, as I needed it and didn't want a fight.

About 10, some fool who had smuggled marijuana and matches in past their search lit up. The guards made no attempt to find out who, they simply shut off the phones again. People who had been brought in at the same time I had, just now getting up to the cell after twenty-four hours, came in and had no way to call.

They still no way to call when I left at midnight.

My name was called on a roster, and I was first at the bars, having moved my mattress to a front bunk during an earlier lull. I lied and said I didn't have a mattress, so someone else would have the use of it. The irony of me lying to a guard to give a prisoner something he needed and decency said he was entitled to was rather bitter.

We were marched downstairs, lined up, processed out in 10 minutes. I was never actually told that my charges were dropped. We weren't actually told we were being processed out until another prisoner asked and was answered.

They opened the locked steel door, told me to go up to the first floor and through the door there. I did so, and was in the lobby of the police department. No warning, no nothing. Through that door and out of our hair, you. To be fair, the guards on this last leg were fairly decent, probably because they knew we were innocent.

Conclusion

CONSIDER THAT ABOUT HALF of those arrested will have the charges dropped. Consider that two thirds of the remainder will be acquitted. That means that five sixths of the incarcerees, more than eighty percent, are innocent. Of the remainder, most are only being held for minor or nonviolent charges, such as Public Intoxication or Driving Without a License. Yet these thugs treat each and every one of them, preemptively, as they would a murderer or rapist.

They planned to leave me in an extra day, to "teach me a lesson." They held me incommunicado, causing suffering for my family, to "teach me a lesson." Despite my cooperation, flawless manners and calm demeanor, they harassed me and threatened me, to "teach me a lesson."

Lesson learned, COs (Correction Officers). I have learned that you are petty, gutless Fascists who are so pitiful as to find solace for your own wretched lives in bullying people with problems, helpless to resist you, until they turn into caged animals for your amusement. I have learned that on the evolutionary ladder, you rank somewhere between child molesters and the bacteria that thrive in septic tanks. I have learned that if I am ever called as a juror for a criminal accused of beating one of you within an inch of your worthless life, I'll need to see some VERY convincing evidence before I'll convict him.

How's that for a lesson learned?

Afterword

NOTHING EVER CAME of any police investigation, as they didn't really do one. About a month later, in response to a written complaint, the watch commander came out, and we talked a few minutes. He apologized briefly, though I don't think he had many options available for correcting the problem. I've had both positive and negative experiences with IPD, and it seems the only positive experiences were when I was the business owner, not a supplicating private citizen.

I still live in the area, but I'm unlikely to move back into Indy proper, and the police are certainly part of the reason.

Inappropriate Cocktails

★★★

Believe it or not, I sometimes do things just to mess with people, and see how they react. Let me mix you a drink and I'll tell you all about it . . .

First came the Scots, who kept the Sabbath...and anything else we could bloody well get our hands on.

Then came the Welsh, who prayed on their knees on Sunday, and preyed on their neighbors the rest of the week.

Next came the Irish, who had no idea what they wanted, but were willing to fight to the death for it anyway.

Last of all came the English, claiming to be a self-made people, thereby demonstrating the horrors of unskilled labor, and relieving the Almighty of a DREADFUL responsibility.

The Challenger

2 oz Vodka with tang powder

In memory of the astronauts.
Drink seven of these and you'll explode.

The Hubble Space Cocktail

3 oz Cuervo 1800
2 oz peach schnapps
2 oz orange juice
2 oz lemonade
Place on a coaster made of sandpaper

It's very expensive, served in a hand-polished glass,
and when you're finished, everything looks fuzzy.
Bonus points for freezing flat, lens-shaped ice.

The Hurricane Katrina

1 oz white rum

1 oz Jamaican dark rum
1 oz 151 rum
3 oz orange juice
3 oz unsweetened pineapple juice
1/2 oz grenadine syrup

Stir until frothy
Serve over crushed ice
Sprinkle shredded fruit and chocolate
on top of the icy froth for debris.

★ ★ ★

★ ★ ★

Fukushima # 1

3 oz melon liqueur
1 oz orange liqueur
1 oz lime juice
This base drink is called a
"Japanese Slipper."

Add two shots of vodka.

Shake vigorously for six minutes
Pour as four big splashing dollops
Sprinkle shredded fruit and chocolate debris
across the froth
Drop a 2" lightstick into the bottom for a cheery glow.

★ ★ ★

The Princess Di

1 oz Vodka
4 oz Orange juice
½ oz Galliano floated on top
Serve on the rocks

2 shot glasses of French brandy

A Harvey Wallbanger with a couple of chasers.
(This goes very well with a Paparazzi Pizza.)
It will give you tunnel vision, and if you drink two,
you'll look back and turn into a pillar of concrete.

***

The Black Klansman

3 oz Kahlua
Float 2 oz 151 proof rum
Delicately create a cross in heavy or whipped cream
Light the rum
It should be served in a glass at least 8" tall
Place on a napkin with eye holes cut in it.

***

The Chappaquiddick

2 oz Irish whiskey
A splash of water
Serve in a glass with a toy car at bottom.

You can't tell anyone you drank it
until after noon the next day.

The Osama bin Laden

2 shots of Maker's Mark
A splash of water

This will really make you feel light-headed.

The Baby Seal

Two shots of Canadian Club
Club Soda
Serve on the rocks.
Pour a pile of fluffy white coconut shavings.
Pour Grenadine into the shavings.
Serve with a wooden stirring stick.

★ ★ ★

Dealey Plaza

Three shots of Irish
One shot of Amaretto

★ ★ ★

★ ★ ★

Flaming Penguin

A wedge of pineapple
Solid block of ice
Kahlua
Cream
151 rum, ronrico preferred
Light

★ ★ ★

The Whitney Houston

3 oz Rum
2 oz Kahlua
1 teaspoon Brown sugar
Coke
Cracked ice.

★ ★ ★